Whenever their paths crossed, that wicked gleam in his eyes beckoned her, and the sensual smile teased her senses. Half the time she wondered what it would be like to kiss him, to run a finger through his mane, or to squeeze his firm backside. Wicked, wicked thoughts she had no business thinking, Cat lamented, not when she wasn't supposed to get too emotionally involved with a man.

A soft sigh escaped her slightly parted lips when her eyes landed on Taj. He was walking toward the storyboard where the step-by-step action and special effects sequences were displayed. If he turned around, she would see his signature two-day shadow. Not that it distracted one from his chiseled, handsome, bronzed features—the high cheekbones, the mysterious eyes with decadently long lashes, the strong nose, and the sinfully sensuous mouth. Combined with the large Harley-Davidson motorcycle he rode to Warner Brothers Studio every morning, it made him look like a renegade, one that every woman would love to reform. The man had the most faultlessly proportioned body, and, unquestionably, the sexiest swagger she'd ever seen. Even now she wasn't the only female on the set watching him.

TIMELESS DEVOTION

BELLA MCFARLAND

Genesis Press Inc.

Indigo Love Stories

An imprint of Genesis Press Inc.
Publishing Company

Genesis Press, Inc.
P.O. Box 101
Columbus, MS 39703

ISBN: 1-58571-148-9
Manufactured in the United States of America

First Edition

Visit us at www.genesis-press.com
or call at 1-888-Indigo-1

DEDICATION

This book is dedicated to all my children; Margaret, Merab, Elijah, Joyce, and Janna. Thank you for enriching my life.

ACKNOWLEDGMENTS

First and foremost, I thank God, Allah, Nyasaye for all of my blessings. To my dear husband and children, what can I say to thank you for putting up with my moods when my creative juices are flowing and when they dry up? I love you guys so much. To my dearest friend Darlene, thanks for your support and being there whenever I need to blow off steam. Friends like you are hard to find (you're a gem). To Cindy, thanks for taking time from your busy schedule to look through the manuscript and 'weed out' the kinks. Cathy, Lillian, Brenda, Miho, and Marjory, thanks for spreading the word. And to my editor, Sidney, thanks for streamlining the story so it flows better. And to the readers out there, I wouldn't be doing this if it weren't for your support, thank you. If I forgot anyone, please accept my apologies; your support is very important to me.

CHAPTER 1

Don't worry if you don't hear from me for awhile, Cat. I'm going to New York. I'll talk to you when I get back. Bobby.

Once again, Cat Simmons reread the brief note her brother had left in her mailbox. A deep sigh escaped her. She didn't know what else to do to help him deal with their mother's death or the events that took place prior to it.

"Rereading it over and over again will not make it go away, Cat," her best friend Jan said from behind her.

Pushing the note into the pocket of her jumpsuit, Cat pivoted around to face Jan. A frown settled on her walnut-brown face. "I know. I've been thinking, though. I want to hire an investigator to help Bobby. He's so obsessed with finding this…this *fictitious* biological father that nothing I say seems to penetrate."

"I thought you said you didn't want to validate his crazy notion that your mother had…." Jan bit her bottom lip, a little uncertain about broaching the sensitive subject.

"Just say it, Jan. That my mother had cheated on my father, and that Bobby was the result of that affair. No, I don't want to. But Bobby believes it's true. He's hurting, Jan, refuses to discuss things with Dad or Kenny. I'm all he has." Cat massaged her temple and took a deep, calming breath. She couldn't afford to be distracted or worked up over this, not when she was about to perform a stunt. Most stunts needed total concentration and precision. Thinking about her personal problems before or during a performance could only lead to disaster. Still, she couldn't help worrying about her little brother. "If I can't convince him to stop this madness, the least I can do is help him. As soon as I'm done here, I'm going to search the yellow pages for a private investigator." She picked up her Neumann's skydiving gloves from the dresser, slipped them on, and adjusted the straps. "What do you think?"

"Sounds like a great idea," Jan said. "Count me in." Cat frowned at her. "Quit scowling at me. That boy is like a brother to me, okay? Besides, private investigators don't come cheap. So count me in."

Emotions blocked Cat's throat. Friends like Jan were hard to find. Jan was one of the few African-American actresses with a lead role in a hit T.V. series. They'd met at a performing art camp at UCLA years ago and had become fast friends. Nevertheless, Cat couldn't allow Jan to pay for something that didn't concern her family. "Thanks, Jan, but I should be able to take care of it."

"Sure?"

Cat nodded.

"Okay. But know that I've got your back covered if things get a little tight." Jan opened a bag of cheese doodles and pushed one into her mouth.

"I know." Cat's eyes followed Jan's hand as it dipped into the bag and pulled out another doodle. "How can you eat that stuff?"

Jan shrugged her thin shoulders. "Easily. Just pop one in my mouth, munch, and swallow. Speaking of eating, are you coming to my dinner party tomorrow night? I have a yummy date for you."

Cat rolled her eyes. "I told you, woman, I'm through dating. No more handsome men with wicked smiles or cute butts. No more dealing with cocky attitudes or excusing bad habits."

Jan pointed an orange-stained finger at Cat. "Cute butts, Cat? Come on, you are a sucker for a guy with a firm behind, and you know it."

"I was. I'm cured." Her ex-boyfriend, Rick, had made sure of that. "Did I tell you Rick used my credit card without my knowledge? And do you know why I didn't see that coming? His cute butt got in the way, that's why." And because she'd allowed her feelings to get involved, she added silently.

"It's been six months, Cat, let it go. Cancel your credit cards and let your lawyer deal with Rick."

"Already did."

"Well, then, that's that. Now about tomorrow's dinner…. If you don't make it, sweetie, I'll have an unpaired male on my hands, a hostess's nightmare." Jan popped another doodle into her mouth, then rolled the bag and dropped it on the table. She turned her famous hazel eyes on Cat. "Please, Cat. Please. I really, really need you."

Cat checked the zippers on her red jumpsuit and then reached for her goggles. "Okay. But you'll owe me big time for this, Janelle Masters."

"Oh, thank you." Jan blew her a kiss and jumped to her feet.

"Bailing you out should be added to my things-*not*-to-do list."

Jan merely grinned at her words.

"So tell me more about this blind date you're saddling me with. What does he do?"

"Works in a bank," Jan answered as she padded to the fridge to get bottled water. She closed the door with her hip and then she leaned against it.

"Good. That means he's conservative, no braided or dreadlocked hair."

Jan rolled her eyes.

"I'm through with men who thumb their noses at society," Cat added.

"Another one of your rules?"

"You've got it. What else can you tell me about him?"

"He went to school with my man, so he's decent."

Cat snickered. "FYI, Miss Movie Star, Doug is as bad-ass as they come. Don't use him as a yardstick." She pushed the goggles up in her hair. She was reaching for her helmet when the masterful purr of a V-twin engine sounded outside the trailer. When Jan looked out the window, Cat asked, "Is that him out there?"

"Doug? Are you kidding? My man knows I can't abide motorbikes. But you'd better take a long, hard look, girl, because if you're serious about all those rules you keep spouting, you're about to miss out."

"Why? Who is it?" Cat asked as she approached the window.

"The kind of bad boy you've sworn to steer clear of."

Cat moved forward to take a look at what had her friend grinning like a well-fed cat.

My, oh my, what a beauty, Cat sighed as her eyes followed the Harley-Davidson with its two-tone sterling-silver and vivid-black lines. What she wouldn't give to ride that, she mused longingly.

Then her eyes moved to the owner of the bike as he switched off the engine and stood up. Watching him dismount sent a thrill through her that had nothing to do with the bike. Now riding that, Cat mused, would be more exciting and dangerous than her most daring stunt.

He was big. All she could see was his masculine back, powerful thighs molded by black jeans, scruffy boots and a leather jacket that had seen better days. Jet black, curly hair fell over his broad shoulders. Wonder how it would feel to run fingers through it? Cat mused.

As if to tease her already heightened senses, the man turned and gave her a profile. Rich chocolate skin, proud bearing, strong nose, and a two-day shadow, she noted. If only she could see the rest of his face. Still, the sigh that escaped her lips was close to a purr.

"Quit licking your lips, Catherine. Go out there and prove me wrong."

Cat's head snapped toward her friend as a feeling close to panic washed over her. That man was too much for her to test her theory on. She stalled. "Prove what?"

"That you're immune to *that* gorgeous hunk. Damn, he makes me want to crawl into his pants."

Me too, Cat added silently. Who was he? An actor?

A knock on the trailer door interrupted her musing. One of the makeup artists, Iryna Chekhov, stepped inside the trailer when Jan bid her to come in. "Sorry to interrupt, Jan. Jed Sutton needs Cat now. The plane will be taking off in ten minutes."

"Thanks, Iryna. I'm right behind you."

As if that were her cue, Iryna stepped down from the trailer and disappeared.

"I've got to go, Jan. No time for testing theories."

"Chicken." Jan picked her car keys up from the table and threw them to her. "Take care of my baby, sweetie. Drop it off at my place tomorrow night when you come to dinner."

Cat caught the keys and nodded. They'd used Jan's car to get to the filming location, but since Doug was picking Jan up, Cat had offered to drive her car back to Los Angeles. As she moved toward the door, the biker outside intruded on her thoughts.

No man was going to turn her into a coward, Cat decided, no matter how gorgeous he looked. "Okay, Jan. Watch and weep. I'm going out there to have a normal conversation with that handsome…*renegade*."

Jan guffawed.

"Then I'm going to leave without a backward glance," Cat added.

"I'll be watching. Make sure you come back in one piece, you hear?"

Cat rolled her eyes. "Please. He's just a man."

"I meant the skydiving, silly. See, he's already making you forget what we're doing here. Look at me, sweetie. We are at Edwards Air Force Base jump field to film a movie." Jan spaced her words as if she were talking to a confused person, and she added sign language for effect. "You are about to hurtle to earth at a death-defying speed, doubling for *moi*, your best friend."

"Very funny." Cat picked up her helmet and opened the trailer door.

"Jokes aside, Cat, be careful."

Jan always wished her good luck whenever she was about to do a stunt, Cat thought with a smile. They were tight like that. "Will do," Cat answered. Then she left the trailer.

Taj Taylor stared with amazement at the people scurrying about the jump field. Were all location film sites this chaotic? How the hell was he going to locate the producer, Dorian McCarthy?

"Nice ride," a voice said from behind him.

His head snapped toward the soft, feminine voice. A stunning woman in a red skydiving suit was standing near the entrance of a trailer, her eyes trained on his bike. As he took in her exotic brown face—the long, graceful neck, the delicately molded short nose, the sensually lush lips, and the high cheekbones—his stomach lurched, as if he were about to take a plunge off an endless precipice. Ignoring the feeling, he murmured, "Thank you."

Cat stepped closer to the bike. "A 1340 Evolution engine?"

Very intriguing, Taj mused. He hadn't met that many women who were interested in motorbikes, let alone able to identify a particular engine. "A modified 1340."

"Impressive. Recorded maximum performance yet?"

She had him totally enthralled now. Who was she? "A maximum of 165 horsepower. You obviously know your motorbikes."

"I've ridden some, modified a few. Yours is a real beauty."

Why didn't she look at him? His bike was getting all her attention, darn it. "Power and beauty are an irresistible combination. I'm a sucker for both."

She flashed a smile his way. "Obviously. How does it handle long distance?"

Still reeling from the effect of her smile, Taj said the first thing that popped into his head. "Purrs like a satiated lover." Her head snapped toward him, and their eyes met. Hers were dark and mysterious. They seemed to sear right through him to his very soul. When her eyebrows shot up, he realized what he'd said. "Handle her with care, and she'll give you the best ride of your life." Damn, that didn't come out well either.

Taj was sure the woman would comment on his sexist remarks, but all she did was shift her slender body until she was facing him. Then she proceeded to study him. A laconic smile passed her lips as she took in his two-day stubble. Made him wish he'd shaved before driving out to see McCarthy. His shoulder-length curly hair received a frown before her eyes ran down his frame. For once, he was happy he hit the gym regularly.

When she said, "Nice chatting with you," and sashayed past him, Taj didn't say anything. Couldn't say anything was more like it. He was still trying to find his balance.

His gaze followed her delectable form. He hoped, no, prayed she would look back. *Come on, baby, just once,* he urged silently. She never looked back.

Taj shook his head to clear it. He didn't know what had just happened, but he was now more interested in what McCarthy wanted from him than before. He hadn't been too keen on taking the assignment, but if it meant knowing the identity of that exquisite creature, he would make time.

"Excuse me?" A man wearing a security badge interrupted his musing. "This area is off-limits, sir."

Taj handed him his card. "I'm here to see Dorian McCarthy."

The guard studied the card. "You need to talk to Mr. Gunter, the unit manager. No one sees McCarthy without going through him."

He'd made the necessary adjustments in his schedule for this detour, Taj reflected, and the last thing he needed was to be given the runaround. On the other hand, he couldn't take out his frustrations on a guy following orders. "Okay, my friend, take me to Mr. Gunter."

"They're actually all together over there." The guard pointed at a group of four men and a woman standing at the edge of the field.

"Which one is McCarthy?"

"Red hair and goatee, hard to miss," the guard answered.

Squinting against the glaring sun, Taj focused his gaze on the group. As the guard had said, it was hard not to notice Dorian McCarthy. He was dressed in white pants and white shirt, and had an unruly mop of red hair. A narrow moustache sat above his lips. He was in his mid-fifties, Taj recalled from the background information he'd gotten over the Internet, although looking at him you'd never guess it. He was of slight build and in pretty good shape.

McCarthy had become a household name in the eighties when he'd produced one action-packed blockbuster after another. Then he'd made the fatal error of switching to romantic comedies. Bad reviews and box office disasters had followed. As if that were merely a prelude to worse times, he'd gotten involved in a scandalous affair with an aspiring actress and ended up in court, fighting for his reputation and his children. His ex-wife, the daughter of a well-known Hollywood mogul, had made sure that he paid. By the time the messy divorce was over, Dorian had become a pariah in Hollywood.

"Wait here, Mr. Taylor." The guard went directly to a gangly man in a Dodgers baseball cap, and handed him Taj's card. After a brief consultation, the man spoke to McCarthy, who looked up.

"Ah, Mr. Taylor, I've been expecting you." McCarthy excused himself from his colleagues, and drew Taj aside. "I'm happy you made it." He paused to study Taj with pursed lips and a thoughtful expression. "Ever thought of being in the movies, Mr. Taylor?"

Taj's eyebrows shot up. "Not really."

"I was told that you're a former FBI agent. Ever consulted for a movie company?"

Taj studied the older man and wondered where the interrogation was headed. "No. Look, Mr. McCarthy, from the message you left with my secretary, I had the impression that you desperately needed my expertise."

McCarthy nodded his head. "But I do, Mr. Taylor. I need a consultant, someone who can give me the inside info on how the Bureau profiles criminals, how a killer's mind works."

Taj's heart sank at McCarthy's words. This was the very reason he had left the Bureau. He'd gotten tired of delving into the twisted minds of criminals. Taj shook his head. "Mr. McCarthy, I've got to be honest with you. I stopped profiling criminals a long time ago."

"But I bet you haven't forgotten the training. I know what you're thinking," the producer said, his eyes sparkling with enthusiasm. "It's just a movie, right? Actors pretending to be agents, nothing like the real thing. Well, Mr. Taylor, we want it to be as close to the real thing as possible. With your help, we can do it. I want the audiences spooked when they watch the antics of the psycho in the *The Guardian*, and rooting for my lead actress and her supporting actor, and I can't do it without you, Mr. Taylor."

Taj's brows furrowed. The last thing he wanted to revisit was his FBI days. But at the same time, there was the exquisite woman he'd met earlier. "What happened to the consultant you had before? I assume you hired one before you started filming."

McCarthy rolled on his heels and gave Taj a wry smile. "Oh, yes, we had one. A friend recommended him, and I went along because he had the credentials. He turned out to be unreliable, irresponsible, and a difficult man to work with. I need your help, Mr. Taylor. Jackie Wilson told me you were the best there is."

Taj smiled. Jackie Wilson was a former client of his, an aging African-American diva who'd conquered Broadway before coming to Hollywood. "I see," was all he said.

"She said I could count on you to see us through this fiasco. Of course," McCarthy hastened to add, "we'll work around your schedule and compensate you for any jobs you could be working on in the next two weeks."

"That won't be necessary, Mr. McCarthy. My people can handle things without me."

McCarthy perked up. "Do I take it that you're coming aboard?"

Taj smiled at his reaction. "Yes."

"Oh, that's wonderful!" He reached for Taj's hand and pumped it vigorously. We're going to have a ball making…oh, excuse me. I need to answer this." He raised the receiver end of the walkie-talkie to his ear. "Yes? Go ahead. Give him whatever he wants…two extra parachutes if it makes him happy."

Dorian turned to whisper to Taj, "I got Pierce Quinn as my lead actor. Lots of talent there. I tell you, he's the next Colin Farrell. Yes?" he murmured into the mouthpiece. "Have Cat talk to him. She already did? Okay, I'll be there." Dorian turned to Taj, "I've got to go. We need to go with the first take on this. Thanks for joining us, Mr. Taylor."

Taj nodded curtly. "I have a quick question, Mr. McCarthy."

"Shoot."

"Is the lead actress doing the stunts with Pierce Quinn?"

"Janelle Masters doesn't do her own stunts, my friend. The woman in red is just a double, a stuntwoman by the name of Cat Simmons. You'll meet them all at the studio on Monday." They shook hands. "Listen, I appreciate your going out of your way today, Mr. Taylor. I'll stop by your offices later and finalize everything."

Taj watched the producer dash across the field to join the people around the plane. He could see the figure in red. She was in a deep discussion with another man. Cat Simmons, stuntwoman.

Just a double wasn't the expression he'd use to describe Cat. In fact, he had known there was something special about her the moment he'd laid eyes on her, Taj reflected as he headed back to his bike. Cat was no one's double. She was special. Even her name, Cat, was unique.

Instead of starting his bike and leaving, Taj settled on it and watched the scene unfold on the field before him. Someone made an announcement, and everyone cleared the field. The plane took off and steadily gained altitude. He could feel the tension and the excitement in the observers. He too felt a twinge of anticipation at the thought of seeing Cat Simmons in action.

CHAPTER 2

"Ready, Cat?" Jed Sutton, the stunt coordinator, shouted above the drone of the aircraft's engine.

Cat looked beyond Jed to the patches of green and brown visible from the window of the Cessna. They were flying at 13,000 feet above the jump area. She smiled and gave him a thumbs-up sign. "Ready," she yelled back.

"Pierce?" Jed asked the lead actor.

"Aye," Pierce answered confidently.

While Jed consulted with the special effects coordinator and the first assistant director who was standing in for the director, Cat studied the lead actor. Most actors and actresses didn't like to do their stunts, but the latest Irish heartthrob, Pierce Quinn, had insisted on doing things his way, including his stunts. So far, he had braved a lot of scenes that would have fazed an amateur stuntman. Was it her imagination or did he appear just a tad nervous about this one?

As if aware of Cat's scrutiny, Pierce glanced at her. "How can you stand doing this over and over, Cat?"

Cat shrugged. "I don't let fear stop me. And it pays bills."

He swept a lock of hair from his forehead. "A dangerous way, though. You've done this many times, right? Skydiving?"

He was nervous, Cat concluded. "Started in my teens. Everything will be fine, Pierce," she reassured him.

"I know. You have my back covered just in case, right?" he added with a grin.

Cat nodded and grinned back. She hoped that her grin hid her tension too. Excitement and nervousness were her two constant companions whenever she did a stunt. Whether she was jumping off a building, riding a motorbike at a death-defying speed, flipping a speeding car, or just fighting on top of a narrow ledge, the two emotions kept her on edge.

Jed interrupted her thoughts. "Everything looks good. The wind velocity, visibility, and cloud ceiling height are perfect. The temperature is about 38 degrees. We've done dry runs, so everyone should be comfortable with it." He looked at Pierce. "Remember, your main chute and the back-up are fail-safe. The ground crew will be waiting for you at the end of the field where you'll be landing." Turning to Cat, he added, "Cat, you go first. Hangman, you'll jump last."

Hank 'Hangman' Heaney patted his cameras and gave a thumbs-up signal. Hank was a legendary cinematographer who filmed free-fall stunts for movies and commercials. How he hurtled earthward at over 100 miles-per-hour with 25 pounds of cameras strapped to his head, and at the same time filmed stunts, was a thing that defied logic. The cameras were mounted on a rig attached to his helmet, and were connected by wires that ran along his arms to hand-mounted controls that allowed him to shoot the aerial sequences.

Jed opened the door and a blast of cold air filled the cabin. "Get into position, Cat," he yelled.

Wind whipping at her clothes, Cat put her feet out on the strut and placed her hands on the wing support bar. Dang, it was cold, she thought. Although her grip was steady, the tempo of her heartbeat shot up. She always got the same buzz when skydiving as she did making love. Her senses heightened, her pulse quickened, and her thoughts got all jumbled up.

Settling into a semi-crouching position, she looked toward the ground. Reality settled in quickly as the 80 mile-per-hour wind pulled at her clothes. The only things between her and a painful death were her experience and the parachutes mounted on her back. And her confidence, she added. That would never fail her.

Jed signaled her.

Taking a deep breath, Cat let go of the wing support. Gravity pulled her toward the surface of the earth as she fell away from the plane. Her descent was rapid. A blurry Pierce appeared in her line of vision as he hurtled toward her. She smiled. He was doing great. Hank wasn't far behind.

For the next several minutes, she swooped, dived and rolled with precise and graceful moves any gymnast would envy. Occasionally, she arched her back and spread out her arms and legs, and achieved stability. Pierce was right behind her, matching her move for move.

A little while later, Cat checked her altimeter. They were approaching the altitude to pull the rip cord and release their parachutes. She signaled Pierce and Hank. Moving her right hand to the rip cord, she released her chute and simultaneously moved her left hand over her head.

The lines jerked her body upwards. Now she could control her descent. This was the fun part of skydiving, Cat mused with a grin. The spectacular view, the fresh air, and the feeling of oneness with nature. As she turned, dipped, and floated toward the ground, Pierce followed her moves. Their landing was smooth.

Thirty minutes later, Cat heard Jed's voice outside the trailer. She was in the stunt crew's trailer now, a far cry from Jan's fully stocked, latest model trailer she'd used earlier. She removed the wig that was streaked with red, just like Jan's real hair, and slipped into her own outfit, a form-filling, stretch denim jumpsuit. It was one of her original designs. She'd only recently started the business, but it was quickly taking off. Turning her head sideways, she checked herself in the mirror.

Satisfied, she ran her fingers through her short curly hair. Reaching inside her bag, she removed a bright red lipstick and applied some to her naturally luscious lips. She pressed her lips, pursed them, and made a "popping" sound before straightening to her five-foot-seven height with a smile. She was ready. Slipping on her high-heeled leather sandals and sunglasses, Cat left the trailer.

Dorian's deep baritone reached her as soon as she stepped down. "That was great, Pierce. Absolutely brilliant. I know it couldn't have been easy, but you pulled it off." He slapped Pierce on the back and added, "Great job."

Jed was waiting for her outside the trailer. But before he could say anything to her, Dorian hailed her. "Hey, kiddo!" He started toward them. "Wasn't she great, Jed?" he directed the question at the stunt coordinator, but didn't wait for a response. "You were awesome, baby." He gave her a warm hug, his moustache tickling her cheek.

"Thank you, Dorian." They had been filming for a month now, and in that short time, Cat had come to know and like the producer. Dorian treated everyone cordially, from the highly paid actors and actresses to the extras. Everyone knew he had a lot riding on this movie. Although he was the executive producer, he was cutting costs by doing the work of a production manager too. Rumor had it that he'd even invested his own money in the movie.

"Take it easy this weekend, kiddo," Dorian was saying. "We have a full schedule next week. Must stick to the schedule. I want you fresh and ready Monday."

"I'll see you on Monday, Dorian," she said with a smile. Something had put the producer in a good mood, Cat concluded. Earlier he'd seemed tense.

"I was going to tell you the same thing, Cat," Jed added, drawing her attention back to him. "Go home and relax. We'll do several dry runs for the helicopter scene at the studio before filming on Wednesday," he reminded her before he bid her good-bye, and disappeared inside the trailer.

Cat put on her sunglasses and headed for Jan's plum red Mercedes. She paused before getting in the car, checking for the man she'd spoken to earlier. He was gone. Disappointment sank in. Why was she interested in that man anyway? Their paths would probably never cross again.

Cat got in and started the car. She automatically reached out to push the CD button. She and Jan had listened to Anita Baker on their way to the base, and the CD was still in the player. She adjusted the volume, and the soothing voice of Anita filtered out.

Soft ballads and classical music or yoga usually relaxed her after a stunt. When those didn't work, mind-blowing sex took care of the excess adrenaline.

Out of nowhere, the image of the man with the Harley flashed in her head. She shook her head, but couldn't dislodge the man's handsome features. She would be crazy to get involved with a stranger. Worse, even, because he seemed like the love 'em and leave 'em type.

———⋙———

Cat was singing along with Toni Braxton when she hit Highway 5 and started for Los Angeles. The convertible was a smooth ride. It was hot, but with the top down and her sleeveless jumpsuit, she was okay. Cool breezes floated past her, teasing her warm skin. Late spring was her favorite time of the year. It was neither too hot nor too cold. But she wished she had brought water. She was thirsty.

As a stunt artist, taking care of her body was her first priority, and that meant keeping it hydrated. Water and a regimented workout, she thought with a grimace. When she was on the road, it was hard to keep a routine, but when at home, she was either at the gym or in her pool. She also tried her best to eat well, although she occasionally binged on sweet potato pie or Rocky Road ice cream, her two favorite desserts.

Two men in a jeep honked at her as she drove past them. She smiled and waved back. Then the musical ring of her cell phone got her attention. When she picked it up, she saw the identity of the caller. "Hey, Jan."

"I talked to Dorian a few seconds ago. He told me you'd left. How was the jump?"

"Smooth."

"Did you see Taj?" Jan asked.

"Who?"

"The hunk with the bike."

Cat's jaw dropped. "You know his name? How did you pull that off?"

"Just walked out there, looked into those gorgeous eyes of his, and asked for his particulars. And you won't believe what I learned."

"He's single and available? Just looking for a serious relationship like all the men you keep throwing at me, right?"

Jan laughed. "No and yes. He's nothing like the others. He's a former FBI agent turned private investigator. Just what you are looking for to help you with Bobby's, uh, situation. And yes, he's also single and available."

Shock rendered Cat momentarily speechless. "I barely mentioned that I plan to hire a P.I., and you conveniently produce one? Yeah, right! And you must be confusing your T.V. character, the Guardian, with the shy Janelle Masters that I know. You aren't that bold, woman. There's no way you approached that man and asked for marital status." Then Jan's giggle teased her ears. "Let me guess what happened. You left the trailer, and he recognized your famous mug, right?"

"Don't you mean my famous jugs?" Jan retorted.

For the first time since the two of them met at the art camp, Cat felt a tinge of jealousy toward Jan's well-endowed chest. Usually she didn't care that her own chest was flat. She stole a quick look at it. Well, not exactly flat, she corrected, merely insignificant beside Jan's double Ds. "So did he want your autograph?"

"Actually, Doug was with me when we spoke. He was waiting for you, you know."

"What?" The car swayed dangerously as her mind absorbed what Jan had said. She regained control of the car as she exclaimed, "Darn it, Jan! Quit throwing one-liners at me. I'm driving your new car."

"Don't you dare crash my baby," Jan admonished playfully.

Cat ignored her. "What do you mean he was waiting for me? Did he tell you that?" And how come I didn't see him after the jump? Cat added silently.

"After our brief chat, Doug and I left him seated on that bike of his with his eyes on the Cessna. So you didn't get to talk with him?"

"He was gone by the time I left."

"Aah, you looked."

"His bike interested me."

"So I noticed. Couldn't you have come up with something more interesting than horsepower and engines, Cat? Then the man tries to flirt with you, and what do you do? Waltz away. You should have at least looked back, girl. He had his hot gaze on you the entire time."

Cat stored that last piece of information. "If you bother to recall, I had an appointment with a parachute."

"Of course, but nothing should pull you away tomorrow night. I'm thinking of inviting him to my dinner party."

Cat was shocked. Jan was so unpredictable, annoyingly so sometimes. But inviting a stranger to her home went beyond that. What was she up to? "You're so outside your mind, Janelle. The man could be a mass murderer, for all you know."

"He put mass murderers behind bars for a living, sweetie. Oh, here's Doug. I've got to go. And Cat? I wasn't really going to invite Taj. Wanted to see what you'd say. But I got his business card. He's really a P.I. Maybe you should give him a call. He might just be what the doctor ordered,. In and out of bed, if you know what I mean."

Cat was left listening to the dial tone. What the doctor ordered indeed. She started to laugh. Jan was such a trip. If I had a man, Cat told herself, girlfriend wouldn't be messing around with my head like this. Jan was always trying to hook her up with some poor guy.

Maybe this time, her meddling might be fruitful. She could hire Taj to help Bobby, couldn't she? With a name like Taj, he was sure to be invincible. He looked invincible. He was big, solid, and beautiful, like the Taj Mahal.

Too bad she was out of the dating scene, though, Cat mused. Taj had a butt to die for. Not that she would ever consider going out with a man like him. Danger oozed from every pore of his body. He was the kind of man who would make her break all her rules, just to put another notch on his bedpost.

Give her a safe banker any time, Cat decided. A banker was predictable and controllable. A banker was not a threat to her heart. When it came to guarding her heart, she wanted to be an expert at playing it safe.

Wasn't that what her Aunt Julia used to advise? *Better to play it safe than rush in like a fool.* Of course, her aunt had meant playing it safe when it came to business, not love. But in her way of thinking, Cat mused, the same philosophy could very easily apply to love.

Growing up in a household where love was used to manipulate and control had taught her a valuable lesson: not to be victimized by love. Her father had selfishly demanded and taken love from her mother until she'd had nothing left to give herself or her children. Not that her mother had been blameless. She'd willingly given in to his demands, putting up with his abusive, manipulative ways to prove her love to him, until the pressure had destroyed her.

There was nothing special about love, Cat had concluded a long time ago. It was a four-letter world often misused. When the time came to choose a mate, she would use her head, not her heart. She would never be a victim of love like her mother.

Thinking about her mother brought a sudden rush of tears to Cat's eyes. How she missed her. Half the time she wondered who she missed the most, her aunty who'd struggled with cervical cancer and succumbed to it a year ago, or her mother, whose recent death after a car accident had left her family in a state of shock.

Maybe the incident she and Bobby had witnessed the night of the accident made letting go harder. As she narrowed the distance to her home, Cat's mind returned to the events of that night.

"Before you drop me off, Cat, can we stop by the house? I need to pick up my laundry," Bobby said.

"Mom is still doing your laundry, baby brother? I wish I'd had it that good in college too. Tuition covered...."

"The inheritance from Aunt Julia paid yours just as it's doing mine, so quit sweating me."

Cat brought her car to a stop outside her parents' house. It was true that their aunt who had neither married nor had children had set money aside for college for all of them, but she couldn't help teasing her brother. Bobby was too darn serious for his age. "No one ever did my laundry or chauffeured me around."

"Maybe you never asked," Bobby retorted.

Cat continued to tease him as they walked to the front door. "Maybe I didn't expect to be pampered just because I'm a genius." Her little brother was brilliant. He was about to graduate with both an undergraduate and master's degree in engineering at the tender age of twenty-one.

"I'm not a genius, smarty-pants. I'm good at what I do. Just as you're good at what you do. You'd never catch me jumping from an airplane, let alone bungee jumping, but you don't see me sweating you."

Cat laughed. Bobby was so intense. She could just see him old and gray, his glasses on the tip of his nose, building some top secret device in some government lab in the middle of nowhere. "Didn't know you scholarly types ever sweated," she teased him.

He tried to give her a side kick, a silly thing they often did when they were together. She skipped out of the way. "Missed."

She was right behind him when he turned the knob and walked into the house. They heard their father's raised voice. "Dad and Uncle Wilkins are at it again," Cat said.

Her father and his best friend, Randal Wilkins, loved to argue about everything, from sports to American education, affirmative action to reparations.

Then they heard their mother's voice. *"Ben, I love you. After thirty-four years of marriage, you should believe me when I say these things."*

"You can't help being who you are, Loretta, so stop lying to me or yourself. You were born a flirt. And your sister is not here to cover for you anymore. Who is it this time? Who are you seeing behind my back? Bobby's father?"

"Not that same tired argument, Ben. This has to stop. Bobby is your son. Why is it that every time we have an argument, you bring that up? Why?"

"I don't know what you do when I'm at work, and Bobby looks differ-

ent from the others."

"*That's crazy, Ben."* There was a pause. "*You know what? I'm through living with someone who doesn't trust me."*

"*You're not going anywhere, Loretta. You belong to me."*

"*I'm leaving you, Ben. Julia set aside money for me, so I don't need you."*

"*I'd rather see you dead, Loretta, than watch you walk away from me."*

Cat saw Bobby's expression. "Bobby…"

"The bastard. Why does he always treat her with such contempt?" He started toward the kitchen.

Cat stepped in his path. "No, Bobby. Don't interfere. They choose to live with each other, choose to call what they feel for each other love. Don't get caught up in their craziness."

Bobby's jaws worked as he tried to control his anger. Then he pivoted on his heel and stormed out of the house. Cat caught the door before it could bang, then followed him outside.

Damn them! When were they going to stop? As far back as she could recollect, their parents had fought. Not frequently, she had to admit, but it was always over meaningless things—her mother talking to some man, the dress she chose to wear, the time it took her to run an errand. The list was endless. But when they weren't fighting, they got so wrapped in each other it was as though no one else existed. They went on trips and vacations alone, attended parties without a second thought for their children. When they couldn't leave them with a sitter, they dropped them off at their Aunty Julia's home. Their love was so exclusive that Cat and her big brother Kenneth had learned at a very young age that they'd never be part of it. Bobby had never learned it. He had often resented them, especially their father.

Cat got in the car and turned to look at her brother. Bobby had pushed his seat back, and was now lying with his eyes closed. "Bobby?"

"Let's get the hell out of here, sis."

"Don't believe things said in anger, Bobby. You know Dad's merely trying to rile her. I know it's…." She stopped when their parents' door opened. Their mother rushed out of the house, jumped into her

Honda Civic, and took off without noticing Cat's car parked at the curb. When their father appeared, Cat got out and braced herself against the car door. "Dad?" she called out.

Their father spared her a glance. "Cat? What are you doing here?" He didn't wait for an answer. He jumped into his truck and took off after their mother.

"Told you we should have left," her brother snarled from inside the car. "They've never cared about us. What they feel, the way they act is so juvenile. But he…he's an insecure, manipulative bastard."

Cat sat down in her seat and closed the door. "Bobby, he doesn't know how to give love because he never received any. Great-grandma Bertha wasn't the most loving of women."

"He's sick. At least now I know why he's never cared about *me*."

"Bobby, don't."

"He's not my father, Cat. You have no idea what a relief that is." He gave a wry laugh and adjusted his seat. "That man is not my daddy."

Cat saw the look on his face and knew it was futile to argue with him. She started the car. The drive to his apartment was accomplished in silence. She would give him a couple of days to come to his senses, she decided. Then they would talk.

But later that night, Cat received a call that their mother was in the hospital. Her car had been involved in an accident, she was informed. As she rushed to the hospital, she kept wondering whether their father had made true his words. *I'd rather see you dead…*

Two days later, their mother died from the injuries she'd sustained. During those two days, their father never left their mother's side. But Cat couldn't stop herself from blaming him for her unexpected death.

Cat snapped from the past as she pulled up outside her house. She entered the combination to unlock her gate and drove into her compound. She unlocked her door, disarmed the alarm system, and sighed as she stepped into the cool interior of her house.

Was it love or guilt that had kept her father by her mother's side? Was there any truth to his accusations of infidelity?

With his gray eyes and light complexion, lighter than hers or Kenny's, Bobby looked very much like their mother. While Cat also favored their mother in looks, she had inherited her father's coloring and dark eyes. Were those small differences in their looks due to different fathers? She didn't think so. Unfortunately, Bobby believed the things he'd heard that night. Since their mother's funeral, he hadn't set foot in their father's house.

Their father had become withdrawn, as though a light had been extinguished from inside. He even accepted Bobby's absence without questions.

Cat wiped the tears from her cheeks and tried to push the negative thoughts away. The truth would never be known, she told herself. Her mother was dead and buried. And her father was barely alive, nursing his heartache and pushing everyone away. The only consolation was that the man who had hit her mother's car was behind bars.

Maybe she should use Taj Taylor to ease some of her worries. As soon as she talked with Bobby, she would see about hiring Taj to help uncover the truth about Bobby's biological father.

CHAPTER 3

Cat searched the movie set for Taj's tall figure. Two weeks had passed since she'd entertained the idea of hiring him. Two weeks since she'd broached the subject with Bobby when he called her from New York and said no. In fact, the impossible boy had said no to everything she'd suggested. No investigators. No speaking to their father. No contribution from Cat or Kenny. This search was his thing, and he was determined to see it through. To her way of thinking, it was becoming an obsession with him. Still, she'd backed off.

The next time she and Taj had met was at the studio when Dorian had introduced him as the new technical advisor. That was the Monday after their first meeting. Jan had been right. Taj Taylor was a former criminal profiler with the FBI, a member of the elite Behavioral Science Unit of the Los Angeles Field Office. He was advising the scriptwriters, the producers, and the directors on how to psychologically assess a crime scene, how to identify and interpret clues, and how to use profiler's terminology. Dorian was determined to make *The Guardian* as realistic as he possibly could.

Since appearing on the set, Cat reflected, he hadn't spoken more than a few words to her. You'd think she would be happy, right? Wrong. It only made her more curious about him. She was reaching a point where all she thought about was that man.

Whenever their paths crossed, that wicked gleam in his eyes beckoned her, and the sensual smile teased her senses. Half the time she wondered what it would be like to kiss him, to run a finger through his mane, or to squeeze his firm backside. Wicked, wicked thoughts she had no business thinking, Cat lamented, not when she wasn't supposed to get too emotionally involved with a man.

A soft sigh escaped her slightly parted lips when her eyes landed on

Taj. He was walking toward the storyboard where the step-by-step action and special effects sequences were displayed. If he turned around, she would see his signature two-day shadow. Not that it distracted one from his chiseled, handsome, bronzed features—the high cheekbones, the mysterious eyes with decadently long lashes, the strong nose, and the sinfully sensuous mouth. Combined with the large Harley-Davidson motorcycle he rode to Warner Brothers Studio every morning, it made him look like a renegade, one that every woman would love to reform. The man had the most faultlessly proportioned body, and, unquestionably, the sexiest swagger she'd ever seen. Even now she wasn't the only female on the set watching him.

As if aware of her scrutiny, Taj's dark eyes locked on her like a heat-seeking missile. Even from afar, Cat felt the effect of that gaze down to the tips of her toes. The bolt of awareness that rippled through her caused her stomach to tighten and her nipples to pucker. Of course, with all the padding she had on for her next scene, she alone was privy to her traitorous response.

"Kind of hard to ignore, isn't he?"

Jan's whisper broke the spell Taj had cast on her. Cat released an erratic breath and turned toward her. "Who?"

"Taj, that's who. He spends his time studying everyone, but you twice as much."

Cat frowned. "He does not."

"Does too. Look at him. He moves around the set, talks to everyone who crosses his path and yet he seems to know exactly where you are. Stops every few minutes to check on you," Jan finished with a knowing smile.

Cat knew Jan was right. But for argument's sake, she shrugged off her comments. "Your imagination is working overtime again, Jan. Like last week when you swore that someone was skulking around your trailer." Jan had run to Cat, and best friend that Cat was, she'd gone back to investigate. And as if he'd known what she was up to, Taj hadn't been far behind. "Made me break into an unnecessary sweat."

"But you saw how fast he followed," Jan added.

Cat narrowed her eyes at her friend. "Another deliberate attempt to bring us together? You're certifiable."

"Sweetie, the whole set knows the man's smitten. I keep wondering why he's not making his move."

That was what had her in jitters too, Cat thought with a frown. Except for a single red rose that was regularly delivered to her every day as soon as she arrived at the set, the man was keeping his distance. Why? Those roses were causing so much speculation among her colleagues she was tempted to tell him to stop. Everyone wanted to know the identity of her secret admirer. She was the only one who was privy to that knowledge. She couldn't even tell Jan that tidbit. Girlfriend might invite him to her house in one of her crazy matchmaking schemes.

Again Cat sought refuge in denial. "Like I said, it's all in your mind, Jan."

"Wear those blinders as long as you want, girl. I have a feeling that when he makes his move, you'd better be ready, 'cause he'll be charging. Look. He's looking over here again."

Cat looked up to see Taj's eyes riveted on her. A shiver ran through her. Was it caused by a premonition that something she couldn't control was about to happen or was it the effect of the fire-retardant gel suit she wore next to her skin?

"Maybe he's shy."

Cat chuckled. "That man hasn't got a shy bone in his body."

"Maybe he's used to women making the first move. Ask him out. It's about time you started dating, anyway. When you're not filming, you're at home working on your designs. Those designs can't replace a good, loving relationship."

They don't hurt you either, Cat thought. But all she said was, "I told you, I have no interest in a relationship." To sidetrack her friend, Cat changed the subject. "We're both off tomorrow. You want to visit a spa? I'm due for a massage and the works."

"Hmm, why not? Doug will be working in the morning."

"I'll make us appointments at the Aqua-Day Spa."

"My treat this time. You took care of our last visit and…." For the first time since Jan sat beside Cat, she looked into her face. A shudder shook her. "Eeew. Every time I see you made up, I get spooked. The voice is the same, but the face is a stranger's."

Cat grinned. Every time she had to double for Jan, the makeup artists and SFX team covered her own natural beauty to make her look as close to Jan as possible. Usually, her face was transformed by adding prosthetic cheeks, using makeup to make her naturally lush lips look less full, and covering her short, curly hair with a flowing wig with red streaks, just like Jan's hair.

"Maybe you need glasses, Jan. I'm supposed to be you."

"Ah-ah, except for the wig I don't see the resemblance."

Their conversation was cut short by the first assistant director's announcement that the stunt was about to be performed. Cat's name was mentioned, along with those of the key personnel involved. Everyone was instructed to stay clear of the area until the scene was wrapped up.

Cat looked up at the makeshift two-story building she was about to jump from. Loren Phillips was staring down at her, a smile on his face. As usual, his curly blonde hair was unruly, and his clothes a little wrinkled. Loren was an assistant to the SFX coordinator, Victor Martins. Cat had worked with other SFX teams before, but none like Victor's. Victor was ingenious, meticulous, and a perfectionist. He often made them practice a stunt over and over again, double-checking everything before the actual performance.

But Loren was assigned to her. His job was to check her readiness, work with her during dry runs, and get her anything she might need for a stunt. The one they were about to perform involved jumping through a glass window of a burning building. At least, that was how it would appear in the final cut. In actuality, an air ram platform was going to catapult her through the window while a rigged charge exploded behind her and ignited the building.

Loren signaled her. Cat nodded and got to her feet. "I've got to go, Jan."

"Take care, you hear? I worry about you sometimes, Cat."

"Don't. We've rehearsed the scene several times. Everything will be cool."

She had no need to worry, Cat told herself. The stunt team and the pyrotechnicians had done a detailed briefing of the stunt. The window she was about to go through was made of sugar glass that couldn't cut her. And Loren had made sure she had the best protection.

Underneath her costume, she wore a thin Nomex suit soaked in fire retardant gel, a raincoat suit to keep the retardant from evaporating, and padding to protect her when she fell. They had the timing between the moment she got pushed off the platform and the detonation of the explosive narrowed to fractions of a second, and she would be way out of harm's way.

"Catch you later, Jan."

"Cat," Jan called, causing Cat, who'd started walking upstairs, to pause and look at her. "I know that when you think no one is looking, you watch Taj too. Give him a chance. I've come to know him these past weeks, and he's really a nice guy." Having said her piece, Jan walked away.

Was Taj a nice guy? Everyone on the set thought so. The men respected him. The women thought he was charming and sexy. Those qualities didn't scare her. What had her in jitters was how she responded to him. It wasn't healthy.

Her eyes found him right away when she looked over at the place where everyone was gathered. His eyes were on her. When he touched a finger to his right eyebrow and saluted her, Cat blushed and continued up the stairs.

Good luck, sweetheart, Taj said silently, although he would have loved to shout it. Heck, he would love to tell her not to do the stunt. There was something about a beautiful woman jumping through a glass window that made him nervous. And the fact that the woman was Cat made it even worse.

Of course he was aware that the window was made of sugar glass, and that the broken pieces wouldn't cut her. He also knew that her landing would be cushioned by the huge airbag beneath the window and the padding she was wearing. Still, seeing her go through one death-defying stunt after another in the last two weeks had been difficult.

Everything about the woman fascinated him: her confidence, her looks, the sexy way she walked. Then there was the mischievous twinkle in her eyes when she smiled, and the vulnerability he glimpsed in them when she was unaware.

Cat Simmons was one amazing woman, and she was meant to be his. He'd known it the first day they met. When he'd looked into her eyes, he'd felt a connection so powerful it had sent panic through him. He had known then that he had found the woman he was going to spend the rest of his life loving.

For two weeks, he'd been waiting for this day to arrive so he could start courting her. Today was his last day of consulting for McCarthy. Call him old-fashioned or whatever, but he didn't believe in mixing business with pleasure, and courting Cat was going to be pure pleasure.

A ripple of anticipation ran through the crew. Taj looked at the window through which Cat was supposed to plunge, and something gripped his chest. There was too much uncertainty in what she did.

What if something went wrong? What if the background fire went out of control? What if the compressed air piston below the air ram failed, and the explosives went off while Cat was still on the platform? What if she got thrown too far and missed the air bag? He hated the negative thoughts, but he couldn't help worrying.

Taj saw the clapper signal the cameramen who were ready to film the scene from various angles. His fingers clenched. Although the urge to close his eyes and shut out what was to follow was almost overwhelming, he kept them fixed on the building.

Fire leaped and licked the windows. Just when the waiting became unbearable, Cat came crashing through the glass window as the charge detonated with a big bang. There wasn't much smoke, but flame shot out after her as she plunged.

Taj's heart almost stopped. He drew a sharp breath in relief when he saw her land on the airbag, then get up and laugh at something the safety crew said. Pride surged through him. *Spectacular.* She was that and more.

As everybody went back to work, Taj scanned the busy scene with a slight smile. The safety crew was at work, deflating the airbag; the camera technicians were checking their cameras; the first assistant director was busy relaying the director's instructions; the art director and his team were getting the props ready for the next scene; the make-up artists, hairdressing, and wardrobe assistants were leaving, probably to prepare the actors and actresses for the next scene; and the SFX team and the stunt coordinator were deep in a discussion with the director near the story board. Even the catering staffs were moving around passing out drinks and food. They'd worked through lunch to get the set ready for the stunt. Crazy as it might sound, he was going to miss it all.

Taj walked over to Dorian and the director and spoke briefly with them. Then he excused himself, stopped by the catering crew's cart for sandwiches and drinks, then headed to the trailer where Cat was.

Cat removed her makeup, scrubbed her face clean, and changed into a pair of jeans and a shirt. She slipped on a pair of high-heeled sandals, picked up her keys and the single rose by her bag, and then stepped down from the trailer.

The first person she saw was Taj Taylor. "Mr. Taylor?"

Taj had told her to call him by his given name, but she wasn't ready to be that casual with him. The smile that settled on his lips was relaxed, as though he found her attempts at thwarting him amusing.

Taj studied her, his eyes taking in her facial features before moving over her shapely form. Finally they touched the single rose she was holding before meeting her stormy gaze. "Cat."

Cat hated the way her body responded automatically to his presence. Her knees become a little bit too wobbly for her liking, and she leaned against the trailer wall for support, took a deep breath, and cursed herself for not being able to fight the attraction between them. She pulled her eyes away from his mesmerizing ones, ignored the wild beating of her heart, and looked toward the set. "Is something the matter?"

"No. I thought I'd bring you your lunch."

Her eyes went to the wrapped sandwiches in his hands.

"One for you and one for me," Taj added.

This was the first time he was asking her to eat with him since he appeared on the set. Why? Cat pushed away from the trailer. "That's kind of you, Mr. Taylor, but you shouldn't have bothered. I'm done for the day."

"I know." He took a step that brought him closer to her. "But I hate to eat alone, and knowing that you worked through lunch, I thought you wouldn't mind joining me." He extended his arm and offered her a sandwich. "C'mon. Take it. I even picked up your favorite—turkey breast on sourdough and iced tea."

How did he know what her favorite sandwich was? Why was she even thinking such a dumb question? The man had spent the last two weeks studying her. He must have noticed that she always requested the same thing for lunch. "No, I think I'll pass, but thanks for your thoughtfulness."

He murmured, "Coward."

Her eyes narrowed. "Are you always this persistent?" The wicked twinkle in his eyes sent warning signals to her head. She knew he was about to say something she wouldn't like. "Never mind." She started to walk around him.

"But I do mind, especially when I want something real bad," Taj stated boldly, easily blocking her path by shifting his large frame.

Cat's eyes snapped to his eyes. Ignoring his blatant, predatory look, she challenged, "And what is it you want, Mr. Taylor?"

"Right now?" After her nod, he said, "I want to spend time with someone I've come to admire these past few weeks. You are an amazing stunt artist, Cat."

If he thought praise was going to get him what he wanted from her, then…he was right, this once. It had been a long day, and she was tired and hungry. "Okay, Mr. Taylor." She took the sandwich he was offering her. "Thank you, Mister…" She stopped. She felt ridiculous calling him Mr. Taylor after he'd brought her lunch. "Thanks for the sandwich, Taj."

A sensual gleam settled in his eyes. "Say that again."

"What?"

"Say my name again."

Cat frowned. "Taj. Why?"

"That was the first time you've used my first name. I like the way you say it. Do you watch what you eat all the time?"

"Not really," she said cautiously, not sure what he would say next. He was so unpredictable. But her caution was forgotten when she dug into her sandwich. "Hmm, this is good," she murmured. Then she looked up and caught his eyes. He was staring at her as if she were a delicacy he wanted to sample. His sandwich was still in its wrapper, forgotten.

"Then maybe we should go out sometime. I know a great Thai restaurant that serves the hottest and tastiest food on the entire west coast."

I don't think so, Cat wanted to say. But after his thoughtfulness, she decided to be accommodating. "Maybe," she murmured, then moved away from him.

"Don't run away."

She laughed. "I'm not running away." She leaned against the trailer.

"Let me get you a chair." He started toward a set of empty chairs.

"Please, don't bother." Cat indicated the trailer's steps. "I can sit here."

A boyish smile crossed his lips. "It's no problem at all."

Cat watched him as he walked way. Every muscle flowed in perfect unison when he moved. What would he look like with nothing on but…?

Cat stopped the thought before it was fully formulated. Why had she agreed to share lunch with him? Spending time with him could lead to things she didn't want to deal with. Although she hated to admit it, she found Taj Taylor too attractive. And from the lazy sensual smile on his lips, he knew it too. "Thank you," Cat said when he set a chair beside her.

"You don't have to thank me for anything, sweetheart." He placed the other chair opposite hers, waited until she was seated, then sat down. "Isn't that better?" he added with a slight grin.

"Yes, it is. Thanks." She waited for him to say something else, but he kept studying her. When his eyes landed on her lips before lifting to meet her gaze, Cat smiled nervously at him. Maybe engaging in small talk wouldn't be such a bad thing. It was better than staring at each other. "So, Taj, have you always wanted to be a detective?"

"Yeah, since I was old enough to play cops and robbers. I was always the cop, of course, while my oldest brother was always the robber. He loved to talk his way out of doing jail time." He removed his sandwich from its wrapper and took a big bite.

"Is he a lawyer?"

He laughed. "You've got it. I was with the Bureau until four years ago. Then I decided to go freelance."

"So the adage, once a cop always a cop, is true?" Cat asked

He flashed her smile. "You could say that. I find it satisfying."

"You don't mind the danger?"

Instead of answering her, he studied her so intently that she felt heat steal up her leg and settle between her legs. She tried to think of something to say to stop him from turning her into a mass of nerves. "I'm sorry, maybe that was too intrusive."

"You don't have to apologize, sweetheart." He pulled a bottle of iced tea from his coat jacket and offered it to her. When her hand closed around it, he didn't let go; he tugged gently until Cat looked at him. "If I answer your twenty questions now, what will we talk about tomorrow?"

His voice was husky and decadently sexy. Was she seeing him tomorrow? "Oh, I'm off for the next couple of days."

"I know." He let go of her drink and pulled one from his other pocket. "And I'm done here."

What did that have to do with seeing her? Cat wondered. Somehow, she doubted that their paths would ever cross. She smiled briefly at him. "I guess I won't be seeing you then, Taj." She carefully wrapped her partially-eaten sandwich. "I'd better be going now."

"I'll walk you to your car."

Cat opened her mouth to tell him not to bother, changed her mind, and closed it. She knew he would walk with her whether she liked it or not. She picked up her things, threw the remainder of her sandwich in a nearby garbage can, and started for her car. He fell in step with her. She shot him a glance. "Thanks for the lunch, Taj."

"The pleasure was mine."

Thoroughly flustered by the intent look in his eyes, Cat hurried to her car. But he easily kept up with her long strides. "Well, it was nice talking with you. If I ever need a P.I., I'll be sure to give you a call," she added as she got into her car.

He pulled out a card from his pocket and passed it to her. When her fingers gripped it, he tugged at it gently until Cat looked up. "This is not good-bye, Cat. I'll be seeing you soon."

No, you won't, she thought.

Oh, yes, I will, his expression seemed to say. Then he did something unexpected. He reached down and dropped a kiss on her cheek. "Take care, baby."

Cat didn't start the car right away. Instead she watched him walk away. What did he want from her? How was she going to discourage him when he seemed so sure of himself? So far, he hadn't said anything definite, just hinted, though that naughty smile and those intense eyes seemed to say so much. Added to that were the roses.

Unconsciously, her hand went to her cheek where he'd kissed her. When she realized that she was stroking the skin where his lips had touched, she dropped her hand, started her car, and eased off the brakes.

CHAPTER 4

As Cat left Burbank behind and headed home, the scene with Taj kept replaying in her head, haunting her. What had he meant by saying he would be seeing her soon? What was she going to do if he said he wanted her? Knowing her, she would probably run in the opposite direction.

She was pulling into her driveway when a squad car sounded behind her. She glanced back with a frown which became a smile when she recognized the police officer. It was her brother Kenny. He'd deliberately put the siren on, the tease. He wasn't even in his unmarked L.A.P.D. Ford Crown Victoria. He was driving his wife's 4Runner.

Cat entered the code to open her gate, drove in, and parked her car. He was right behind her. She stepped out of her car and then turned to smile at him. "Hey, big bro! Are you trying to get me evicted by sounding that thing around here?"

Kenny grinned at her as he unfolded his six-foot-two frame from his car. He was dressed in blue jeans and a mauve polo shirt. His head was shaven clean. She'd always thought that her brother, with his quiet ways and easy smile, was the epitome of masculinity. That had changed the day she met a rogue by the name of Taj Taylor.

Kenny threw the portable siren back into his car. "You were speeding."

"Was not."

"Was too."

"So cuff me, officer."

"Don't tempt me. But it wouldn't do to haul my only sister in. The guys at the precinct would never let me live it down." He opened his arms.

Cat walked into them and received a warm hug. "Hmm, I needed that." She grinned at him. "How are you? How's Bri...Jamie?" Kenny and his wife Brianna had recently celebrated their second anniversary. Jamie was their eight-month-old son.

"Doing great." He pulled a lock of her hair and added, "Find yourself a man, sis, then you won't need hugs from me."

She punched his stomach playfully, to which he gave a mock grunt. "I'll always welcome a warm pooh-hug from you, baldy, whether I'm involved with some man or not." She stretched her back and smiled. "Jeez, I'm beat. We've been filming like crazy these past few weeks. I used to meet Bri every Wednesday at the Copper Mill for lunch, but these days I'm lucky if I eat."

Kenny draped an arm around her shoulder. "You need a regular job, sis, instead of jumping off burning buildings." He studied her face. A frown crossed his handsome features. "How are you doing?"

"So-so." Could he tell that she was stressed out? Worrying about Bobby and Taj's constant presence at the set had frayed her nerves. But thank goodness Taj would be leaving now that his contract was over. As for Bobby, he'd called her a week ago to let her know that he was back in town, but he'd still missed the Sunday dinner at their father's. She had no idea whether he was still trying to locate his imaginary biological father. "You want to come in?"

Before Kenny could reply, a voice called, "Hi, Catherine."

Mrs. Lucille Lambert, Cat realizedher next door neighbor. Nothing ever happened on their street without that woman's knowledge, whether it was new neighbors, renovations, houses for sale or newborn babies.

"Ms. Busybody is at it again. When are you going to tell her to stop spying on you and eavesdropping on your conversations?" Kenny whispered to Cat.

Cat nudged her brother in the ribs. "Not so loud, Kenny. She could hear you."

Kenny dropped his arm from her shoulder, and they both turned around to face Mrs. Lambert. She was peering at them from the gate.

"Hi, Lucille. How are you and Jonas doing?" Cat asked.

"We're doing great, my dear. I heard the siren and wondered what was going on. But I see it's your brother. Hello, Kenneth."

Kenny studied Mrs. Lambert's beaming expression, perfectly styled hair, and the designer outfit she had on. "Mrs. Lambert, you're looking very fetching this afternoon. Going anywhere special?"

The woman blushed all the way to her coiffed ash-blonde hair. "Oh, you…you're such a flirt, Kenneth. I merely slipped on this old thing for afternoon tea with my bridge friends."

"Well, you're looking mighty fine in that 'old thing,' Mrs. Lambert. I hope you'll have a wonderful time with your friends."

"Thank you, Kenneth. Bye. See you later, Catherine dear." She walked back to her gate.

Kenny waited until they heard her door close before he said, "Do they still use their high-powered binoculars to spy on their neighbors?" A brick wall separated Cat's house from the Lamberts'.

Cat opened her door, disabled the alarm, and pulled Kenny inside the house. "Those are for bird-watching. How soon you forget that poor Jonas is wheelchair-bound."

"I'm sure the birds that *poor Jonas* watches are the two-legged kind, preferably those of the female persuasion, although one can never tell these days. The wheelchair-bound old man's preferences might be different."

Cat wagged her finger at him as she kicked off her sandals. "Only kind words, please. Lucille takes care of my plants when I'm out of town. She may be nosey, but she's harmless. Besides, my bedroom window faces the other side of my compound. Let the others worry about being spied on." She dropped her purse and keys on a table in the foyer.

They left the foyer and walked along the hallway, passing an arched doorway opening to the living room, and another to their right leading to a formal dining room. They headed straight for the kitchen.

"So, how is the movie business and Miss Janelle?"

"Keeping me busy…and Jan is fine, as usual." Cat opened the fridge and pulled out bottled water. "Want a drink?"

"Sure. When will you be done filming?"

"I'm not sure, but it'll be sooner than Dorian had anticipated. Did I mention to you that he hired a consultant to help with the crime scenes?"

"Yeah. The one who was delaying things by asking for more props."

"*He* was fired a couple of weeks ago. Dorian brought in a new guy who simplified things considerably. Taj worked with the scriptwriters and the director to straighten out some of the mess his predecessor created, coached the actors, and even brought in his people to work with the art director and the prop team."

"Did you say Taj?"

"Yes. Ex-FBI Taj Taylor. Do you know him?"

"Persistent-to-the-core Special Agent Taylor is now a consultant? I'll be damned."

Was that admiration she was hearing in her brother's voice? Kenny wasn't given to admiring just anyone, Cat thought as she reached for a bottle of the Heineken she kept for when her brothers visited. She slid it across the counter. Kenny caught it and followed her to the living room, where she flopped onto a lounge and sipped her bottled water. Kenny opened his beer and took a long swig before sitting down opposite her.

She was beat, but it was good to be home. The warmth of her home seeped into her. Although the Spanish-style house was part of her inheritance from her Aunt Julia, Cat had refurbished it, put her personal stamp on it and made it as comfortable as possible. There were plants and flowers everywhere and lovely watercolors on the walls. The décor soothed senses.

"The guys at the precinct will get a kick out of that," Kenny said with a chuckle.

Cat pressed the cool bottle against her temple. A headache was brewing behind her eyes. "Out of what?"

"Taj Taylor turning consultant. You could say he rubbed a couple of people the wrong way when he was stationed here in the L.A. field office. He wasn't very good at following orders. Liked to do things his way. But he's sharp and relentless. The best criminal personality profiler I've ever worked with. Rumor has it that he took a bullet meant for some prime minister, even got invited to the White House to receive a commendation from the president."

Bullet, huh? Sounded like something Taj would do. Could that be why he decided to leave the Bureau? And how the hell did they get on the topic of Taj anyway? Time to change the subject, Cat decided. "So, did you stop by for a visit or was there some purpose?"

Kenny grinned. "I know that tone. You're about to kick me out, aren't you?"

"Oh, no, big bro, you can stay as long as you want." She eyed his feet which were now resting on her coffee table. She was too tired to ask him to put them down. "I, on the other hand, must soak my weary muscles in a hot, bubbly, scented bath or go stark raving mad."

"You work too hard, baby girl."

She wrinkled her nose at him.

"Okay, this is one of the reasons I stopped by. Dad's retirement party has been tentatively set for Friday the 21st, three weeks from tomorrow. The details are still sketchy." Their father was retiring as the Deputy Chief of Operations, West Bureau of L.A.P.D. Kenny worked directly under him at the precinct on West Venice Boulevard. "And could you baby-sit for us?"

Because their parents had often left them with sitters while they were off partying, Kenny hated to leave his only child with strangers. His wife Brianna was a stay-at-home mother, and if they had to go anywhere, Jamie either went with them or stayed with Cat. "Hmm, you weren't thinking of tonight, were you?"

"N-no! Pardon the language, sis, but you look like shit. I wouldn't dream of leaving Jamie with you when you're obviously tired."

"You're so good for my ego. FYI, I don't mind watching that cherubic bambino anytime. Except for Saturday night, I'm home."

"What's happening Saturday night?"

"Dinner party at Jan's."

"Another one?"

Cat just shrugged.

"Lots of company?"

Cat cut him a suspicious look. "Yes. Why do you ask?"

"You don't go out much, sis. Have you dated anyone since that shmuck Rick?"

Cat gave her brother a withering look. "I'm not discussing my dating habits with you, Kenneth Simmons."

"Yeah. Whatever. But there's this new guy at my precinct who…."

She closed her eyes and shut him out. Why did everyone feel they had to fix her up with a man? It wasn't as if she were lonely or desperate. Okay, maybe she got a little lonely sometimes, but it was better than the alternative. She'd gone through one man who cheated on her, and another who stole from her. She was better off without one, thank you very much.

"Okay, sis, I'll back off." He stood up. "So tomorrow is cool?"

She nodded. "Are the two of you going somewhere special?"

"We're thinking of catching a movie, then dinner. Bri works so hard that I need to wine and dine her once in a while."

Cat knew that her sister-in-law had been cooking and taking food to their father's place regularly since their mother died. "You found yourself a gem there, big brother. And yes, tomorrow is fine with me. We're not filming until next week. Jan and I are hitting the spa in the afternoon, and that's about it."

"I owe you one," Kenny said.

"I'm not doing this for you. I love my nephew, and enjoy having him around."

"Until you have yours, huh?" He wiggled his eyebrows.

Cat rolled her eyes at him.

"Thanks. I better head home. Bri wants you to call her." He started for the door.

Cat got up too. She was tired, but she had been taught to always see her guests to the door. "I will. Have you seen or heard from Bobby lately?"

"Not since last week when he was at our house. Bri gave him plenty of food to keep him going for a while."

"That boy needs to learn to cook."

Kenny laughed. "You try telling him that. I'll stop by his apartment and check on him tomorrow." As they got to her front door, Kenny paused to say, "Sis, you need to update your security system, okay?" He pointed at her door. "What you have now is too basic. Lately we've had cases of break-ins, and most of them have involved single women. I'd hate to see something like that happen to you."

She'd been meaning to upgrade her system, but work always got in the way. "I'll take care of it, Kenny. Thanks for reminding me. Now give me a hug." He laughed as he hugged her. She loved hugs, always had, even as child.

Kenny tugged her curls, and teased, "Find your own bear-man to hug, sis."

"Yeah-yeah," she murmured.

Cat smiled as she watched him drive away. How proud she was of her brother, she mused. Despite their parents' example, Kenny was a doting father and a wonderful, loving husband. The two of them had sworn that when they married, they wouldn't repeat their parents' mistakes. They wouldn't neglect their children or use them to hurt their spouse. Kenny was fulfilling that vow. He doted equally on his wife and son.

She, on the other hand, wasn't sure if she would ever marry. What if she turned out to be just like her mother? What if she got so wrapped up in pleasing her man that she neglected her children? The very thought sent a shiver of apprehension through her.

No, if she ever considered marriage, she'd use her head to pick a mate. None of that head-over-heels-in-love nonsense. Nosiree, she would not be ruled by emotions or feelings. Too much passion was unhealthy; her parents had taught her that

Cat picked up Kenny's empty beer bottle from her coffee table. She'd forgotten the coaster and now there was a wet ring on the glass-top. She threw the bottle in the trash can and wiped the table with a paper towel. She glanced at the clock. She was going to take a long bath, order some take-out, then crawl into bed.

Cat inserted an Alicia Keys CD in her player, adjusted the volume, then headed to the bathroom. Getting her candles, aromatic beads, and oils, she went about getting her bath ready. When it was set to her satisfaction, she stripped and sank into its frothy depth, turned on the jets, and let the churning water massage her achy body. A sigh escaped her lips as she closed her eyes.

As much as she liked what she did for a living, at times it took a toll on her poor body, Cat thought as she sank deeper into the scented water. The soothing bath soon had her in such a state that her mind started playing tricks on her.

The jets of water against her skin felt like a lover's soft caresses and kisses. Heat spread along her lips, and an ache started in her belly and pooled between her legs. Her thoughts turned to former agent, decorated hero, Taj Taylor. It was his hands she now imagined on her skin, his lips on hers, his hair caressing her body as he kissed her. Cat's eyes snapped opened. She sat up in the tub and shook her head.

She didn't want to think about Taj, not now, not ever. Unfortunately, her mind betrayed her. Even as she catalogued reasons why she shouldn't let him bother her, a part of her was intrigued enough about the man to wonder and fantasize. Taj defied all her rules. She wanted her mind to reject him. It wasn't working. And her body was following her mind blindly.

Cat became restless. The music that usually calmed her down after a stunt wasn't working. Maybe yoga might do the trick, orWhat exactly had Taj meant by saying he'd be seeing her soon?

Taj secured his motorcycle outside his office building. Tucking the helmet under his arm, he entered Hawkeye Plaza, the five-story building he'd bought three years ago and renovated. He'd changed the name to Hawkeye after his granddaddy, a fact that had pleased the old man to no end.

Instead of heading to the elevators, he walked across the lobby, past the statue of a hawk balancing on a globe, to the doors of Ying an' Yang Flower Boutique. He needed to get flowers for Jackie.

He had been discussing the last scene with Dorian when his assistant, Mrs. Dunlop, had called him with the news that Jackie Wilson had been rushed to the hospital with lacerations on her face and several broken ribs. The perpetrator was none other than her ex-boyfriend.

Taj had seen her a few minutes ago, and the poor woman's face was a mess. Hopefully, the doctors could do something for her. Just thinking about the situation made his chest tighten with anger.

Jackie was a former client. He had closed her case nearly a month ago. Her ex-lover had been stalking her until the day Taj caught him slashing the tires of her BMW. As her hired P.I., Taj had told Jackie to press charges. But the soft-hearted, aging diva had refused to inflict more pain on her besotted ex-boyfriend.

Not another black man behind bars, Jackie had insisted. Instead, she had reasoned with the man, showed him the error of his ways. Her words, not his. And for two weeks the man had left her alone. But Taj had dealt with enough psychos to know that they didn't change overnight. So he had asked one of his guys to keep an eye on the man. But when Jackie found out, she had been livid. Taj had been forced to close the case. And now this.

Taj pushed open the door of Ying an' Yang and walked in.

"Ah, Mr. Taylor, how do you do?" Mr. Yang hailed heartily with a bow.

"Evening, Mr. Yang. Could I get a bouquet?"

Mr. Tang quickly left the flowers he was tinkering with, and walked toward Taj. He dismissed his assistant. "I'll take care of Mr. Taylor. Roses?"

Taj shook his head. Every couple of days for the last two weeks, he'd picked up roses for Cat from Mr. Yang. "Something else, I think," Taj murmured, looking around. "Ah, that one." He pointed at a bouquet in a violet vase. It contained flowers of different purple hues;

tulips, irises, roses, and violets.

"Perfect. What's the occasion?" Mr. Yang asked.

"They are for a sick friend."

"Maybe you add a teddy bear or balloons, yes? Make a perfect get-well gift?"

Taj looked around. He didn't know anything about flowers or get-well gift baskets. He did know that purple was Jackie's favorite color, and that was the reason he was getting her a purple bouquet. Cat, on the other hand, loved roses. The scent seemed to surround her, he'd noticed.

Taj forced thoughts of Cat from his head and answered Mr. Yang, "I think some balloons sound wonderful."

"Good choice."

"How is your wife doing, Mr. Yang?" Taj asked as he pulled out his wallet.

"Better. I tell her, no go skating, you old to start learning. She says, 'This is America, Liu, age no matter.' My daughter says, 'Mommy right.' I tell them, 'Okay, fine.' Then she hurt her hip." He finished with a shrug.

Taj tried not to laugh at the florist's narration. "I hope she feels better soon."

"I hope she listen to me, eh?" Mr. Yang added.

Taj paid for the flowers, then headed upstairs. After he'd finished refurbishing the building, with the help of Sheryl, his oldest brother's wife, he had been worried that he might not fill it with tenants. But within a month, the stores downstairs were leased by Mr. and Mrs. Liu Yang for his flower shop, a forty-something-year-old woman, Olga Chavez, for a clothing store, and a Jewish couple for a jewelry store. A real estate company took over the entire second floor. Several offices and companies were on the third and fourth floor. His agency, Hawk Detective Agency, was on the top floor.

He walked into the office, opened the door to his right, and saw Mrs. Dunlop's grey hair peeking above a cubicle. She was on the phone. "Still here, Mrs. D.?"

She looked up and smiled. "Mr. Taylor. I didn't expect you back. Mr. Orlandi would like to have a word." She waved the phone in the air.

"Thanks, Mrs. D. I'll take it in my office." But instead of walking into his office, he pulled a carnation bloom from the bouquet he was carrying and passed it to Mrs. Dunlop. "For telling me about Jackie. I don't know what I'd do without you."

The fifty-three-year-old woman blushed with pleasure. "I'm sure you'd survive just fine, Mr. Taylor. Thank you for the flower."

"No, we wouldn't, Mrs. D., and you know it." He had tried to make Mrs. Dunlop call him by his given name, but she was from the old school. An "everyone and everything in its place" kind of a woman was Mrs. D. Taj had called her Mrs. Dunlop until they'd been together for a couple of months. He'd found out that her staid exterior hid a nurturing and kind heart. Now everyone in the office called her Mrs. D. "Go on home, Mrs. D."

He used the connecting door to gain access to his office. He sat behind his desk before picking up the phone. "Nat? What's happening in Napa Valley?" Nat Orlandi was his friend from college. He owned a small vineyard in Napa Valley.

"Nothing but growing grapes and winemaking. What's up, detective?"

"Keeping busy. Work is good. Can't complain. What's going on with you?"

"The West Coast Wine Competition is being held this weekend. Just wanted to tell you I'm flying in tonight."

"Ah, your first harvest. Congratulations, Nat."

"We've been damn lucky. With all the problems we encountered in the last year, it's a wonder we made enough to break even."

"Winemaking is in your blood, Nat. You were bound to succeed." Nat had been a happy-go-lucky broker in New York when he was told that he'd inherited land in Napa Valley, and had to claim it or lose it. He'd cashed in his stocks and the ones he'd invested in for Taj, and left for California. And because he had done it before the dotcom crash, he'd made both of them a tidy sum of money. While Nat sank most of his wealth into his vineyard and winery, Taj had bought this office building and built a home in Simi Valley.

"So, are you planning on staying at my place? Annie Mae would love someone to fuss over." Annie Mae Johnson was his housekeeper. She was always complaining that Taj paid her for nothing, since he rarely spent time at his house.

"Thanks, man, but I'll have to pass. I'm bringing my mom and a few of my people. I don't want to inconvenience you or Ms. Annie Mae."

"She'll be disappointed."

"I won't tell her if you don't. I've got to run, Taj. Let's plan on having dinner sometime this weekend. We can celebrate my victory. I intend to net a few gold medals." When Taj laughed at his presumptuous attitude, Nat added, "I'll bring you several bottles. I'll call you when I get in."

"Sounds like a plan, Nat." They hung up after that.

Taj stretched his neck, trying to ease the tension on his upper back. Mrs. Dunlop walked into his office with a manila file in her hand. He looked at his watch. It was after six. "You should be heading home. Mrs. D."

"I was just finishing up. Mr. Norris left this report for you." She passed him a folder with Godfrey Norris's name on it. "Young Mr. Solomon said he might not come in tomorrow until late afternoon. His son isn't feeling well."

Taj nodded. In his employ were two junior detectives. One was Mike Calhoun, a twenty-seven-year-old high school drop-out who, at Taj's insistence, was back in school. Mike had just passed his GED and was now studying photography at a nearby junior college. Solomon Dawson, at twenty, had recently had a baby and needed to work full-time. Then there were the two senior detectives, Godfrey Norris and Frank Clark. At fifty-nine, Frank was the oldest member of his team. Godfrey was a few years younger at fifty-five. Both were former military police. Frank was the surveillance gadgets expert, while Godfrey was good at tailing people. Five-feet-five and reed-thin, Godfrey tended to blend into the background. The five of them made an impressive team.

"Thanks, Mrs. D.," Taj said as he flipped through Godfrey's report.

Mrs. Dunlop's eyes went to the flowers Taj had set on his desk. "Did you get to see Ms. Wilson?"

"They were still working on her when I got there. I promised to stop by later." He knew he didn't owe Jackie Wilson anything, but he couldn't forgive himself if he didn't go in to see her. Other than her assistant and companion, Moira, Taj had a feeling that Jackie didn't have many people she called friends.

"I hope her injuries aren't serious," Mrs. Dunlop said before she turned toward the door. "I think I'll head on home now, Mr. Taylor. I'll see you tomorrow."

"Have a good evening." As the door closed behind Mrs. D., Taj leaned back in his chair and closed his eyes. What a day. Thank goodness it was over.

A pair of flashing black eyes set in a smooth walnut-brown, exotic face floated in his head. Cat Simmons. A smile touched his lips as he recalled in detail their earlier encounter. He couldn't wait for Saturday to arrive. Anticipation ran through him at the thought of seeing her again. Jan had invited him over to her house with the promise that Cat would be there. He wished it were tonight, though.

You're getting impatient in your old age, Taylor.

His hand went to his chin. He got off his desk and headed to the bathroom.

When was the last time he'd shaved? Three days ago? Most likely. Whenever he was busy, shaving and making the long drive to his house in Simi Valley became the least of his concerns. After prowling the streets at night, it was much easier to crash in the bed in the room off his office than to drive miles away to his house.

Taj looked in the mirror. *You look like a bum, Taylor.* He was surprised Cat hadn't run for cover when they'd spoken earlier. He picked up his shaving cream. Darn, it was empty. He'd have to shave when he got home

Picking up Jackie's flowers, Taj left his office. After seeing Jackie, he was going to head home to a decent meal cooked by his talented cook and a nice, long, uninterrupted sleep. In two days, he was going courting.

CHAPTER 5

"I cannot believe I did that," Jan wailed as she and Cat left Dialog.

"Burn it off tomorrow, Jan," Cat quipped as they waited outside for Jan's ride. They had spent half the day at Aqua-Day Spa being pampered by the most expensive hands in the entire Los Angeles area. Then they'd stopped at Dialog, Jan's favorite coffeehouse. As usual, girlfriend had over-indulged on various mouth-watering pastries.

"It's easy for you to say. You have the metabolism of a horse. Never gain a pound."

"That's not true. I work out like crazy, that's my secret. Besides, you're reed-thin. I don't know what you're complaining about," Cat chided her.

"It's good for my spleen," Jan retorted as she looked up and down the street. "Where's that man of mine? I can't move an inch. If he doesn't appear soon, take me home, Cat. I need to lie down and digest this, slowly."

Cat giggled. "It's not my fault your mouth and stomach don't always agree when it comes to sweets."

Jan looked back at the shop. "This is the last time, I promise. Look at the display. The rolls seem to say, 'Eat me. Come and sink your teeth into me.' "

Cat laughed. "Quit complaining, girl. You know you enjoyed every last one of those rolls and horns." The soft purr of an engine made her look up. "Oh, here's your man."

Doug's silver Benz slowed down and stopped beside them. He rolled down the window. "Hey. Do I know you honeys from somewhere?" Cat dismissed his comment with a wave while Jan stuck out her tongue at him. "Sweetheart, looks like you overdid it again," he told her with a knowing grin.

Jan made a face at him. "I don't know what you're talking about."

Cat laughed. Jan swung her bag at her and she skipped out of reach. Doug left his side of the car to open the door for Jan. "Need a ride, Cat?"

"No. My car is parked down the street." She waved at them. "See y'all tomorrow."

"Hey, Cat, about your date for tomorrow…"

She stopped to glare at him. He was just as bad as Jan and Kenny. Always trying to fix her up with someone. She pointed at him. "Back off before I get ugly, Doug Hayes."

"You haven't met him yet, Cat. Gary's a real nice guy."

"Hmm-mm, so was your banker of two weeks ago. His tongue was hanging all over the place…. I thought Hannibal Lecter had acquired a tan and was on the prowl." She shuddered with revulsion and pointed an imaginary gun at him. "Pow! Jan, tell him to back off or I'm off your guest list."

"Let her be, sweetie," Jan told Doug.

Cat turned to stare at her best friend suspiciously. Usually Jan supported her boyfriend's matchmaking schemes. Why was she taking her side this time? What was she up to? "Thank you, Janelle. I think."

Jan winked at her. "You're welcome, Catherine." She turned to Doug. "Baby, I need to lie down before I become sick all over your leather seats." They waved at Cat as their car left the curb.

Cat started toward her car in high spirits. A couple of hours spent pampering her body often did that to her. Yesterday, she'd been tense and emotional. Now she could conquer the world.

She was close to her car when she heard, "Hey, baby, wait up."

Her steps faltered. That voice was familiar. Could it be Taj's? Or was her imagination playing tricks on her? She kept on walking.

"Why is it you're always running away from me, woman?"

It was Taj, all right. Cat turned around with a frown. The frown disappeared when she took a proper look. *Oh, my,* she thought as her eyes widened. A soft whistle escaped her lips as an appreciative gleam entered her eyes.

What had he done with his bad-boy image? He had shaved, and he looked devilishly handsome in tan slacks and a mauve polo shirt. It wasn't that she hadn't liked what she'd seen these past few weeks. Taj would always look sexy, masculine, and dangerous, dressed up or not. "What did you say about running away?"

His eyes roamed her glowing face. "You're always running away from me. Am I such an ogre?"

"No."

"Diseased?"

She smothered a giggle. "Of course not."

"Unsightly?"

She raised an eyebrow and pursed her lips. "Fishing for a compliment, detective?"

"Dying for attention, baby. But right now, I'll settle for a kiss." When she grinned at him impishly, he leaned down and pressed his lips to her cheek. "How are you?"

Her cheek tingled from his kiss and his clean masculine scent filled her nose, overwhelming her senses, making her feel a little weak in the knees. But she recovered fast enough to say, "Great. What about you? No bad guys to catch today?"

"A break now and then doesn't hurt. I was dropping off a friend at his hotel when we decided to stop here for a decent cup of coffee. Do you want to join us?" he asked, indicating the coffee house.

Cat was tempted. But she couldn't forget her resolution. Taj Taylor was someone she had to keep at arm's length. Her gut feeling told her that he could storm through her defenses with little difficulty. "I just left the place, Taj. Maybe some other time."

"Was that another brush-off?"

She smiled and took a step away from him. "No. Jan and I were in there for at least an hour." She looked at her watch. "And I must head home."

"Going out tonight?"

"No, staying in."

"May I join you?" he said in a husky voice.

A shiver ran up Cat's spine. The man could seduce with words alone, she thought. And his dark eyes were filled with a hunger she couldn't afford to acknowledge. "No, you can't," she replied.

"Why not? I want to get to know you better, sweetheart. But I can't if you keep running from me or pushing me away."

"I'm not running away. I happen to be baby-sitting for my brother and his wife tonight. I don't want to disappoint my eight-month-old nephew by being late."

His brows shot up. "Baby-sitting? I'm impressed."

"Why?"

He grinned charmingly. "If I tell you, promise not to laugh?"

She shrugged. "Promise."

"I had this crazy idea that you spent your weekends racing bikes, skydiving, and that sort of thing."

Cat laughed. She did her share of those when she wasn't filming. "I do those too, but I also baby-sit." She looked at her watch. "I really must leave now, Taj."

"What about later tonight? I can stop by for a drink." She shook her head. "Late dinner? You have to eat when you baby-sit, don't you?" She shook her head again and smiled. He wiggled his eyebrows wickedly and asked, "Dessert?" His eyes dropped to her lips. "I know the best dessert in the entire world. I promise you, you'll enjoy it."

From the glint in his eyes, she knew exactly what he was thinking. The man was shameless. Would kissing him be a worthy dessert or a prelude to something much more decadent? Somehow she knew his kisses would lead to bed. Tangled limbs and sweaty bodies floated in her head. "I'd love to, Taj, but I can't. Maybe some other time," she murmured coolly.

"*Maybe some other time.* I'm truly beginning to dislike that expression. Okay, baby, I wouldn't want to deprive you of such a noble undertaking as baby-sitting. Call me when you need help with your nephew."

Cat gave him a slightly provocative grin. "And what do you know about babies, Detective Taylor?"

He smiled at her with a wealth of masculine charm. "Get to know me, and you'll find out."

The promise in his voice sent tremors up and down her spine again. "Yes, well, I won't keep you. I'm sure your friend is wondering where you've disappeared to."

"Nat will understand. I'll walk you to your car."

She laughed. "It's less than a block away, Taj. What can possibly happen to me in broad daylight?"

He took her arm, draped it over his. "Thugs don't need darkness to accost a beautiful woman, sweetheart."

Her arm tingled where their skin touched. Cat tried to ignore it. It wasn't easy. "Taj?"

"Yes, baby?"

"I'm not your baby, or sweetheart, or whatever," she said with a slight smile, robbing the words of their sting.

"I know. You look like a sweetheart, though," he replied with a naughty gleam in his eyes. He reached out to stroke her cheek.

Cat shifted her head, and his hand dropped. "I bet you tell that to all the women you meet." To her chagrin, her voice was unsteady.

"I'm not dignifying that with an answer."

She wrinkled her nose at him.

"Can I at least have your number?" When she frowned at him, he added, "I can't call you if I don't have your number. You did say we could share dessert sometime in the near future, didn't you?"

It was only a number, no big deal, Cat told herself. She could always say no. Before she could think up any more excuses, she wrote her number on a piece of paper and passed it to him.

"What's your nephew's name?"

"Jamie. Why?"

"I'll call later tonight to see how you and Jamie are doing, if it's okay with you."

Cat shrugged. "That's fine. We usually have a slumber party with lots of games and story time. He's a mild-tempered baby. But give us a call anyway. He loves to coo on the telephone."

"Good." He waited until she opened her door, then casually

dropped a kiss on her cheek, lingering as he inhaled her scent. "Hmm, roses. You sure smell good, Catherine Simmons."

Cat's eyes widened at the casual way he'd dropped the compliment. Her eyes flew to his. Sensual heat simmered in their depth, and she found herself responding to it. His eyes dropped to her lips, and his head dipped as though he intended to kiss her.

Cat blinked rapidly as reality crept in. What was she doing? She couldn't allow this man to touch her. "Good-bye, detective."

"You don't like compliments?"

His voice was decadently sensual, his eyes watchful. "Oh, I love them. I'm just not into flirtatious games these days."

"Why? Are you involved with someone?"

Instead of answering him, Cat started the car. "Talk to you later, Taj." Taj stepped back, his eyes promising her something she didn't want to deal with.

"Have fun with Jamie," he added with a salute.

Cat waved as she eased off the curb. Taj had better keep his hands and his endearments to himself, she thought as she headed toward her home. He was too free with both. She had no intention of starting a relationship with anyone, even if the man after her was blessed with a sexy body she couldn't ignore, a smile that was so naughty it made her sensitive parts tingle, and lips that were perfectly molded for kissing.

What would it be like to be kissed by those lips? her wicked side wondered.

Don't go there, her reasonable side warned.

Next she would be wondering what kind of a lover he would make. Yes, she needed to control her wayward emotions. Taj was a forbidden fruit she shouldn't be thinking of sampling.

Cat was done eating her dinner when Kenny and Brianna arrived with little Jamie in tow.

"Wow, you guys look quite gorgeous this evening," she said as soon as she opened the door. Her brother's wife was a beautiful, cinnamon-complexioned woman with a dimpled smile and vivacious personality. She complemented Kenny's calm, serious nature perfectly.

"You like?" Bri asked as she twirled around, the skirt of her red dress curling and frothing around her shapely calves.

"You look sensational, Bri." Her outfit suited her rounded body. Brianna still hadn't regained her pre-pregnancy size, but she carried the extra weight very well. At five-foot-eight, the extra weight was distributed evenly above and below her waist.

As Brianna showed off her outfit, her brother's gaze stayed riveted on his wife. To be so in love, Cat sighed inwardly as she studied her brother. Kenny looked quite dapper in tailored gray pants and maroon-and-gray silk shirt. Jamie was safely cradled in his arm.

"Come on in, guys," Cat said. She turned to look at her nephew as soon as they got inside. "Hey, sweetie pie, come to Aunty Cat." She took Jamie from Kenny and kissed his plump cheek with a loud smack. She was rewarded with a smile. "Oh, what a beautiful smile. Aunt Cat loves you too, pumpkin." She gave him another kiss, then caught the indulgent looks Brianna and Kenny were giving her. She blushed. "Where are his things?"

"In his bag," Brianna answered, putting the blue baby bag beside Cat. "He's been fed and bathed. But he didn't eat very well, so I brought a bottle and some food. Just in case."

Cat peeked in his bag. "Look, sweetie, Aunty gets to feed you some yummy, solid food. Promise not to blow bubbles and mess up my dress. I still haven't gotten rid of the carrot-orange of last month, and," she nuzzled his neck, "it's all your fault, pumpkin—and truth be told, a little bit of mine." She smiled at Brianna. "I think we've got everything we need. Pacifier, toys, books, drink, change of clothing, diapers and wipes, and finally, the playpen Kenny just brought in."

Cat cradled the baby against her side as she ushered her brother and his wife to the front door. "Okay, people, out. Good-bye. Go have fun. Don't worry about us." She stopped in the doorway.

Brianna kissed Jamie good-bye. "Bye, sweet pea. Be good to your Aunty Cat." She looked at Cat and mouthed, "Thank you. You know where to reach us in case of emergency."

"No, I don't. For the next few hours, you're going to forget this baby exists. Now go."

Kenny kissed Jamie too. "Bye, buddy. Take care of him, Cat."

"I always do, brother dearest. Have fun." Cat nuzzled Jamie's neck as she watched them. Kenny opened the door for Brianna and stooped low to kiss her before walking to his side of the car. When they waved, Cat lifted Jamie's chubby hand and made him wave too. She waited until they drove away before she walked into the house.

"It's just you and me, pumpkin. What do you want to do?" She picked up his bag and walked to her bedroom. Spreading his blanket on the floor, she put some of the toys on it, and settled him on it. She lay down on her stomach beside him, and tickled him on his tummy. He rewarded her with a wet, toothless grin. "Talk to me, sweetie pie. You're growing so fast. Soon your mom and dad may want to give you a little sister or brother to play with."

She pulled out some books from the bag and started reading. She exaggerated the sounds, made it as interactive as possible until Jamie started to fuss. She picked him up, and put him on her stomach as she lay on her back. She started to sing, bouncing him up and down. A grin split his face. "That's a million dollar smile, Jamie. You'll have women swooning at your feet before you can walk." Like Taj Taylor's smile. *I wonder how many women have found him irresistible.*

Now why was she letting Taj intrude on her thoughts? She had succeeded in keeping him out the last couple of weeks. Maybe seeing him today had something to do with it. *That and his wicked smile.*

Jamie started to fuss again. "Okay, sweetie, let's see if you're hungry." She got up with him, and went to warm his bottle.

Cat was burping Jamie when her gate's intercom buzzed. It was her brother Bobby. She searched his face as soon as he stepped into her foyer. *No good tidings there,* she thought. "Hey, stranger."

"Hi, sis. Hey, big guy." He touched the baby's cheek, but did not take him the way he usually did. But Bobby distracted Jamie, and he stopped fussing.

"Sis, do you have anything to eat around here?" Bobby asked as soon as they entered the kitchen.

"In the fridge. Warm up anything you want." Cat sat by the counter and watched as he removed one covered plastic bowl after another. Her brother had one hell of an appetite. Her mother used to cook for him, but now that she was gone he was relying on her or Brianna to feed his lanky frame. Twenty-one years old and couldn't cook a lick. She was going to make him take cooking lessons if it was the last thing she did.

"How's college, Bobby? I called a couple of days ago, but Joe said that you weren't in." Joe Gainers was his roommate and best friend.

"I've been busy. I'm defending my thesis in a month's time, remember?" He piled food on a plate, covered it with a paper towel, and shoved it in the microwave. Then he turned to look at her. "Don't worry, sis, I'll be graduating this year as planned."

But Cat couldn't help worrying. It had always been hard to read Bobby, and ever since their mother died it was nearly impossible to know what went on in his head. He was becoming so secretive.

"What's up with you, sis? Still filming *The Guardian*?"

She talked about her work while he ate. He was through eating when he dropped the bombshell.

"I went back to New York, Cat."

"What? Why?" She screeched so sharply that Jamie started to cry again. She put him on her shoulder and paced the kitchen floor, her eyes riveted on Bobby. Of course she knew why he'd gone to New York. She just needed to hear him say it.

"You know why," Bobby said calmly. "The first time, I had to come back immediately because I had a job interview with a local engineering firm. This time I stayed longer."

"Oh, Bobby," Cat sighed. Because Jamie had stopped crying, she sat down again and studied her brother's set expression. "You need to let this go, okay? You already have a father. He may not be perfect, but he's still our father. You have to stop this."

"I can't, Cat. I've tried to these past weeks, but his words haunt me. I can't stop thinking about them."

Why was he fixated on this? Cat wondered. It was okay when he stopped going to their father's. She'd thought he blamed him for their mother's death, for fighting with her those few hours before the accident. So had she, for that matter, but she'd let it go. Blaming their father wasn't going to bring their mother back, she'd concluded. But Bobby was more disturbed than her with what had been said before the accident.

It suddenly dawned on Cat that the reason he couldn't let go was that it helped him rationalize their father's indifference. All their lives, their own father had been mostly concerned with two things: his career and their mother. They had always been somewhere at the bottom of his list when it came to showing love or appreciation. Bobby would love to have a reason for that lack of attention.

"Don't believe the nonsense Dad spewed that night, Bobby. The words didn't mean a thing. You've heard them go at it before. It was his way of controlling her." Cat frowned. "Or maybe he was just insecure about their relationship. I mean, you have to admit that Mom did tend to flirt a lot." She leaned forward and looked into his eyes. "Bobby, you, Kenny and I are siblings, okay? Same father and mother."

Bobby merely shrugged and walked to the fridge to get a drink.

Jeez, he was so stubborn, Cat thought with frustration. "How did you know who to talk to in New York? You weren't even born when we left there. Heck, I don't think anyone we knew still lives in the old neighborhood."

"You'd be surprised. I was given the name of a priest who headed the church you used to attend. I figured that Mom might have talked to him."

Cat tried to recall the faces of the priests at St. Augustine, their church in New York. There was Father O'Keefe, a funny Irishman with thick glasses. Who else? "Did you get to meet this priest? What's his name? What did he say?"

"Nothing. He's not in New York anymore." For the first time since he walked into her home, excitement rang in his voice. "He's here in L.A., Cat."

"Have you talked to him or tried to locate him? What if he tells you he doesn't know anything?"

"Then I'll ask Dad." His voice was firm, determined.

Bobby and their father never saw eye-to-eye about anything, Cat reflected. And from the sound of things, talking to their father would be his last resort. She sighed. "You're blowing this out of proportion. You know that, don't you?"

He raised an eyebrow. "You want to tell me that you're not curious about what was said that night?" He shifted on his stool to stare at her. "Look at me, Cat, and tell me that if our situations were reversed you wouldn't be doing this."

Would she be running all over the country trying to find her real father if the situations were reversed? She answered honestly, "I don't know." When Bobby made a derisive sound, she sighed. "Okay, maybe I'd be curious. But I would be careful about whom I talked to, and how I went about investigating the entire thing."

"That's what I did...am doing. Now I've got a question for you. How many people name their children after their fathers?" A watchful expression entered his eyes.

Not knowing where the question was heading, Cat shrugged. "Quite a few, I'd say. Your friend Joe is named after his father. A few boys I went to school with had the same name as their fathers. So?"

"Mother named me after a priest."

A shiver ran down Cat's spine. "What are you saying?"

"The priest I'm trying to find is called Robert John Forster. The only thing we don't share is a last name."

Cat shook her head. "Bobby, lots of people name their children after priests. That doesn't mean...."

"What if it does, Cat?" Bobby interrupted. When Cat shook her head, he nodded vigorously. "What if *he* is my father?"

"Then he probably wouldn't want to talk to you. He's a priest, for chrissake."

Bobby just shrugged. "I have to find him and talk to him. I have to know. And if he isn't, he might know something."

"When are you going to speak with him? Do you want me to be there?"

A look that could only be described as fear flashed across Bobby's face. "There's something I haven't told you yet, Cat."

Premonition that she wasn't going to like what followed swept through her. "What?"

"Father Robert Forster has disappeared. I have been asking around the center where he works but no one is willing to talk to me. He ran the St. Vibiana Center for Spirituality, but the women were sent to a different center two weeks ago. Three days ago, I went there in the evening, hoping to find some answers."

Cat couldn't believe her ears. "Find some answers, Bobby? Are you saying you broke into the center?"

Bobby looked sheepish for a beat. "No, I was hoping to find someone, anyone who could talk to me." When Cat made a derisive sound, he said, "Okay, so I'd intended to snoop around, but I didn't get a chance. I surprised two men and a priest who were loading things into a black Honda van. They saw me, and for some reason started to yell at me. When one of them, a bulky man with a weird tattoo on his arm, came after me, I didn't stop to hear what he had to say. Not that it would have made much difference. The man was speaking too fast in Russian for me to follow."

What had he gotten himself into? Cat wondered. "Let me hire a P.I. to help you with this, Bobby. You're supposed to be studying, not running from a bunch of Russian crooks. I know this P.I. who'd be perfect for...."

Bobby cut her off with, "I'll stop, sis. As soon as I speak with

Father Forster, I'll stop." He stared at his hands, then shot her an uncomfortable look.

Cat raised her brows questioningly. "What is it?"

"I have a feeling that the black van I saw that night has been following me."

She gawked. "Okay, that's it. We're talking to Kenny and Dad."

"No. Don't do or say anything to either of them, please. Not yet. I promise I'll stop searching if the priest doesn't know anything. If Dad or Kenny finds out what I've been doing, I'll look like a damn fool. It's just the van that's bothering me. Give me two days, sis. If the van's still on my tail, I'll call you and we can forget about the whole thing."

Somehow she doubted that her brother would ever forget the words he'd heard that night or the possibility that he might have a different biological father. Cat sat back and released a deep breath. "Okay, Bobby, two days. If I don't hear from you by Sunday night, I'm stopping by Kenny's or Dad's place."

Her brother reluctantly nodded.

A few blocks from Cat's house, Taj was enjoying the company of Nat Orlandi and his mother. They had just finished a very satisfying dinner and were now lingering over coffee.

Mrs. Doreen Orlandi was a dignified, petite woman who doted on her only son. She had married the youngest son of a prominent Italian-American family in Napa Valley against his family's wishes, borne him a son and daughter, and never once expected the patriarch of the family to accept her children. But her husband had believed that one day his children would inherit his share of the Orlandi Vineyards and had encouraged their interest in the wine business. When he died, she had carried on his wishes and kept exposing her son and daughter to the world of winemaking, making them work in and around vineyards in California during the summers, and even sending them to friends in

Italy for more intensive education in the wine-making business. But while their grandfather was still alive, Nat and his sister had been denied their inheritance. The Orlandis took pride in their lineage, and Nat and his sister, being of mixed race, hadn't fitted the image they wanted the world to see. Unable to fight the powerful Orlandi family and claim their inheritance, Nat had become a stockbroker and his sister had taken modeling assignments abroad. It wasn't until their grandfather passed away and their grandmother took over the running of the vineyards that they were given their inheritance.

Taj watched the pride shine in her eyes as they talked about the varieties of wines—Chardonnay, Merlot, Pinot Noir—Nat had submitted for the West Coast Wine competition.

Then their conversation shifted to marriage and love. "I'm hoping that Nat will soon look for a wife to work alongside him," his mother added. "Every established man needs a good woman by his side."

Nat frowned at his mother. "Mom, I told you I'll cross that bridge when I meet someone special."

She turned to look at Taj. Taj knew what was coming. Mrs. Orlandi had known him since he and Nat met at UNLV and had begun to hang out together. As their friendship had become stronger, they'd often spent time visiting each other's homes. Taj knew there wasn't much about him that Mrs. Orlandi didn't know. And like his mother, Mrs. Orlandi often spoke her mind. So he wasn't surprised when she said, "What about you, Taj? Have you met someone special?"

Taj grinned. "She doesn't know it yet."

"Doesn't know…what's there to know? People meet, fall in love and get married. Nat's father and I, we knew at our first meeting that we were meant to be together. Nothing and no one was going to keep us apart."

"Well, she's a very stubborn lady. It's taking me a little longer than I'd expected to convince her to see things my way."

"Keep telling her that you love her until she gives in. If that doesn't work, abduct her and keep her in bed for a week."

"Mother!" Nat was shocked by his mother's bluntness.

His mother patted his hand. "Despite my being your mother, baby, I'm a woman. And only a woman would know certain things about women." When Nat threw up his hands in surrender, his mother turned to Taj. "Don't waste time, my dear. Find out whatever is stopping her from loving you and fix it. Maybe then you can help Nat find himself a wife."

"Mother," Nat said in exasperation.

She smiled at him and excused herself. "I know you young people might have plans for the evening, so I'll wish both of you goodnight."

Since they were dining at their hotel, Nat got up to escort her to her room. As Taj watched them weave their way through the restaurant, he reached a decision. He was going to call Cat. As Mrs. Orlandi had said, he had to find out whatever was stopping Cat from going out with him.

His eyes went to his watch. It was still early. Would he be intruding on her time with her nephew? He hoped not. He would keep the conversation brief.

Before he could change his mind, Taj took out his cell phone and dialed Cat's number. She answered after two rings. In the background, he could hear her nephew screaming. "Cat? What's going on over there?"

"Who's...Taj?" he heard, followed by, "hush, sweetie. C'mon, baby. Don't cry, please."

"Is everything okay?" Taj asked.

"Yes...no. Jamie started crying ten minutes ago, and I can't seem to stop him. I've checked everything. His diaper, temperature, made sure he's not too hot or cold, but he keeps crying. I don't know what else to do."

She sounded close to tears, he thought. "Where are his parents?"

"Out...I don't want to bother them...I promised not to. Hush, sweetheart. Ooh, he threw up. Listen, I've got to go."

"Have you checked if he's teething?"

"Uh, hmm, his mother said he was late. I tried to check, but he wouldn't let me."

"How about his stomach, is it rumbling or bloated? He could have eaten something that doesn't agree with him."

"How the heck do you know so much about babies?" Cat asked disagreeably. There was a pause, then, "I'm sorry about that. I'm going so crazy here trying to find out what's wrong with him that I...listen, I need to calm down. I can't help him if I'm losing it. I've taken care of him before, but he's just never been this colicky. If he's teething, I'll run to the store and get him Tylenol or something."

Now he was sure she was crying. "Do you want me to stop by and help? I have taken care of my brothers' kids, so I know a thing or two about babies."

"A-hmm, I don't know." There was silence as though Jamie had stopped crying. "Oh, I think we'll be okay. I can handle it." There was another pause as she talked to her nephew. Then Taj heard a fresh bout of screeching. "Oh, my. Okay, get here as quickly as you can. Here's my address."

Taj dropped enough bills on the table to cover the meal and the tip, then went in search of Nat.

CHAPTER 6

What do I know about children? Taj wondered as he jumped in his car and started for Cat's home. Not much. In fact, what he knew couldn't fill a page. The suggestions and the questions he'd fired at Cat were what he'd heard his sister-in-law and brother discuss when their children, Liana and Alex, were ill. Now he needed a dose of advice.

Taj dialed his brother's number. Aaron answered after a ring. "Hey, Aaron, where is Sheryl?" Taj asked immediately.

"Little brother, what happened to 'hello, how do you do, how is work?' No one is courteous anymore."

Taj sighed. The last thing he needed was his brother acting as if he were in a courtroom. "We talked last weekend, Aaron. Listen, I'm in a hurry. Where is Sheryl? I need her advice."

Aaron laughed. "I'm the lawyer in this house, and no one ever asks my advice on anything."

"I need a woman's input on this, big brother."

"Aah, a woman problem?" Taj heard him call out Sheryl's name. "My brother wants advice on how to handle a woman."

Taj grinned when he heard him. Trust Aaron to reach that conclusion. When he wasn't extolling the virtues of married life, his brother was laughing at their mother's desperate attempts to find Taj a wife. Whenever their mother visited him, Taj often called San Diego to talk to Aaron. Or he called Montana to complain to Jerry. His other brother, Jerry, operated a horse ranch in Montana.

Aaron interrupted his thoughts with, "She's coming. So, is Mom at it again?"

"No. As far as I know, she's in Montana."

"Then what's the problem? You've met somebody?"

He wasn't about to tell Aaron anything. If he did, within twenty-four hours every member of their family would know about Cat. Then his mother would want to come down and meet her. After all the mess their mother put his brothers' wives through, Taj wasn't having her anywhere near Cat. "Actually, counselor, it's not a woman. It is a boy."

"Oh. Who's this boy? Is he in trouble with a woman? Is that why you need Sheryl's advice? I know if he was in trouble with the law, you'd come to me."

"Quit giving him the third degree, Aaron." It was Sheryl. "Taj, how are you? What's this about a woman?"

"That's your man trippin'. Listen, what could cause an eight-month-old to cry incessantly?" There was a long silence. Taj waited. "Are you guys still there?"

"You have a child, Taj?" Aaron asked.

"Sweetie, stop interrogating him. Taj, whose child is it?"

Taj sighed. "A girl I know is..."

"You're involved with a woman with a child?" Aaron interrupted.

"Sheryl, get him off the phone if he can't shut up. In fact, both of you need to stop asking questions and listen. This lady I know—her name is Cat, in case you were about to interrupt and ask—she's baby-sitting her nephew; unfortunately, the little boy started to cry, and she can't seem to console him."

"Aaah," Sheryl and Aaron sighed in unison. Then Sheryl added, "Well, if he's not running a fever, there are two things to look for: teething or upset stomach. This is what you'll need to do or have...."

Taj listened as he drove. He stopped by a grocery store near Cat's house, bought the medication that Sheryl had recommended, and added a few things that might fascinate a fussy eight-month-old baby. Five minutes later, he was outside Cat's gate.

Taj was so eager to go to Cat's rescue that he didn't notice the black van following him. When the gate opened and he drove through, the van continued down the street, passing slowly as Taj drove into the compound. As Cat opened the door, the van went past her gate once again before going back to the end of the street, where the driver parked it.

Relief flashed through Cat when Taj arrived. Jamie was screaming at the top of his lungs, his arms and legs flailing with distress. "He was okay, then suddenly he started wailing." It was right after Bobby left. Maybe Jamie had sensed that she was troubled by the discussion she'd had with Bobby.

"Here, let me take him." Taj put his purchases down and scooped the child from Cat's arms. He lifted him up until they were eye-to-eye. Jamie stopped squirming long enough to stare at him. "Okay, Jamie, my boy, we are going to stop the ruckus this very minute and behave, okay? You're waking up the neighbors."

The baby stared at him suspiciously. His eyes were shiny, nose runny, and his fingers clenched. His breath was still uneven, a testimony of his earlier tantrum.

Taj folded the baby into his arms placed him on his chest so he could see his face as he walked toward the kitchen. Jamie was quiet, his eyes riveted on Taj's face.

Cat stared after them in disbelief. She muttered, "I can't believe it. I thought I was in a madhouse a few seconds ago, and now look at him." She picked up the paper bag Taj had dropped on the floor and followed them.

"Don't count your chickens yet, sweetheart. He'll get tired of my face soon enough and start again." He sat on a stool by the kitchen counter. "Okay, let's take inventory." He touched Jamie's head. "No fever. You're big for your age, Jamie, one healthy boy." He patted his diaper. "Your aunt already changed you. She also made sure you're comfortably dressed." He stopped to look into Jamie's eyes. "You, big guy, need to treat her with the utmost respect. Not only is she special, it's not easy to take care of a disgruntled member of our gender. Now, big guy, let's take a look at those gums." He looked up and caught the look on Cat's face. "What?"

"Nothing." She was amazed and impressed.

"Could you hold him while I wash my hands?"

Apprehension sliced through her. The two of them were doing great without her. What if he started to cry again? Her ears still rang from his previous screams. "Are you sure you want me anywhere near him? I don't think he likes me."

As if on cue, Jamie whimpered. "The novelty of having me around is about to wear off, so we'd better act quickly." He shifted Jamie to his shoulder. "Why don't you wash my hand for me?"

"Oh, okay." Cat walked to the sink and turned on the water. The thought of touching Taj…

It's just a hand, Catherine.

She took his hand in hers. Her hands were small against his, which was strong, large, and rough—an outdoorsman's hand. Her heart pounded as she started lathering it. She wrapped her fingers around each one of his and slowly rubbed each to the tip. She washed the sensitive skin between his fingers. There was intimacy in the simple act that was a little unsettling. A weird sensation invaded her lower region as she imagined his hands on her body, slowly stroking it. Her body temperature shot up a notch. When she heard him take a deep breath, she didn't dare look up. Who would have known that something as simple and mundane as washing a hand could be so intimate, so arousing

"There…done," Cat mumbled in a breathless voice.

"Thank you."

The husky timbre of his tone made her look up. His eyes were hot. She felt their pull to the tips of her toes. He shifted his body. Only then did she realize how close they were. All he had to do was move an inch, and they would touch.

The look on his face indicated that he wanted to kiss her. The heat from his hard body beckoned her, his masculine scent teased her senses, and the longing in his eyes tugged at her heart. And she was sure that the excitement and the need in his eyes were mirrored in hers. When his hand reached up to pull her closer, she leaned forward too.

Jamie let out a screech, and the moment was lost. Taj stepped back and went back to the counter. "Okay, big guy, tell me what's wrong? Where's the pain?" He put Jamie on the counter. "Can you hold him while I check his gums?"

She hurried to his side and wrapped her arms round her nephew. But she was also aware of Taj's body next to hers. His arm brushed hers as he reached for Jamie's mouth. Her body trembled.

"Uh-hmm. No wonder. The gums are swollen. Did his parents bring medication or anything?"

"No. Earlier, I tried to give him one of his toys to chew on, but he wasn't interested."

"I stopped by Yucca Supermarket and bought a few things, including teething medication." He nodded at the paper bag. "Check out the stuff in the bag and see if there is something you could give him for pain." He stood up with the baby, whose crying had subsided somewhat.

Cat looked at Taj with amazement mixed with gratitude. "Wow. You're more amazing than Houdini, detective." Taj smiled at her. Her heart skipped a beat.

She grinned as she fished the medications out of the paper bag. He'd bought four different brands of pain medication, and two brands of teething gels. She picked out what she'd seen at her brother's house—Tylenol for pain and Orajel for teething. Then she saw a disco light nightlight in his purchases and paused. "Taj? Is this…did you pick this up just now?"

"Yes. I thought the colors would entertain him. Children like flashy things."

She gave Jamie some Tylenol, and let Taj rub Orajel on his gums. "Okay, detective, what's your secret? How did you know what to buy on such short notice? I don't…never mind." She was about to say that she didn't know any man who could shop for a baby the way he just had. Even her brother was clueless around his only child.

"No, tell me. Don't ever be scared to tell me what's on your mind, Cat."

"I'm not scared. You've surprised me. That's all." When he raised an eyebrow, she added, "In a nice sort of way."

"Good. I want to surprise you, only you."

Cat looked at Taj, really looked. He was cradling Jamie in his arms, his large hand slowly patting the baby's back while a smile played on his lips. He had never looked more handsome or sexy than he did at that very moment, Cat thought with awe.

Could he be real? Was he some mirage sent to tantalize and seduce her? She didn't know what to believe anymore, because the man was slowly showing different facets of his personality that were very interesting. "How come you know so much about babies?"

He lifted a silken eyebrow, the sensual smile widening. "I told you that you should get to know me better."

Okay, I walked into that one, Cat thought with a smile. "I owe you one, detective."

His eyes snared hers. "I'll collect with interest."

The promise in his voice wasn't lost on her. She blushed.

While Taj stretched with Jamie on the lounge, Cat plugged in the disco nightlight and switched off all the lights in the living room. Jamie's eyes followed the myriad of lights dancing on the walls and ceiling. He was totally mesmerized, just as Cat was mesmerized by this bold, large man with gentle hands. Taj Taylor.

She stared at them, the child and the man, and her defenses started to crumble. Panic seeped in. Here she was, wishing that she was her nephew, wishing that she was the one lying on Taj's broad chest and listening to his heartbeat.

Cat shook her head and went to sit on the couch. Her eyes stayed on Taj and Jamie, though. She shouldn't want this man. He made her feel too much, and that was scarier than anything she'd ever faced in her thirty-one years.

To stop her wayward thoughts, Cat went to the bedroom to prepare the playpen for Jamie. When she came back to the living room, she wasn't surprised to find the child sleeping.

Cat transferred Jamie to the playpen in the bedroom, but left the flashing disco nightlight on, and the door open. She joined Taj outside on the patio. He was seated on one of her patio chairs, but he got up as soon as she joined him. He pulled out a chair for her.

"Thank you," she murmured as she sat down, feeling a little uneasy now that they were alone.

She cut him a discreet look. He was such an enigma. For two weeks now, she had admired him from afar, run from his mesmerizing glances, and watched him interact with people. He wasn't arrogant or pushy, just confident and persistent. He was also charming and witty. And from his interaction with Jamie, he was a natural-born daddy.

Why didn't these thoughts please her? Why did they make her more apprehensive? "You're full of surprises, Taj."

His perfect teeth flashed as he smiled roguishly at her. "Good. I wouldn't want to start boring you so early in our relationship."

"Do we have a relationship?"

"Oh, yes." He said firmly. "You and I had a relationship way before we met, Cat Simmons."

"What do you mean?"

"I knew you were out there waiting for me. You don't believe our meeting at the base was unplanned, do you?"

So maybe he was a little delusional, Cat concluded, but after helping her with Jamie, she could afford to be accommodating. "I think my mechanic planned it by not fixing my car sooner. If my car hadn't been at the shop, I wouldn't have gone to Jan's trailer to get her keys, and you and I wouldn't have met." Then there was the dare from Jan, but he didn't need to know about that.

He grinned at her. "'Ye of little faith,'" he said in a preachy tone. "I was thinking of a higher power than that, but if you believe it's the mechanic, then I owe the man a drink."

"Sorry to disappoint you, but my mechanic is a woman."

He laughed. "I'll buy her a drink, invite her husband, if she's married, and their children too, if they have some. Does that meet with your approval?"

"Hey, I'm not the one who believes in higher intervention." To change the topic, she indicated the house where Jamie was. "Tell me where you learned so much about babies?"

In the dim light, his gaze caressed her beautiful face and her body in the loose dress. The dress had a split neckline, giving him a glimpse of her satiny skin and enticing cleavage. He cleared his throat before saying, "I have done my share of baby-sitting my brothers' children."

"Really? That is impressive. I love my brother dearly, but he's basically clueless around babies." She saw the way Taj's eyes seemed to move over her face and chest. She'd completely forgotten that she had no bra under her kimono, and that the top had a split neck. She stilled the urge to reach up and cover the split. "So how many nephews and nieces do you have?"

"Four. Liana and Alex belong to Aaron and Sheryl, and of course, Jerry and Angela's twins, Jon and Josh."

"You must have a large family." When Taj's gaze locked on her hands as she folded them in front of her on the table, Cat wondered if he was remembering their hand-washing episode. She couldn't get it off her mind. It seemed like a prelude to something more intimate. "How many in all?"

"I have three brothers, and then there's Mel," he reached for her hands and trapped them with his. He stroked her skin.

Sensations shot up her arms and down her body as he caressed her skin. It didn't cross her mind to pull her hands away. "Who's Mel?"

"My baby sister, Melissa," he replied, a soft smile playing on his lips.

"That's a strange way of shortening her name."

"She has wanted it that way ever since she was old enough to resent being born a girl. Most of my cousins in Montana are male. To hear her, it wasn't fun being the only girl in a family of boys. Now she says it helps fool people in her line of work." Cat raised an inquiring eyebrow. "She's a reporter with the *Chronicle* in San Francisco. She claims that people take her articles seriously when they see her byline."

She heard the love in his voice as he talked about his sister. What would it feel like to have this man's love? Cat pushed aside those thoughts. She shouldn't be thinking of relationships in connection to Taj Taylor. He would have her so wrapped up in him there wouldn't be room for a thin razor blade. Even now, she was too curious about him. What was his family like? What were his ambitions? Did his hair feel as silky as it looked? And how would it feel to be kissed by him?

You need to get a grip, girl, before you make a fool of yourself, Cat told herself. She pulled her hands from underneath his. "Would you like something to drink?"

"Thanks, baby, but I should be heading home now."

Disappointment ripped through Cat. What was wrong with her? She was wary of being with him and yet she didn't want him to leave. "I appreciate what you did tonight, Taj. It was very sweet."

He winked. "Why don't you show me how appreciative you are?" he asked, flames leaping in his eyes. He got up and gently pulled her up.

Was he going to demand a kiss? Cat wondered. Did she want him to? Her heart beating wildly, she looked into his face. "What do you want?" she asked, anticipation running through her nerves.

He moved closer until their bodies were a few inches apart. "A hug."

"Ooh." She hadn't expected that. Again, she felt a ripple of disappointment. Pushing the feeling aside, she wrapped her arms around his waist and laid her head on his chest. His arms came around her, pulled her closer.

Mercy me, Cat mused, but it felt wonderful having those strong arms around her. She wanted to burrow and never come up except for air. When he buried his face in her hair, she felt that she now had the right to do something she'd been fantasizing about ever since he walked through her door. Her eyes closed, Cat burrowed deeper into his chest and filled her lungs with his clean, masculine scent. For a few seconds, she felt surrounded by him, part of him.

"Have dinner with me tomorrow night?" Taj whispered from above her.

Cat stiffened. Taj's arms tightened about her, as if to force his will upon hers. She knew that she wouldn't mind having dinner with him. But would it stop there? She found him attractive, but had no interest in having an affair with him. Could they have a platonic relationship?

Platonic, Catherine? Are you out of your mind? No one could be friends with such a virile man. What would the two of them discuss? No, she was definitely crazy to contemplate being friends with Taj Taylor. "I'm sorry, I can't."

He stepped back and stared at her upturned face. "Can't or won't?"

"I can't." What excuse would she give him that didn't make her sound plain crazy? She remembered Jan's party. "I made a commitment to attend Jan's dinner party."

He smiled. "So did I, but I was going because she promised me that you'd be there," he countered back. "We can call her together and ask to be excused."

"I don't think that's a good idea."

"Why not?"

She was running out of excuses and said the first thing that popped into her head. "Because you want something from me that I'm not capable of giving."

Taj murmured, "Look at me, sweetheart." He caressed her cheek with his knuckles, then lifted her chin with his forefinger until she was looking into his eyes. "You and I are meant to be together, Cat. You can't run from it. And don't ever believe that you're incapable of giving me what I want. You have a lot to offer me, a lot more than you think. And I want it all. When it comes to you, I'm a very greedy man."

She stared at Taj, totally enthralled by his boldness. What could she possibly say to such assertive statements? Cat thought as she chewed on her lower lip. She should be scared by his resolute stance, yet all she felt was excitement, as though she were about to embark on a journey filled with wonders and new discoveries.

She was still struggling with her thoughts when the gate's intercom interrupted her. "Excuse me." She stepped away from him and started for the door.

"Cat," Taj called out, his voice filled with frustration. She paused to look at him. His hand was extended toward her. "Go out with me tomorrow."

Cat wanted to run back and take his hand in hers. She wanted to yell yes. But she just couldn't do it. He was wrong for her. He evoked feelings in her that were too overwhelming for her to deal with. And she wasn't used to losing control like that. She had to think about this first. "We'll talk. I need to let my brother and Bri in."

Kenny and Brianna appeared happy and relaxed. That changed when Cat explained about Jamie and the teething. "How did you get him to calm down?" Brianna asked, hurrying inside the house.

"I had help from a friend. Taj stopped by with helpful hints and things he'd picked from the store, including a nightlight that your son absolutely loved. Oh, here he is. Taj, my brother, Kenny, and his wife, Brianna…Kenny, Bri, Taj Taylor."

Kenny and Taj greeted one another like old friends. Immediately, they started talking about police work. "Can I keep the light?" Brianna interrupted them teasingly as she studied the disco nightlight with fascination.

"Please do. And the medication too, if you like, Mrs. Simmons," Taj told her.

"Thank you." Brianna checked his purchases with a practiced eye. "This is amazing. You even bought gas medication? You are a very useful man to have around, Mr. Taylor."

"Please, call me Taj. I've had some experience with young children, Mrs. Simmons. That helped."

"Call me Brianna or Bri. Any man who knows anything about babies is a rare gem." She winked at her husband.

Kenny grinned. "You didn't tell me that was a criterion when we got married, love."

"No, sweetie, you had a lot more going for you," Bri answered sassily.

Cat watched the exchange between them with a smile. A sensual glint entered her brother's eyes as he looked at his wife. Brianna blushed. Kenny grinned and told Cat, "We need to head home, sis." Everyone knew what was on his mind. "Thanks for taking care of Jamie."

"Except for the crying bout, he was a darling."

Brianna added her thanks to Kenny's. "We'll see you on Sunday if not before. You should invite Taj home to dinner some time, Cat," she told her with a wink, but not loud enough for Taj to hear.

"Maybe," Cat whispered back as she ushered them out of her house. The last person she wanted to take home to dinner was Taj Taylor. She couldn't keep their relationship platonic if she took him to their biweekly dinners. Not only that, it would also be the first time she brought a man home. Her father might read a lot more into it than was warranted.

As soon as her brother and his family left, Cat walked back to the living room. Taj was waiting, his jacket already on. "So, are we on for tomorrow?" he asked right away.

He was persistent if anything. Why not have dinner with him? It wouldn't hurt. And maybe she could use the chance to talk to him about Bobby's priest.

When she didn't answer him right away, Taj asked, "Are you afraid of me, Cat?"

"No," Cat replied promptly. Why should she be? She was maybe afraid of her feelings, but she didn't think he would physically harm her. "No, I'm not afraid of you."

"Then why won't you go out with me?"

She looked into his eyes and sighed. He wasn't going to give up until he got his way. "Okay, Taj, I'll have dinner with you tomorrow."

"Great."

She grimaced at the satisfied look in his eyes. "You love to have your way, don't you?"

A glint entered his eyes as he looked into hers. "There is always a certain amount of satisfaction in getting what I want. And I want...." His eyes moved back to her face. They seemed to catalog her features.

"There are lots of things I want, baby. I'll tell you all about them tomorrow," he promised huskily.

Cat blushed at the promise in his voice. "You believe in being blunt, don't you?"

"It eliminates doubts, gets the message across." His shimmering gaze stayed riveted on her face. "I also believe in going after what I want."

And he'd said that he wanted her, hadn't he? Would she be able to resist him? "What if the thing you want is unattainable?"

"That has never stopped me, especially when I know it was meant for me."

Did that mean he truly believed she was meant for him? "You are a very unusual man."

"Is that a compliment?" Taj asked as he started for the door.

Heat suffused Cat's face. She hadn't realized that she'd voiced her thoughts aloud. Her embarrassment was complete when Taj turned around and grinned at her.

"No, it was a comment."

"Oh, but I rather like being unusual, extraordinary, remarkable, amazing, outstanding, incredible," he added without embarrassment.

"Don't leave out odd, weird, peculiar, abnormal, or strange."

He stopped. "I like my words better. Yours aren't very flattering."

He wore a wounded face that was so comical she started to laugh. "You have no modesty whatsoever, Taj Taylor."

"Yes, I do." He kissed her cheek. "I'll see you tomorrow, baby. Is seven okay?"

"Sure. Have a good night."

"You too. Have nice dreams." *With me in them,* his eyes seemed to convey.

Cat laughed. He was so cocky. *But you like him anyway, don't you, Catherine?* a voice teased in her head. Yes, she had to admit she liked Taj Taylor. Hopefully, he would help her find Bobby's missing priest.

As the gate closed behind Taj's Range Rover, a vehicle sped past the gate. Taj, who was about to pull onto the street, braked sharply. From her position, Cat gave it a passing glance and immediately forgot about it as she closed the door. If her mind hadn't been filled with thoughts about Taj, she would have noticed that it was a black van.

CHAPTER 7

Damn, she looks hot! Taj thought when he came to pick up Cat the next evening. She had on a black, ankle-length, chiffon number with a halter neckline which showed off her shoulders. The gathers under the sternum curved around her tiny waist. On her feet were leather-heeled shoes with gold baubles. Matching her dress was a leather clutch. Pearl and sterling earrings adorned her ears.

"You look magnificent," he said as he dropped a kiss on her cheek. He wanted to kiss her naked shoulders, the space between her breasts, her lips. He wished they were staying in instead of going out.

"Thank you. You don't look bad yourself," she replied, studying him. He had on a pair of tailored black pants, a light-blue dress shirt, gray, woven cashmere tie with plaid striping, and black wool, three-button sport coat.

"I'm happy you approve. These are for you." He handed her a dozen red roses.

While she put the flowers in a vase, he waited in her living room, taking time to study the pictures displayed above the fireplace. He noticed that Cat favored her mother, who was quite a looker. He recognized her father from his FBI days. There was also a picture of Cat and an older woman who looked very familiar. He studied the older woman's features, her regal posture, the dramatic flare of her attire, but he couldn't remember where he'd seen her.

"I'm ready," Cat said from behind him.

He turned to look at her, his gaze admiring. He loved the revealed expanse of skin between her breasts. It looked so soft and inviting. He saw her breasts heave as she took a deep breath. As if aware that he was staring, he smiled and glanced at her face. "I'm sorry for staring, baby, but you look gorgeous in that outfit. I keep wondering whether I should share you with the gawking male population out there or stay in and keep you to myself."

Cat blushed. "Maybe I should change," she murmured cheekily.

"Oh, no, please, I love that dress." *I'm a glutton for punishment,* Taj added silently. The dress did interesting things to his blood pressure, and he vowed that any man who was bold enough to ogle her was in for trouble. "Don't mind me."

He took her arm and led her outside the house. Hmm, she smelled good. He wanted to hold her, even if just for a second. As soon as she engaged the security system and locked her door, he said, "May I have a hug?"

Cat frowned.

"I really need to hold you, baby, like right now," he added before pulling her into his arms. Taking a deep breath, he closed his eyes. When she put her arms around his waist, he was sure he was going to burst with wanting her. "Hmm, I needed that."

Cat smiled. "My brother complains every time I tell him the same thing after a hug."

He caressed her chin, then let his hand slide down her arm until it closed around hers. "Any time you need a hug, call me." *Or when you need a kiss, or someone to laugh, cry, or make love with,* Taj added silently. He wanted her to depend on him for everything, however big or small.

Cat didn't say anything to his remarks. But she didn't pull away either.

Taj noticed her lack of response and sighed. She wasn't giving an inch. Would he know why before their date was over? He led her to his car and opened the door. He waited until she was seated before walking to his side of the car. "Are you comfortable? Not too hot or too cold?"

"I'm okay, thank you." She glanced at him from under her lashes. "So, where are we going?"

"It's a surprise. But I promise that you'll like it." Taj waited until they were away from her house then said, "I saw a couple of pictures of your family at your place. Are you an only girl?"

"Yes. You've met Kenny, of course. Then there is Bobby, our last born. He's at UCLA."

"What a coincidence. My little brother Blake is at UCLA too."

"Really? What's his major?"

"Premed."

"Blake Taylor," Cat murmured thoughtfully. Then she laughed and turned to look at Taj. "Not the basketball wonder boy, Blake Taylor, 'the doc'?"

"I'm not sure who started calling the little runt 'the doc.' The boy will never see the inside of medical school with all the time he spends playing basketball."

Cat laughed. "You call that six-foot-six boy a runt? I caught some of his game. He's really good. He dribbles as though the ball is an extension of his arm."

"Don't let him hear you say that. His ego is big enough as it is."

"Actually my brother thinks highly of him, which says a lot about Blake. Bobby is never easily impressed."

For the next few minutes, the conversation stayed on family and siblings. Taj mentioned that his other brother Jerry had played for the L.A. Angels before he retired. "Who was that lady with you in one of the pictures?" he asked. "She's wearing a gold outfit, and a fancy hat. I had this weird feeling that I had seen her somewhere."

"That's my Aunty Julia. She was a stage actress before she decided to try Hollywood. She didn't fare too well in the movie industry, though"

"Was she ever in Broadway plays?"

"Oh, yes. Numerous. Kenny and I never missed any of her plays when we lived in New York. She had a presence, a voice that made people stop and listen. I remember watching her in *A Raisin in the Sun* and marveling at her talent."

Taj's mind raced as he tried to remember her face. "Julia…Julia. Not Julia Rainier?" Taj asked with disbelief. Cat nodded. "Julia Rainier was your aunt?" Cat laughed at his expression. "Oh, man, my mother loved her. When we lived in New York, which wasn't for long, she took us to every play Julia Rainier appeared in. Then she just disappeared. I didn't know she came out to Hollywood."

"Hollywood wasn't ready for her. She wasn't dark enough in most cases, and of course, she wasn't light enough for the rest."

What a waste of talent, Taj thought with a slight frown. "Did she ever get angry or try to get back on stage?"

"She had her moments, but Aunt Julia wasn't the type to stay angry. She kept busy. Within two years of living in California, she had a small real estate company. She poured her energy into it and made it a success. She used to say if she couldn't get into Hollywood, she would make sure Hollywood came to her. For a while there, she was the real estate agent for the movers and shakers in the movie business. Then she was diagnosed with cancer. She lingered for a couple of years, but in the end the cancer won."

"That's sad. But I now know where you get your talent. It runs in your family."

She blushed at the compliment. "Thank you. She and her good friend Jackie Wilson were the ones who got me interested in the movie industry."

Wasn't that something? Taj mused. That was the third thing they had in common. They'd lived in New York at the same time, watched the same shows, just missed bumping into each other, and they both knew Jackie Wilson. If they hadn't met at Edwards Air Force Base, they would have met at Jackie's place. He didn't believe in coincidences, not in his line of work, and definitely not when it came to love. He had been right all along. Their meeting was predestined.

"Jackie was my client until a few weeks ago." Taj quickly explained what had happened to the aging actress.

"Poor Jackie. I must stop by and visit her. She's one of the last in a long line of talented stage actresses who didn't fare well in Hollywood."

"What about your mother? Is she in the business too?"

"No. My mother was a kindergarten teacher. We, eh, we lost her two months ago."

He hadn't meant to bring up a painful subject. He took her hand in his and brought it to his lips. "I'm sorry, baby, I didn't know." He was surprised when she curled her hand around his.

"How could you? Anyway, it's been tough going these past weeks. Sometimes I wonder if I'll ever get used to not having her around. Whenever I visit my father I always expect her to come to the door." Her voice ended with a wobbly note.

Taj regretted bringing up the topic. He didn't want their first date to start on a morbid tone. Still, he found himself squeezing her hand and trying to soothe her. "It's hard to accept a loved one's death. All I can tell you is that the pain lessens with time."

Cat glanced at the outline of his handsome face. "Have you lost someone in your family?"

Taj nodded briefly. "My father was shot in broad daylight by some punk. I was ten when it happened, but I still miss him. I remember the things we did together. He used to coach our neighborhood basketball team, and loved to take us to the Lakers games. Even now, whenever something important happens in my life, I wonder what he would say or do if he were alive."

Cat couldn't hide her reaction at his words. She stared at him, as though surprised by his revelation.

Aware of her scrutiny, Taj wondered if perhaps he shouldn't have told her about his father. The lights from the street fell on her face as he brought the car to a stop. He saw how solemn her expression was.

She must think you're a wimp, Taylor, a sap, a weakling, an oh-I-miss-my-daddy-sissy. When she kept staring at him, Taj asked, "What?"

Cat smiled. "Yesterday when you were cooing to my nephew…"

"I did not coo," he protested.

She touched his arm. "There is nothing wrong with that, Taj. As I was saying, yesterday when you were helping me with Jamie, I was convinced you couldn't be as sweet as you seemed."

"Ouch! That's the second time you've referred to me as sweet. No one has ever called me sweet and lived to talk about it."

She laughed at his teasing voice. "Deny it all you want, Taj. Underneath that bad-boy image you've perfectly cultivated, you really are a sweet guy."

Sweet sounded bad, very bad indeed, he thought. But all he said was,

"Bad boy?"

"Oh, you know, week-old stubble, motorbike, scruffy boots, long hair…I keep wondering where the tattoos are hidden," she teased.

"I'll show you mine if you show me yours," he teased as he leaned toward her, his eyes on her cleavage. Cat moved back, her face a picture of shock.

His hand moved toward her chest as though to touch her. He was aware that Cat had gone still, and that her breath had become suspended before it rushed out of her lungs. His hand hovered above her skin. Then without touching her, he traced an imaginary line with his finger down to where her dress fell in folds. "Do you have one around your belly button?" he whispered huskily.

Cat took a deep breath, then another, causing her chest to heave. Then Taj spread his fingers in front of her chest and said, "What about your chest?" Her eyes locked on his hand.

He might as well be touching her, Taj thought, because the effect was the same. He felt the heat from her skin, saw her nipples pucker and push against her dress in anticipation. Or was it invitation? His arm trembled, and his finger accidentally grazed the swell of her breast.

Cat's body jerked. Her eyes snapped to his.

Her gaze was uncertain, Taj noticed, but the unbridled arousal was unmistakable. His lids lowered as his eyes moved to her chest. He wondered what she would say if he were to slip his hand down her dress and cup her breast. Would she moan and welcome him?

Taj knew he was playing with fire. Cat's instantaneous reaction to him was thrilling, but the way he felt while watching her was killing him. He was hard as a diamond, but he couldn't stop. She was going to slap him for this, he was convinced.

He touched her skin. It was like dipping a finger in molten gold. Her skin was hot, soft, and smooth. This time, he traced the plunging neckline of her dress, his head dipping. "So sweetheart, can I take a look," he whispered huskily.

Cat gulped. His words seemed to break the spell he'd kept her under. She slapped his hand, and made a sound that was a cross between outrage and bewilderment.

He tried to diffuse the situation by saying, "Oh, I guess that means no." Her eyes narrowed dangerously. He grinned, trying to charm a smile out of her. Slowly she thawed, then she rewarded him with one.

"You are a tease, Taj Taylor."

His brows shot up. "Does that mean you wanted me to look?"

The smile disappeared from her lips. "No, it doesn't."

"You want to gut me?"

She took in his contrite expression, belied by the lazy smile on his lips. She wrinkled her nose at him. "I'm thinking about it."

He leaned back on his seat. "I'm sorry if I've offended you."

"I doubt that you feel a scintilla of remorse, Taylor."

He peered at her face. "You think you know me that well?"

"I'm beginning to," was her reply.

He grinned disarmingly. "Good. I want you to know me. So, are you ready to go in?"

Cat glanced at the throng of people around the well-lit entrance of Soul Palace. It was the hottest spot in town, frequented by most young hip-hop, R&B, and jazz fans. Quite a lot of artists performed there too. The restaurant part of it served a variety of cuisines which drew many customers every night. "Um-mm," she murmured.

"We're going to use the back entrance. I'm not strong enough to brave that queue."

Cat turned her head to look at him. "You know the owner?"

"Archie and I go way back," he said as he started the car. He drove to a gate with a glaring yellow sign warning trespassers to keep out. He pulled out his cell phone, pressed buttons, and spoke briefly.

He'd barely finished talking when the gate opened automatically from within. He drove through and parked his Range Rover next to a silver T-bird. A door opened behind them and light flooded the parking lot.

A tall, large man stood in the doorway, dimming the light with his girth. He spoke with an indistinct foreign accent, "Ma man, Taylor! I ax around why ma boy ain't visiting me. Dey say he's too busy for the likes of us. What's up widut?"

"Now you know that's not true, Archie," Taj replied. They clasped hands, thumped shoulders, and patted each other's back. "What's happening, ma brother?"

"Whatever it is, it ain't hap'ning here," Archie replied. Then his eyes fell on Cat. "Wha'chuhavhere?" He said it as though it were one word. "A lil'angel for me?"

Taj laughed. "This is a friend of mine, Catherine Simmons. Cat, allow me to introduce…West Indian Archie Payne."

Cat smiled as she extended her hand to greet the man. But Archie surprised her by shaking his head and spreading his arms. "I don' shake a pretty girl's hand, lil'angel. A kiss, yes?" He leaned forward to look into her eyes.

Cat looked beyond his heavily scarred face to the gentle smile and the twinkle in his eyes. *Here was a face that has seen and been through a lot, but still manages to convey a pleasant openness that makes one feel comfortable,* she thought. She reached up and kissed his cheek. "Nice to meet you, Mr. Payne."

"She calls me, Mr. Payne, Taj. Hmm, I like her. Come into my humble dwelling." Talking rapidly, he led them into the building. His accent had disappeared along with the broken English. Now he sounded like any educated American.

As they climbed the stairs to his office, he asked, "Tell me, Cat, have we met before? I always remember faces, and yours is unforgettable." He glanced back at Taj and winked. "Am I right or what, Taylor? So, my sweet angel, have we met before?" he asked as they continued up the stairs.

"I've been to your club before, Mr. Payne."

"No, no, sweetie, you call me Archie. So, you've been to my club, huh?" He stopped outside a door and stared at her upturned face. She grinned at him. "Yes, you have. The memory eludes me, but it'll come back." He pushed open a double door and said, "Welcome to my oval office."

His office was indeed oval and tastefully done in blue—dark-blue plush carpet and plaid sofas in various hues of blue. Huge wall-to-wall velvet curtains—now tied to the side—covered one section of the room. The other part of the room had T.V. screens. Half-naked women gyrating to the music appeared on several of them. A waiter carrying food to a table, guests at various tables appeared on another. Cat could see that nothing escaped Archie Payne's attention. He obviously monitored his entire operation from his lofty office.

Archie led Cat to the window—or the glass wall—to show her the beautifully displayed interior of Soul Palace. The office appeared to be hovering above the bar. Cat could see people moving and shouting, but no sound penetrated the walls to Archie's office. Like his office, both the club and the restaurant were elegantly furnished in different shades of blue. The club was done in electric blue, while the restaurant had soothing pale-blue wallpaper with musical instruments on the borders. The club had a huge stage for performances and various niches for his professional dancers. The various dance floors were wide and oval in shape. The DJ's platform was strategically placed opposite Archie's office. Along the walls, Cat could see numerous well-lit exit doors.

"You have a beautiful club, Archie."

"Thank you, my dear." He led her to the sofa and asked, "May I get you something to drink?" He indicated the bar where Taj stood, ready to fix her a drink.

Cat gave Archie a gracious smile and said, "Anything non-alcoholic, thank you."

"You don't drink alcohol?"

Cat shook her head. "Doesn't agree with my profession. I need a clear head when I work."

"Don't tell me a delicate flower like you operates heavy machinery," he teased. Cat laughed.

"Not exactly delicate," Cat answered, flexing her biceps.

"Oh, go on with your bad self." Archie laughed, then slapped his head with glee. "I remember now...New Year's Eve...you were with that actress, Janelle Masters, and a couple of your friends, right?"

Cat blushed. She remembered the day as though it were yesterday. That was the day she found out that her boyfriend, Rick Rawlins, was two-timing her. And on top of that, he was also trying to hit on Jan. An ugly scene had followed. She recalled punching Rick in the nose and telling him to get lost. When he'd tried to hit her back, Archie's bouncers had gotten to him first. Cat couldn't recall Archie being there, but he must've witnessed the entire incident on his monitors. "Don't remind me. That was a very horrific evening."

"I thought you handled yourself wonderfully, my dear, very admirably. That punk got what he deserved."

Cat looked up to find Taj staring at her and Archie with amusement. She blushed harder. "Yes, he did. Thank you," she added as she took the glass of Perrier from Taj's hand.

Taj smiled at Cat and said, "Will you excuse us, please, baby."

She nodded, refusing to look at him. How much of their conversation had he heard? She hoped not much. Her ex-boyfriend Rick was someone she didn't much think about, let alone discuss. Whenever thoughts of him did cross her mind, self-directed anger was the uppermost emotion. Rick was the ultimate player—lying, cheating, and using emotions to control women. And she had almost become his victim.

Was Taj a player too? Did he cheat, lie, and misuse women? She was so helpless to control her feelings when around him it scared her. She recalled the events in the car, and shame washed over her.

She'd wanted his touch, had anticipated it. Her nipples had puckered as though inviting him to cup her breast. And when he hadn't, a tinge of disappointment had sliced through her. She hadn't known whether to be mad at him for toying with her, or herself for being such a weak fool. Later, when he'd teased her, she'd realized it wasn't his fault she was so weak. She and she alone had let him get to her.

What was happening to her? How could an attraction be so immediate and explosive? And how could she want him when her gut feeling told her he was bad for her? Truly, her reaction had her totally bewildered. But from now on, Cat vowed, she would be on her guard.

Taj entered the room and interrupted her thoughts.

"Where's Archie?" she asked when she realized he was alone

"He's making arrangements for our dinner. It's more private and quiet to use his office than go downstairs to the restaurant."

The words barely left his mouth before two waiters and a waitress appeared and started to transform the room. A table was set for two with the best linen, polished silver, and china plates. They added Waterford crystal and Varga amber glasses. A bottle of non-alcoholic cider was set in a cooler on the bar. Curtains were drawn, lights dimmed and replaced with candles. A single rose sat majestically at the center of the table.

Cat watched everything with amazement. She stole a glance at Taj. He was busy consulting with one of the waiters. Had he planned all this for her? If he'd set out to impress her, he was succeeding.

Taj asked her what she wanted as soft jazz music played in the background. They consulted the menu and picked varied dishes—a southern spicy crawfish dish, shrimp jambalaya, wild rice, and sautéed asparagus.

Using the cider, Taj proposed a toast, "Here is to you, my beautiful companion, and to our future."

Cat went along with the toast. Whether they'd have a future or not didn't matter. She was too mesmerized to care.

While they waited for their meal, Taj regaled her with stories about growing up in San Diego, his college days at UNLV, and why he'd decided to join the Bureau. She stared at his handsome face, made more so by the flickering candlelight. He was full of masculine charm. The curve of his sensual lips seemed to beckon her. And his eyes sparkled with fire that made her imagine so much.

I'm in deep trouble, Cat thought with dread. She wasn't going to be able to resist Taj Taylor, not for long. Who could have believed they would be having a private, candlelight dinner in the hottest club in town and yet not be bothered by the sound from the club or other patrons?

The first course of their meal arrived. While they nibbled on hot rolls and stuffed mushrooms, the waitresses delivered the main course. The dinner was delicious, the atmosphere intimate, the companion compelling. He had her so enthralled that she temporarily pushed aside the thoughts of her brother, her father, and her misgivings about having anything to do with Taj, and just enjoyed herself.

She revealed a lot about herself as she talked about college, how she and Jan met, how they trained for their chosen careers while attending college, and the breaks she'd had in show business.

The meal was enjoyable. Cat's eyes sparkled as she asked Taj questions or laughed with him over silly anecdotes. She teased him when he was being cocky or silly. The setting was friendly; the tiny gestures they exchanged, a touch here, a smile there, were all prelude to something more intimate.

It was almost nine o'clock when they were done. As if Taj had waved a magic wand, the waiters appeared to clear the table. Soon after, Archie stopped to check on them. They complimented the chef, and he promised to pass their message to him.

"Dance with me," Taj requested huskily, taking Cat's hand in his and pulling her into his arms. He inhaled slowly, sucking in a dose of her feminine scent. But he didn't say anything, just closed his eyes and held her closer. Sometime during the dance, he dropped a feathery kiss on her brow.

Heat stole from where his lips had grazed and pulsed through Cat's body. His natural clean scent, mixed with whatever cologne he was wearing, teased her nose. She inhaled slowly. Everything about him was seductive, and she was helpless to fight him, Cat thought.

Could he feel the tremor that shot through her? she wondered. Or hear her changed breathing? It was as though he were already making love with her. The slow dance, the intimate setting, and the bodies pressing against each other were all part of the foreplay. One song after another, they stayed in each other's arms, their heat mingling and their passion building. Their dessert was delivered, but they hardly noticed.

After a while, Taj opened his eyes, leaned back, and stared right into Cat's aroused ones. She stared back at him, and hoped that he couldn't read her thoughts. She wanted him to kiss her. Yet when his head dipped, she inched away.

Taj's arm tightened about her waist and her body landed smack against his. "Where are you going, sweetheart?" he murmured huskily.

"To sit on the couch and rest my feet," she whispered.

He looked down at her feet. "Are the shoes the problem?" He went down on his knee and started to undo her sandals.

"What are you doing, Taj?"

He looked up and grinned naughtily into her eyes. "Removing the offending shoes," he replied.

He lifted her feet, one at a time, and slowly released the straps. She had worn no panty hose or tights, and his palms were drawn to her warm, walnut-brown, satin skin. He caressed her calf, her heel, the arch of her foot, and her toes. Her toes were painted scarlet, matching her nails and lipstick.

Cat knew she was going to fall flat on her face with desire. She wanted to stop him, but couldn't voice her thoughts. Speech had deserted her as soon as he'd gone on his knee. When he'd lifted her first foot, her hand had gone to his head for support. Now she moved her fingers, enjoying the feel of his black, curly mane against her palm.

At the back of her mind, a voice tried to remind her that Taj was too bold, was bad for her, and oh-so-naughty. But she'd stopped caring. She wanted him, desperately wanted to be in his arms.

When she was shoeless, Taj got up. Cat, who was about to remove her hand from his hair, found her hand trapped under his. He pressed her palm into his scalp, moving it in his hair seductively. Then she looked into his eyes and froze.

I have to flee. Her hand clenched and her body tensed. There was need, and there was need. What she saw in Taj's eyes scared the hell out of her.

"Taj?" she whispered achingly.

He stared at her lips. "Yes, sweetheart?"

Cat's nerves went wild at the predatory look in his eyes. She wanted to push him away, but didn't seem to have the strength. Her mouth went dry and her stomach tightened with desire. "Don't start anything we'd both regret."

His eyes roamed her face. "I could never regret claiming what's mine."

Her eyes snapped to his. He was crazy. "Don't, please." His head dipped. "Taj, don't you dare."

"Babe, you dare me with every breath you take," he murmured as his lips closed on hers.

The caress was tentative at first, as if he were giving her a chance to push him away, slap his face, or whatever. When she didn't, he went in for the kill. He surged into the embrace. When she gasped, he pushed his tongue in to mate with hers.

Sensations invaded Cat's body. He was everywhere. When she inhaled, it was his scent that filled her nose. When her arm moved, his hard, warm body was in the way. And his taste invaded all her senses. Any words or thought disappeared from her head when he shifted his body so they fitted chest to chest. The timbre of the kiss changed then.

The thrust of his tongue and the suction of his mouth bespoke of a hunger so great that Cat whimpered. His desire for her was evident. She found herself responding to it, pressing closer.

Then he released her and stepped back. Cat stared at him with desire mixed with bewilderment. "Why…?"

"Let's go," he croaked. He cleared his throat and repeated, "Let's go home."

Reality kicked in, loud and clear. "What?"

"Thing are inevitable between us, sweetheart. We need to get out of here and finish this at home."

Cat sputtered. "You…you…" She stopped and glared at him. "It was just a kiss, Taj."

"That wasn't *just* a kiss, baby. That was a promise of more to come. It wasn't the first, and it won't be the last."

She frowned at him. "What do you mean 'it wasn't the first'?"

He grinned wickedly before saying, "Every time I look at you, I kiss you with my eyes. Everywhere my gaze touches is a caress, a promise."

Now she knew he was nuts. And he scared her. No, she scared herself. The wanton feelings he generated in her were abnormal. "Take me home, Taj. This was a mistake."

Taj stared at her without getting angry. As if he knew she was afraid, he answered in a gentle voice, "It wasn't a mistake, baby. It's destiny."

"Do you ever listen to yourself? There is no divine intervention, no preplanned or predestined anything in this world. You make choices, and you live with them."

Taj took her hand in his and pressed it against his heart. "You hear that? That is my heart beating with excitement. It's doing that not because we kissed, but because whenever I see you, whenever I'm with you, I feel happy. We were meant to be together. You were meant for me, Cat. You're my destiny."

Crazy man, Cat thought as she looked around for her purse. He wasn't her destiny. And she definitely wasn't his. Oh, he made her so mad, and so confused, and so…hungry. She wanted him with a hunger that scared her. But she refused to let history repeat itself. To be obsessed with a man like her mother had been with her father wasn't healthy. She wasn't letting her emotions interfere with her reasoning. Taj was bad for her.

She found her purse and picked it up. When she turned around, he was still standing where she'd left him. Her eyes went to his face. He wasn't angry, just watchful and patient. Annoyance slashed through her. "What do you want from me, Taj?"

His eyes darkened, exuding strong sensuality. "I want you to love me, Cat."

Cat had opened her mouth to give him a sharp retort, but what he said registered. Anger drained from her. Slowly, she sank on the couch, her eyes still locked with his. His words echoed in her head, so clear, so bold, and so scary.

CHAPTER 8

Taj studied Cat's expression. That she was stupefied by his statement was very much obvious. He moved forward and sat beside her. Not too close, though. He made sure there was enough space between them so as not to crowd her in. "Cat, you know how I feel about you, don't you?"

She shook her head, looking at his face with a puzzled expression. "You want me?"

"There's no doubt about that. But I'm talking about my innermost feelings."

"Taj, you don't know me. How can you possibly have feelings for someone you hardly know?"

"I knew from the first day we met that you were meant to be mine, Cat. I recognized you." He touched his chest, "Right here. My heart belongs to you." When her eyes widened, he added, "I love you, Catherine Simmons."

Cat shook her head. "You can't."

"I can, and I do."

She got up and put some distance between them. From a few feet away, she turned around to look at him. "Taj, what you feel is a healthy dose of lust, nothing special about that."

He knew he ought to be offended that she was reducing his feelings to basic lust, but she didn't know any better. He had to make her understand the situation. "It's deeper than that, Cat. I don't deny that I want you every time I see you or think of you, but what I feel is much deeper and much more lasting than lust." When her eyes indicated denial, he got up and walked to her. He cupped her chin, searched her beautiful eyes and saw the struggle going on inside her. "Kiss me."

"What?"

"I said kiss me."

"I don't want to...."

He cut off her words by covering her lips with his. When she didn't struggle, he slowly ran his tongue along her lips until she opened them and let him in. Gently, he showed her that he wasn't after conquering her, but loving her. It wasn't long before she was moaning and gripping his shirt. The kiss deepened and sizzled. When he stopped, she was hanging on to him.

He lifted her chin, watched her as she slowly opened her eyes. "What we have is special, Cat. How can you deny it when we feel it every time we look at each other, touch, or kiss? How can you refuse to see what's so right and so beautiful?"

She took a step back and walked to the couch. "It's wrong to have such overwhelming feelings," she murmured.

He heard her and sighed. "There is nothing wrong in loving someone or wanting to be with them."

"You don't understand, Taj. That kind of overpowering emotion destroys everything in its path, everything it touches. It doesn't nurture."

His eyes stayed riveted on her face as he went to sit beside her. "Make me understand, baby."

"If I do, will you leave me alone?"

"I can't promise that. I can never promise that."

She sighed. "If you'd grown up in my house, you'd understand. My parents were so passionately in love and so wrapped up in their own world no one else mattered." She frowned as she looked at him. "That kind of passion is ravaging. I saw what it did to us. I saw what it did to them, how they were incapable of loving anyone except each other. They were often jealous of one another, possessive and distrustful. There was so much drama in our house…" She shook her head. "I swore I'd never again go through anything like that."

She spoke calmly, her voice firm, but he felt her pain and loss at not getting the parental love she'd deserved. Taj also knew she believed what she was saying. He couldn't invalidate her feelings by telling her she was wrong, or that her parents had been selfish and immature. He had to show her that love could be unselfish, generous, and good.

His hands gripped hers. "I will never abuse any gift you entrust to me. Your heart. Our children. Never. Whatever we feel for each other will be spread evenly to include them because they come from that love."

"Children? What….Didn't you hear anything I said?"

"Yes, I did."

"Then you know I can't enter a relationship that I know will destroy me."

"I agree with you, baby. You should never ever consider doing that. But ours will not be like that. You and I will make sure it is pure and healthy." When she opened her mouth to argue again, he reached up and silenced her with a finger. "We'll work on our problems, Cat, together. You can teach me to be patient, and how to love you better. And I'll show you that I'm sincere, that I'd never ever hurt you or our children, and that love can be steadfast, true, and generous." He extended his hand to her.

Myriad expressions crossed her face as her mind warred with itself. Finally, she sighed and put her hand in his. When he pulled her up, his arm went to her waist. She gripped his hand and seemed ready to speak, but a brief knock at the door interrupted her.

"How was dessert?" Archie's voice called from the doorway.

Cat and Taj looked at the two plates of *tiramisu,* then at each other. They smiled guiltily.

Archie followed their glances, took in the closeness of their bodies, and grinned. "I see you didn't need the dessert."

Cat blushed.

Taj merely grinned. "Archie, Cat and I would like to thank you for the use of your office. We were just about to come and find you. Maybe we should personally thank Jacques too; otherwise, he won't ever let me forget that I didn't touch his famous *tiramisu.*" He turned to Cat. "What do you think, sweetheart?"

Cat smiled and nodded. "Sure, why not."

Archie led them to the immaculate kitchen where Jacques Montville was busy chopping and dicing while shouting orders to his willing minions. Despite the French name, Jacques was a dark-skinned man who was powerfully built like a boxer. They watched as he instructed a young woman on the right amount of wine to add to Lord-knows-what dish. Archie explained that Jacques was from Haiti. With relish, he recounted how he had lured him from some five-star hotel in Florida.

But what was obvious was the respect Archie had for the man. He waited until Jacques was ready to talk to them, then performed the introductions.

"Ah, our honored guests from upstairs, Monsieur Taylor and Mademoiselle Simmons." Jacques gave her a brief bow. "I was told you liked my food, mademoiselle?"

"Every dish was wonderful, Monsieur Montville."

He bowed again, a smile on his pleasant face. "Then you make sure you come again. Next time, you try my island cuisine, *oui*?"

Cat nodded.

Taj apologized for not tasting the dessert, but Jacques forgave them after they asked if they could take the two pieces with them.

※

"Thank you for a wonderful dinner, Taj," Cat said as Taj maneuvered his car through Archie's gate.

"You are welcome." He watched her stretch her back and smiled. He liked to see her relaxed and happy. "Want me to come in, have the dessert Jacques was kind enough to wrap for us, and rub your back?" he asked with a devilishly sexy grin.

"You can come in for the dessert, but I think I'll pass on the back rub."

"You don't know what you're missing, baby. I've been told that my massages are to die for."

She shook her head. "I'll take your word for it."

"Not even a quick one?"

She shifted her body sideways to face him before asking, "You're saying that you'd like to have me entirely naked under a sheet for a quick scalp-to-toes massage?"

Although her sultry voice made his stomach knot with desire, he grinned at her as they entered a side street. "Maybe quick is the wrong word. We could make it a slow one." When his eyes went to the rearview mirror, though, a frown chased the smile from his lips.

As Cat noticed his preoccupation with something in the rearview mirror, she checked the side mirror. Several cars were behind them. "Is something wrong?"

"Hmm?"

"Is someone following us, Taj?"

He heard the worry in her voice. "No. Maybe we should work on each other after dessert." He tried to keep her mind on their repartee as he stepped on the gas. There was no need to make her panic. He had to make sure that the threat was real first. Was the Lincoln following them? Or was it the black van?

"I think I'll take a rain check," she answered, but her eyes were on the side-view mirror. Then she turned to look behind them. The lights from the cars behind them blinded her.

"Which vehicle is following us, the Lincoln or the black van?"

"I'm not sure." Then he cut a left on the next street and the van followed with screeching tires, cutting in front of the Lincoln.

Who were they? What did they want? He repeated the same move, but the van stayed behind them. "Yes, we have a tail. Brace yourself." He hit the gas.

She braced herself on the dashboard as Taj gunned the engine. The black van made a wild left turn, barely missed an oncoming car. They drove fast on a straight road with dead-end side streets, the van not far behind, barreling down on them like death. Tires screeching, the van matched them turn for turn.

Cat couldn't bring herself to watch the black van anymore. She faced forward and fixed her eyes ahead. Her chest heaved as she took deep, calming breaths.

Taj shot her a quick look. He couldn't offer her any comfort, not yet. He had to lose the rampaging black van first. Eyes narrowed, his handsome features rigid with tension and his hands steady, he performed one maneuver after another. After several blocks, he careened right and turned into a street with few pedestrians. Even though the Range Rover ate up the pavement, the van kept coming on strong. Block after block, the van matched his moves. Suddenly Taj made an unexpected right into another side street, barely missing a parked car before swerving back onto the street.

"Are you okay?" he asked Cat.

"Yes. Just get us out of here alive."

"I intend to," he replied as he shot straight ahead.

They were now on a busy street. Bars and clubs were open on both sides of the street, and people were milling around. They drew attention and received curses from other drivers as Taj swerved and banked between cars. The van fell back as Taj sped away. After a while, he entered another side street and backed up into an alley.

The tension in the car mounted as they waited. Who was in that van? Taj wondered again. What did they want? He didn't look at Cat, but he knew the same questions must be running through her head. She was probably scared, too. Although what she did for a living was dangerous, it was nothing compared to this. This was real life, not staged actions for the cameras.

They both stiffened when the van passed the entrance to the alley, cruising at full speed, probably hoping to catch up with them ahead.

The windows were so dark he couldn't see the driver's face before the van disappeared. "Are you all right?" Taj asked.

Her breath came out in spurts. "I'll live."

He looked at her, smiled briefly, and nodded. She was quite the trooper, he thought. No screams or screeches from her. The question was, who was behind the wheel of that crazy van? Moreover, what and who were they after?

"Did you glimpse their faces?" Cat asked.

"Windows were too dark." After a few minutes passed, he inched the car forward. At the curb, he paused to check the street before pulling out.

As Taj used side roads to cut through residential areas before heading toward her house, Cat looked into the night and tried to bring her breathing back to normal. She was wired. The chase had adrenaline pumping through her veins like water down a chute, the same kind of reaction she got after a dangerous stunt.

She stole a glance at Taj. He was concentrating on getting her home fast, driving a little above the speed limit, his eyes fixed on the road with a fierce intensity. The occasional drumming of his fingers on the steering wheel was the only indicator that he wasn't as calm as he looked.

After a while, Cat couldn't stand the silence. "Do you think those people were after us?"

"Maybe," followed by a shrug, "or maybe not."

Very eloquently put, Taylor, Cat thought with frustration. "It was a black Honda minivan wasn't it?"

Taj frowned at her. "Yes. Do you know anything about a black van?"

She nodded. Now that the time had come, she didn't know how to start telling him about Bobby and the missing priest. "We'll talk when we get to my place."

Taj frowned at her. She could tell that he wanted to ask her what was going on, but instead of speaking, he reached for her hand and held it tight. His touch was calming.

In no time, they were at her house. After she locked her door, she led him straight to the kitchen where she busied herself fixing coffee, getting out mugs, cream, and honey, and laying them on the counter, then taking out forks and plates for their dessert. She transferred the *tiramisu* from the cardboard boxes to the plates and poured each of them a cup of coffee. "Cream?" she asked him.

"No thanks,, black."

Cat tried to organize her thoughts. There was no subtle way of revealing the mess in her family to Taj. Taking a seat opposite him, she looked into his face and said, "I'm ready now." He was about to take a sip of his coffee, but he stopped when she spoke. "Remember when I talked about my family earlier?"

"Yes, I do."

"What I didn't mention were the fights. My parents fought on and off. Nothing physical," she said as she warmed her hand on her coffee mug, "just words. The night my mother had the accident, they'd had a major blowup." Cat retold the incident, how Bobby had reacted to the words, his search for the person he believed was his biological father. Cat paused to search Taj's face for signs of revulsion. Relief filled her when she saw none, merely curiosity.

"I spoke with Bobby last night about it," she continued. "His search started in New York and has now led him to Father Robert Forster of St. Vibiana Center for Spirituality here in L.A. Because they share the same first two names, Bobby thinks that the priest could be his biological father. However, this priest has disappeared."

"What about the black van? How does it fit in everything?"

"Four days ago, Bobby went to St. Vibiana to locate Forster." She repeated everything Bobby had told her the night before. "He saw a black van parked behind the church. Then he saw a priest and two men transfer crates into it. One of the men spotted him and started to yell. The next thing he knew, he was being chased. When he came to see me yesterday, he was convinced he was being followed by a black van." Cat sipped her coffee, then glanced at Taj. "Do you think it could be the same van that chased us tonight, that maybe they followed him to my house? Or maybe that they're hoping I'll lead them to Bobby?"

Instead of answering her questions, Taj appeared to turn over the information in his mind. Finally, he said, "I'd like to have a word with your brother."

"I don't know how he'll react to you. I tried to convince him earlier to hire a private detective to help him with the investigation, but he refused. This is a very sensitive subject with him. Yesterday, I promised him that I'd give him until Sunday night before talking to my father or Kenny about it. After this, I don't think I can wait." She paused to sip her drink again. "Maybe I should be with you when you talk with him."

But Taj was already shaking his head. "I was planning on paying him a visit tonight or early tomorrow morning."

"He won't talk to you, Taj."

"I've been known to be persuasive."

Cat sighed. "Why won't you let me help?"

"First, apparently you haven't been listening to the news. St. Vibiana Center for Spirituality has been all over the news. Someone torched it three nights ago, the same night Bobby saw the men outside the church." Cat gasped. "Chances are that he saw the people who did it. And now we come to the crucial reason you can't help. I can't knowingly put you in harm's way and live with myself. Surely you must understand that. It is my right to protect anyone I love and care about."

Cat rolled her eyes in exasperation, totally disgusted by his attitude. "I don't recall appointing you as my guardian angel, Taylor."

"Comes with loving you," he replied and got up with his empty plate. He put it in the sink, along with his mug, and turned to contemplate her annoyed expression. "You'd better get used to it, too."

"I wish you wouldn't go on and on about loving me, either. It's not true. It's not possible."

"We'll just have to see about that, won't we? Now about Bobby. Where does he live?"

The man was annoyingly stubborn. But then again, the center had been torched the night Bobby was there. That was a sure warning that they could be dealing with bad-ass people. "Bobby lives off-campus with a couple of his friends. I'll give you his address." She reached for a pad by the telephone on the counter. While she scribbled Bobby's number, she thought of ways to convince Taj to see things her way. "You know something, Taj, there's not much difference between what you do and what I do for a living. I put my life on the line every time I do stunts. I'm trained to hold it together under stress."

Taj moved to where she sat, draped his arm around her shoulder, and kissed her forehead. "Sweetheart, what you do is child's play compared to this. There are no props or safety gadgets in case of a serious fall. Think about tonight. What if the men had tried to knock us off the road? What if they'd had guns?"

She shrugged his arm off. "I don't scare easily, detective. Maybe their intention wasn't to hurt us. Maybe they hoped that we would lead them to Bobby. Of course, that's assuming that the van is the same one Bobby saw. What if it's not? What if they were after you or me for some other reason?"

Taj wrapped his hand around the back of her neck. "I know what you're trying to do, sweetie pie, but it won't work. As I said, you're not used to this kind of thing. This is my job. I get paid to put up with this crap."

"Good. Then I'll just pay you to let me tag along. End of story."

"Cute, Cat, very cute. You couldn't pay me enough."

While Cat sputtered with anger, he planted a brief but hot and possessive kiss on her lips. "Goodnight. I'll keep you posted."

She ignored the tremors that shot down her spine with his kiss. He had left his taste on her, and she unconsciously licked her tingling lips before saying, "Taj, you're not being fair about this."

Taj grinned at her behavior. "What's your schedule like for the next couple of days?"

"Why?"

"In case I need to get in touch with you. Oh, could I have a recent picture of your brother?"

"Okay. I'll be at the Sequa Club in the morning. It's down the street from here. After lunch, at about four, I'll be at my dad's." She wrote down her cell phone number and her schedule for the next week on the telephone pad. "Here." She tore off the sheet and handed it and a small picture of Bobby to him. "Promise to call me if you learn anything."

He saluted her. "Scout's honor." He took the note, then caressed her cheek. "I'll be working on this for the next couple of days." He dropped a kiss on her cheek, then moved his lips to hers and nibbled gently. She didn't push him away, but neither did she respond.

He moved his lips closer to her ear and whispered, "Think about me while I'm gone." He kissed her again. "We'll talk soon."

CHAPTER 9

Taj didn't waste time after leaving Cat's house. He dialed Godfrey Norris's number as he drove toward Bobby Simmons' off-campus apartment. The phone was picked after one ring. "Godfrey, I hope I didn't catch you at a bad moment."

The older man chortled. "Your timing couldn't be more perfect, boss. You might save me some money if you get me out of here. I'm playing poker with a bunch of thieving, conniving geezers. What's going on?"

"You don't live far from St. Vibiana, right?"

"Two blocks."

"What's the buzz on the fire?"

"Officially, nothing. The fire department is still checking things. But I've heard trickles of rumors that it could be gang-related."

Taj recalled something Cat had said. Bobby had seen a tattoo on the arm of one of the men. "What kind of gang?"

"Russian, Georgian, or something. They all sound the same. Encino has a large population of Eastern Europe immigrants."

"Can you find out what's going on?" Taj asked as he pulled up in front of Bobby's apartment.

"Sure. I know this old man who lives down the street. He works at the center, or used to, now that it's half gone."

"Good. Call me tomorrow if you have something."

Taj hung up, sat back, and studied the apartments. It was a typical Saturday at student apartments. Several parties were being held at the same time, rap music competing with rock to see which one could be more loud and annoying. Some students were hanging out in the parking lot, drinking or making out.

He got out of his car and walked to the building. The lights were on in Bobby's apartment. That probably meant that someone was home. But it didn't necessarily mean it was Bobby. Taj pulled out his phone and dialed Bobby's number. He waited patiently, his eyes on the well-lit apartment.

No one picked up the phone, yet he saw movement in the apartment. He hung up, waited a few seconds, then redialed. This time it was picked up after the second ring.

"Bobby, please," Taj said.

"Who's this?"

"Taj Taylor, I'm a friend of Cat, Bobby's sister."

"Bobby's not here. Haven't seen him in days." Then the person hung up.

Damn. Taj studied the apartment. If the boy who answered the phone was Bobby's friend, he probably knew where Bobby was and why. He dialed the apartment number again.

"Man, I told you he ain't here," the voice said belligerently.

Okay, so they had caller I.D. "I know. Could you give him a message? Tell him to call his sister. She'll vouch for me. Then have him give me a call." Taj left his number and hung up.

There was no point in sticking around now that he knew Bobby wasn't home, Taj decided. And if he were home, the boy wasn't going to talk to him anyway. He was scared.

Putting his phone in his pocket, Taj walked back to his car. A couple of students looked his way, then went back to their activities. Next stop was Archie's place, Taj decided. Archie might be a respectable man now, but it hadn't always been so. His friend was deep into the street. He knew everything that went down. If there was a new group, local or foreign, strutting their stuff in public, Archie was the man to talk to.

Sleep eluded Cat that night. After checking the TV news for information on the fire at St. Vibiana Center and finding none, she switched off the TV and turned on her computer. Finding articles on the fire wasn't hard, but the information was sketchy. There were no witnesses. The police and the fire department were still conducting their investigation. Arson hadn't been ruled out.

She went over everything Bobby had told her about the black van. If these people were the ones who started the fire, they might believe that Bobby could identify them. And if they believed that Bobby might report them, they could harm him. Was that why they were following him around? Were they waiting for a chance to silence Bobby? This missing priest business was getting too dangerous, and she didn't know who to blame—her father for what he'd said that night or Bobby for obsessing about it.

When sleep finally claimed Cat, she dreamed about Russian priests chasing her in a black van. She came awake in cold sweat. Who had Bobby seen that night?

She didn't go back to sleep after that. When her clock chimed at six, she got up, dressed, packed her things, and jumped into her car. She would sweat out her fears at the gym. One good thing about her gym was that it was open every day from five to midnight.

After several hours of burning fat, Cat took her time in the steam room, showered, then dressed. On her way home, she stopped by the grocery store and picked up a few things. She was supposed to prepare several dishes for the dinner at her father's.

When Cat turned onto her street, the first person she saw was Taj leaning on the intercom outside her gate. Excitement exploded through her even as she wondered what he wanted. Then she remembered Bobby.

"Hey," she called out when she pulled up beside his bike.

"I was beginning to worry when no one answered. I called you several times on your cell phone too."

"I try not to answer it when I work out." Actually, she hadn't carried her cell phone this morning. "Come in." She opened her gate, drove into the compound, and parked her car. Taj was right behind her.

As she got out of the car with groceries, he got off his bike and said,

"Let me help you with those."

He took several bags from her arms, stooped low to give her a brief kiss on her lips, then followed her into the house.

"So what brings you here so early in the morning?" she asked.

"It's ten o'clock, sweetheart, hardly early."

She put the bags on the kitchen counter, then turned to study him. The playful mood of yesterday was gone. He seemed preoccupied, on edge. "Have you talked to Bobby yet?"

"I tried last night, but his roommate said he wasn't home. I asked him to give Bobby a message. He hasn't called you, has he?"

"No. But then again, I didn't have my cell phone with me this morning. Let me check my answering machine." She reached across the counter to press the message button on her answering machine.

When she turned, she caught Taj's eyes on her backside. She was wearing a miniskirt that seemed to suddenly have a life of its own. It rode high on her thighs, making her want to pull it down. When her eyes connected with Taj's, she caught the heat burning in their depth. For a beat their gazes locked. Then Bobby's voice came to her rescue. They both turned to stare at the answering machine.

"Sis, some guy called my place last night, claimed to know you. Name is Taj Taylor. Do you know him? Call Joe. If this Taylor guy is legit, I'll return his call."

"Who's Joe?" Taj asked.

"Bobby's best friend and roommate. He was probably the one who answered the phone yesterday. I don't like this missing priest mess or the way Bobby's acting."

"I think he's acting pretty normal for a guy who's scared."

Cat frowned. "Oh, yes, I see. He's covering his bases in case the people in the black van were the ones calling his place. Give me a sec, and I'll clear everything with Joe." She walked to her fridge door where she had a paper taped. She found Joe's cell phone number right away. As she dialed it, she turned to study Taj.

He didn't look like he'd had much sleep. What had he been doing? She hoped he hadn't been up late working on Bobby's case.

As if aware of her scrutiny, Taj looked up and zapped her with his roguish smile.

"Would you like a cup of coffee, detective?"

Taj looked at the coffeemaker. "You talk to Joe. I'll warm some."

"The cups are…"

"I remember from last night," he interrupted.

She smiled and turned just as Joe came on the line. "Joe, where's Bobby?"

"I don't know, Cat. Did you get his message?" Joe asked, making it obvious that he knew where Bobby was, but was refusing to tell her.

"Yes. Tell him that there's been a new development, that we need to talk. Tell him that he can trust Taj Taylor. Taj will explain when they meet."

"I'll tell him if I see him. Bye, Cat."

Cat shook her head. So much drama. "I supposed he thinks the phone is tapped or something," she murmured.

"Why?" Taj asked.

"He didn't admit that he knew where Bobby was, yet he knew that Bobby had left me a message this morning."

Taj removed the cup of hot coffee from the microwave and placed it on the counter. He looked at the steaming coffee as if evaluating something, then looked up. "Do you want to go for a ride?"

She looked at him, then at his bike, which was visible from the kitchen window. Excitement spiraled through her. "On your bike?"

A flicker of amusement touched his lips at her tone. "Yes."

Her eyes rounded. "I get to be the driver?"

"No." When she pouted, he added, "C'mon, you'll get your turn one day. Just not today."

"Where are we going?"

"To get some breakfast. I'm famished."

"Okay. Let me change." She dashed into her bedroom while he stayed in the kitchen. The thought of wrapping her arms around his waist and hugging his body sent a bolt of excitement through her. In no time, she'd changed into a pair of jeans and picked a light jacket to put over her shirt. "Ready." He gave her a swift smile of approval.

Outside, she put on her helmet and sat behind him. When the time came to wrap her arms around his waist, she didn't hesitate. She could feel the ripple of his lean muscles as he moved. His musky smell filled her nose. Automatically, her body responded.

"Hold on tight, baby."

Cat pasted her body against his and pressed her cheek against his back. The ride was short but enjoyable. Within ten minutes, they were seated on the patio of a restaurant she'd driven past often but never thought of going in. It looked like a grandmother's cottage from the outside, and was quite cozy on the inside. The proprietor knew Taj by name.

Cat looked around with interest. Surprisingly, there were quite a number of customers. "I guess you eat here a lot."

"When I work late, yes. The food is wonderful. Wait until you try her Texas-style omelet."

She wrinkled her nose. "Is that the one with beef galore?"

"Oh, yes. Reminds me of the ones my grandma makes. Grandma Martha makes the best breakfast steak in the whole of Montana."

Cat laughed at his blissful expression. "You're definitely one of the cattle people. I can't imagine eating steak for breakfast."

"When you're rounding up calves, strays, or branding, you'd better have something substantial in your stomach, baby. Otherwise, you'll fall flat on your face after a few hours. Ranch work is gruesome."

Cat cupped her cheek and studied his smiling expression. "Have you really branded cows, Taj Taylor, or are you putting me on?"

"Branded, birthed, slaughtered. You name it, I've done it. My grandparents own a cattle ranch in Southern Montana. Every summer, as far back as I can remember, we visited them and worked alongside the ranch hands. Do you ride?"

"Yes, part of my training. I've had to perform a couple of stunts on horseback."

"Then you'd have no problem fitting in at South Creek Ranch. They spend more time on horseback than in a car or on their feet."

"Here we go, my dear." The proprietor, whom Taj had introduced as Mrs. Winters, placed a mouth-watering omelet topped with cheese and a red sauce before Taj. "And for the young lady," she added and put a plate before Cat. "Enjoy."

Cat stared at her plate. Her two egg breakfast and toast suddenly looked unappetizing beside Taj's omelet. She stole glance at his plate as he cut into it. Sauce oozed out, making her mouth water.

"Want some?" Taj asked teasingly.

Her eyes collided with his. She blushed. "No."

She made a show of cutting her eggs, but her eyes followed Taj's fork as it moved from his plate to his lips. When he opened his mouth and placed it in, she swallowed. She put a bite of egg in her mouth and chewed.

"Baby," Taj said.

Cat looked up. A twinkle was in his eyes. "What?"

"Open your mouth." He cut another piece of his omelet, then held it to her lips. "C'mon."

Cat didn't argue. She accepted his offering and savored the taste. It was delicious. For the reminder of the meal, he shared part of his omelet with her. They were sipping their coffees when Taj surprised her by asking, "When's Bobby graduating?"

"This year. In fact, he'll be defending his thesis in a month. He's getting his master's degree at the same time as his bachelor's."

Taj whistled softly under his breath. "I guess that means he can't take a week or so off."

"Actually he has a very flexible schedule this semester. The two classes he's taking are being offered via the Internet, and his thesis goes with him wherever he goes. It's in his laptop. Why?"

"My guess is that Bobby is in hiding because of the people in the black van. If he needs to go somewhere where nobody can find him, I happen to know the perfect place."

"Where?"

"My brother's ranch in Montana."

Cat frowned as she digested the information. She would be relieved if Bobby were safely tucked away, but at the same time she wondered if Taj wasn't blowing the incident of the black van out of proportion. "Do you really think he's in serious danger?"

"I can't say for sure, but his behavior indicates that he's scared. And you wouldn't worry about him if you knew he was safe."

Cat massaged her temple as she thought the matter through. It was sweet of Taj to want to ease her anxiety. "Why don't you see what he says about what happened that evening? If you think he should lay low, I'll talk to him. Does your brother have Internet access? Oh, what am I talking about? Of course he doesn't. He's a horse breeder." Then she noticed the wide grin on his face. "What?"

He shook his head. "Don't worry about Internet access. Angela owned a computer design company before she married Jerry. Last I heard, she was still running it from the ranch. I believe they have wireless Internet access."

Maybe it wouldn't be a bad idea for Bobby to visit the ranch for a week or so, Cat mused. For one, Jerry's ranch sounded modern. He could still attend his classes and write from there. And secondly, a break from everything that reminded him of their parents might knock some sense into his thick head. This biological father thing of his was causing too many problems.

The sound of a cell phone ring interrupted her musings. She automatically assumed it was hers, and was reaching for her purse when Taj's said, "It's mine, baby." He slapped the phone to his ear. "Hello? Where are you, Godfrey? You're breaking up."

"I'm in the basement at St. Vibiana Center. You need to come here now before he wakes up and alerts somebody that I have his key."

"Before who wakes up? And what keys?" Taj asked even as he pulled out his wallet to pay for their brunch.

"The keys to the basement door. Remember the old man I mentioned last night, the one who used to work at the center? I had late drinks with him, was at it until two. The man couldn't hold his liquor, though. He told me quite a bit about the center, including the fact that he had a copy of the basement key at his home. By the way, the fire didn't touch the basement, and from the looks of things, it's the one place with one too many secrets. Better get here ASAP, boss."

"I'm on my way." Taj looked at Cat when he hung up. "We've got to go."

"What's going on?"

"Godfrey, one of my men, found a way into the basement at St. Vibiana. He wants me to meet him there. He thinks there's something there that might interest me."

She picked up her jacket. "Then we'd better go."

"Oh, no, you're not. I'm taking you home." He put down enough money to cover the bill and a tip.

"What if the old man wakes up? Taj, you'll be wasting valuable time taking me home, then driving over there." She smiled innocently. "I promise I won't be in your way."

"I know I'm going to regret this," Taj murmured as he took her arm and started for the door. He waved at Mrs. Winters as they exited the restaurant.

"You won't. If you want me to wait outside, I'll do it. I'm very good at following orders."

"Humph! I find that very hard to believe."

Cat didn't argue with him. Listening to Bobby weeks ago instead of hiring a P.I. had been eating at her. Had she gone ahead and hired Taj, Bobby wouldn't be running around L.A. and hiding from a bunch of Russians with questionable reputations. The only way she was going to ease her conscience was by getting involved in the investigation.

St. Vibiana Center for Spirituality was a two-story house located behind St. Vibiana Catholic Church. According to what he'd found on the Internet, Taj recalled, the center housed and counseled women in dire domestic situations and pregnant teens. It was run by Father Forster, the pastor of the church.

Taj had also checked on Forster to see if he'd been involved in anything that could explain his sudden disappearance. The zero-tolerance policy adopted by the Catholic Church required that any priest with a substantiated abuse case had to be removed from the priesthood. Forster, though, was squeaky clean. In fact, the man was a boy scout. He'd done more things to better the condition of poor Encino families than government and charity organizations put together.

When Taj brought his bike to a stop at a gas station a block from the center, he and Cat just sat and studied the layout. There were lots of trees around the center, but that didn't mean that anyone walking to and from the buildings would go unnoticed.

There were very few people around, which made sense since it was Sunday morning. With the church damaged and no services being offered, the parking lot was empty. Parking there would draw attention to them, Taj concluded, the last thing he wanted.

"We have a problem," Taj told Cat. "If I walk to the center alone, I'm bound to attract attention. But if we're seen together, people will think we're just a couple out for a stroll."

"I see your dilemma. We'd better get going then, before we attract attention by sitting on the bike for too long."

They got off the bike, then hand in hand headed in the direction of the center at a casual pace.

When they reached the trees, Taj pulled Cat into his arms, then pulled out his cell phone and called Godfrey. "We're at the southeast side of the building," he said. "Where are you?"

"Follow the path to the north corner of the church. You'll be directly in front of the center's front door. The door looks bad, but it's functional. Walk in. I'll be waiting."

Taj looked around, every sense alert. No one seemed to be paying them much attention. "Let's go. If you see anyone, squeeze my hand but try to act naturally." He gave the order briskly and Cat nodded.

He led them down the path, past the parking lot. They could see the partially cleared debris from the fire, bare trusses and damaged walls. The pulpit, chairs, and some pews were piled outside the church.

"The damage was substantial," Cat murmured.

"But not as bad as at the priest's house. It was nearly burnt to the ground."

The center looked as though someone had taken a chunk out of it. Most of the damage seemed to have occurred on the second floor. The south part of the second floor, to be more precise. But that didn't mean the first floor ceiling or walls were stable. Wherever there was fire, the firemen's water usually added its share of damage too. Taj felt Cat shiver. "Are you okay?"

"Hmm. I can imagine how ominous this place must look at night. What exactly do they do here?"

"The center provides spiritual guidance to victims of domestic violence and teenage mothers, and helps them get a new start in life. Forster started it. According to sources on the Internet, the Father has an unorthodox way of doing things. Cardinal Mallory puts up with him because he's very successful at everything he starts, and he knows how to get donations for his projects."

Taj led Cat toward the entrance. He turned the knob and the door swung on its hinges. There was gray water, charred wood, and shingles on the floor. "Godfrey!" he whispered.

"Over here." The older man was standing in a doorway. His eyes moved from Taj to Cat and then back to Taj again. "I didn't know someone was coming with you."

Taj performed a quick introduction. "How are the floors and the walls?"

"The floors are intact, but the walls are a little unstable in some places. Watch your step, Ms. Simmons. Some of the broken trusses have nails sticking out of them."

With Godfrey in the lead, Cat in between him and Taj, the three of them walked along a narrow corridor to the middle of the house. Godfrey pushed open a door and disappeared down some stairs. Cat wasn't far behind. "Lock the door, boss, just in case."

Taj locked the door behind them, and joined the other two in the basement. The basement's nondescript brown carpet was soaked with water and there was nothing in the room except for a bookshelf with a few old towels. "Looks like they packed way before the fire," Taj commented dryly.

"You mean the women who lived here? They were moved nearly two weeks ago." Godfrey walked to a closet. He pulled two flashlights from the top shelf and passed one to Taj. "Sorry, Ms. Simmons, I don't have another."

"That's okay, Mr. Norris. But why do you need the flashlights?" Cat asked.

"For entering here." He turned on his flashlight and pointed it at the wall of the closet.

"A secret room?" Taj asked. Godfrey stepped aside to make room for Taj. Immediately, Taj felt a draft of air. Before he could say anything, Godfrey knelt down, grasped the bottom corner of the back wall, and pulled. "I'll be damned," Taj murmured when he saw what was behind the wall. "A nice little nest for secret trysts for the good Father or for something else? Did you enter it, Godfrey?"

"Nah. As soon as I saw it, I knew you'd want to check it out. It doesn't look damaged and it's still fully furnished." Godfrey stepped back.

The floor of the room was a little higher than that of the closet, which explained the lack of water on the floor. Taj directed the flashlight around the room. There were vents in the ceiling, but no windows. Since there was no electricity, the flashlights would provide adequate light.

Taj started to enter the room, then turned to Cat. "Stay here, please."

Confident that she would obey, he turned back and entered the room. His flashlight revealed an unmade bed with sheets that seemed free of dust or stains. However, the indentations on the bed indicated that a relatively short person had recently lain there.

He stopped beside a trash can and, seeing a newspaper and magazine in it, he pulled them out and checked the dates. "Last week," he grunted.

He flipped the pages of the magazine, stopping when he found the corners of several pages turned down. "Fashion, perfume, and hairstyle pages," he noted.

Moving to the vanity mirror and table, he placed the flashlight opposite him on the table, and knelt down to study the surface. "There were bottles and jars on this table, and the dust pattern indicates they were swept off the table, not picked up one by one." He imitated the sweeping motion. "She must have been in a hurry to leave."

Taj walked to a tiny closet and opened it. Empty. He studied the floor of the closet and spotted a scrap of paper, which he picked up. It was part of a letterhead, an official letterhead with a complex logo. Superimposed on the center of a black and white cross was a goblet having a white dove crest. "Ever seen anything like this, guys?"

Cat, who'd been observing him from the doorway as he worked the room, walked to his side and studied the logo. "Must belong to some Christian order," she said and looked at Godfrey.

"Nuns," Godfrey said. "There was a bunch of them here a couple of weeks ago. About the time the women living in this center were moved."

Taj stored the information for later. "What about the women who worked here with Forster?" Taj asked.

"I know a couple of them, but they're all tight-lipped about Forster and the fire."

"What church are they attending now that this one is out of use?"

"St. Patrick's Catholic Church, two streets from here," Godfrey answered. "It's bigger than St. Vibiana, but not as successful. Father Forster had a way with people. He dismantled gangs around this neighborhood, founded programs for the youth, mentored them, and found jobs for them. He wasn't afraid to challenge businesses to offer young people jobs. Beyond offering spiritual guidance, he cared about what happened in people's homes, the future of the children. People referred to the women he housed here as lost souls."

"He must have stepped on someone's toes because this fire wasn't accidental," Taj said. "And since his lost souls were conveniently out of the way when it happened, he must have known about the fire in advance."

Taj rocked on his heels and gave the room a once-over. Walking to the bed, he picked up the pillow and shone the light on it, looking for hair. He found a couple of strands and put them in a small evidence bag. Dropping the pillow back on the bed, he then pulled off the bedding. Nothing interesting there. When he lifted the mattress, however, something fell on the floor. He stooped low and picked it up.

"What is it?" Godfrey asked.

"An audio tape of some kind, label looks to be in Russian." Taj turned the tape over in his hand. "You don't happen to speak Russian, baby, do you?" He glanced at Cat who had walked to the vanity table and was now busy studying it. "What are you doing?"

"Trying to figure out how you drew some of your conclusions." She looked up as Taj chuckled at her behavior. "And no, I don't speak Russian. But Bobby does. He took a class in his freshman year in college."

"That brother of yours is beginning to interest me. I'll have him listen and translate this when we meet. I guess we're done here." He turned to Godfrey. "Keep me informed if you hear anything, Godfrey. I'd love to know where Father Forster is hiding."

"I guess if you find the women, you'll find Bobby's priest," Cat said softly as she looked behind the vanity and reached to pick up something shiny.

"What is it, Ms. Simmons?" Godfrey asked.

Cat was holding an object between her fingers.

Taj peered at the object. "What is it?"

"Mascara. It was trapped between the table and the wall."

Taj took it from her, checked it for dust, and found nothing. "Hmm. Is this an American brand?"

"Maybelline?" Cat asked. "You can buy it in any drugstore across the country."

"Is it expensive?"

"Not as far as makeup goes."

"Hmm. Thanks, baby, I knew you'd be useful."

"That's not what you said," she answered.

Amusement flickered in his eyes. "A man is allowed to change his mind." The three of them left the room. Taj handed Godfrey the flashlight and said, "I'll see you in the office tomorrow, Godfrey."

"Aye, boss."

Taj took Cat's arm, and they started up the stairs. "I think I'm going to drop you off now. If I don't hear from your brother by this afternoon, I'll give you a call, okay?"

Cat nodded. "May I ask you a question, detective?"

"What is it?"

"I saw you work that room thoroughly, and you were kind enough to share a few observations. But what's your conclusion?"

"The woman who last occupied the room was about five-six, slender, with long blond hair, and was very fashion conscious."

Cat gawked. "How could you possibly know all that from looking at that room? All I saw was the unmade bed, a garbage can, a dresser, and the mascara."

"Don't forget the magazine and the newspaper. The pages she'd turned down had to do with clothes and perfume. There were strands of long blond hair on the pillow, and the indentations on the bed gave approximate height and size."

"Amazing," was all she said as they left the building.

CHAPTER 10

After Taj dropped her off, Cat spent some time cooking. Scenes from St. Vibiana kept playing in her head, though. Now she understood why her brother Kenny respected Taj. His total transformation from playfulness to utter concentration had amazed her, and his deductive prowess was remarkable. She'd enjoyed watching him work, liked helping him a little. Maybe Taj would ask her to go with him somewhere again.

Cat checked the clock on her microwave. What was Taj doing now? she wondered. Was he with Bobby? It was going on three, and she hadn't heard from either of them. Or maybe he hadn't found Bobby yet. She knew she could call either of them, but she didn't want to appear pushy. But Kenny might be able to tell her a thing or two. When he had visited her on Thursday, he'd mentioned that he would stop by Bobby's place.

Cat called her brother's home. "What are you guys doing, Bri?" she asked as soon as Brianna picked up the phone.

"Trying to cook a few things...baby, don't put that in your mouth." There was a pause as she tsked and made the meaningless noises mothers make to calm their babies. Cat waited. "Sorry about that, Cat. Your nephew is getting into everything. It's as if learning to crawl gave him license to tear my house apart. Anyway, I'm still working on my dinner dishes. Are you done already?"

"Hmm. I was thinking of stopping by for a chat. Is brother-man home?"

"He actually left early to go to your dad's. He mentioned getting the barbecue ready, but I think he wanted to spend some time with him before we got there."

"Do you know if he saw or talked to Bobby yesterday or this

morning?"

"If he did, he didn't mention it to me. Actually, he would've mentioned it. He's a little worried about him."

If only they knew the whole story, Cat mused. "Want me to come over and help?"

"Sure, Cat," Brianna said with laugh. "You know you don't have to ask. Besides, you could watch Jamie for me. He's still cranky."

Within thirty minutes, Cat was parking her car outside her brother's house. The door opened when she tried the knob, and Jamie's screams welcomed her into the house. "Are you murdering my only nephew, Bri?" she yelled as she followed the racket to the kitchen.

"I swear when he starts, there is no stopping him. I've given him Tylenol, rubbed Orajel on his gums, given him something to gnaw on, and he's still at it. How can such an angelic baby screech like this?" Brianna asked in a frustrated voice.

Cat stared at her nephew's weepy eyes and reddened cheeks. "Poor baby, he's got it bad." Her presence distracted Jamie long enough to halt his tantrum. "Hello, cutiepie. Your teeth still bothering you, huh?" She looked at her nephew's tear-stained face and turned to glance at Brianna. As Cat had been two nights ago, Brianna was close to tears. "You need a break, Bri. Has he been like this for long?"

"Since Friday."

"Why don't you sit down while I keep him company, huh?"

"But the food...."

"Can wait." She took Jamie from Bri's arms and pointed to the living room. "Go and put your fanny down, Bri. I'll make you mint tea." Brianna hesitated. "I'd take a broom to your backside, but unfortunately, with the padding you got there, girl, you might not feel a thing."

Brianna laughed. "Oh, Cat, I'm so glad you're here."

"So am I. Now go on while I lay down a few ground rules for junior here." She waited until Brianna was gone before she turned to stare at her nephew. He looked ready to start howling. "Now, sweetie-pie, you know I love you. But after Friday, I've got to tell you, I'm in no mood for mess." Jamie continued to stare at her, his mouth pulling down as if he were about to start crying. "Now look here. You take some advice from your never-had-kids-but-knows-all-about-them aunty. Don't stress Mom out. That's the number one rule. When she's unhappy, the whole house suffers. Think. No food, no diaper change, no midnight feeding, and no kisses or hugs...oh, and unwashed clothes. I know you're in pain, but that medicine should be kicking in soon. Now give me some love." She kissed him on his chubby cheeks. When she didn't get a reaction, she lifted him up, put her face on his tummy and nuzzled it. She was rewarded with a weak gurgle.

She tucked Jamie in front of her and murmured, "Now behave yourself, baby, while I make Mommy tea." While she poured water in the cup, microwaved it, and added a mint teabag, she kept chatting with her nephew. "You know something, sweetie. Your mother is one special lady. She puts in a lot of quality time with you, your daddy, this house, and your grandpa but, she needs her own space sometimes. She needs to rest too." She carried the tea to the living room.

Brianna was sitting in a rocking chair, her legs propped up and her eyes closed. "Here, Bri," Cat said as she handed her the cup of mint tea. "No, don't get up."

Cat took the seat opposite Brianna's rocking chair. Jamie sat in her lap, chewing on a toy. A frown creased Cat's brow as she looked at Brianna. "Are you feeling any better?" She'd noticed the bags under her eyes.

"Umm-mm, it's been rough. Last night was hell."

"I can see that."

"You think I look like crap? You should see Kenny. He stayed up with him most of last night." Brianna sighed and sat up straighter. "Now I have the strength to finish the cooking. Do you think you and Jamie can play a little longer while I finish?"

Cat shook her head. "I have a better idea. Why don't you tell me what needs to be done, so I can do it while you and heavy-eyed Junior here lie down for a spell? Close the curtains and turn on the disco nightlight or something. That should charm him to sleep."

"That nightlight has been a blessing. I have to thank that man of yours again."

He's not my man, Cat wanted to say. Instead, she looked at her watch and said, "I'll wake you up in an hour."

"Sure you don't mind, Cat?"

"My contribution to tonight's meal was easy to fix. Now take Jamie and go nap together." Cat smiled briefly when Brianna thanked her.

Two hours later, they were at their father's house. The men already had the barbecue going. Cat gave their father a kiss. He smiled absent-mindedly and patted her hand. Their father's hair had grayed prematurely, but their mother's death had taken a toll on him, making him appear older.

His closest and oldest friend, Randal Wilkins, was already nibbling at some of the food. Cat swatted his hand and said, "Not yet, Uncle Willy."

As far back as Cat could recall, Randal Wilkins had always been in their home, never missing a special occasion or the meals their mother had loved to cook. He was a childless widower and the retired principal of a local school. Cat had never understood why he never remarried after he lost his wife. He was distinguished-looking, with his salt-and-pepper hair, a nicely trimmed goatee, and a slim body. He worked out regularly and was in great physical shape for a man in his late sixties. If he dated, no one had ever met his women. But he was around Cat's family so much that she and her brothers just referred to him as Uncle Willy. It had started when they were little, and the name just stuck.

Her father looked a lot more chipper than usual, Cat thought as she stole glances at him. No one could stay withdrawn in Uncle Willy's presence, though. He was funny and liked lively, intellectual debates.

Kenny was playing with his son as Cat and Brianna set the table. Cat stopped by his side. "Do you think Dad looks more relaxed than usual, Kenny?"

Kenny shrugged. "Hmm, I think so." He pulled something from his son's mouth and added, "So, sis, do you have something going on with Taj Taylor?"

Taj was the very last person she wanted to discuss. And they didn't have anything going on except Bobby's case. "No, we're just friends."

"Friends don't help each other out the way he did Friday night. Not that I'm complaining, you understand? I think he's a great guy perfect for you, if you must know."

"Why, big bro, thanks for telling me how you feel. The fact still remains that we're just friends, okay?"

"Jeez, baby girl, don't bite my head off. I was just giving my opinion." But the grin he wore on his face indicated his amusement.

She stuck her tongue out at him and went inside the house. Just as they were about to sit down for the meal, Bobby arrived. Cat gave him a hug and went to set a place for him.

"Hey, little brother. What's up?" Kenny said when he saw him.

"Just busy, big bro," Bobby replied, then looked at Kenny's head. He grinned. "What's up with the hairdo, Kojak?"

Kenny grinned back. "Bri likes it." He wiggled his eyebrows. "A major turn-on, she says."

Bri swatted the back of Kenny's head. "I heard that, you big oaf."

Bobby laughed at them as he gave Bri a hug. "Tell him to grow his hair, Bri." Then he ruffled Jamie's curly hair. "What's happening, Jamie? You have more hair than your daddy now." He said hello to Randal Wilkins before stopping beside his father. "Good evening, sir."

His father looked at him for a few seconds without saying a word. Then he nodded. "Where have you been, son?"

Everyone went quiet and waited to see what was going to happen next. Cat saw Bobby's jaw flex. Although Bobby hadn't attended any of their biweekly dinners since their mother died, no one had men-

tioned it until now. Would Bobby be rude? The last thing they needed was a row between him and their father.

Cat was surprised to see Bobby smile. He said, "Just busy. I'm
defending my thesis in less than a month."

Their father frowned at him. "Good. But that shouldn't stop you
from being with your family, son. Sit down, we're about to have dinner."

Bobby stared down at him for a few seconds and then he moved
to the place Cat had set for him. Cat sighed with relief.

Dinner was delicious. Cat had cooked macaroni and cheese,
mashed potatoes, and gravy, and bought from the store sweet potato
pie and peach cobbler. Brianna had brought meatloaf, collard greens,
and corn bread. The men had barbecued chicken and racks of lamb.
The conversation kept flowing smoothly, despite their father's silence.
Even Bobby joined in.

It wasn't until after dinner that Cat got a chance to talk with
Bobby. "Hey, you. I didn't know you were going to make it tonight."

Bobby shrugged. "I wasn't going to, but I kind of changed my
mind."

Cat looked at his face, trying to read his mood. "Did you get my
message? Did you see Taj?"

A smile touched his lips. "We had lunch together and talked."

Cat nodded at a chair. "Do you mind? I'm getting a crick in the
neck looking up at you." At six-one and still growing, Bobby was tall.
He pulled out a chair and sat down. "So, what did you two talk
about?"

Bobby looked toward the dining room as though to check for
someone eavesdropping on their conversation.

"Don't worry. They're playing chess in the patio."

"I told him what I'd told you. He asked for details about the three
men, the black van, and what I knew about Father Forster."

"And?" Cat prompted.

"He told me what happened last night. I'm sorry about the black
van chase. I haven't seen it in two days now, but I'm sorry I put you in

danger, Cat."

Her frown deepened. "Bobby, we don't know if it's the same van, okay? And even if it is it's not your fault they came after us. We just have to figure out who they are and what they want."

"You should let Taj take care of this, sis. I don't want something to happen to you."

He sounded so much like Taj that Cat had to ask, "Did he tell you that?"

"Who?"

"Quit playing games with me, Robert Simmons. Did he tell you that I needed to be protected from the big bad wolves in the black van?"

Bobby looked sheepish for a second and then said, "He does have a point, though. I should've confided in Kenny instead of running to you with such problems. We have to protect our women, not vice-versa. In fact, I'm planning on talking to Kenny about it tonight."

I'm going to kill him, Cat swore to herself. "That's up to you, Bobby, just as it's your decision to talk to me when you need someone to talk to. That's what siblings are for."

"I know. So, are you dating him?"

Cat stiffened. "What? Did he say something to give you that impression?"

Bobby shrugged. "He just seemed a little overprotective. He's an interesting guy, though. Some terrorist tried to off the Israeli Prime Minister, and he actually took a bullet for him."

Cat sat back and frowned at the obvious admiration in Bobby's voice. First Kenny, now Bobby. Taj was charming all the members of her family, one by one. "Hmm-mm, I knew that."

"He told me about his family in Montana, and how he spent part of his summer with his cousins on the reservation when they were growing up. His grandpa is this wise man who takes them up the mountain for days at a time and teaches them survival skills."

"Did he ask you if you want to stay there for a while, at least until it's definite that there's no threat from the people in the black van?"

"Yeah. I told him that I'd think about it. So, are you and Taj involved?"

Cat ground her teeth, but her voice was calm when she said, "No, we're just friends."

———ᘑ———

The telephone was ringing when Cat walked through her door. She threw down her keys and bag on the table and reached for it. "Yes?"

"Miss me, sweetheart?" Taj teased.

A smile crossed Cat's face. She almost said yes. She wanted to ask him where he'd been, and why he hadn't called her sooner. Then she remembered the conversation she'd had with Bobby. "Good evening, detective. What can I do for you?"

"No need to be so formal, baby. Did you just get in from your dad's?"

"Why do you ask?"

"You sounded breathless, as though you ran to the phone. And I called several times this evening, the last time five minutes ago, and you didn't answer the phone. How was dinner?"

"Scrumptious. You should have been there." Now why had she said that? Other than Jan, she'd never taken anyone to dine at her parents' house. And the last person she wanted around her family was Taj Taylor. Not that it mattered. He'd already won over four members of her family—Kenny and Bobby acted like he walked on water, and Bri and baby Jamie couldn't see beyond the disco nightlight.

"Tell me what you ate."

Cat reluctantly listed all the dishes and tried to downplay the occasion.

"Sounds like good home cooking to me. Okay, invite me next time, and I'll be there."

"I was just kidding, Taj, okay?"

"Sorry, sweetheart, you've whetted my appetite now. I've got to savor the flavor and the essence of what you have to offer," he finished huskily.

She shook her head. He had a knack of making everything sound sensual, even food. Or wasn't he discussing food anymore? "So, you got to talk to Bobby?"

"Did he make it home for dinner?"

Cat frowned. Was he responsible for Bobby's appearance at their father's tonight? "Did you have a hand in that, detective?"

He chuckled, a deep, rich, sexy sound that sent shivers up her spine. "Hey, we talked. Whatever he decided to do after that was his own decision. He's a cool kid."

"He's my brother too. Where do you get off telling him that he shouldn't come to me with his problems?" She didn't raise her voice when she spoke, but her words carried a sting.

There was silence from Taj's end. Cat waited and waited. Wasn't he going to say anything?

"Are we having our first fight, Cat?" he finally asked.

Cat rolled her eyes. He couldn't even give her an excuse to be mean and nasty. "No, we aren't having a fight, Taj. But I want you to stop interfering in my relationship with my brother."

She heard a deep sigh before he spoke. "I'm sorry, sweetheart, if I offended you. We talked about the chase, and what could have happened. I just think that it's my right as your man to protect you from any danger."

You're not my man, Cat wanted to tell him. But she couldn't make herself go after him like that. What if he didn't care about her? What if he put her in danger by being careless? Would she be happier? Which one was better, a caring and loving man or a selfish and indifferent one? Cat sighed. This man was making her rethink a lot of things, see things from a different perspective, and she didn't like it. He was wrong for her, darn it. "Taj? Are you still there?"

"I'm here, love."

"I'm the one who needs to apologize. You're a natural protector. I may not agree with your way of handling things, but I respect it." Cat paused and smiled. "I'm sorry for trying to stop you from being your-self."

He chuckled. "Baby, you don't have to apologize. We're getting to know each other, right?" There was a pause before he added, "Now I wish I was right there with you."

"Why?"

"I need one of your hugs."

She wouldn't mind a hug either, but she wasn't as open about her needs as he was. "Have you found anything interesting yet?"

"I guess no more sweet talk, huh?"

"Bad timing."

"Yeah, the story of my life. I don't know if Bobby told you, but the title on the tape we found in the secret room at the center is *English for Dummies*. That means that whoever was in that room was someone who's trying to learn English, maybe an immigrant."

"Interesting. Quite a number of Russian immigrants reside here in L.A. Did you hear about the ones who were involved in that kidnap-ping-gone-wrong two years ago?"

"Baby, they're into everything—prostitution, racketeering, mur-der-for-hire. You name it, they run it."

"I hope that whoever was in that room is not connected with all that. I'd hate to see Bobby cross their path. Russian mobsters are ruth-less people."

"Have you heard from him since you left your dad's?"

"I just got home. Why?"

"He agreed to visit Montana for a week or so. He said he would call you before he left."

Thank goodness. She wouldn't have to worry about him anymore. "No, I haven't heard from him. He'll be okay, won't he?"

"Oh, yes. I already talked to my brother Jerry. Bobby's supposed to call the day before he leaves L.A., so someone can pick him up at the airport and drive him to the ranch."

Cat frowned. "You're sure he won't be a bother, Taj? I remember what you said about ranch work. They might be too busy to take time off for a city slicker like my brother."

Taj tsked. "Do you always worry about things this much? I already said it was okay, baby. Bobby will be fine, and my brother will watch over him as though he were his own child. Now, what else did I need to tell you? Ah, do you remember the paper I found in the closet?"

"The one with a cross and a goblet? Yes, I remember it."

"The insignia is associated with the Corpus Christi Convent."

"They are nuns, aren't they?"

"That's right. There's a convent in Menlo Park. I'm planning on driving there tomorrow. Want to come? We could…."

Could do what? Not that she wanted to go with him anywhere. She was going to be busy the entire week. Still, she waited for him to finish the sentence. But as if he had hung up, there was no sound. "Taj? Are you still there?" There was no response. Panic set in. "Taj!"

"I'm here, sweetheart. Something's come up, I've got to go."

Relief flooded her. "I guess if you gotta go, then you gotta go."

"Don't sound so dispirited. If you dream about me, you won't miss me too much."

"What makes you think I want to dream about you, detective?"

"Because I'll be dreaming about you," he replied.

"You are so perverse."

He laughed. "Goodnight, sweetheart, have wonderful dreams. Make sure I'm in them."

Cat put the phone down, rolled her eyes, and started laughing. That man was scandalous.

Though Taj spent the evening with Nat, he couldn't keep Cat off his mind. As Nat had predicted, his wines netted several gold medals and a few silver ones at the West Coast Wine Competition. After the competition, Nat visited Taj, bringing along a box of his winning Chardonnay and Cabernet Sauvignon, as well as two very attractive female wine enthusiasts.

But Taj couldn't master an ounce of interest in either of the women. Somehow a short-haired witch with flashing eyes kept appearing in his mind. He had no interest in bedding any woman but his Cat.

The next morning, he held a meeting with his people. He quickly explained what had happened over the weekend. "We are helping Ms. Simmons' brother find Father Forster. Solomon, find a way to become a new member of St. Patrick's Catholic Church in Encino. Be their new lawn boy or help clean the church. Do whatever it takes to get you close to the main players. Identify the women who worked at St. Vibiana Center. They're likely to be doing exactly the same thing that they did at St. Vibiana. See what you can find out about the whereabouts of the women they cared for before the fire. I'm hoping Forster will be with them, wherever they are. Right now, I'm betting on the convent in Menlo Park, but I need confirmation. Keep your ears open. Anyone mentions Father Forster or anything to do with him, eavesdrop." Women tended to open up to Solomon, Taj mused. Solomon insisted it was his charms, but Taj believed it was the boy's unassuming manner.

Taj turned to Godfrey. Godfrey had a friend who worked at the Department of Motor Vehicles. "They know your face around Encino, Godfrey, so we'll let Solomon do this on his own. But I want you to contact your buddy at the DMV. We need a list of people in Los Angeles and the surrounding area who own a black Honda Odyssey. See if he can give you information on each owner—what they do, where they live, and their marital status."

"Frank and Mike, you're still on the Dorgan case, right?" Frank Clark and Mike Calhoun often worked well as a team. Presently they were helping Dorgan Security Company test the efficiency of their surveillance system by trying to break into facilities armed with their security systems.

"We're making them rethink their protocols," Frank said with a wry grin.

"You keep doing that and they'll get better. We all need a safer world." He turned to Mrs. Dunlop. "Mrs. D., I need you to make calls, lots of calls, to dioceses, small churches, and even to His Eminence Cardinal Mallory. We need to know where Father Robert Forster might be hiding, who his closest friends are. He lived behind the church, but the house got burnt down to the ground."

As everybody filed out, Taj reminded them, "My cell phone will be on twenty four/seven. Get in touch anytime you get anything to share. Otherwise, we're concentrating on these two cases in the next week."

After everyone left the office, Taj sat back with a frown. He was worried about Cat and the significance of the black van. Could it be the same van Bobby saw outside St. Vibiana? Why had they stopped tailing Bobby? And what was the driver's beef with him and Cat?

What if the van had nothing to do with Bobby? The one epidemic he'd encountered in the last three years was stalking. People became obsessed with their ex-girlfriends, public figures, or co-workers. If the black van were driven by a stalker, then was he or Cat the target?

He couldn't be sure until they knew more about the case. And extra help from his other sources wouldn't hurt either. He picked up the phone and dialed his friend Raymond Delaney. Ray was with the FBI.

He and Ray went way back to the days when Taj had been an agent with the FBI. The two of them had met during their training days in Quantico. As the only African Americans in their class, they had watched each other's back. Even after they'd been assigned to different field offices, they had kept in touch. Ray had joined the L.A. Field Office the year before Taj retired. He was now one of the rising stars in the Organized Crime Division, and Taj knew he could always depend on him for information.

Ray's voice interrupted his thoughts. "Delaney."

"Hey, Ray. How's Uncle Sam treating you?"

"Could be better. How's the private sleuthing game?"

"Interesting, at times predictable," Taj answered. "Ray, is Cipher still with the Bureau?" Cipher was the computer whiz kid in Ray's department.

"Yes. Why do you ask?"

"I need to know what businesses or groups St. Vibiana Center in

Encino is in bed with. Anyone Father Forster, that's the priest who runs it, has had dealings with in the last year, anyone he's pissed off, however big or small, okay?" There was a long silence from Ray. "Ray? Are you still there?"

"Yeah, I'm here. Isn't that the church that got burnt down?" Ray asked. "I think they're still investigating it."

"So I heard, but I'm investigating something else entirely. I'm trying to locate the priest. He's disappeared."

"Oh, okay. I'll see what I can do. Anything else?"

"No, but thanks for helping a brother out."

"Hey, I'm only returning old favors. Oh, Taj, I won't be in my office or at home for the next couple of weeks because of a case, so the only way to get a hold of me is through my private cell phone."

"Sounds hush-hush. Are you guys cracking down on a group?"

"Sorry, I can't discuss it. I'll call you with the info you wanted." He hung up.

Taj frowned. Ray had to be on a very sensitive case not to want to discuss it with him, he decided, although that had never stopped him before. He put the phone down and grabbed his keys, Ray's strange behavior all but forgotten.

His next stop was a clock shop tucked away somewhere in Pasadena. The man who ran it was a former marine who specialized in electronic devices. Taj had a plan and he needed military-standard, clandestine surveillance equipment.

CHAPTER 11

Taj didn't get a chance to call Cat until Tuesday evening. She answered after two rings, her voice soft and melodious. Just hearing her voice filled him with need. "Hey, baby, miss me?"

"I've been too busy to miss you," she replied sassily.

"Ouch! Okay, tell me what you did today." He smiled as he listened to her talk about her work. He teased her about Loren Phillips, the SFX technician he thought was sweet on her. When he was on the set, he'd noticed how Loren always stuck close to Cat. He hadn't let it bother him before because he knew the blond-haired kid was no threat to his goals. But now he couldn't discount the admiration he'd seen in Loren's eyes. Could that puppy love become obsessive? That was what stalkers were, obsessive. That was something he would check into later, after he got back to Los Angeles.

"You didn't see any shady characters in a black van today, did you?" he asked Cat when she finished talking about her day.

"No, although I checked for it on my way to Burbank and back. Do you think it was the same van that had followed Bobby? I'm beginning to believe it was a case of mistaken identity."

He didn't believe in coincidences. Maybe his stalking theory was off-base, but the car chase was too fresh in his mind to dismiss it as nothing. "Maybe."

"Where are you, Taj?"

"Menlo Park."

"Ah. Visiting with the nuns. Are they being helpful?"

"Are you kidding? Sister Mary Head Honcho saw me for about two minutes. As soon as I mentioned St. Vibiana, I was quickly dismissed. However, I still managed to give her the mascara and the *English for Dummies* tape. I told her that one of the women from the center left them behind, and that I was sent to return them. When she didn't tell me to take them back, I knew I'd hit pay dirt."

"Do you really think Father Forester is living there with those nuns, Taj?"

"I can only hope. I asked around, and Solomon, who's assigned to St. Patrick's Church, confirmed that the women who worked at St. Vibiana were transferred here. Now all I have to do is sit back and wait."

"Is someone supposed to get in touch with you?"

"Oh, no. I planted two micro transmitters on the items I left with the Mother Superior. One is under the tape label, and the other one is under the tiny mascara label at the bottom of the tube. They're so tiny they'll never see them. I plan to eavesdrop. If Forster is there with her, I should be able to hear him."

"Impressive."

"I told you to get to know me better, sweetheart. So, what are you doing now?"

"Do you really want to know?" Cat asked with a giggle.

"I asked."

"I'm having a bath."

He closed his eyes and imagined her soft skin wet and glistening with soapy water. He wanted to be there with her, touching and kissing that satiny skin. "Bubbles?"

"Yes," she replied with suppressed laughter.

"What scent?"

"Hmm, wild roses. I'm partial to it."

"I know." He loved that scent on her skin. "I love roses, especially their scent on the skin of a beautiful woman. Do you have them tattooed on your lovely body?"

"Hmm, a few here and there," she said with a sultry laugh.

Okay, you walked into that one, Taylor. He imagined making love to her on a bed of rose petals. "You're killing me, woman. You lit some candles too?"

"Yes," she answered.

The gentle purr of her voice teased his senses. "You've got the jets on?"

"How did you know?"

"The sounds you're making." She was driving him crazy.

Cat giggled. "I need to scrub my back, detective, so get off the phone."

Now that was deliberate. He wanted to be the one scrubbing her back, kneading her muscles, licking her silken skin. "You are a tease, Cat Simmons."

"You invented the word, detective. When are you coming back?"

"Tomorrow at the latest. I don't think my back can endure another night in a sleeping bag," Taj said with a dry laugh.

"Sleeping bag? Where in Menlo Park are you, Taj?"

"Definitely not in the Stanford Park Hotel." He looked around him. He was surrounded by redwood trees. After two days, he was beginning to hate the damn trees. "I've set up a base camp at a nearby private campground, but presently I'm perched on a fork in a tree near the convent, my binoculars hanging around my neck, and the receiver set to pick up sounds from the transmitter."

"Jeez, Taj, you need to be careful. What if someone sees you?"

He looked at his black shirt and pants. "I've done my best to blend in with the background. I guess it would be hard to explain why I have binoculars trained on the convent." He saw the tape start to record. "I've got to go, sweetheart. I'm picking up a signal."

"Be careful, okay?"

Ah, she was beginning to care. Good. "Will do. I'll call you tomorrow."

As soon as he hung up, he put the headphones on. A slight grin played on his lips as he listened to the Mother Superior. She was conversing with a woman who spoke English with a heavy accent.

Cold, Cat held the blanket tighter as she waited for a signal from the first assistant director. She was tired of doing the same scene over and over again. The jumpsuit she was wearing on top of the wet suit was still wet from the last scene. Although the scene involved a simple sequence, the director wasn't happy with the effect.

They were at the Santa Monica beach. Motorboats were being used to create fake waves, and giant fans to create a gale. Through the camera's lens, however, it would look as though there was a real storm. Unfortunately, the director thought the five motorboats weren't causing enough turbulence in the water, and the two giant fans on the pier, simulating wind, weren't producing the desired effect. He wanted more boats and another fan. Victor, the SFX director, was beginning to pull his hair, and Dorian...poor Dorian was ready to have a stroke.

"What's going to happen now?" Cat asked Loren, who was seated beside her near the helicopter.

"The director needs stronger wind and bigger waves and that's what he'll get. If Dorian doesn't get to him first."

A shiver raked her frame. From the sound of things, they were going to be at the beach much longer than she'd anticipated. Such was the nature of filming, she thought with a sigh. The director always had the final say. "At this rate, I swear I'm going to catch a cold," Cat murmured.

"Do you need an extra blanket?" Loren asked eagerly.

"No, thanks. The sun will warm me up soon...I hope." Another shudder shook her body. She'd already made three jumps into that churning water, Cat mused. One more and she would definitely be sick. The cold seemed to be seeping into her bones.

"Do you need a drink? I can try to get you something warm."

"Loren. Sit. Down. I don't need anything." The young man sat back with a sheepish grin.

As Cat stared at the scene before her, her mind wandered. What was Taj doing? Had he gotten what he wanted from Menlo Park? Bobby had called her last night, right after Taj had hung up, to tell her about his impending trip to Montana. He'd left this morning with the promise that he would call when he got there. At least she didn't have to worry about his safety for the next week.

The sound of a truck intruded on her thoughts. She turned to see a large moving truck backing up to the end of the pier.

"The fan's here," Loren said from beside her.

"Thank goodness," Cat added.

As the fan was wheeled down the ramp from the truck, from the other end of the pier came sounds of motorboats. Then the engines went silent and they waited. For the next few minutes, the SFX team worked to place the fan beside the other two.

Just before the boatmen revved the engines, Cat heard a familiar sound. She looked up to where a crowd had gathered to watch the filming. A grin lit up her face when she saw Taj pull up on his bike. Within seconds, their eyes met. She waved and he saluted her.

"Are you seeing Taylor?" Loren asked from beside her.

Cat's head snapped around to the SFX assistant. "Are you asking me if I'm dating Taj?"

The boy blushed. "Uh-hmm, yes."

"And you'd be interested because…?"

His blush deepened. "He's a dangerous man. I mean, what he does is dangerous."

Cat smiled. "Taj is not dangerous, Loren. He used to put bad people away when he was with the FBI, but not anymore."

"Still, he makes enemies as a private investigator, doesn't he? People who hate him and want revenge? As his girlfriend you have to think about that. You could get hurt because of him."

She couldn't tell whether Loren was concerned for her or whether he merely hated the idea of her seeing Taj. Could Taj be right? Could Loren be sweet on her? "How old are you, Loren?"

"Twenty-five. Why?"

"I have six years' headstart on you, my friend. Let me give you a bit of advice. Never let fear stop you from living or doing what you love. For starters, if I let fear dictate how I live my life, I'd be out of a job. The bottom line is that Taj is the good guy; the villains he put away are the bad guys. Always root for the good guy."

Loren shrugged his narrow shoulders. "I just think it's important for you to remember that a man like him has enemies. His enemies could become yours."

Cat frowned. What was the man trying to tell her? "Then I'd take on his enemies any day."

Loren opened his mouth to speak, but the first assistant director cut him off with, "One more take!" A cheer went through the crew.

While she'd been conversing with Loren, the team in charge of the fans had switched them on. Now, combined with the churning water by the motorboats, the effect was a perfect storm.

Cat pushed aside the conversation she'd been having with Loren and stood up. She smiled at the helicopter pilot, who gave her a thumbs-up sign. With Loren's help, and under Jed Sutton's watchful gaze, she once again checked the harness around her waist, thighs, and shoulders, making sure that everything was secure. When she was ready, she and Jed got in the helicopter and it took off.

While the helicopter hovered in the air above the turbulent sea, Jed signaled her. Cat moved from her seat and stepped onto the helicopter rail. Her eyes were watering from the wind gust from the fans. The helicopter bobbed in the air, but she didn't worry about falling. The harness around her body was attached to both the rail and the ladder.

Gripping the rail, Cat started down the ladder. The flimsy ladder swayed dangerously under the helicopter. She concentrated on getting to the bottom. When she got to the bottom, she hung on to the rope ladder with one hand for about ten seconds before letting it go. The distance to the water wasn't far. She hit the water, then swam to the boat standing by. Loren was waiting for her with a blanket.

"It's a wrap," Loren told her as they sped toward the shore. Cat nodded as a shudder shook her body. A sneeze followed, then another. She was happy the scene was finally done.

Taj was waiting for her when she left the set. "Tell me you had a harness on when you were dangling over that water," was the first thing he said when she reached him.

She laughed at his tone. "Of course."

"Whew!" Before Cat could guess his intentions, his arm snaked around her waist and he pulled her into his arms. Her eyes widened at the public display. "I swear I aged ten years watching you do that." Then he fused his lips with hers.

Cat's hands came up to push him away. But when her hands connected with his warm, hard chest, desire uncoiled in her midsection. Bolts of pleasure crashed through her senses. Searing heat chased away the cold that had crept under her skin. A soft purr replaced her protest, and instead of pushing him away, her fingers balled his shirt and pulled him closer. A whistle from a bystander finally drew them apart. Cat hid her face on his chest.

Oh, this was scandalous, Cat thought weakly. He was turning her into a wanton, an indecent hussy with no regard for conventions.

"Hey," Taj whispered from above her.

"You're bad for me, Taj Taylor," she murmured.

"What did I do this time?"

She heard the smile in his voice. She leaned back and glared at him. "It isn't funny. I'll have you know that I've never acted like this in public."

"I should hope not. It's scandalous."

Cat laughed. Then she jabbed him hard in the ribs.

"Ouch!" All at once he peered into her eyes. "Are you okay?"

"Why?"

"Your eyes look a little red, and," he touched her forehead, "forehead is too warm."

Cat opened her mouth to answer, but a sneeze got in the way.

"I guess that answers my question. Are you done for the day?"

"Oh, yes. You have no idea how happy I am that it's over. That was the fourth take. Everyone was starting to get cranky and acting weird." The conversation she'd had with Loren floated back into her mind.

"When did you," she stopped to sneeze, "get back?"

He frowned at her. "This morning. I spent a little time at my office, and I'm leaving for Mexico in," he checked his watch, "in less than two hours. Where's your car?"

"I came on my bike."

A frown crossed his face. "Are you sure you feel like handling your bike with that cold? Maybe someone ought to drive you home. Where's that boy Loren?"

She nudged his ribs. "It was just a few sneezes, Taj. And I don't want to ask Loren. Why are you going to Mexico? Has this anything to do with the case?" She'd taken to calling Father Forster's disappearance 'the case.'

"Yes. I'll explain later. Are you sure you're up to your bike? Surely one of these people could drive it home, and you could ride with me."

"Jeez, the way you go on, you'd think I was about to die." She eyed her bike, then turned to contemplate his. "How about we see who gets to my place first?"

His brows shot up. "You want to race me?"

"Eh, no…yes. Yes, why not? Not that it would officially constitute a race since we'll be on the highway and there are speed limits, but yes, let's race. I believe that my baby can handle your Harley any time."

Taj laughed. "Are you serious?"

"Scared?"

"Please. It'll be like taking a candy from a baby. What are you riding?"

Cat pointed at her red Kawasaki motorcycle. "Ninja ZX-6."

Taj turned to study her bike. "Not bad, baby girl, not bad at all." His grin widened. "Okay, it's on. What does the winner get?"

She hadn't thought that far ahead. But from the smile on his lips, he was way ahead of her. "Homecooked dinner?"

"No time. I'm leaving in a few hours."

"You'll eventually come back, won't you?"

He draped his arm around her shoulder. "Baby, you lack imagination. I can think of something much better than food."

He would, the sexy devil, Cat mused. "Okay, the winner decides what we do the next time we meet."

"Now we're talking." Then he gave her a quick kiss. "See you later, gorgeous."

Within minutes they were on their bikes, starting their engines. Cat glanced at Taj. He waved to her to go ahead. Oh, he thought he was that good? She was going to make him regret patronizing her. Cat took off, and within seconds she was on Santa Monica Boulevard, heading toward 10th Street.

For awhile there, Taj was visible in her rearview mirror. But as soon they passed West L.A., she picked up speed and left him behind. She grinned with glee. She continued until North Doheny Drive, where she turned left, then straight on toward West Sunset Boulevard. When she turned into her street, her eyes widened with disbelief when she saw him waiting outside her gate.

How did he do it? she wondered as she pulled up beside him. "You cheated," she said as soon as she switched off her engine.

"Now why would I do that, sweetheart?"

"Because…," she stopped. Because he wanted her in his bed and he was finally going to get his way, she thought. "There was no way you beat me without speeding."

"Never knew you could be such a sour loser, sweetheart. I won fair and square." He nodded at her gate. "C'mon, unlock the gate before you fall flat on your face. You're sick. Can Jan keep an eye on you while I'm gone?"

She dug in her heels. "First tell me what you want."

"Now?" he asked in disbelief.

"Yes, now."

Taj studied her tense expression and wry amusement flickered in his eyes. "You can cook for me next time we meet."

Cat's jaw dropped. Was that it? It was exactly what she'd suggested. Didn't he want her anymore? She stole a glance at his face and encountered an unreadable expression. What was wrong with her anyway? Why should she be disappointed when he didn't try to take advantage of the situation? Then her eyes narrowed. What was his game?

"Are you done pondering my motives?" When she stared at him in amazement, he chuckled and tapped her forehead. "I know how that mind of yours works, okay? Now be a good girl and open the gate."

She grabbed his hand. She was through trying to figure out how his mind worked. He was too unpredictable. She punched in the codes to open the gate. Then they wheeled their bikes in, locked the gate, and entered the house.

Cat's head was pounding now, and she was sneezing every few seconds. She should have listened to Taj and hitched a ride. So much for her foolish pride.

"Okay, what remedies for a cold do you have around here?" Taj asked as soon as they reached the kitchen. He dropped his hands on his hips as he turned to look at her. "I'm talking Nyquil, Tylenol, anything to knock you out for a couple of hours. You don't look good at all."

"Jeez, thanks. You sure know how to make a woman feel good. I have grapefruit in the fridge which, by the way, I can get all by myself."

"Said the little red hen." He took her arm and led her to a stool. "Sit. Don't move."

"I'm beginning to notice how bossy you get sometimes, Taylor. I let it slide when we were at St. Vibiana, but you'd better watch it. I don't take kindly to being ordered around."

He grinned at her tone. "You must really be feeling crappy." He opened her fridge door and retrieved a grapefruit from the bottom drawer. "Do you want me to run to the store and get you real medicine?"

"There's nothing—" sneeze, "—wrong with grapefru—" sneeze. "It has a gazillion doses of vitamin C."

"Hmm. Poor, baby. You have it real bad." He cut the grapefruit in two, placed the halves in a bowl, then he removed a spoon from a drawer. "C'mon, let's go."

Cat didn't argue. She followed him to her bedroom.

"Do you have warm pajamas?" She frowned at him. "Personally, I love to sleep in the nude, but it never hurts to have something handy for times like this."

Okay, so he was trying to cheer her up, but didn't the silly man realize he was only making matters worse? His *sleeping in the nude* brought to mind an image of his splendid body wrapped in nothing but red silk sheets. Need rose in her, sharp and quick. Oh, no. She was sick and weak and horny after that crazy stunt. She needed Taj gone before she did something regrettable. "Taj, go."

"Actually, I was thinking of postponing my flight to Mexico. I'll let Mike go ahead without me."

"No, you're going. I'll call Jan or Bri." Of course, she wouldn't dare call either of them because Jan was filming the rest of the week and couldn't afford to be sick, and Bri would only infect Jamie if she caught her cold. Suddenly feeling sorry for herself, Cat felt tears burn her eyelids. "And yes, please, can you get me some Nyquil from the store? I'll eat the grapefruit while you're gone."

Taj stared at her for a few seconds, then nodded. "I'll be back." When he leaned to kiss her, she turned her head away.

"You don't want to catch my cold," Cat murmured.

He grabbed her chin and held it in place. He studied the teary eyes, the trembling lips. "I already kissed you before, baby, so what's one more kiss?" He rubbed his lips softly against hers. "I'll be back."

Taj picked up two of six different cold brands, five boxes of tissue, mint tea, and honey. On his way back, he placed a call to his office. He spoke briefly to Mrs. D. When he came back to Cat's house, she was in bed, wearing long-sleeved cotton pajamas.

She looked vulnerable and lost in her big bed; her nose was shiny and her eyes were red from crying, which he knew she'd done while he was gone. The near-empty box of tissues beside her was a dead giveaway. He'd never loved her as much as he did now, Taj thought with smile.

"How's our patient doing?"

"I'll live. Can I have the Nyquil, please?" Her voice ended in a wobbly tone.

He heard it, but ignored it. He already knew what to do. "Sure." He used the lid to measure the right amount. After she finished drinking it, he asked, "Do you want mint tea with honey?"

Her eyes watered afresh. She pulled a tissue and made a play of cleaning her nose. "Thank you. That would be nice."

Taj left for the kitchen. He had to go to Mexico, he knew, but he wouldn't concentrate on his investigation knowing that Cat was so ill and alone. Despite her words, he knew she wasn't going to call Jan or her sister-in-law. And if he insisted on staying against her wishes, she would nag him and get all pissed. Oh, let her fume. He was staying. He carried two mugs of mint tea to her room. He noticed that she was more composed.

"Here we go," he said as he placed the tea on her nightstand. He made sure she was propped up against the pillows before giving her the tea. Then he pulled a chair closer to the bed and sat. "So, what do you want to know?"

Another sneeze shook her. She pressed the tissue to her nose. "What did you find in Menlo Park?" she asked with a nasal twang.

Darn, she sounded bad. "Before I tell you about the deplorable conditions of my campsite, the cramps I got from sitting in that damned tree for hours, you have to know that it was worth it. I actually heard Mother Superior and a woman with a heavy accent, presumably our mysterious guest, discuss Father Forster. According to what I picked up, the good father is in Veracruz, Mexico, at a monastery or a church called the Santa Maria. That was what Mother Superior kept telling the woman she called Ms. Kovalenko. 'They are at the Santa Maria. Father Forster will get them. Don't worry. Father Forster will get them.' I have no idea who 'they' are, but Ms. Kovalenko seemed very distraught about them. I thought I'd fly down there and meet Father Forster before he disappears again."

"Of course, you must go. When's your flight?"

"I spoke to Mrs. D. a few minutes ago. I should be there by tomorrow," he said smoothly.

Cat frowned at him. "You told me you'd be leaving in less than two hours over an hour ago." Her eyes touched the clock by her bedside. "You've changed your flight, haven't you? Because of me?"

Taj shrugged. "I would've been totally useless if I'd left knowing you were sick." He put down his mug and rubbed his hands together. "Now, what else do you want to know about my trip?"

"I told you I'd call Jan or Bri." Her voice sounded annoyed despite the roughness caused by the cold.

Taj offered her a small smile. "No, you wouldn't have called them."

She sniffled. "You think you know me that well?"

He shrugged. "You're a caring person, Cat. If Jan caught your cold, she wouldn't be able to work. And Bri has Jamie…teething Jamie with a nasty cold would be a tough customer. Pig-headed, but caring, that's you. Now where were we?"

She put her cup on the side table and slid back under the blankets. "Tell me about your campsite. I thought San Mateo area is supposed to be beautiful all year around."

While he exaggerated his two-day camping trip in Menlo Park, Cat became drowsier and drowsier. He moved close enough to take her hand in his. When sleep finally overcame her, she had a tiny smile playing on her lips. Taj left her bedroom to call his office.

"Did you change the ticket, Mrs. D.?"

"Yes, Mr. Taylor. Your flight will be leaving tomorrow at ten-thirty. Mr. Calhoun is presently on his way to the airport, though. He said he'd call you as soon as he got there."

"Thanks, Mrs. D. And thanks for the offer to stop by and bring Cat your cold remedy. She'll like that." He hoped.

"Is evening a good time to stop by?" Mrs. Dunlop asked.

"Evening would be perfect. I'll talk to you later." Taj hung up the phone, then walked to the bedroom to check on Cat. She was fast asleep.

CHAPTER 12

Taj flew to Veracruz, Mexico, the next day. After checking in at the El Convento Hotel, he followed Mike's directions to the boardwalk along the harbor.

He didn't know why Mike had picked the El Convento Hotel, which seemed to be *the place* for visiting homosexuals. A few men had smiled at him when he came downstairs. One had even been bold enough to invite him out for a drink. He hoped the look he'd given the man was enough to tell him that he didn't swing that way.

The harbor's boardwalk was only two blocks from the hotel. Along it were small shops, bars, cantinas catering to tourists and sailors. It was early afternoon and the sidewalk was filled with vendors hawking their wares, harp and marimba players offering up their tunes, spiffily uniformed sailors, male tourists in *guayaberas*light, short-sleeved shirts with small pleats and a straight bottom hem that was worn loose and women in jeans or skirts and embroidered blouses. Maybe it was the music, but there was an Afro-Caribbean feel in the air.

Taj saw Mike immediately as he approached *el gran café de Parrquai*. If it weren't for his height, Mike would have blended with people around him. He was conversing with a young Mexican woman in a red-and-white skirt and an embroidered top. Taj shook off a vendor hellbent on selling him a *guayabera* and approached Mike's table.

Mike looked up. "Hey, cousin." Before Taj could ask him why he was calling him cousin, Mike turned to his companion. "Violetta, this is Tito, the cousin I was telling you about. Tito, Violetta Sanchez." After Taj smiled and said the appropriate words to the woman, Mike added, "We'll call when we're ready to order. Thanks, Violetta."

"I see that you're already on first name basis with waitresses, *cousin*."

"Can't help it if the *senorita* likes my ugly mug," Mike said with a sardonic grin. "Plus, she's full of information."

"Is that so?" Taj looked at Mike's cup. "What are you drinking?"

"Local Veracruz coffee, strong and sweet."

"Is it any good?" Taj asked.

Mike shrugged. "Coffee is coffee. To my palate, all coffees taste the same."

Taj called the waitress over and ordered a cup. "So why are we hanging out in the quay sipping local brew and masquerading as cousins? Has your *senorita* helped you find the church yet?"

"Yes she did, except the *Santa Maria* is not a church or a monastery. It's a ship." Mike looked around him, then leaned forward. "The ship is owned by a local shipping company. It also happens to be docking tonight. It's coming from Eastern Europe."

A thoughtful expression settled on Taj's face. "Passenger ship or cargo?" he asked.

"Cargo."

The conversation between the Russian woman and Mother Superior played in Taj's head. What would a priest want from a cargo ship? "I wish we could find our way onto that ship."

"We will, tonight." When Taj's brows shot up, Mike explained. "Violetta introduced me to this guy last night. Don't sweat it, boss. She thinks we're hiding here for one reason or the other. That's why I'm Randy and you're Tito."

"Okay." Taj smiled briefly when Violetta brought him his coffee. "Thank you." He waited until the woman was gone before he said, "So we'll be helping with the cargo?"

"Yes. And here's another interesting fact I learned last night. The *Santa Maria* is known for bringing in special cargo."

"What kind of special cargo?"

"Illegal immigrants from Asia and Eastern Europe," Mike dropped the bombshell with a triumphant smile.

Taj knew he'd found the 'they' the Mother Superior had been talking about. The Kovalenko woman must have people she held dear in that ship, and Forster was here to get them.

Saturday morning, Cat woke up early. Instead of hurrying to the gym as she usually did, she stretched and reminisced about the last two days.

For starters, she felt great. It was as though she hadn't been laid out with a nasty cold for two days. Mrs. Dunlop's brew had worked wonders. And the person to thank was Taj Taylor. That wonderful man was beginning to make her rethink a lot of her personal choices.

That Taj had stayed an extra day to be with her merely because she'd had a cold had touched her. But her reaction to seeing his face first thing in the morning as he'd slept in the recliner in her bedroom had made her wonder if he'd been right all along, that they were meant to be together for always. The man was slowly working on her defenses. And it was becoming harder and harder to resist him.

Then Mrs. Dunlop had appeared at her gate and uttered his name. That was all it had taken for Cat to let the woman into her home. Cat smiled as she recalled how the older woman had cajoled her into doing her bidding. Mrs. Dunlop had made her drink chicken broth despite the fact that she hated canned broth. Her bed had also gotten made while she was in the shower. And could the woman talk, Cat mused with a chuckle. Throughout her brief stay, Mrs. Dunlop had regaled her with one office anecdote after another. To Mrs. Dunlop, Taj was a cross between a saint and a wizard.

But it was later, after Mrs. Dunlop had charmed her and lulled her into a false sense of security, that she'd given her the vile concoction she called her 'magic brew.'

Cat had cursed Taj to hell and back while she drank it. Then she'd called herself a fool over and over again for opening the gate when Mrs. Dunlop had come a-calling. Who but a fool would think she could trust anyone who evoked the name of the man she was falling in love with?

Cat left her bedroom and padded to the kitchen. Time for reminiscing was over. As she fixed herself toast, her mind went back to Taj. Since he left her place on Thursday, she hadn't heard a peep from him. Was he okay? What was he doing that he couldn't pick up the phone and call her?

She was in the middle of packing her gym bag when she decided to call him. She pulled Taj's business card from her purse and started dialing. The office telephone went unanswered. Frowning, she called all the numbers listed on his business card. No answer. She started pacing the floor. Where the hell was he?

Thoroughly annoyed with herself for worrying about him when there was no way of easing the worry, she grabbed her gym bag, jumped on her motorbike, and headed to the gym.

Two regulars were sharing a treadmill on her right. She said hi to them as she got on the Stairmaster beside them.

An hour and a half later, she was collecting her CD player and water bottle when the whispering of the two women sharing a treadmill reached her ears.

"Oh, Melanie, look what the sun brought in? I could crawl into those jeans and never leave," one of them said.

"I like the hair. Wouldn't you love to have him at your salon, Amber," her companion added.

"No, girl, I'd prefer that hair spread over my pillow."

Cat's stomach clenched when she heard their exchange. Surely Taj couldn't be here? Her head snapped toward the front desk.

Ah, but he was. Her heart lifted at the sight of him. What was he doing in her gym? Why hadn't he called her? And where the hell had he been?

The women were right, she concluded. Taj looked sexy as hell in black jeans and a black shirt. The shirt didn't hide his biceps or the chiseled planes of his chest. His hair was pulled back in a ponytail, baring his handsome face. He looked yummy.

Suddenly Cat was aware of the sweat trickling down her back. Her hair was sticking to her scalp and her face was dripping. Why did he have to see her at her worst? Who was she kidding? The last time Taj had seen her, she was in bed with a temperature, no makeup, runny nose, and bloodshot eyes.

"Hey, sweetheart." Taj's cheerful voice interrupted her thoughts.

Her heart did a jig at his voice despite her thoughts. His beguiling smile reeled her in, made her forget her sweat-drenched body. "Hey," she murmured.

She stepped off the machine and straight into his arms. His arm went around her waist, then he pulled her against his body. She didn't offer any resistance. Didn't want to, Cat mused, to be honest. She wanted to devour him with more than just her eyes.

"Hey to you too, sweetheart. How are you feeling?" he asked huskily, his eyes on her face.

"Better."

"I've missed you,"

The rumble of his voice rolled up her spine. A flicker of desire started to grow inside her. "You didn't call," she whispered, her voice nearly failing her at the sensual heat in his eyes.

"I couldn't." He didn't explain. Instead, his head dipped. Then his lips fused with hers.

The kiss was deep and hard, his mouth possessive, hot, and moist. Not caring that everyone in the workout area could see them, she welcomed the attack on her senses. When they came apart, her wits were gone. Her body ached and hurt. She hadn't wanted him to stop, and at the same time, she felt ashamed for losing control right in the middle of her club. She wasn't used to losing control, not in any given situation. But around Taj Taylor, she was always on a rollercoaster of emotion.

She said the first thing that came to her mind. "Mrs. Dunlop came to take care of me."

A lazy smile crossed his lips. "Good. Are you ready to leave?"

"I have to shower first." She moved back to pick up her towel from the rail of the Stairmaster.

He took the towel from her hand and wrapped it around her neck. Then he tugged it slightly until their bodies touched. He gave her another long kiss. "Run along then. I'll wait for you by the desk."

Cat nodded, flashed him a smile, and hurried to the women's changing room. She skipped the steam room, showered quickly, put moisturizer on her skin, and dressed in black Capri pants and a red-and-black silk shirt. Using the curling iron, she quickly styled her hair. After adding mascara and a dash of her red lipstick, she hurried to the lobby where Taj was waiting.

He was conversing with the man behind the counter. Her gaze caressed his smooth, dreamy skin, his silky eyebrows, the curve of his mouth, and his strong jaw line. She was mesmerized by his sheer magnificence, but scared of his expectations.

Should she be scared of how she felt when with him? He filled her thoughts and her dreams. And she worried about him whenever he was away from her. As for wanting him, he didn't have to be around for her to crave his kisses.

It was ridiculous to deny that they wanted each other, Cat decided. But could she survive an affair with him? What kind of a lover would he make? He was strong, patient, playful, and sensitive. Those traits would translate into meticulousness when it came to loving, wouldn't they? Could she let him go after being with him?

He looked up and saw her. He pushed against the counter and moved toward her. "Done?"

She nodded. When he was close enough, she noticed a few things that she had missed earlier. He looked tired. The whites of his eyes had rivers of red running through them. And his hair was still wet from a shower. "Didn't have time to blow dry your hair?"

"Never do." He touched her hair and caressed her cheek. "I was in too much of a hurry to get here. Maybe I need a haircut."

"Oh, no, don't." His eyebrows shot up at her outburst. Cat blushed. "I mean, eh, of course, you can cut it if you want to. It's your hair. But, it's…. You know what, forget I spoke."

"You rather like it like this, right?" he asked with a gleam in his eyes.

She smiled and wrinkled her nose. "Honestly? I do." Then she swept a hand down his head, followed the wet strands to his back where they landed in spirals and ripples. "When did you get in?"

"This morning." He took her bag, slung it over his shoulder. Then he took her hand in his as he led them outside. "It was crazy down there, but we made it out in one piece."

She didn't like the way that sounded. What were they doing in Mexico that was crazy? "You look tired. Did you find him?"

"Yes and no. Let's talk at your place. Can you take pity on me and feed me? Brunch at your place, perhaps?"

She laughed. "Of course. Remember the bet?" A confused look crossed his face. "The race before you left? I was supposed to cook for you because you won."

"Oh. That one. You didn't take it seriously, did you?"

At the time, yes, Cat mused, but not anymore. "Not really. Okay, brunch at my…" She paused when she looked over his shoulder and saw the black van. It couldn't be. She shook her head. Not now. "Taj. It…it can't be," she whispered.

"What is it?"

Before he could turn to check what had her so alarmed, she threw herself at him, catching him unprepared, and knocking him down flat. Her arms went around his head as her body covered his. She whispered, "The black van…oh, they found us."

—⁓—

Even as Cat's words registered, Taj realized something else; she was protecting him with her body. He twisted his body, reversing their position. Pain ripped through him as he used his elbow to get them behind his car. He heard the crunching sound of wheels on the gravel of the shoulder, followed by a popping sound.

Were they shooting at them? Or getting out of the car for better aim? He covered Cat's head and held on tight.

Then he heard the popping sound again. He waited, but nothing happened. The bastards were shooting at them and yet nothing ricocheted around them. Why? The third time the sound came through, he frowned. Was it his imagination or did it sound like a BB gun? Why would they be shooting at them with BB guns? What the hell was going on?

Taj lifted his head, looked at the near-empty parking lot between his car and the club building. Nothing suspicious. No club member heading to his car. He pressed his lips to Cat's temple and murmured, "Don't move."

He let her go, easing her to the ground and making sure her head was cushioned by her arms. Then he crept upwards. He used his car for cover as he tried to see beyond it.

There it was. The damned black van. It was parked directly opposite them on the gravel shoulder. No one was getting out, and the windows were closed. The tinted windows were too dark for him to see the driver. But it was the same van all right.

Then he heard the popping sound again and ducked. The sound hadn't come from the van, he realized. His gaze shifted to the left. He saw them, two young boys playing with BB guns. One of them jumped out of the road as a tan Lincoln took off from the end of the parking lot.

His gaze shifted to the van. Why weren't they getting out? Were they waiting for them to get in their cars or were they trying to tell them something? Taj started to get up.

"Taj? What do you think you're doing?" Cat asked from the ground, her hand snaking around his ankle.

"Let go, Cat. I want to know what the bastards want."

"Now is not the time to play hero, detective."

He heard the tremor in her voice. It wasn't the time to panic. He'd rather have her angry than panicky. "Stop being such a ninny, Cat. Stay put while…." But as if his warning had galvanized her, she scrambled to her feet. "What do you think you're doing?"

"No one calls me a ninny, detective."

Revving engine and screeching tires drew their attention. The van was taking off. They stared after it as it sped away, cut a wide corner, barely missing an oncoming vehicle, and disappeared around a bend.

"Didn't I tell you to stay put?"

Still staring at the corner where the van had disappeared, she replied distantly, "Didn't I warn you I don't like to be ordered around?" Then she turned on him. "Why did you expose yourself like that?"

"They didn't seem dangerous."

"What? And for that you got up? I swear, if you pull something like that again, I'll put you in the hospital myself."

He was getting ready to say she didn't stand a chance in hell when he realized that she was shaking. He put an arm around her. "You got up too, love."

"That's beside the point. But how did they find us? Why is it they only come after us when I'm with you?"

He smothered a curse as he looked at her pinched face. She'd made a valid point, though. While he was in Menlo Park or Mexico, they hadn't followed her. Now that he was back, the black van was around again. Was he missing something? And how did they find him? He'd made sure he wasn't followed, retracing his route and taking unnecessary side streets to lose anyone who might be on his tail. There had to be another explanation.

"Where is your car?"

She mutely pointed at her motorcycle.

"C'mon, in the car you go."

A shiver ran through Cat. "I'm not so helpless that I can't ride my bike," she complained.

"I know. You're a heroine. You protected me with your life." He led her to the passenger side, made sure that she was buckled up before loading her bike onto the motorcycle carrier rack on the rear of his Range Rover.

He wasn't ready to tell her that the popping sounds had come from

BB guns. Maybe he ought to, but he wanted them gone before the van came back. Somehow, he knew it would. Maybe the children's presence had prevented them from carrying out their mission.

But now he was truly pissed. They'd put the fear of death in Cat once again. That was unforgivable. And to do it in front of him was a personal insult. It was time for some major reinforcement, he decided as he pulled out of the parking lot.

Along the way to Cat's house, he placed a call to Ray, his friend from the Bureau. Taj explained what happened.

"Why does the van only appear when you're around?" Ray asked. "I think you may have a stalker, Taylor."

"That's what I fear too," Taj said. "Could you check if any of my old cases have been reopened or if one of the guys I put behind bars is out on parole?"

"Will do." There was a brief paused, then Ray added, "Maybe you need to stop seeing your stunt lady until you figure out who's after you, my friend. Not that you need me to explain to you how a stalker's mind works. You were a member of the prestigious Behavioral Science Unit."

They hung up soon after, but something about the conversation with Ray bothered Taj. He just couldn't put a finger on it.

During the short drive, Cat stared at her fingers. Tears burned her eyelids. They'd almost gotten killed. *Oh, Bobby, what did you get us involved in?*

When they reached her house, she watched with amazement as Taj punched in the codes to open her gate, then disengaged her house's security system. "How?"

He spared her a glance. "I was with you on Wednesday when you disabled them." He headed straight for the bar as soon as they were inside and poured her a snifter of brandy.

"Here." Taj pushed the drink into her hand and wrapped her fingers around the snifter. "Drink it!"

She took a mouthful and sputtered. "Argh! I told you I don't drink alcohol."

He poured himself a shot and downed it in one gulp. Then he poured another shot and headed toward her. "I know, but you need something strong now." He sat beside her and pulled her against him. "Are you okay?"

"I'll live. But I don't know how long I can put up with these people. I didn't see them while you were gone, and all of a sudden they're back." She touched his face, then his knuckles. "You have cuts that need to be cleaned."

"I know. And because of what? BB guns."

"What?"

"The sounds that you heard outside the club? They were from toy guns, not real guns."

Toy guns? "Are you sure?"

"Yes." He sat back and pressed the glass against his furrowed brow.

Cat processed the information. "That's strange. Why would they shoot at us with toy guns?"

"They didn't. The two boys at the end of the parking lot were playing with them." He shot her a glance, caught her stupefied expression. "Sorry, baby, I didn't want your heroic efforts to go to waste."

Cat's eyes narrowed. Why hadn't he said something before? She hadn't done anything heroic after all because there were no real bullets to begin with. She recalled the stark fear that had stunned her. The thought of being chased by men with guns had been horrifying. The relief now was so heartfelt that laughter bubbled inside her and spilled over. "Why you...you sly fox. Why didn't you say so then? And what was that about heroic efforts?"

The corners of Taj's mouth lifted as he glanced at her. "Actually, it's Hawkeye."

"What?" she asked between bouts of laughter.

"Sly Fox is my oldest brother's middle name. Mine is Hawkeye," he said with a deadpan expression.

She looked at him as if he'd suddenly lost his mind, then convulsed with more laughter. He pulled her onto his lap. When her eyes locked with his, laughter disappeared from her face. Her eyes rounded; then she blinked. Her heart picked up tempo. The transformation from laughter to passion was swift. "Taj?"

"Yes, baby?"

She reached out a hand and touched his cheek. She couldn't turn away. Yes, she wanted Taj, and it was time she did something about it. She didn't want him forever, just for a little while. When it was over, they would go their separate ways without regrets. "Kiss me."

Taj didn't need a second bidding. His lips closed over hers, tasting, savoring, teasing. Then he angled his head and deepened the kiss. His mouth was hot, molding her lips while his tongue showed her what he would like to do to her lower anatomy. He slid down the couch, taking her with him until their bodies locked comfortably. Then his hands swept down her body to cup her ample buttocks.

For a moment, there was nothing but heavy breathing as the adrenaline rush from the incident outside the club translated into lust. They strained against each other. Hands were everywhere; mouths connected, came apart, and reconnected.

His hands were driving her crazy. The length of his glorious body felt beyond good. She could feel his erection pushing against her stomach and she pressed against it. She wanted only one thing now, to be skin to skin with him, to have him in her so deep she couldn't tell where she ended and he began. Just thinking about it made her moan and burrow deeper into his body.

His hand moved upwards. She trembled as her nipples tightened painfully in anticipation. Those centers of sensual pleasure demanded attention, and his fingers took notice. He reduced them to tight pebbles, left her gasping for breath. She could feel his body straining against hers, wanting release. He shifted their positions until his thigh was over her hips, trapping her.

Cat welcomed his weight. Feelings ruled her head. Ecstatically, she threw her head back, giving him access to her sensitive neck as she pulled him closer. The warmth radiating from him invited her. Her hands roved his body, his arms, and his chest. Thoughts took over as she imagined what she wanted to do to him. Her hand went to the waist of his pants, to yank his shirt off. The shirt wouldn't cooperate.

As if aware of her needs, Taj pulled the shirt out of his pants and guided her hand to his flesh. His muscles contracted and a shudder shook him at the contact. He groaned. Then, as if to give her a dose of her own medicine, his rough palms slipped under her shirt, grazed her stomach, and left an invisible burning trail in their wake.

His hands on her bare skin made Cat jerk. Pulsating heat shot from her skin to her core, creating an ache that demanded satisfaction. When his hand slipped under her bra and found her nipples, her body trembled.

A ringing sound went off in her head. She wasn't surprised. The man had kissed her to the point where she was hearing bells. The sound came again, this time long and uninterrupted.

Cat froze. Her head stilled to find the source of the intruding noise. When it came again, she lifted her head, and the kiss was broken. It was the intercom from her gate.

Reluctantly, they moved apart. "Saved by the bell comes to mind, don't you think?" Cat said weakly.

"Did you want to be saved?" Taj's voice was hoarse, but his eyes were steady and serious.

Cat shook her head, and said confidently, "No."

His eyes searched hers. "So we're not moving too fast for you?"

She got up and pulled down her shirt. She stared at him sprawled on her sofa, looking so devastatingly handsome and sexy. "Sounds like you want to bail out, detective."

"Are you kidding? I've waited forever for you, woman."

She leaned down and brushed her lips against his. She was tempted to deepen the kiss but the intercom beeped again. "Hold on to that thought. I'll be right back."

She ran outside to see who was at the gate. There was no one there. Strange. She opened the gate and checked the street. A few people were walking on both sides of her street, but she didn't recognize anyone. There were no strange cars nearby, either. No black van in particular. She sighed with relief.

Then she saw two boys running away and looking back. *Crazy kids.* Could they be the ones who had pressed her intercom?

Frowning, she stepped back into the compound and locked the gate.

"Who was it?" Taj asked.

She shook her head. "No idea. I came out and they were gone. But I saw two boys running away, playing tag or something."

"Want me to go after them?"

"Hmm, no, but I need to check something with Lucille."

When she walked past him, Taj turned and followed. "Who's Lucille?"

"My next door neighbor." She picked up her phone, dialed, and waited. Lucille knew everyone who lived on their street. "Oh, hi, Lucille. I hope I'm not bothering you."

Lucille Lambert laughed softly. "Oh, no, my dear. What can I do for you, Catherine?"

"I need to check something with you. Two young boys, about nine and ten, are running up and down the street, goofing around." She quickly described what they were wearing. "You don't happen to know who they are, do you."

"Must be Fay Faulkner's boys. What did they do this time?"

"Just pressed my intercom and ran away. I was wondering if they pressed yours too."

"Oh, I wouldn't know, dear, because our bell is broken. I've been meaning to replace it."

"Oh, okay, thanks, Lucille."

"Do you want me to have a talk with Fay about her boys?"

"No, you don't have to, Lucille, but thanks for the thought. Bye." Cat hung up and turned to look for Taj. He had poured himself a drink and was sipping it while scribbling on a piece of paper.

He looked up and asked, "Well?"

Cat shrugged. She walked to where he was seated. "Lucille identified the boys as a neighbor's sons, but there's something else that keeps bothering me." She chewed on her lower lip. She hated this, knowing that there was something she was missing and yet not being able to see it. Maybe if she went back to the gate it might become clearer.

Taj watched her. As if reaching a decision, he asked, "Do you want to come with me to the Camaldoli Monastery? I need to try to locate Father Forster's brother."

Cat looked up hopefully. "Oh. We never got around to talking about your trip, did we? I'd love to come."

He grinned at her eagerness. "Okay, then let's hit the road."

She looked at his face and grinned. She knew they could be in bed this very minute instead of…no, she wasn't going to torture herself with that. *Our time will come.* "Better come with me." She took his hand in hers and led him to the bathroom where she got a face towel, wet it, and pressed it into his hand. "Clean your face first."

He took the face towel with one hand, and wrapped the other arm around her waist. He pulled her to his body and landed a brief, possessive kiss on her lips. "Thank you."

"For what?"

"Caring."

She opened her mouth to say she didn't, then changed her mind. She did care about him. "You're welcome," she answered. Then she took the cloth from his hand and wiped the dirt from his face while he grinned with some inner male pride she couldn't begin to fathom.

CHAPTER 13

Thirty minutes later, they were on the Pacific Coast Highway heading north. Cat opened the pamphlet Taj had gotten from a souvenir store and read aloud the history of the Camaldoli hermitage.

"Founded by St. Benedict in the sixth century, the lifestyle was brought to the United States in 1958, with the founding of New Camaldoli Hermitage in the Santa Lucia Mountains," Cat read aloud. "The Second Camaldoli Hermitage was finished forty years later near Morro Bay." She read silently for a moment, then said, "They advocate privacy for personal prayer and contemplation, group prayer and work on the monastery, and growth of meditative spirituality in the outside world." She turned to Taj. "It amazes me the lengths people are willing to go to find peace."

"Don't knock it till you try it, baby. Meditation is a powerful tool."

"You've gone on a retreat before?"

He nodded. "My grandpa, Hawk, loved to take us boys up in the mountains for days on end. He taught us survival skills that have been passed down for generations. But most important of all, we learned that solitude is not something to be feared."

"How old were you when you first did this?"

"About five, Jerry was seven, and Aaron nine. You have to meet Grandpa Hawk to appreciate his wisdom. He's half Crow Indian and strongly believes that communicating with the gods can only be accomplished on top of a mountain."

Cat looked at Taj with interest. Every time they conversed, she learned something new about him. "Tell me more about your grandparents. You said your grandpa was half Crow. What is the other half?"

"Irish. Grandpa Hawk was raised on the reservation in Billings until his father died—boat accident—without leaving an heir. Then his grandfather had no choice but to bring him to South Creek and acknowledge him as his grandson. As you can imagine, my great-great-grandfather wasn't too pleased to leave his entire estate to a half-breed. However, he was determined to beat the '*heathen, Indian ways*' out of him, and make him as Anglo as he possibly could. That's Grandpa's quote, not mine. To hear Grandpa tell it, the battle began before they ever laid eyes on each other, and it never stopped until my Uncle Cyrus was born."

"How did your grandparents meet?"

"Grandma Martha came north with her father as his cook and stayed on after he died. She continued to run her father's restaurant/bar/boarding house until the day she met Grandpa Hawk. Here is where their stories differ—Grandma says Hawk came to her restaurant acting cocky and full of himself, and demanded the best room in the house. He says he was half-starved and had run away from his grandfather rather than cut his hair or get rid of his bear-claw necklace. He had joined the rodeo to pay his way to Helena. When he stumbled into Grandma Martha's establishment, he was tired, hungry, and pissed off. But he says that she was the loveliest woman he'd met in a very long time, and he fell in love with her over a bowl of soup and bread she gave him. They were married within a month. When my infamous great-great-grandpa heard about the marriage, he almost had a heart attack. Not only did he have a half-breed for a grandson, but his great-grandchildren were going to be black. First he tried to buy Grandma off. When that didn't work, he tried to ruin her business. By then she was pregnant with Uncle Cyrus. Also, Hawk gave him an ultimatum: accept their marriage and they would go back to South Creek. Continue to give them problems and they'd move as far away from him as possible. He caved in, and here I am."

"That's an amazingly romantic story," Cat commented dreamily. Suddenly, she sat up. "The road to the monastery should be coming up now. Ah, there it is," she exclaimed when she saw the big wooden cross. The sign underneath it—Second Camaldoli Hermitage—seemed insignificant by comparison.

They turned and headed inland, away from the highway and the ocean. The road was long, narrow, and bumpy, the terrain rugged. To their left was a rocky embankment. The land sloped gently to their right, with bits of grass, shrubbery, and rocks.

Her mind went back to the story Taj had just shared with her. "Taj, you've no idea how lucky you are to have both your grandparents alive."

Taj took Cat's hand in his and said, "I know. Wait until you meet them. They're wonderful people. Grandma Martha rules South Creek with an iron hand, but the hands respect and like her. She's getting old, though, and so is Hawk. They've worked hard to make the ranch a success. But what's kept them going all these years is their love and total devotion to each other."

"Did your great-great-grandfather live long enough to see this?"

"Oh, yes. He came to love and respect them. The one thing he told Hawk before he died was that they'd taught him a valuable lesson, that people should never let others define who they are or limit what they can be."

"Who helps them run the ranch now?"

"My mother and her husband, Luke."

Cat shifted her body until she was facing Taj. "You haven't told me yet what you learned at the monastery in Mexico? Or why we're going to this one."

"*Santa Maria* isn't a monastery, baby. It's a ship."

"What?"

"Oh, yes. It's owned by a local businessman in Veracruz. Apart from picking up regular cargo in ports in Eastern Europe, it also carries illegal cargo, namely beautiful, young Russian women. These girls pay exorbitant fees to make the trip only to arrive here and be put in brothels. You should have seen the spaces they were crammed into. As soon as I found out about them, I knew Father Forster was there on a rescue mission. Two of those girls must be the ones Mother Superior was discussing with Ms. Kovalenko. Anyway, Mike and I found a way to get inside that ship. You should have seen the reaction of the men who came to pick up those girls when they found them missing. I don't know how Forster did it, but he removed those girls way before that ship reached Veracruz harbor."

"How strange. This case keeps getting weirder and weirder."

"And my respect for Father Forster keeps getting higher and higher. He has the making of a good detective."

"I can see why you'd appreciate his ingenuity. You aren't bad yourself, detective."

He wiggled his eyebrows and flashed a smile. "Why thank you, love."

"You don't need to thank me, Taj. I'm merely stating a fact. Why are we going to this monastery? Is this where he brought them?"

"I don't think so. Camaldoli is for monks, not nuns. When they found the girls missing in that ship, the name they kept yelling was Sergey. We assumed that this Sergey was working with Forster and had helped the girls escape. Now I know that Sergey is a common name in Russia, but when I called Solomon this morning and he informed me that Father Forster had a brother with the same name, I knew it couldn't be a coincidence. According to his source at St. Patrick's, the Father's brother is a monk with the Camaldoli Hermitage. I also spoke to Ray, who told me that Forster's records indicate a strong affiliation with the hermitage. What does the map show? Are we getting closer?"

"Just around this curve at the top of the hill," Cat said as she consulted the map.

The road was even narrower as they got closer to the top. Taj slowed down and approached the bend cautiously. When they reached the top, the ocean was visible to their left. Directly in front of them was an oak forest. They drove through the trees, rounded a curve, and saw the monastery.

It was on the nearly flat surface of the hill. Directly in front of them was a gated entrance. On the left side of the gate was a map of the compound. They got out of the car to stretch their legs.

According to the posted schedule, the gift shop was open every day. It was due to close at five, because they had solitary prayers called

'Lectio' at five-thirty. Taj looked at his watch. "It's four-thirty. We'd better go in before the gift shop closes. After that we might not see anyone to talk to."

They got back into the car and drove through the gate, and along a road lined with trees and shrubbery. It led directly to a one-story beige building with a stained-glass window in the top. The sign near the entrance indicated that it was the gift shop. Beside it was a white plaster building with an archway that led into an enclosure. A sign said, PLEASE DON'T GO BEYOND THIS POINT. It was also written in Spanish.

To their right was another one-story house. The signs indicated that it was the house where guests could stay during retreat. Below the retreat house, along the hillside, were several trailers. According to the brochure, retreants were given the choice of either the house or the trailer hermitages during their stay.

"It's beautiful, isn't it?" Cat whispered as she looked around. The ocean and the woods gave it a calm tranquility conducive to a monk's contemplative way of life.

"Can't argue with you on that, but it's also isolated and secluded. Anyone can hide here forever." He parked his car, and they got out of the car.

"You don't think Father Forster is here, do you?" she asked in a low tone.

"Anything is possible." He took her elbow and led her toward the gift shop.

There was a foyer-like entryway with a statue of the Virgin Mary. In the gift shop were two monks in brown robes with leather cords around their waists. One of them was behind the counter, ringing up merchandise for a customer. Another customer was browsing. Cat noted that the store included a bookstore and art gallery.

"Have you seen anything you'd like to buy, sweetheart?" he asked Cat in a carrying voice as he pulled her within his arm. "We're being observed," he whispered in her ear. He hoped that to the others they would appear to be nuzzling. Taj checked his audience. Everyone was now looking away. "Buy something and then engage the brother behind the counter in conversation. I need to pick the brain of the one over there."

Cat nodded and stepped back. Since the monk was still serving a customer, she browsed while waiting. She'd heard that most of the monks had led normal lives and held professional jobs before choosing a life of solitude in the monastery. Now all their talents were dedicated to two things: knowing and serving God. Literature and audiotapes on meditation, and beautiful artwork packed the shelves.

The famous fruitcakes and date nut cakes pulled her to the east wall of the shop. They were on display behind a glass case. As she picked up one of each and read the ingredients, she heard someone murmur thank you and looked up. The monk was done with the man, and the couple was leaving the shop.

Cat carried her meager purchases to the counter, a pleasant smile on her lips.

"We need to leave, now," Taj said a little while later, taking her arm.

They hurried out of the building. "What's the big hurry?" Cat asked, brushing against a monk who was coming in, his hood over his head, and his head down. "Excuse me," she said to the monk.

"Get in the car, please." Taj opened the passenger door, closed it after she got in, and practically ran to his side of the car.

"Will you stop scaring me and tell me what's going on?"

"Oh, nothing," he lied. His conversation with his monk had been very illuminating, but toward the end he'd had a funny feeling that it was all staged. "Brother Patrick told me it was time to leave after he realized he couldn't convince me to spend the night."

"You, too? My monk also tried to convince me that we should spend the night."

He picked up speed as they left the gate. "So, what did you charm out of the redheaded monk?"

"Brother Cornelius? I found out that the monastery owns two vans: a white one for transporting their fruitcakes to the nearby hotels, and a black Honda Odyssey."

"What else?"

"That's about it. What about you? What did you learn?"

"One, a lot of these monks used to be ordinary Joes before they decided to hibernate in there. The one I was talking to, Brother Patrick, was a cop. I knew he would be suspicious if I started asking about Father Forster. I mentioned that I wasn't Catholic, but I was thinking of joining their monastery. He told me I had to become Catholic, get involved with my community for two to three years, repay any moneys I might owe—in other words, I have to be free of any financial obligations, including school loans—and I must be over twenty-eight years old. I was happy to tell him that I was thirty-four and just happened to live close to St. Vibiana, Father Forster's church. Of course, I made sure I casually mentioned that the church is closed for repairs, but that I've been trying to get in touch with the good father to no avail. He started talking about what a great priest Father Forster is, how he has worked with at-risk children in his area, and that I couldn't have picked a better church. I added my two cents as he continued to talk about gangs the good father had dismantled. And check this out."

"I'm listening."

"Some of them were Russian gangs. The leader of one of the gangs, Sergey Krylov, joined their hermitage. Everyone calls Sergey Father Forster's brother even though they aren't related. When I asked Brother Patrick if I could talk to this Sergey, he told me that Sergey left the monastery a couple of weeks ago."

Cat frowned. "He's no longer with them?"

"He is, but he apparently went back home to Mother Russia to visit his family. He's supposed to be back by the end of the week. According to the card he sent his brothers at the hermitage, he was working his way back on a ship."

"Let me guess, the *Santa Maria*."

"That's right."

"That ties up well with what you learned in Mexico."

"Very nicely, but where's he now? For that matter, where's Forster? I asked Ray to inform me when they reenter the country. He promised to keep tabs on the U.S./Mexican border for me."

Cat glanced at the speedometer. "Taj, you need to slow down. The road is getting narrower and steeper."

"Right." He stepped on the brake pedal.

"What the…."

He pushed on the pedal again. It went all the way down to the floor and the car wasn't slowing down. *Please, let it be a leaky circuit,* Taj thought as he pumped the brake pedal. Nothing happened. Damn. Someone had tampered with his brakes.

Who? When? Who wanted them dead? And how the cotton-picking hell had they known they were coming to the hermitage?

The questions raced through his mind at warp speed as he searched for a way out. To their right was a high rock face. To their left was a grassy, flatter area, but it was littered with boulders and rocks. But he had to stop the car.

How? The parking brake? Maybe, if it worked. Scrape against the embankment if it didn't? No way, Cat was on the embankment side. Throw the vehicle into reverse? That might work.

Cat interrupted his thoughts. "Unless you want to crash, Taj, you'd better slow down."

"Sorry, babe, but someone tampered with my brakes. I have to make an emergency stop." He spoke calmly, but inside, anger clenched his gut. *Damn them!*

"What? When?" Cat screeched.

"I don't know."

"I can't believe this. What's going on? What did Bobby involve us in?"

Taj had no time to vent his anger or frustrations or answer her questions. "I'm going to use the hand brake. Brace yourself." He grabbed the hand brake and pulled with all his might.

But the car didn't even slow down. In fact, it was gaining speed as the road sloped more steeply. They were approaching a section of the road with granite embankments. It was now or never, he decided.

"Brace yourself." Taj shouted again. He reached for the gear stick and pushed it in reverse. The car shuddered and started to spin out of control. "Hang on, baby."

He hung on to the steering wheel. The distance between his car and the granite wall narrowed, and the closer they got to it the rockier the terrain became.

"We're slowing down, Taj!" Cat exclaimed with excitement.

But they weren't going to escape scraping the granite, Taj thought, struggling to bring the vehicle under control. Rather his side of the car than Cat's, he thought. "Hang on, Cat." Even as he spoke, the truck struck the granite wall.

The jolt of the impact was hard but somehow not strong enough to cause the side airbags to inflate. As the truck scraped against the granite, it shook and shuddered, then finally came to a complete stop.

CHAPTER 14

Anything broken? Cat wondered as she took a deep breath. Lungs and ribs seemed okay. She wiggled her body experimentally. A deep sigh of relief escaped her. She was okay.

Taj!

Her head snapped toward the driver's seat. Taj was slumped over the steering wheel. The airbag hadn't inflated. She reached out a hand and touched his shoulder. "Taj?"

There was no response. Then she saw the crack in his window. Had his head made that crack? Blood. She saw blood. His temple was cut and bleeding. With her heart beating like tom-toms, she put fingers on his neck and felt a pulse. Her eyes filled with tears. They both had made it out alive.

"C'mon, baby, talk to me. Are you okay?" He didn't answer and she felt a fresh wave of fear.

The cut on his head looked bad. "Wake up, baby. Please tell me that you're okay. Oh, God, let him be okay." She wasn't even aware that she was talking as she rummaged through her bag for a small First Aid kit she usually carried with her. Finally she found it and removed sterile gauze and pressed it on the bleeding cut. Did he break something or have internal injuries? "Taj! I can't tell how badly you're hurt if you don't talk to me."

She was beginning to panic. Taj was deathly still, yet he was breathing evenly. Then she started to get mad. "Damn it, Taj! Don't you dare quit on me now." Tears rolled down her cheeks. "You wake up this instant. We need to get out of here." A sniffle followed. He still didn't move.

Get a grip, Catherine, think, she admonished herself. "I'm going to call for an ambulance. Whoever did this is going to be one sorry bas-

tard. And I'm sorry for yelling at you earlier, baby. Please, wake up."
She pulled out her cell phone and dialed 911. After explaining the situation, where they were, and what had happened, she dropped the cell
phone into her purse.

Her eyes went to Taj's head. "I'm sorry for getting you involved in
this mess. If something happened to you, I don't know what I'd do."
The sentence ended in a hiccup.

"Don't cry, sweetheart," Taj whispered, lifting his head.

Her eyes flew to his face. "I thought I'd lost you. I thought you
were never going to wake up." She started to laugh and cry at the same
time.

Taj touched his temple. When he removed his hand, there was
blood on it. He looked at Cat and frowned. "Why are there two of you?
You don't have a double. You can't. You're unique."

Her grin disappeared. He was seeing double. That wasn't good.
"Of course, I don't have a double, baby. Do you remember what happened? Someone tampered with our brakes, and you had to…."

"To swipe the embankment to stop, I remember." He tried to
straighten up.

"Don't try to sit up, Taj," she yelled. "Stay put until you feel well."
What the hell was she talking about? "I'll help you, okay?"

"You shouted," he murmured, squinting at her.

"What? I'm sorry…your head. I'm just worried about you." She
put her arms around his shoulder to restrain him. "The ambulance is
on the way."

"We need to get out of here."

"Don't try to be a hero, please, not now." But he was determined
to sit up. "Okay, slowly," she urged as she helped him.

By the time he was fully upright, he was breathing hard, and his
eyes were shut tight. She took more gauze from her kit and replaced the
soaked bandage with a fresh one. She held it in place until he took over.
She eased back toward her seat, but her eyes were locked on his face,
ready to intervene.

"How the hell did I crack my head?" He sounded more coherent now.

"I thought you said you knew what happened," Cat screeched.

He squinted at the crack in the window. "Yes, I do. I was just wondering why the damn side airbag didn't inflate."

Jeez, she'd thought that he had amnesia or something. "Don't you ever scare me like that again, Taj Taylor. It's bad enough I got you into this, almost got you killed. No more. You're not to continue with this investigation. Your life is not worth whatever Forster knows about Mom. Bobby will just have to get over his disappointment."

He turned to grin at her. "My grandfather was right," he murmured.

"About what?"

"You know that a woman loves you when she feels your pain and cries over you. You were crying."

She gawked at him. She was going crazy with guilt, and he was talking about love? "Really, Taj, this is hardly the place or time to be talking about such things."

He pulled her into his arms. "Love is what holds us together and keeps us going, baby. There's no time or place we can't embrace it. And you're not getting rid of me that easily," he whispered.

She started to cry all over again as he held her close to his heart. *We're alive.* The phrase kept repeating itself over and over again in Cat's head.

"How are you feeling?" Taj asked some time later from above her head.

Cat patted his chest. "I'm okay now. I'm sorry, I made your shirt wet."

"Nothing but a drop in the bucket," Taj said softly. "Tear stains aren't worth worrying about." He lifted her chin, flicked a tear from her cheek. "Did you get hurt?"

She shook her head. "You saved us, Taj. You saved me." She didn't know how to start thanking him, as if she could ever repay such a debt.

He touched her lips with a finger and said, "Just taking care of my own."

Cat smiled. Those words weren't as irritating as they once were. Maybe he was beginning to make a believer of her. Maybe she was truly meant to be his.

She moved to check his wound. It didn't seem to be bleeding anymore. "How are you feeling? You passed out, Taj. That spells trouble."

"I'll be fine."

"It needs to be sutured." She held his face in place with one hand and the other flitted all over his face, touching and checking for more injuries.

"I have a head of steel, sweetheart." He touched his temple and winced. "I'm not even dizzy."

"Good, but you still need to be checked thoroughly. There might be injuries that you don't know about."

Taj closed his eyes. Her voice was soft, and her breath grazed his face as she moved from one place to another and murmured soothing words. Her touch was infinitely light and gentle.

Cat wondered what was going on behind Taj's closed eyes and serene expression. His handsome face, with its stubble and rakish smile, was battered and bruised. She found herself closing her eyes, leaning forward, and pressing her lips to his. His eyes snapped open. He was surprised that she'd kissed him, she noticed. "I'm happy we're okay," she whispered.

Taj leaned slightly forward and kissed her back. There was no passion in their kisses or urgency in their embrace, just a celebration of life. They had made it out alive. When a shiver ran through Cat, he muttered, "I need to get us out of here."

"I already called the police. They should be here any minute."

His eyes locked with hers and a smile touched his lips. "Good. Let me call my people, too." He searched his pocket, found his cell phone intact and functioning. "This won't take but a minute."

Cat partly listened to Taj's firm voice as he mobilized his people. He called someone named Frank, and told him what had happened and their location. The next one was Mike, whom he told to contact a tow-truck company to pick up the Range Rover. Then he turned toward her.

"What do you want to eat tonight, baby?" he asked as he pulled her close.

The mention of food made her stomach to growl. "If I could get away with it, I'd eat a horse." She felt his smile against her temple. "Whatever you order will be fine with me."

"Chinese?"

"Sure, hmm, shrimp with broccoli for me."

Taj punched in numbers, and then put the cell phone to his ear. "Dolores? How are you doing? Good. How is Pete doing? Oh? That's good news. Could I talk to Solomon?" As he waited for Solomon to come to the phone, he rested his chin against Cat's head and closed his eyes. "Solomon, did I catch you at a wrong time? Are you sure? Good." He explained what had happened and what to pick up for them for dinner. "We may not be there for another hour or two, so take your time. Bring it to Ms. Simmons' house." He gave her address. Then he put the phone away and wrapped his arms around Cat.

For a while, they just held each other and waited, neither of them wanting to talk about what had happened.

After a while, staring at the rocky hill became monotonous for Cat. "Tell me about Frank, Mike, Dolores, Pete, and Solomon," she murmured. "Who are they? What do they do?"

For the next thirty minutes, Cat listened as Taj talked about his employees. From his tone, Cat concluded that he was closest to Mrs. Dunlop and Frank Clark, and that he had a great deal of respect for them, as well as Godfrey Norris. He worried about Solomon Dawson, who had become a father at a young age.

"But Solomon married Dolores and he's taking care of her and Pete," he added.

The pride he felt in Mike Calhoun's achievements was apparent, too. Mike was going back to school to get a formal education. He spoke of each and every one of his employees with affection, knew the names of their spouses and children, and in the case of Frank and Mrs. D., their grandchildren too.

In no time, the police and the paramedics arrived. While the paramedics sutured Taj's head and checked for other injuries, he talked to Officer Dilbert. The officer was friendly, especially when he learned that Taj was once with the FBI.

Taj didn't mention Bobby and the investigation or why they were visiting the monastery. Instead he told Officer Dilbert that they were sightseeing when they'd decided to stop by the monastery's gift shop.

Cat followed their conversation as they speculated about the faulty brakes. When Officer Dilbert teasingly asked Taj if he had enemies, Taj answered casually, "I've sent so many bad guys behind bars that I can't say who wants to get at me first."

They laughed at his comment, but Cat didn't find anything humorous about it. What if Taj was the target? He'd probably put away murderers and drug dealers who could easily arrange his death. Her chest constricted with fear and something else she refused to analyze.

She didn't interrupt their conversation, but she tightened the blanket around her and moved closer to Taj. When he reached for her hand, she gripped his.

Frank Clark pulled up just as the paramedics were leaving. He looked Taj over and shook his head. "Are you feeling as bad as you look, boss?"

"Not really, but thanks for pointing it out." Then he introduced Cat.

"Nice to meet you, Ms. Simmons," Frank said.

They thanked Officer Dilbert, and within ten minutes they were on their way back to L.A. Taj spent the time explaining to Frank all that had happened. He downplayed the incidents, but they still sounded awful.

Maybe it was time she talked with her father and brother, Cat thought. They were cops, had connections and the manpower to help Bobby. They would never forgive her if something happened to her or Bobby when they could have prevented it. She would talk to Taj about it, she thought drowsily as the effect of Taj's comfortable chest and the soothing rumble of his voice lulled her to sleep.

Frank watched them in the rearview mirror. When Taj looked down at Cat and kissed her hair, Frank frowned.

"Where are the keys, baby?" Taj's voice woke Cat up a little while later.

Cat looked up. They were at her home, parked in the driveway. Taj had already opened her gate. She rummaged through her purse until she found her keys.

A few minutes later, they were inside the house. "I'll let you gentlemen entertain yourselves while I freshen up. Please make yourselves at home." She would have loved to have a soaking bath, but with these two in her house and two more to come, she would have to settle for a quick shower.

"Food should be here by the time you come out, okay?"

Cat nodded, then disappeared into her bedroom.

Frank waited for her to leave before he turned to contemplate his boss. "Tell me again what happened today, because I can't believe that delicate woman actually shielded you from a stalker's bullet."

Taj threw him a look.

"Yeah, well, BB guns," Frank said, "but it's the thought that counts."

"She's a lot stronger than you think." Taj walked to the bar and asked Frank, "Want a drink?"

"Whatever you're having will be fine," Frank replied, relaxing on Cat's plush couch and looking around with interest.

Taj brought back glasses with ice and directed Frank to the bar. After they each got a drink, they walked back to sit around the coffee table. Taj picked up a writing pad and pen from a side table, and started to write.

"We need a strategy for tomorrow, Frank. By the time Solomon and Mike get here, we should have an airtight plan on who's doing what and where."

"So I'm off the Dorgan case?"

"Tired of mock breaking and entering?" Taj asked.

"Just a little too old to be crouching for long periods of time, sprinting, and leaping over ledges. Plus, I hate dogs. Some of these people have the nastiest damned dogs you ever saw."

"Then you're off the case." A frown crossed Taj's face. "Is your cousin still looking for a job?"

"Carlton? Oh, yes. He got a temporary position with a security firm downtown, but he doesn't seem to like it very much. The hours and the pay suck."

Taj passed Frank his cell phone. "Get him. I think we need extra hands, ears, heck, even eyes. Work with him. Show him the ropes in the next couple of days. After that, we'll see how it goes." He kept busy scribbling while Frank spoke with his cousin.

When Frank passed the phone back to him, Taj got up and walked to the pool deck. He quickly outlined to Carlton Johnson what he expected from him. He walked back into the house as he explained that it was a trial period, but if Carlton was willing to work hard, there could be a job for him at the end of that period.

"Finalize things with him tomorrow, Frank. Monday we're hitting the streets." He passed the phone back to Frank.

Taj sat on the sofa he'd vacated earlier, stretched his back, and rotated his head to ease the tension in his neck and upper back. This wasn't just a case of a missing priest anymore. The bastards had made it personal by trying to kill him.

His head throbbed and his stomach growled with hunger every few seconds. But nothing gripped him like the smoldering anger. He was going to draw the bastards out and make them pay. From the information he now had, he was convinced that the person after them was not Father Forster. The priest was not a murderer.

Somewhere along the way, he and Cat had become the target of some crazy man and he didn't know why. His gut instinct told him there was something he was missing, something that could glue the whole thing together.

Could someone he'd put behind bars have a contract on him? He might have joked about his past coming back to haunt him with Officer Dilbert, but it was a possibility. In his days with the Bureau, he'd put away murderers, Mafioso and street gangs, drug lords and serial killers. Could one of them be on parole, and want to punch out his lights?

What about Cat? How was he to make sure she was safe while he was busy? Taj turned his head toward her bedroom. The water had stopped running.

He was worried about her. He wasn't sure how well she was holding up. Would they ever have time alone without worrying about her brother, the Father, or the people in the black van? Despite the fatigue, the headache, the dirty clothes, he wanted her. Nothing could take away the horror of the last several hours like good loving. But he would have to be an insensitive cad to make love to her tonight. They were both tired and bruised.

Also, he had to come up with a plan for tomorrow before he hit the showers or crawled into bed. There was no doubt that he was going to spend the night at Cat's house He wasn't leaving her alone in this house, not tonight, not after what had happened.

"Done," Frank said, interrupting Taj's thoughts.

"Good. Now where do we start? We need to find out why someone wants us out of the way. Who would be scared enough to want to hurt me or Cat? Why?"

"Maybe the Simmons boy saw something he wasn't supposed to see," Frank suggested. "You mentioned the crates that were being transferred into the black van outside the church. Maybe those are the people who torched the center, and they fear Bobby could identify them."

"And since he came to see Cat, these people assume that she knows about them too. And it doesn't take a stretch of the imagination to conclude that she's hired me, a P.I. to check into things for her brother. What a mess."

"But it makes sense," Frank added.

"Unfortunately, yes. What about the possibility that this has nothing to do with Bobby at all?"

"You did put quite a number of scumbags away in your days, didn't you?"

Taj rotated his neck again to remove the kinks. "I've thought about that, even asked Ray to check into it. He's also checking into Forster's activities. It's one thing to want to save the souls of all the scumbags in the word, but quite another to put your own life on the line too. Father Forster is one *loco* priest. At least that's the reputation he has among some local people in Veracruz. It appears he does these rescue missions quite a bit. If Ray comes through, I should know just how many Russian crimelords he's pissed off."

They discussed scenarios and possibilities while sipping their martinis. Mike was first to arrive. Solomon came fifteen minutes later, laden with Chinese food.

—m—

Cat didn't join the men until they were almost done with their discussion. She had changed into a yellow-and-orange tie-dyed African kimono. Her hair was still wet, but she'd swept it back to hug her skull. It curled enticingly at the base of her neck. The men stopped talking and stood up when she walked into the living room.

"Please, don't mind me. Go on with your discussion."

But they stayed standing until after Taj finished with the introductions. She felt dwarfed by the four of them. They were all tall and big men.

"The food is in the kitchen, baby," Taj informed her.

"Does anyone want anything?" she asked, although they each had a drink in front of them.

The men murmured no, except Taj who said, "Could you fix me a plate, sweetheart?"

All the men's eyes moved from their boss to Cat and then back to their boss. Taj was oblivious to the interest he was generating with his harmless endearments. Cat wasn't. She fought a blush. "Sure," she replied.

"Thanks," he replied absentmindedly.

Cat hurried to the kitchen as the men went back to their discussion.

She warmed the takeout before fixing their two plates. She was famished, she thought as she carried in a tray with two bowls of hot and spicy soup and two plates brimming with shrimp and broccoli, cashew chicken, fried rice and egg rolls. Discussions ceased again when she walked into the room. She placed her bowl and plate on the side table, near the leather lounge, and took the tray to Taj.

"Thank you," he said. "We're just about done here."

"That's okay. Don't mind me," she murmured.

Cat walked back to her seat, sat down and tucked her feet under her. She kept an ear on their discussion and watched the four men while she ate. She studied them, one after the other. Taj had described each of them while they were waiting for the police at the scene of the accident, but he had left off a few details only a woman would notice.

Mike Calhoun was buffed up, but had an angelic face. He had once aspired to be a boxer, but according Taj he was turning out to be a great investigator. Taj had praised Mike's sharp mind and keen sense of observation. Frank, the most seasoned warrior and the oldest in the group, had a hard, weathered face, and sharp intelligent eyes. Taj had mentioned that he was the surveillance gizmos and gadget expert in the group. Cat could see that despite his age, Frank's bearing was still very much military. And for the youngest member of the team, there was only one word to describe Solomon: pretty. He had incredibly curly lashes, big grey eyes, and arched eyebrows. He had no hair on his head, but a well-trimmed moustache.

Her eyes finally went to Taj. She studied his bruised face, the intelligent eyes, the high cheekbones, the long hair, and the sensuous lips. Who was the real Taj Taylor? she wondered. The intense detective who could single-mindedly pursue a case without respite? The tease who audaciously expected women to fall into his lap? Or the sensitive man who talked about his family with affection and had a kind word for all his employees? Who did she want him to be? She had seen him change from one person to another with ease and confidence. She might have said it teasingly before, but he was one unique man.

They were winding up when she excused herself to go to the kitchen to make a cup of herbal tea. A few minutes later, she heard the front door open and close. Then Taj walked into kitchen.

"Done already?" she asked, eying him from under her lashes

"Yes." He swept a hand on his nape. "Listen, baby, I don't want to leave you alone tonight. Do you mind if I crash on your couch?"

A sigh of relief escaped Cat as she nodded. She had been nervous about spending the night alone, but had refused to dwell on it. She wanted to sleep with him. She wanted to be held in his arms and to feel safe, but all she said was, "I have a spare bedroom you could use."

She studied his tired face. Involuntarily, her hand reached up to touch his cheek. He turned his head sideways and dropped a kiss in her palm. She smiled.

Taj watched the gentle sway of her hips as she led him to the spare bedroom, which was beside hers. Only a bathroom separated them. "Thank you."

She nodded. "I, uh, will see you in the morning. If you need anything, you know where to find me."

"Sure. I'll come tell you goodnight when I'm done."

"No, Taj. I'll probably be…." He'd already disappeared into the bedroom. She didn't get a chance to tell him to help himself to the shorts her brothers had left behind, but she hoped he would use them.

Oh well. Cat shrugged and headed to her room. Changing into nightshirt and shorts, she crawled into bed. She finished her tea and switched off the light, hoping that Taj would take it as a hint that she didn't want to be disturbed.

As if tuned to his every movement, Cat knew when Taj got out of the shower, when he went to the bedroom, and when he left it to come toward hers. She closed her eyes tight, as if that would make him not knock on her door. When he walked by without stopping or saying anything, she sighed with both relief and disappointment.

She heard him moving around the kitchen. He must have called someone because she heard his deep baritone. A few minutes later, he was walking toward her door again. This time he paused and knocked gently. Cat held her breath. Would he leave?

"Sweetheart, I know you're awake."

She sighed and turned on the light. Why couldn't the man just let her be? She was tired, achy, lonely, and horny. She was likely to jump him. "Come in," she said, thoroughly annoyed with him and herself.

He opened the door, and whatever objections Cat had disappeared. If God had ever sent a man to tempt women, it was this man. A sigh escaped her lips as her eyes roamed his body. He wore only shorts, courtesy of her brother Kenny. The sculptured expanse of his chest was bare. His wet hair fell in waves around his shoulders. He looked handsome, sexy, sinfully tempting. Heat engulfed her as she stared at him staring at her. "I see you found my brother's shorts," she said softly.

"I wondered who they belonged to." He leaned against the door frame and studied her. The soft bedside lamp bathed her features, creating shadows around her eyes and cheeks. "Can you fall asleep okay or do you want a back rub?"

She could do with a back rub, Cat thought, but she wouldn't want him to stop there. "I'm fine," she lied. "Did you find everything?"

"Do you happen to have a spare toothbrush?"

"Sure," she said. She flung off her coverlet and nearly ran to her bathroom.

Taj's eyes followed her figure as she left the room. Air rushed out of his lungs when she disappeared into the bathroom. He straightened his frame when she reappeared.

"Here." She passed him a new toothbrush in a plastic wrapping.

Taj took it and then stepped back. "Thank you." He looked at her face. "Come here, sweetheart," he said and reached for her. She met him halfway.

They kissed hungrily, with a tinge of desperation. After what they'd experienced, that wasn't surprising. They both knew that they would both welcome the release if they made love.

Taj was the first one to break contact and step back. "Goodnight, baby," he said in a husky voice.

Cat stared with amazement as Taj walked away. How could he leave her like this, so aroused she was close to exploding? She closed the door and crawled into bed. Tears burned her eyelids as she willed sleep to come. She knew the timing was wrong. Both of them were tired and feeling very vulnerable. Still, she couldn't help feeling rejected.

When sleep claimed her, the nightmare started. A monstrous figure wearing a monk's habit was chasing her down a maze. Everywhere she turned he was there, laughing hysterically while holding out a fruitcake. She was close to the exit when a figure suddenly stepped in front of her, wearing a black robe and a mask. In his hand was a gun, and behind him, waiting silently, was the black van. Cat screamed.

"Cat…sweetheart, wake up." Taj was shaking her.

She sat up with a cry, recognized Taj's face, and jumped into his arms. "He was after me…he wore a monk's robe…then he changed and became somebody else. He was waiting to take me to the black van."

"Hush, baby, it was just a dream, okay? Just a dream, a figment of your imagination, a culmination of all the crazy adventures we've had today, nothing else." Taj talked and rocked her until she calmed down. Then he said, "Move over. I think I'll stay with you and keep the bad guys away."

"But…."

"Shush. I just want to hold you tonight. I also need to keep my demons away." Before she could come up with an argument, he'd already slid in beside her, cushioned her head with one arm and wrapped the other around her waist. Then he pulled her against his chest.

Cat felt the hard chest and the warmth of his body and sighed. "Thank you," she whispered. "I thought you didn't want to be with me tonight."

Taj squeezed her. "I'll always want you, baby. Don't ever doubt that."

"You left, walked away," she whispered drowsily.

"The timing wasn't right for us. Soon, I promise." He kissed her hair.

She smiled. "Yes, soon," she murmured. Then she slid her hand into his and interlaced her fingers with his. "Promise me something, baby."

"Anything, love."

"Stop investigating this case, okay? It's not worth losing your life for. I don't know what I'd do if something happened to you."

Taj frowned in the dark. "Let's talk about it tomorrow, okay?"

"Okay. Good night." Sleep claimed her fast.

CHAPTER 15

Taj woke up and started to stretch. A warm body tucked into his chest prevented it. He looked down. Cat had somehow turned around to face him. Her head was on his shoulder, but under the light blanket her leg was draped across his groin. His member was painfully swollen as she cradled it in the back of her knee.

A grimace crossed his face. He had spent the night with the woman he'd been fantasizing about for weeks, and hadn't touched her sexually. That was a first.

He could have, though. She'd literally thrown herself into his arms, admitted that she wanted him. But he'd known that fatigue and vulnerability were doing much of the talking. When they made love, Taj vowed, it would be for the right reasons, with both of them cognizant of the implications. He wanted exclusive rights to her body, now and forever. He didn't share or play games.

He stared at her face, perfect in repose. Her lashes formed shadows on her cheekbones. Her mouth was slightly opened and each breath she exhaled fanned his skin, sending sensual ripples down his chest. He wanted to wake her up and devour her.

Then he noticed the bruise on her shoulder where her shirt's neckline had dropped. She must have gotten that outside her gym, he concluded. Frowning, he lifted the cover. Her shirt and shorts had ridden up, baring her back and upper thigh. He saw the darkened spots on her buttock cheek. He couldn't help it; he reached down and touched the damaged skin.

Damn. Seeing her bruised body killed his desire quick. Slowly, trying not to wake her up, he removed his arm from underneath her. Then he lifted her leg from his groin. Carefully, he slid off the bed.

He turned to look at her. His movements hadn't woken her. *Soon, baby, soon I won't be sneaking out of your bed. Soon I'll be waking you up with a kiss and loving you like there's no tomorrow.*

Taj went to the guest room, stripped off the shorts, and got into the shower. After an invigorating hot shower, he changed into his clothes of the previous day. He wished he'd asked one of his people to bring him a change of clothing. Then his eyes fell on the clock beside the bed and a curse emanated from his lips.

He'd asked Archie to loan him one of his men to watch over Cat. Archie surrounded himself with former military or police officers, and at a time like this they came in handy.

Taj walked outside, but no one was at the gate. He opened the gate and checked up and down the street. No parked black van or unsavory characters lurked nearby. He closed the gate and headed back to the house.

His eyes touched the flowers blooming in beds around Cat's house. By rule, he wasn't a flower person, Taj thought as he walked toward the rose bushes. He was more likely to buy a girlfriend sexy lingerie than bring her flowers. But Cat was different.

He recalled when he'd started bringing her a rose every day at the set. She'd always found him in the crowd and thanked him with a nod and a smile.

Smiling at the memory, Taj stooped low to pick a red rose. He had a hard time breaking it from the parent plant, pricked his fingers several times and cursed the air like crazy, but he eventually won. What he put up with for his woman, he mused, sucking his thumb.

He made himself a cup of coffee and sipped it while he wrote her a note. He knew that she wanted him to stop the investigation, but he couldn't, not now, not when they'd made it personal.

He was looking through the window later when Frank's Tacoma pulled up at the gate. He finished his drink, checked on Cat, who was still sleeping, and left the note and the rose on her bedside table. When he opened the gate, he saw a grey Explorer beside Frank's truck.

Frank was talking to Mack Greer, West Indian Archie's man. Both men had steaming cups of Starbuck's coffee in their hands. Mack pushed his back against his truck and straightened his body. Frank watched him with an unreadable expression.

Taj looked at his watch. " 'Bout time y'all got here." And that set the tone for the rest of the day. "I need a change of clothing before we go anywhere, Frank. Mack, I appreciate your presence. I would have loved to introduce you, but Ms. Simmons is still sleeping. I need to meet a friend ASAP and work on getting the bastards who pulled that shit on us yesterday." Just thinking about it made his blood boil.

Mack touched his chest with a fist and pointed at Taj. "I feel you, my brother. You go do your thing. I'll wait out here for the little lady."

"Thank you. I left her a note, so she'll know you're here." He got in Frank's truck.

Soon they were heading toward his office where he shaved and changed, then called Ray and agreed to meet with him at a coffee shop not far from his house.

Later, Taj waved when he saw his former buddy walk into the coffee shop.

"Damn, man, you look like shit." Was Ray's greeting. "Someone caught you with his woman?"

"Jealous, Ray? You're spending too much time behind the desk, man. Going soft around the gut," he teased, although his friend was anything but soft. He waited for Ray to be seated before adding, "Now that we're done with the pleasantries, let's talk."

"None of your cases has been reopened, so the skunks after you aren't seeking revenge," Ray explained.

Taj nodded. Then he explained what had happened outside the hermitage and in Mexico. He only paused when the waitress brought Ray a cup of coffee. "I need you to do me a favor. Check if there's a Russian mob operating in California with the Siberian tiger as its insignia. A tattoo on the right arm to be more precise. Bobby said the Russian priest he saw outside the church had one on his arm. I'm assuming the person wasn't really a priest. Check their activity level. Who they work for. Don't give me that look, Ray. I know the Bureau never misses a thing when they profile a syndicated gang. Your dossier on each member is usually complete. I think Father Forster may have pissed off their boss or someone higher up. I too will check with my usual sources."

"You may want to start with these." Ray pulled computer printouts from inside his jacket. "Business associates and enemies of Father Forster. You might find a thing or two in there that's useful. So, do you think the priest planned your little accident outside the hermitage?" Ray asked with a slight grin.

Taj frowned. He didn't know whether he was imagining things, but he could swear Ray was enjoying his predicament, which didn't make sense at all. "Honestly, no. I don't see what he would gain by killing us. And I highly doubt that he's into anything illegal. Father Forster is a cross between Robin Hood and a cat, nine lives and all that. In Mexico, some think of him as a hero while others think he's crazy. Apparently, he rescues illegal immigrants on a regular basis down in Veracruz."

"Hmm, interesting. Maybe I should have a chat with this priest of yours once you find him. Call me when you do. We've broken a couple of smuggling rings, racketeering, prostitution run by Russian Mafioso, but they keep sprouting like daisies all over the goddamn place. Have you figured out how they traced your whereabouts yesterday afternoon? You were never that careless."

Taj ignored the dig. "I don't know how they did it, but I'll find out. In fact, I'm heading back to the garage to have another look at my car."

"You're thinking they're using a tracking device of some kind?"

"If I'm dealing with a Russian mob, anything is possible. I think Bobby saw something he wasn't supposed to see. Because the only person he contacted was his sister, they've turned their attention to her. Needless to say, they saw me with her, checked my background. If they know I'm a P.I. and former agent, they might think I'm dangerous. Heck, seeing me with you now could confirm their suspicions. I don't think she's the target, Ray. I think it's me they want. That might explain why they only appear when I'm around. How they've managed to find me twice puzzles me, though." When it wasn't pissing him off, he added silently.

"Sounds like you have a vengeful stalker on your hand, my friend. How's your stunt lady taking it?"

Taj smiled. "Cat is pretty cool about it, but I'm afraid they might use her to get to me."

"No one can pass Archie's men unless they're exceptional."

Taj made a derisive sound. "There's nothing exceptional about a psychopath or a delusional stalker, Ray."

"Yes, well, this one seems to have the upper hand, doesn't he?"

Taj frowned at Ray. Was he mocking him?

Ray interrupted his thoughts. "So, you finally met your match."

"What?"

"This stunt lady, Cat Simmons, sounds like she made quite an impression on you."

Taj grinned. "Am I that obvious?"

"To someone who knows you well? Yes."

Taj looked sheepish for a brief moment. "Remember how you knew the first time you met Diana that she was the one? That's how it was with Cat."

Ray leaned back on his seat with an unreadable expression. "Yeah, Diana was all right."

"She was more than…" He stopped when he saw Ray's jaws flex and his fingers tighten around his coffee mug. Ray had given him the impression that he'd gotten over the death of his fiancée. Could he still be mourning her? Diana had committed suicide five years ago. "Man, I'm sorry I brought her name up."

Ray glanced up. "No problem, man. I just don't like discussing her." He shook his head, then perked up. "So when do I meet Cat?"

Taj smiled briefly. "S-soon, when this madness is over."

Ray laughed. "That hesitation could only mean one thing, Taylor. You're losing your touch. In the old days, she would be warming your bed the very day you met her. You must be getting soft in your old age." Ray added as he got up, "Still, I'd like to meet her, the woman who's bringing you down." He pointed at him and grinned.

"Do I look downhearted?" Taj replied as he dropped change on the table.

"No, you look like a man who doesn't know what hit him or where he stands. I hope she makes you sweat. You owe for all those easy conquests."

Taj gave him the finger. Ray only laughed harder. That was the Ray he knew, Taj mused, uncomplicated and carefree. He must have been imagining things earlier. "When do I hear from you, Ray?"

"Soon. Call me when you catch up with your priest. He might help us with some of our cases. Are you hitting the streets?" Ray asked as they left the coffee shop.

"It's the best place for more information, especially now that I know none of the thugs I've put behind bars is on the loose. Get in touch as soon as you find something." His friend waved and headed back to his car.

Next on his agenda was the mass at the cathedral, Cardinal Mallory's domain. Maybe he would get a chance to talk with the cardinal, ask him for Forster's whereabouts. But first, he had to check on Cat. He pulled out his cell phone and dialed her number. The phone went unanswered. He checked his watch. It was almost nine o'clock.

Cat opened her eyes. Instead of seeing the face of the clock telling her the time, she saw a single rose. A smile touched her lips as she recalled sleeping in Taj's arms, feeling safe and loved as his warmth surrounded her.

She was beginning to believe that that man truly loved her. Yesterday, he'd put his life in danger to save her. And last night, he could have made love to her, yet he'd held back as though aware of her vulnerability.

Where was he, anyway? she wondered as she reached across the pillows to pick up the flower. Her nose picked up his musky scent. She inhaled deeply and smiled. Then she saw the note beside the rose.

Frowning, she sat up and picked up the note. She twirled the flower under her nose as she read the note.

Hey Sweetheart,

You looked so peaceful and exquisite I debated whether to let you sleep or wake you up and start where we stopped…dang, we didn't start anything last night. We'll have to do something about that soon.

I have a surprise for you outside. Appreciate it. Take it easy. I'll see you later.

I love you.

Affectionately,

Taj

(P.S. enjoy the rose)

'I love you.' How natural he made it sound. Was she crazy to want to love Taj? What if their love became obsessive and unhealthy? Would they use it as a weapon to control and hurt each other?

Cat sighed. She didn't want to think negative thoughts, not today. She wasn't her mother, and Taj was definitely not her father. It was time she stopped using her parents to push Taj away.

Now what surprise did that man have waiting outside? Cat grabbed a robe and slipped on her slippers. She peeked through the window, but saw nothing. Maybe it was outside the gate, she thought as she headed outside.

Blocking her entrance was a grey Ford Explorer. Moving closer to the gate, she saw that a burly man was seated inside it, drinking coffee and nodding his head as though listening to music.

Who was he? Was he the surprise? She started to move away, unaware that the man had seen her. Cat was hurrying back into the house when the man spoke.

"Ms. Simmons? Wait up, Ms. Simmons."

Cat turned around. "Yes?"

"Taj, eh, Mr. Taylor, said I was to guard you until he returns. He mentioned leaving you a note?"

Cat's eyes took in the man's casual posture, hands linked in front legs apart, shoulders relaxed, but she wasn't fooled. Two cops in the family had taught her enough. He was poised for any quick movement should a threat suddenly appear. Then there were the sharp intelligent eyes which shone brightly against his mahogany skin. She would bet that those eyes missed nothing, including the fact that she was reluctant to talk to him.

Was Taj out of his damned mind? Who did he think he was to hire a bodyguard for her without consulting her? But her thoughts didn't show when she said, "I see. Would you excuse me, Mister, eh…?"

"Greer…Mack Greer, ma'am," he supplied.

She smiled briefly. "Mr. Greer, could you give me a moment, please? I'll be right back." She pivoted on her heel and headed back to the house. Eyes narrowed, each step indicating her increasing ire, she entered the house and headed straight for the phone. She picked up the card with Taj's number and started dialing.

Oh, Taylor, you're going to be sorry you did this to me. Mr. Greer…Mack Greer out there didn't look like someone who could be intimidated into leaving. He was big and mean-looking. He had bodyguard written all over him, for crying out loud. Where was she to put or hide him? How long was she supposed to keep him?

She had a scene to shoot on Wednesday, and there was no way the producer was going to allow Mr. Greer on his precious film set. And if, by some miracle, Dorian agreed to let her bring him in, everyone would know exactly what he was, a bodyguard. Then the questions would start. Why did she need a bodyguard? What happened? Where? When?

Taj wasn't in his office. Where was he? she fumed. She checked the back of his card where he'd scrawled his cell phone number and punched it in.

He answered after two rings. "Taj, I have a strange man parked in my driveway. Explain, please."

"Ah, my sleeping beauty finally awakes. Did you sleep okay? You gave me quite a scare last night. Thought someone had broken into your room."

"I'm not discussing anything, Taj, until you tell him to leave."

"Don't you want to know how my night was? I slept peacefully, like a baby. Must be because I had you in my arms." He was trying to tease her out of her bad mood. "I love holding you in my arms and seeing your lovely face first thing in the morning," he added huskily.

"Taj, I…." She stopped. She couldn't stay mad with him when he talked like that. "Thanks for the rose. It was very sweet of you."

"You're welcome. I pricked my fingers a couple of times getting it. You, my lovely lady, are worth bleeding knuckles any day. So, what were you saying about Mack?"

She sighed. How could she resist him? How could she stay angry after what he'd just said? "Why did you hire a bodyguard for me?"

"Because I can't keep an eye on you while I'm out here. I don't know who we're dealing with, and until I do, I want you under constant guard."

"I thought we agreed that you were off this case." She took a deep breath and added, "I couldn't bear it if anything were to happen to you. Please, stop investigating this." She waited for a response. Taj was quiet for so long she started to worry. "Taj? Are you there?"

"I'm here, sweetheart. Listen, this is now personal. If they were only stalking us, that would be different. But when they mess with the brakes of my car and try to kill us? No, no, that's a different ball game."

Cat rolled her eyes. Men and their egos. "What if these people aren't connected with Forster at all? What if they're after you for something you did? As a P.I. you must piss people off right and left. It could be a vendetta or…what does the Mafia call it? Ah, a contract on you. I heard your conversation with Officer Dilbert."

"I've just finished speaking with a friend with the Bureau, baby. There's nothing to fear from those quarters."

"If you say so. Still, be careful out there. Listen, about the bodyguard…."

"You don't have to keep him if you don't want to," he interrupted.

"You mean it?"

"Go on outside and tell him. Mack is a reasonable man. He'll understand if a lady doesn't need his protection. In fact, he is too highly trained to be babysitting anyone. He was in the marines, you know, an expert at what he did until he sustained an injury on some secret, mission-impossible type deal. Now he can't find decent employment, a damn waste of his God-given talents." There was a pause, then, "Baby, are you still there?"

"Are you trying to make me feel guilty, Taj?"

"Is it working?"

She chuckled. "Aren't you just so witty in the morning? Don't go away, I'll be right back." She heard him mutter, 'ungrateful, pigheaded woman' just before she put the phone down. She smiled. But her smile was gone by the time she arrived at the gate where Mack Greer was waiting patiently. "Mr. Greer…."

"Call me Mack, please, Ms. Simmons."

"Mr. Greer," she said firmly. "I'm sorry but I won't need your services after all. I just got off the phone with Mr. Taylor. He knows that I'll be okay." She smiled to soften her words.

"You will be," Mr. Greer said with a firm nod.

"Oh, good. Then we have an understanding. Well, eh, have a nice day, Mr. Greer. And sorry for making you come out here on a Sunday morning." She turned to walk away.

She had taken a few steps before she realized the man hadn't moved an inch. He was watching her with an inscrutable expression. Was he hard of hearing? Maybe his ears got hurt in the hush-hush mission Taj mentioned. If it were true, she added to himself. She moved closer and said in an overly loud voice, "It is okay for you to leave, Mr. Greer."

"I can't do that, Ms. Simmons."

Frustration mounted in her. "Why not?"

The man shrugged nonchalantly. "Because I promised that I'd watch out for you until this situation is resolved."

"But didn't I just say that you were released from that promise?"

"Yes, you did, Ms. Simmons. But I don't take my orders from you or Mr. Taylor. He knows that."

She took a deep breath and counted backwards from ten to one. When she felt she was calm enough, she asked, "May I have the name of the person you take orders from, Mr. Greer?"

"I'm not at liberty to give it, ma'am."

She pivoted on her heel and headed back to the house. "Taj, who the heck does he work for? Let me guess, the FBI. You got the freaking FBI to guard me?" she snapped into the phone as soon as she got back in the house

"Actually I had nothing to do with it. I told Archie what had happened, and he said he was sending someone in the morning."

To say that Cat was tongue-tied by Taj's statement was putting it mildly. Why would West Indian Archie care about her safety? They'd only met once. "Thanks a bunch, detective. Maybe if you hadn't opened your mouth, I wouldn't be in this predicament." She couldn't very well call Archie and tell him that she didn't appreciate his gesture. Taj probably knew it, too. "You're so overbearing."

"You are right on both accounts, sweet buns. Did I tell you that yours are perfect for my hands? Firm and yet rounded…."

"Good-bye, detective," she interrupted him, thoroughly annoyed that she was stuck with a bodyguard she didn't want, and all he could think about was making love.

"Are you still there, sweetheart?"

"I'm hanging up," she warned.

"Next time we spend the night together, don't wear anything. I rather like the feel of your…."

She pressed the off button and cut him off. *Arrogant, impossible, makes-me-want-to-scream man.* To cool her frayed temper, she prepared a soothing bath and settled in the tub. After the water had done its magic, she started making calls. Whether Bobby liked it or not, it was confession time.

The first person she called was her father. No matter what their problems were, they were family. She needed to know he was doing okay, and it was time for her to come clean. She couldn't keep Bobby's secret any longer.

Cat sighed when the answering machine started. He wasn't home. She left a message.

Then she called Kenny. Brianna answered the phone. "Hi, Bri? Did I catch you at a wrong time?"

"No, just trying to do laundry while feeding your nephew breakfast. What's up?"

"Wanted to talk with that husband of yours. Is he home?"

"You just missed him. He and Bobby were having this huge discussion in the backyard. I could hear their raised voices. They both wore stormy expressions when they came inside. Kenny refused to explain, said we'd talk later. Soon after that they both left."

"Oh, well, tell him to call me as soon as he gets home, okay?" Damn, Bobby was back from Montana already? His timing couldn't have been worse. But at least he was confiding in Kenny. That ought to ease things on her a little.

Cat looked around her living room after she hung up. What was she to do now? If she went to Jan's, Mr. Greer would have to go with her. Same with the gym. She was stuck at home, a prisoner in her own house. She could slowly smother Taj to death for doing this to her, she thought in an unusual fit of frustration.

Forgetting that she had on sandals, she kicked the leg of a side table. She cursed at the inanimate object and her stupidity as she hopped on one leg.

Her gate intercom rang. "Darn, I'd forgotten Mr. Greer," she muttered. She went to the receiver, pressed it, and asked, "Yes, Mr. Greer?"

"There are two men out here who claim to be your brothers."

Great, just what she needed on a Sunday morning. "I'll be there, thanks."

She found them talking with Mr. Greer. She ignored the bodyguard and concentrated on her brothers. Neither of them was smiling. Tough. She was in no mood for a lecture. They each gave her a hug, but didn't speak in front of Mr. Greer.

Cat looked at her unwanted bodyguard and sighed. It wasn't his fault he was here, she admitted grudgingly. She walked to him and said, "Mr. Greer, why don't you pull your truck in and park it inside the compound? I'll bring you a fresh mug of coffee."

"Thank you, Ms. Simmons."

"You're welcome." She turned to find Kenny and Bobby watching her. She raised an eyebrow, then indicated with her head that they should precede her into the house.

As soon as they got inside, Kenny started with, "Was that a body-guard? Why didn't you tell me what Bobby's been up to? Of all the half-brained…."

"Please," Cat interrupted him with a raised hand. "Let's get comfortable and then talk. I wish you'd told me you were planning on coming back, Bobby. Things aren't getting any better around here. We have a lot to talk about."

After she took Mr. Greer his coffee, Cat and her two brothers settled around the counter with coffee mugs. Cat started with, "I don't want any interruptions until I'm done talking, guys, okay? Then we can discuss what to do next."

She saw the shock, the disbelief, and finally anger register on her brothers' faces as she narrated everything. When she was done, Kenny spoke first. "We need to tell Dad what's happening."

Bobby jumped in with, "No!"

"I agree with him on this, Kenny. We have no idea what the priest knows about Mom."

"I'm not talking about *that*. What's more important is your safety, Cat. Dad will be ticked off that you were in danger and we didn't tell him."

Would he? she wondered. "If you say so. I've left him messages, but he doesn't seem to want to talk. Anyway, we don't know if the people after us are the same ones who chased Bobby. Taj is checking into it right now, despite the fact that I told him to stop investigating the case." She threw Bobby a hooded look from under her lashes.

Bobby flushed. "I think he should stop too. I didn't know things would get this ugly, sis. I swear." He was clearly distressed by the turn of events.

"I know," Cat said soothingly.

"He can't stop now," Kenny added.

Cat glared at her brother. Trust him to support Taj. "How do you figure that, Kenny? We almost died yesterday. Lord knows what else they have in store for us."

"My point exactly. Sis, whether Taj goes after them or not, they'll still come after you guys. They must want something real bad to do this. Taylor needs to find out what they want. That means catching them before they get cocky and do something real stupid." He jerked his thumb toward her window where Mr. Greer's truck was visible. "And getting you a bodyguard was a good first move."

Cat's eyes narrowed. She stopped short of snapping at him. "I don't like his high-handed attitude, and you aren't making the situation better by supporting him. What am I supposed to do with Mr. Greer, huh? I can't go anywhere with him around."

"Good," Kenny answered, getting up from his seat. "Do you have Taj's contact? If we can't get Dad involved, I'd like to see what I can do to help." He turned to Bobby. Compassion crossed his face. "We'll find Father Forster, Bobby."

"No," Bobby said, shaking his head. "I want Taj to stop with the investigation, Kenny. You were right. It was a foolish idea to begin with." He looked at Cat. "I should have listened to you, Cat. You might have been seriously hurt because…." He stopped and cleared his throat. "Just tell him to stop with the search, okay?" He got up and left the kitchen.

Cat looked at Kenny. "Will he be okay?"

Kenny nodded and reached for the phone. "Yes. He and I talked. Listen, sis, I need to talk with your man about this mess." When Cat didn't deny that Taj was her man, Kenny added, "You chose well, sis. Taj Taylor is a good man."

Cat frowned at him. Of course, Taj was a good man. Any fool could see that. He was witty, handsome, and hard-working. He was sensitive and patient, calm and efficient when the need arose. But she didn't choose him. He chose her. But she didn't want to think about that, not now. She wanted to know that he would be safe.

Kenny interrupted her thoughts. "I've got to go, Cat. I'm meeting

Taj downtown in an hour." He put the phone back in its cradle.

"Watch his back for me, Kenny, will you?" Cat said in a soft voice.

"Sure, sis." Kenny left.

CHAPTER 16

That afternoon, Cat came back from Jan's to find a metallic grey Jaguar parked inside her grounds. Whose was it? And how did they get past her gate? The only people who knew the combination to her gate and house were she, her brothers, and Taj.

Her question was answered when Mr. Greer muttered, "Looks like Mr. Taylor is here."

As she got out of Mr. Greer's car, she caught Mrs. Lambert shamelessly spying on her house through the fence. "Good evening, Lucille. How are you today?"

The woman looked flustered at being caught snooping. "Ah, Catherine, I, eh, I'm doing okay. Is everything okay?"

"Sure. Why shouldn't it be?"

Her eyes went to Mr. Greer. "I see you have a bodyguard now, or is he your chauffer?"

Nothing ever escaped Ms. Busybody's prying eyes. Cat touched Mr. Greer's arm as she said, "I've been having car problems, and my cousin was kind enough to drive me around." When the woman's eyes went to the Jaguar, Cat knew she was through answering her questions. "See you later, Lucille." Then as an afterthought, she added, "If you see a black Honda Odyssey lurking around my gate, Lucille, could you give me a call? I'm expecting a guest from out of state, and I don't want him to end up at the wrong house."

The woman stared at her as if debating whether Cat was serious or not. "Sure, Catherine. Oh, I had a talk with Fay Faulkner too. Her boys won't be bothering you again. She said that they swore they never touched your intercom, but with those imps, you never can tell."

"I see."

"My bet is that they did, but didn't want to get in trouble with their mother by admitting anything."

"Thanks for talking to her, Lucille. Bye."

"That woman has been watching me. Gives me the creeps," Mr. Greer complained to Cat as soon as he parked his car.

"She's quite harmless, Mr. Greer," she answered before entering her house.

Her eyes found Taj as soon as she entered the house. He was in the kitchen, draining a cup of coffee. Her heart skipped a beat and a smile leaped to her lips. "Hey."

He looked up. A sensual glint entered his eyes as they ran down her spaghetti strap sundress. Then an irresistible, wicked grin flashed across his lips. Slowly, he walked toward her. When he reached her, he wrapped his arms around her and gave her a long, hard kiss. "How's my girl?"

"Wondering why you're putting your life in danger after she specifically told you not to."

"It's the principle of things. Besides, they won't stop now, not until we find out what they're after." He angled his head and kissed her again. "Don't want to talk shop. Not now."

"What is it you want, detective?" she asked boldly as her fingers sank in his hair.

He grinned. "This," he murmured on her lips and kissed her again and again. "You taste good."

She licked his lower lip and murmured seductively, "You too, baby." Then she pulled his head lower and kissed him. She was through running away, Cat decided. She would enjoy Taj until the attraction lessened, then she would walk away with no regrets. No *I-wish-I-had-done-this-and-done-that* mess.

"Cat?"

The seriousness of his voice made her eyes snap open. The naked hunger in his gaze took her breath away. "What is it?"

His eyes caressed her features, then settled on her mouth. "I need you," he said hoarsely.

"Kiss me." And he did, with a thoroughness that left her clinging to his shoulders.

"I want you," he whispered on her shoulder, his lips creating a sensual line toward her breasts. His hand slid down her waist and cupped her behind. He pulled her closer against his hardness.

"I want you too, Taj."

At her words, he crushed her mouth with a searing kiss that left her whimpering. The heat that had started in her stomach turned into a raging inferno. Her legs turned to jelly, and the throb between her legs intensified. She wanted his hands on her skin. When he paused, she gasped, "Oh, baby, don't stop."

"I don't intend to." His hands moved up to cup her breasts, to tease her taut nipples.

Cat shuddered. She ran a hand from his neck, down his back to his buttock cheek. The other hand closed on the other cheek. She squeezed. "I'm sorry for making us wait, baby."

He tilted her chin and looked into her eyes. "Are you sure now?"

"Oh, yes," she breathed.

He dropped a brief possessive kiss on her lips. "Can you wait here and not move an inch? I've got to take care of something."

She caressed his cheek. "Changing your mind already?"

"Hell no! I've got to let Mack go. From now on, I'm your bodyguard."

"Hmm, I've always wanted a personal guard. Hurry back."

Taj nearly ran from the house. He talked briefly with Mack Greer, then went to his car to retrieve the box of protection he'd bought. He walked into the living room and froze.

Cat was halfway through undoing the buttons on her dress. She wasn't wearing a bra., and the swell of her breasts beckoned him. He caught a glimpse of a rosebud tattoo on her right breast and around her belly button.

She looked up, a seductive smile on her soft lips. She'd waited for this man for so long, oh, so long. Smiling, she beckoned him with a finger. Taj didn't waste a second. He closed the gap between them, dragged her to him, and lifted her up. Their lips met in a deep, desperate kiss. She eagerly wrapped her legs around him.

Cat was caught in a whirlpool of sensations as Taj showed her his hunger. A shiver ran through her as her senses smoldered. Her hands reached up, sank in his long hair and held his head in place. But it wasn't enough. She moved against him.

He yanked his mouth from hers to growl, "We're not going to make it to the bedroom."

"There'll be time for that. I want you now."

She lowered herself from him, pulled his shirt from his pants, and yanked it off his body. Heated flesh meshed as he took a forward step and brought them to the edge of a leather lounge. They tore at each other's clothes as they stumbled backward onto the lounge. There was no time for gentleness or exploration. The hunger that had been building in them demanded satisfaction.

"Hurry," she urged.

"Yes," he answered. He readied himself and entered her in one swift move.

Primal instinct to mate and conquer took over. She wrapped her legs around his flank, dug her nails into his muscles, and urged him on. His grip on her hips wasn't gentle as he drove in her again and again. Echoes of their passionate moans and groans reverberated around the room. There was wildness in their joining, desperation as they strained against each other, and finally, cries as their bodies shuddered in climax.

Cat couldn't think. Aftershocks of sensations still rippled through her body. Her arms tightened around Taj's body as the crests shook him. They hung on to each other for what seemed like eternity before Taj shifted his frame and wrapped her in the cocoon of his arms.

"That was wonderful," she murmured a little while later.

"You think so?"

"Hmm," she murmured.

"It was just the beginning."

"Is that so?"

Laughter rumbled from deep inside his chest. "Ready to take this to the next level?"

"Oh, yes." Then she kissed him.

He got up and lifted her in his arms. He deepened the kiss as he walked with her to the bedroom. Gently, he laid her on the bed, reached down and caressed her cheek. Their eyes locked. "Now I want to touch and taste every inch of you, baby."

His gaze made her feel hot and cold at the same time. "And I you," she whispered.

He bent low and nibbled her lips, retreated, and nibbled some more. Then he angled his head to deepen the kiss. His lips memorized her face, then moved past her chin to her satiny neck. She tilted her head back, giving him better access. The action also pushed her breasts forward. His hand lowered and covered one. "Perfect."

When Taj started playing with her nipple, Cat's breath stilled, then rushed out of her. The sensation was overwhelming. Then his mouth replaced his fingers, and a cry emanated from her mouth. When her nipple became a tight pebble of sensations, he began alternating between her two nipples. Tension built within her. Then he stopped. Cat opened her eyes to see what he was doing.

Her eyes locked with his. He had been watching her all along, his eyes smoldering. Slowly, his hand moved to her inner thigh. Cat inhaled jerkily. When he moved to cup her, she gulped. But Taj still didn't say anything, nor did he break eye contact.

The anticipation was becoming too much for Cat. She didn't know whether to tell him to get on with it or stop. Her body was like a wire, taut with tension. How much of this could she take?

Then, as if he read her mind, he slid a finger into her, and her senses exploded again. He smiled at her cry, groaned at the tightening of her muscles around his finger. His mouth closed on a nipple. He slid in another finger, then another, stretching and familiarizing himself with her most intimate part. His lips continued their downward journey.

Her eyes glazed as his mouth replaced his fingers. She buckled and smothered a small scream. Her back arched, her legs trembling, and she caressed his sweaty body. Still, he didn't stop. Wave after wave of sensation flowed through her body, building up in volume until she fell apart. Only then did he join with her.

With each stroke, a tear squeezed from her eyes. With each stroke, he pushed her higher and higher. Her hands were all over his body, tearing at his flesh, wanting to get lost in him. When she thought she couldn't take it anymore, her body snapped and lights exploded in her head. Her inner walls contracted, sucking him into her mysterious depth. Then he yelled out her name and quivered in her arms.

"Are you okay?" Taj asked a while later.

He had loved her till she turned blind, Cat thought with wonder.

"Open your eyes, sweetheart." She slowly opened her eyes. "See, you're not blind."

She'd spoken her thought out loud, Cat mused. She smiled at him. She was in more trouble that she'd anticipated. She couldn't get enough of him.

—⟋⟋⟋—

The smell of eggs and freshly-brewed coffee woke Cat up later that evening. She padded to the kitchen to find Taj, looking decadently sexy in shorts and no shirt, cooking at the stove. His hair was still wet from the shower. His masculine shoulders invited her hands to explore. With every movement he made, his muscles rippled underneath his dark skin. She felt hot and tingly just watching him.

"Hey, baby," she said, slipping her arms around his waist. She rubbed her face against his warm back and kissed his smooth skin

"Hey, sleepyhead." His smile was wide as he turned around to kiss her.

He tasted good, Cat thought with a smile. "Why didn't you wake me up?"

"You needed to rest."

"What are you cooking?"

"A little something—eggs, turkey bacon, and scones, all from your fridge." He poured her a cup of coffee. He even remembered how she liked it, with a dash of French vanilla creamer.

He kissed her nose and passed her the coffee. "Do you want to spend the next couple of days at my place?"

"Oh, where is that?"

"Simi Valley. I'll make sure you're at the studios on time every morning."

"I'm not starting rehearsals until Wednesday. We're filming on Thursday and Friday."

"Okay. We should be back by Tuesday night at the latest." His eyes twinkled charmingly and a lazy smile formed on his lips. "So, what do you say?"

She blew him a kiss. "Sounds like a wonderful idea. Maybe if the people in the black van come a-calling, the empty house might make them rethink their lunacy."

He frowned slightly. "They won't be anywhere near your house without someone knowing about it. Here, dig in. We can make it home by ten if we leave in the next hour."

Taj checked his rearview mirror one more time as they drove on Interstate 18. No cars behind them. He'd retraced his route and used side roads since leaving West Hollywood. He had promised her total privacy, Cat mused as he left the interstate and headed north on Sequoia Avenue. He'd assured her that his home was secluded, that the security was tight, and that no could possibly get past his dogs.

He got to Presidio Drive, then turned left. He must have called ahead because someone opened the gate from the inside. They drove through. The house was a French-Norman style, done in stone with brick accents and a slate roof. The entrance portico had an arched transom window and there were curved windows within the front door itself.

"Looks like we have visitors," Taj commented when he saw a Toyota Sienna and a Durango parked side by side near his garage. They both had rental plates.

Cat stared at his home with interest. "Who are they?"

"Probably my brothers." He parked beside the Sienna instead of in the garage. "We don't have to stay here, baby, if you don't want the company. My family likes to descend on me unannounced from time to time. We could go to a hotel near here, relax, and just be alone."

"That's so sweet, baby, but not a good idea. They've come to be with you."

"Don't you want to rest and…?"

She put a finger on his lips. "Meeting them, spending time with them, might be what we need. It will certainly take our minds off things."

"Are you sure?"

She nodded.

"Thank you."

"No, I'm the one who should be thanking you for being patient with me, and for being there whenever I've needed you."

Taj kissed her. Then he took her hand, and they walked together toward his front door.

Before Taj could unlock the door, it was yanked open from the inside. Yelling children and adult laughter teased their ears. The tall man standing in the doorway looked at them with a grin. "About time, little brother. We were about to send out a search party. We left countless messages at your office that we were on our way. What took you so long?"

Instead of answering him, Taj asked Cat, "Did we take a wrong turn, baby? This madhouse couldn't possibly be mine."

Cat grinned, looking into the caramel eyes of the man who'd opened the door. He was blatantly studying her. Before she could say anything, the man asked, "Cat?"

Surprised, she answered, "Yes."

"Aaron Taylor. It's a pleasure to finally meet you. And about time

Taj stopped keeping you to himself." Then he gripped the hand she'd extended, leaned forward and planted a kiss on her lips. "Let's not be too formal, darlin'."

"Quit kissing my woman, Aaron. Where is Sheryl? She ought to be keeping tabs…." His brother cut him off when he enveloped him in a hug.

When Taj stepped back, Aaron saw the bandage on his head. "What happened to you?"

"A little cut…all in the line of duty," Taj answered easily.

"Anything serious?" Aaron asked, his gaze steady on Taj.

Cat heard the worry in Aaron's voice.

"Just a scratch, big bro," Taj murmured as he led Cat into the house.

As soon as they cleared the door, three pairs of adult eyes zoomed in on them. Two women and a man who could pass for Taj's twin were in the foyer. The man and the taller of the women each carried a baby. Judging by the babies' sizes, they had to be the twins Taj had mentioned to her a week ago, Cat concluded.

Before Taj could perform an introduction, a screech came from upstairs, followed by running feet. Cat dragged her eyes away from the adorable twins to look toward the stairs. "Uncle Taj? Uncle Taj! He's going to get me…save me…."

"No running down the stairs, Liana," someone reprimanded.

But Taj had moved to the foot of the stairs, just in time to catch the little girl in a pink nightdress who practically flew down the stairs. "Aye, Princess Liana, what a welcome," he said as he swung her up in the air, turned her around, and gave her a resounding kiss. "Who's going to get you?"

"Mean old Alex. There he is!"

Cat took in the activities with bemusement. Yes, this was what she needed to keep her demons at bay. With Taj's family visiting, she wouldn't spend time worrying about Bobby or the psycho in the black van. And it was great to see Taj interact with his family. He looked so happy.

Cat turned to watch a boy, two or three years older than the girl, walk down the stairs with dignity. He was three steps away from Taj when he decided he wasn't about to be left out. He flew into his uncle's arms.

Taj turned around with them, then put his nephew down first. "What has your mommy been feeding you, Alex? You're huge." Then he leaned down to look into his nephew's face. "Is that a moustache you're sprouting, my man?"

Alex laughed. "I'm too little for a moustache, Uncle Taj."

Taj grinned and gave him a mock punch on his chin. Then he winked at his niece. "And you, my little princess, you look ready for college."

"Oh, Uncle Taj, you're so silly. I just started first grade. I've got twelve more years to go. That's what Mommy said. But Daddy said I can skip grades cause I'm sharp as a tack. I don't know what a tack is. Do you know what it is, Uncle Taj?" Liana didn't wait for an answer, especially when she realized that she had the attention of all the grownups. "I promised Daddy to work very, very hard, go to law school and be just like him. I'll have a big, big office with a window, and a chair that goes round and round like Daddy's. But mine will be pink, not black like Daddy's."

There was a burst of cheering and groans from the grownups. Cat smiled. What a precocious child, she thought.

Taj shook his head at his brother. "You better add this young lady's name to your law firm, Aaron. This is the next generation of Taylor lawyers."

"What happened to your head, Uncle Taj?" the children asked simultaneously.

"I was out slaying dragons...."

"That means bad guys," Liana interrupted with a giggle.

"When I received a minor cut," Taj finished in a jocular tone. "This is a badge of honor."

"Can we see it?" Alex asked with awe.

A woman whom Cat assumed was the children's mother cut in.

"C'mon, sweethearts, you can talk to your uncle tomorrow. He's brought home a guest whom everybody is dying to meet." She looked pointedly at Taj.

Taj looked at Cat. He took the children by their hands. "Excuse us, Sheryl." He led them to Cat. "Liana, Alex, I want you to meet a very special lady, Catherine Simmons. Cat, these are my niece and nephew, Liana Maya Taylor and Alexander Winston Taylor."

"Nice to meet you, ma'am," Alex replied charmingly.

Definitely the next Taylor heartbreaker, Cat mused. "The pleasure is mine, Alexander."

"Are you the love of Uncle Taj's life?"

At least two voices shouted, "Liana!"

The men hooted with laughter.

Liana ignored them. "Daddy said that Mommy is the love of his life. And when I asked Uncle JT, he told me Angela was the love of his life. When I grow up I will have a handsome prince as the love of my life. So I hope you are the love of Uncle Taj's life, 'cause every man must have a special woman."

"I'm enrolling her in an etiquette class," Sheryl moaned. Her husband protested.

But Cat couldn't help liking the child. And neither could she bring herself to admit that she was Taj's special woman. She had barely adjusted to the change in their relationship. "It is a real pleasure to meet you, Liana."

"It is a pleasure to meet you, ma'am." Thankfully, Sheryl intervened before Liana could point out Cat's lack of response to her question.

"I don't know where she gets her outrageous behavior. I apologize," Sheryl said.

Cat shook her head. "Don't, please. She's adorable."

"Thank you. I'm Sheryl." Then she surprised Cat by giving her a hug. "My husband, Aaron, is the Casanova who stole a kiss from you in the doorway."

"Nice to meet you, Sheryl," Cat said, blushing furiously.

"I'll take these two upstairs," Sheryl told everybody. "C'mon, children, it's bedtime."

"But Mom, Uncle Taj just arrived, and we haven't really...," Liana started.

"He'll be here tomorrow. Come along, Liana. Alex. Tell everybody goodnight."

"Uncle Taj, can you read a book to me?" Liana asked with an adorable pout.

"Really, Liana...," Sheryl started.

"It's okay, Sheryl," Taj interrupted. "You know I've got to, or she'll never let me live it down. I'll be up shortly, princess."

Sheryl mouthed, "You're spoiling her."

Taj gave her a hug and whispered in her ear, "Don't worry, I'll soon have mine to spoil and leave yours alone." Sheryl raised an eyebrow. Taj grinned cockily and walked to where Cat was standing.

The children said goodnight, then kissed everyone, including Cat, before they were led upstairs by their mother.

Taj finished the introductions. Cat met Jerry, the former L.A. Angels player turned horse breeder, and his wife Angela. She thanked them for letting her brother stay at their ranch. There were hugs from everyone, making her feel as though she were family. She thought the twin boys, Joshua Cyrus Taylor and Jonathan Hawk Taylor, were adorable.

Thirty minutes later, after reading to the children and tucking them in, Taj came downstairs to join everyone in the family room. Cat made room for him on the couch, and didn't mind when he sat close and put an arm around her waist.

As they sipped drinks or hot cocoa, conversation flowed easily. When they included Cat, it was as if they'd known her forever. Cat smiled and participated. When conversation flowed around her, she quietly studied the Taylor family.

The Taylor women were warm and friendly, the men tall, handsome, and charming. Jerry favored Taj in looks much more than Aaron, but still, anyone could tell the three were brothers. Sheryl, Aaron's wife, was of medium height and always on the move. She was not beautiful in the classical sense with her dimpled, round cheeks. Her long mane suited her face. Angela, on the other hand, was gorgeous—from her slightly slanted eyes to her perfectly shaped body. She was very tall, Cat had noticed, at least six feet. What was apparent to Cat was the obvious affection between all of them.

From the list of facts Taj kept dropping in her ear, Aaron and his wife Sheryl had been married for eight years. It was easy to see that they adored each other. They touched frequently. Angela and Jerry were in their third year of marriage and still acted like newlyweds. They were constantly giving each other special looks and smiles. They doted on their twins who were now in Taj's and Cat's arms.

"When Taj called me for the third time," Jerry was saying, "and spent the entire time talking about you, Cat, I knew I had to come to California and meet the woman who had my brother so captivated."

Cat locked eyes with Taj. She mouthed, "Captivated?"

He grinned back. "Totally."

Aaron interrupted them. "You should have heard him a few weeks ago. He called us in the middle of the night to ask us what to do with your nephew, Cat."

"Oh, this ought to be good. He went ape when we left him with the twins for an hour three months ago," Jerry added. "What happened?"

"He was panicking because Cat's nephew was crying and he didn't know what to do. Sheryl, love of my life and mother extraordinaire," he kissed his wife, "shared with him her words of wisdom."

When Cat looked at him with a knowing grin, Taj pressed a kiss on her hand. "I had to win some points, babe."

"Were you impressed, Cat?" Angela asked.

"Oh yes, very much. He purchased this disco nightlight that had my nephew Jamie totally spellbound." She too had fallen under his magic spell that night, she thought with a smile. And today, he'd shown her that the two of them could create a different kind of magic together. As if he'd read her thoughts, a glint appeared in Taj's eyes.

Angela interrupted their silent exchange. "What was wrong with your nephew, Cat?"

Cat looked away from Taj's eyes, caught the knowing looks they were receiving from the others, and blushed. Thankfully, the baby in her arm stirred, drawing everyone's attention away from her. "He was teething. Taj was wonderful with him."

"That, I would've loved to see," Sheryl murmured.

"Me too," Angela added.

"Hey." Taj raised his arms in surrender. "At times a man has to go the extra mile in order to win. Now can we talk about something else? Like what brought you guys to California, Angela?" He shot his brother a look. "I'm not buying your husband's explanation."

"We're here for the Del Mar National Horse Show in San Diego. But we also haven't seen you in a while, Taj. Hawk was beginning to worry." She moved to Cat's side to take the child who was starting to cry. "Let me take him. It's close to their feeding time."

"He had one of his visions," Jerry added as he took his other son from Taj's arms.

Taj explained to Cat about their grandfather's gift. Whenever Hawk said he was worried about someone, it usually meant he had foreseen danger dogging that person's footsteps.

"I'll call him tomorrow," Taj told the room.

"Talk to Mom too, little bro," Jerry urged. "She wanted to come, but changed her mind at the last minute. Actually, she acted quite peculiar. For an entire week, all she talked about was coming to see you. Then two days before we left, she changed her mind."

Taj smiled mysteriously. "Mom and I have already spoken."

"I'm beat, guys. I've got to keep up with my little terrors tomorrow at sunrise," Sheryl said, extending her hand to her husband who got up and put his arm around her waist. "So goodnight, everybody. It was nice meeting you, Cat."

"Likewise," Cat replied.

"See y'all in the morning," Aaron added.

They watched the two of them leave the room.

"So, how long is the show in San Diego going to run?" Taj asked Jerry, who was standing by his wife.

"Three weeks. It starts next week and goes till the first week of May. I have Elegance and several of my fillies entered." Jerry wanted to explain about his horses, but the twin in his arm started to cry. "Feeding time. How about we talk about my mares tomorrow, Cat?"

"Tomorrow will be fine," Cat said.

"Don't let him get started, Cat. He could go on the whole day. Those animals are his pride and joy," Angela added.

"No, sweetheart, you and the boys are my pride." He winked at Cat, then bid her and Taj goodnight. They heard him say to his wife as they walked away, "But you, my love, are my joy." Angela's giggles echoed behind them as they disappeared in the hallway.

"Alone at last," Taj murmured. "I love having my family around, but when unexpected they can be a bit overwhelming."

Cat shook her head. "They were not."

Taj pulled her into his arms. "So, you don't mind having them here?"

"No, I loved watching you interact with them. They're nice."

They started walking toward the foyer. "They are loud and boisterous, and tend to say what's on their minds. If they become annoying, let me know, and I'll throw them out."

Cat giggled. "You're silly, Taj Taylor."

He took her hand. "Let's go get our bags from the car and go to bed."

They used a side door that led through the library. Cat paused to admire its mahogany bookshelves and paneling, a huge mahogany desk, and leather chairs.

"You have a beautiful home, Taj," Cat said.

"Thank you."

In no time, they were unloaded. Then Taj took a look at Cat's tired eyes. "I'll show you around tomorrow, but right now let's get you into bed."

They went upstairs to what was obviously the master bedroom. He opened the door, turned on the light, and extended a welcoming hand to her.

Cat took it and walked into the room. She looked around with appreciation. The décor surprised her. With his love for motorbikes and leather, she'd expected his bedroom to be done in strong dark colors. Instead, it was a restful palette of muted tones. Everything—the walls, the duvet cover, the curtains, the watercolors—was very calming. The bed was impressive. From the little that she knew about antiques, she guessed it to be a Louis XV piece. "The room is very soothing."

"That was what I wanted, and Sheryl accommodated my wishes." Taj showed her where everything was.

A door from his room led to a short hallway. On the left was a closet filled with towels and on the right a room-size walk-in closet. The door in the middle led to the bathroom.

Cat put her small makeup bag beside the sink and looked appreciatively at the upholstered ottoman. She liked the room, especially the marble counter and floors, large mirrors, and the huge tub.

Taj let her use the bathroom first. As he took his turn, Cat got into bed. He came into the bedroom a few minutes later wearing only his briefs.

Cat admired his physique as he walked toward her. His hairless chest had a few water drops she wanted to lick. And his powerful thighs beckoned her to touch and kiss them. When her eyes landed on the bulge between his legs, she saw it stir. Her eyes snapped to his.

Taj paused to puff out his chest, and wiggle his eyebrows. "Like what you see?" he teased.

Cat pursed her lips and checked him from head to toe. Then she indicated with her finger that he should turn around. "Nice. Anything else?"

He started posing as though he were a body builder at a show. He showed his abs, his pectoral muscles, and his biceps.

"Hmm," she murmured, throwing off the cover and kneeling on the bed. "Come closer, baby, I think I need a closer inspection of the merchandise before I can give my final opinion."

His eyes took in the two-piece red teddy she had on. He walked to her outstretched arms and grinned. "That's some outfit, love."

"I'm happy you like it. I wore it with you in mind."

His hand caressed and then closed around a breast. "Us in mind." His lips touched her cheek, then her neck and her collarbone. Finally, he reached her nipples. The lacy number she had on offered no barrier to his questing lips. He suckled on her nipples and took tiny sensual bites.

"Taj?" Cat whispered achingly.

"Sweetheart, don't bother a man when he's savoring his favorite meal," he murmured.

Seeing his hair spill around her chest, feeling his wicked mouth turn her insides into jelly, she almost told him then that she loved him. Why didn't the thought bring a barrel of panic anymore? She glanced down at his head, the play of muscles on his shoulder, and every thought disappeared from her head except the urge to touch him. "I want to touch you."

His head shot up. "Oh, please do."

She ran a hand down his back and then pulled off his underwear. His swollen manhood stood proud and bold. Her hand closed around him, gently stroking and squeezing. He sucked in air and exhaled in short spasms. "You like that, huh?"

"Oh, yes."

"Then you're going to love this." She kissed his neck, then moved to his chest. Perfectly formed, she thought as she licked, sucked, and bit his nipples. When his body jerked, she grinned. It was her turn to tease and torment him. When his breathing became harsh, she prepared him and boldly straddled his hips. Slowly, she started their next sensual dance.

Honed from years of physical training, her muscles contracted around him and released. With each movement, she squeezed and pulled him further in. She felt the change in his rhythm before his eyes snapped opened.

"What are you doing to me," Taj whispered as he stared into her passion-glazed eyes.

"The same thing you do to me," she whispered back, loving that she could watch him watch her touch him. He met her thrust for thrust. Then he lifted her off him and turned her around.

His hands spread around her hips. When he entered her, she pushed back for deeper penetration. It was hard for her not to scream, but other people were sleeping nearby. The sex was wild, mind-blowing, a mingling of pain and pleasure. When they both peaked, he was the one smothering a scream.

CHAPTER 17

Taj woke up before Cat. Turning his head, he studied her as she slept. He wanted to wake up every morning with her by his side, he thought with a smile. Truth be known, he would have proposed to her by now if he'd thought she would accept him. But they were making progress. In fact, he suspected that Cat loved him. Everything she did or said pointed to that. If only she could say the words too.

That was one of the reasons he hadn't wanted his mother to visit, Taj thought with a frown. One glance at him, and his mother would have known things weren't completely kosher between him and Cat.

He'd made the mistake of mentioning to his mother that he'd met a special lady, someone he was planning to bring home to meet her and the grandparents. Beyond that, he'd refused to discuss Cat, except to say that he loved her. After grilling him nonstop without getting anywhere, his mother had concluded that a visit to personally check out Cat was in order. But after all the crap his mother had put Angela through before she married Jerry, Taj didn't want her anywhere near Cat. He had told her to trust his judgment and accept that he'd found the woman he wanted to marry. She must have believed him because she hadn't traveled with Jerry and his family.

Making sure not to wake Cat up, he made a few phone calls and then showered. When he walked from the bathroom a few minutes later, Cat was just waking up.

He smiled at the way she stretched and moaned. Their lovemaking last night had been vigorous. He too had a few bruises as testimony. "Aches?"

Cat looked up and smiled. "Bearable ones. What time is it?"

"Almost twelve." He studied her face. She looked well-rested, he thought, and had the look of a contented woman. That was what he wanted to see every night before he fell asleep and every morning when he woke up.

What would she say to going to Montana for his grandfather's birthday? He'd been thinking about it since speaking with his mother. The old man was sickly, so they all tried to attend each of his birthdays as if it were the last one. His grandparents would love Cat, her spirit.

Cat's eyes followed him as he walked to the bed. "Did you rest at all?" she asked.

He gave her brief kiss. "Like a baby. That's natural after all the demands you made of my body."

She giggled and jabbed his side. "How's your head?"

"Healing."

"Let me take a look." She removed the bandage and checked the sutures. The wound was dry. "Were you planning on going somewhere without me?"

"No, love. Today we'll stay at home and rest. But if you want to be alone, let me know. I can arrange it. If you want to go anywhere, I'll drive you. I'm here to fulfill your every wish."

And for the rest of the day, he did exactly that. He started by introducing her to his housekeeper, Annie Mae Johnson, and her husband, Duke Johnson, before leading her to the patio where a buffet lunch was laid out on the table.

As they ate, they watched his niece and nephew frolic in the pool. The pool itself had stone geyser-like fountains at the edges, providing water sounds that were very soothing. Stones were strategically placed along the pool's perimeter, softening it with a touch of nature. At the other end of the pool was a gazebo. There were trees along the fence and all around the compound, creating a sense of seclusion.

While the other grown-ups joined the children in the pool, Taj took Cat on a grand tour of his house, beginning with the living room and dining room on the main floor and ending with the unfurnished bedrooms upstairs.

The living room was done in a controlled color palette of cream, tan, and brown. Cream-colored plush chairs and sofas with pillows of brown and tan mixed perfectly with the metal and smoky-mirror coffee table. The side tables were made from mahogany, the floor covered by a beautiful, large Oushak carpet. Instead of chandeliers, the room had wall, floor, and side table gilt lamps. Arched windows added subtle flair to the room. Cat loved the spacious room, the timelessness of the furniture.

The dining room had a striking Baccarat crystal chandelier above a majestic mahogany table which would sit at least eight people. Cream damask upholstered chairs complemented the dining room color and the drapes. Works of art opposite a gilt mirror lent more elegance.

Upstairs, Taj skipped the three bedrooms that were being used, but showed her the two unfurnished rooms. He explained, "The nursery and the playroom."

"You have a beautiful home, Taj. Did Sheryl do the entire house?"

"Yes. She's an amazing interior designer."

"Do you ever worry about someone breaking in?"

"Not really. I have Annie Mae and her husband watching things. The dogs aren't friendly either."

―――ww―――

For the rest of the day, Cat relaxed and had fun with Taj's family. Part of the afternoon, it was just Cat, the two Taylor women, and the children. Taj had given Annie Mae the day off, and the men went shopping for a cookout dinner they planned.

"Tell us how you got started in your career," Angela asked Cat as they sat on the deck and kept an eye on the twins in their playpen and the older children playing computer games in the family room.

"And how did you and Taj meet, Cat?" Sheryl added.

Cat laughed. "Can I answer the last question first?" She received vigorous nods. "My friend Janelle dared me to talk to him when he pulled up on his Harley."

"And what did you two talk about?"

Car blushed, remembering Jan's comments about her choice of topic.

"Bikes and engines."

Sheryl and Angela laughed.

"Must have stupefied him," Sheryl said. "Taj is not used to women who like what he does. What happened next?"

"He gave me a single rose every day for two weeks without asking me out. He later claimed he never mixes business with pleasure." She quickly explained the reason Taj had been at the set. "On his last day at the set, he asked me out. I was determined to resist him, but he wore me down."

"The Taylor charm. And now you're so in love," Sheryl said dreamily, smiling with nostalgia as she remembered her own courtship. "Then we'll have another wedding in the family."

Cat blushed. She couldn't deny her love for Taj any more than she could stop breathing. And Taj had shown her over and over again that he cared about her. Marriage, on the other hand, was something she wasn't ready for. It was such a big commitment. "Do you really think he's ready for that?" she asked Sheryl hesitantly.

Angela and Sheryl looked at each other, then nodded emphatically.

"Absolutely," Sheryl said. "He's crazy about you, Cat."

"You should have heard him when he called us. All he did was talk about you. Cat this and Cat that," Angela added.

"Can I ask you something, Cat?" Sheryl asked.

Cat nodded.

"There are two rooms upstairs that are unfinished. Did Taj tell you what those are for?"

"A nursery and a playroom."

Sheryl leaned forward to whisper, "Do you know what he told me when I did this house for him? He swore that only the woman he intended to marry would ever know what those two rooms were for. I'd asked him to turn one of them into an upstairs library and another into a media room."

Cat didn't know what to say to that or what she would say to a marriage proposal from Taj. It was something she just wasn't ready for. To change the subject, she said, "Tell me how you two met your husbands. How did you know he was the one?"

Sheryl turned to Angela, "Do you want to go first, Angela?"

"Oh, no."

"What happened?" Cat asked.

"C'mon, Angela," Sheryl urged. "Tell or I will."

Angela wrinkled her nose at Sheryl, but the twinkle in her eyes indicated she was eager to tell all. "Okay, I thought Jerry was responsible for the death of my sister, so I found a way to be part of his household so that I could find something I could use to bring him to justice. Aaron and their Uncle Cyrus had hired me to help him with his records. Unfortunately, Jerry didn't want…how had he put it…'*another incompetent female wasting his goddamn time.*'"They burst out laughing. "He told his foreman to take me back to wherever I'd crawled from."

"Oh, no, he didn't," Cat said, genuinely shocked.

"Yes, he did. He was so infuriating." She glanced quickly to where Alex and Liana were playing before lowering her voice and adding, "I kept wondering how it would feel to kiss him the entire time." They hooted with laughter again.

"Mommy, what's so funny?" Liana yelled.

"Reminiscing, sweetheart," Sheryl answered. "Go back to your game."

Angela patted Sheryl's arm. "It's your turn, Sheryl girl. Tell Cat what Aaron did when your dad locked you up in that monstrous mansion you called home."

Sheryl giggled. "Don't let my mama hear you. That monstrous mansion is her pride and joy." Then she said, "I've got to tell you how we first met, okay? I walked into Aaron's office, and he confused me with a girl from an escort service."

"What?" Cat screeched.

"Seriously. Lord knows how he jumped to that conclusion since I was dressed in a wrinkled business suit, had minimal makeup and my hair in a severe bun"

"But an escort service? Why?"

"You have to understand something, Cat. Aaron Taylor was San Diego's number one playboy—an upcoming criminal lawyer, gallant, charming, handsome…every mother's nightmare, but a rebellious girl's dream man. I was more than ready to rebel against my parent's rigid codes of conduct when we met. He saved me. Every function he attended, a different woman was on his arm. Little did I know he acquired them for the evening for a hefty fee paid to Social Savoir-Faire, Inc., a company providing businesses with male and female models for social functions."

"What happened?" Cat asked with a grin.

"In under an hour, he had me dressed in the latest couture and my hair done by the best hair stylist in San Diego. When I discovered the bad-boy image he so loved to flaunt was false, I was more than intrigued. Then I decided that he was perfect for a torrid, scandalous affair."

"Did you have one?" Cat asked, looking at Sheryl's dreamy expression.

"Oh, yes. And what a scandal."

"She's saving the best for last, Cat," Angela jumped in, her eyes twinkling.

"Aaron, with the help of your man and Jerry, planned and executed the perfect elopement."

"How romantic," Cat exclaimed.

Sheryl giggled. "I didn't think so at the time. A cousin convinced me that Aaron had done something terrible. Made me question his love. And the fact that my parents hated his guts also made the situation worse. But the impossible man decided to scale my dad's wall, climb through my window, and take me away. The rest is history."

Cat liked the Taylor women. They were full of warmth. The day passed quickly as they got to know each other. The men finally returned to barbeque. It wasn't until later, after dinner, that Taj filled her in on what his investigators had discovered.

Taj was in a mellow mood. Cat was lying on his chest and their hair was slightly damp after a bath together. He kissed her forehead and murmured, "I had an interesting talk with your brother Kenny today."

She looked at him through her lashes. "I completely forgot you were going to talk with him. You don't mind that I told him everything, do you?"

"No, sweetheart, I don't. In fact, he's been very helpful. He assisted my people with a few things today."

"What did they find?"

"Frank spoke with the two monks we met at the gift shop the other day, Brothers Patrick and Cornelius. They said Sergey was back in the country, but was in solitude. My source in the state department also informed me through Mrs. D. that Sergey and Father Forster entered the country through Tijuana Saturday afternoon. That confirms that they had nothing to do with what happened to us that morning. However, they weren't alone. They had two young girls, ages ten and twelve, and an older man."

"Could they be the ones that the woman in Menlo Park was referring to?"

"Possibly."

"I'm glad to know, though, that Father Forster wasn't the one trying to scare us or hurt us. He sounds like a nice person. And if he turns out to be Bobby's biological father, it wouldn't be such a bad thing."

Taj kissed her forehead. "Maybe not."

—m—

The next day, the two of them followed Taj's family to the Burbank airport. After seeing them off, they headed for L.A. First they stopped by the offices of A.P.P. Alarm and Video Security Company, where Cat purchased a house security system. It was so expensive that it put quite a dent in her savings account, but it was money well spent, she thought when they got back to her house. The company had promised to send its people the same day to start installing the system.

Taj gripped Cat's hand. He was leaving for his office, and she'd walked him to his car. "If these guys weren't installing your security system today, I'd insist you come with me." He looked toward her gate, then turned to face her. "Promise me that you won't go anywhere without letting me know. Until we know who's after us, I want you to be careful, okay?"

"You too." She ushered him toward his car.

He stopped to kiss her one last time. "I love you, baby. I don't think I could bear it if something were to happen to you."

It was at the tip of her tongue to tell him that she loved him, too. But years of being cautious won. "I'll be careful, I promise."

Taj didn't seem bothered by her lack of response, or if he was he didn't show it. "I'll call in a couple of hours to see how things are going."

Cat watched him leave. Why was she such a coward? She loved that man with all her heart. Why, then, couldn't she vocalize her feelings? Oh, she knew why. She wasn't ready to deal with the implications. Taj believed in happily-ever-after, but she still had her doubts. He believed that she and she alone was meant to live that life with him. She wanted to believe him, but old habits died hard. Admitting her love to him was equivalent to giving him power over her. Could she trust him with her heart? She surely hoped so, because he already had it.

Slowly, Cat walked back to the house and closed the door

Less than an hour later, the security company employees were at her gate, ready to start working on her new security system. She spoke briefly with them and then rearranged her sewing room, where the monitor was going to be set.

As she watched the men work, something kept teasing at her mind, a memory. She was talking to one of them about motion-triggered security lights when a white van drove past her gate. Suddenly it all came back to her.

On the evening Taj had helped her with Jamie, a black van had driven past her gate, too. Could it have been the same van that was now following them around or was she becoming paranoid? She decided to ask the Lamberts if they'd seen a black van parked along the street or if someone on their street owned one. Lucille was bound to know such things.

Cat called her neighbor. Lucille was in the shower, her husband informed Cat. But they wouldn't mind if she stopped by in an hour or so, he added. Cat thanked Jonas and hung up. Then the phone rang.

"Where have you been, woman? I've been calling your place but no one picked up the damned phone," Jan said disagreeably. "I'm coming over."

"Good morning, Jan. How are you? Thanks for asking after my health. I'm just doing great. And you, Ms. Movie Star, aren't my keeper."

"Ooh, you're in a nasty mood."

"I'm cooped up in here, and it's slowly driving me crazy."

"Cooped up? What's going on?"

Damn, the last person she wanted to talk to was Jan. Too late now. "Aren't you supposed to be rehearsing today?"

"Not until later. Don't you want me to visit, Cat? I haven't seen you in days."

"Miss you too, girl. Listen, I'm having my security updated so don't freak out when you see a bunch of half-naked men in my yard."

"Now I'm definitely coming over." There was the jiggling of keys. "By the way, how is Taj?"

"You won't know unless you come here."

Jan made it to her house in record time, causing Cat to push aside her worries. After exchanging hugs and getting soft drinks, they settled on the couch.

Without exaggerating, Cat told Jan about everything that had happened the last week—the car chase, the scare outside her club, and the runaway Range Rover. When she finished, Jan was staring at her with rounded eyes.

"Ohmigod, Cat. What did Bobby see that night?"

"It's a question of who he saw that night: Russian hoodlums."

"I hope Taj gets them. These people sound dangerous."

Cat smiled at Jan's expression. "Oh, he will," she answered with confidence. She was fast finding out how tenacious Taj could be when he wanted something.

As soon as Taj arrived at his office, he started piecing together everything he knew about Bobby's case. He drew charts.

The top one had an arrow from the black van to Bobby. The facts as he knew them were that Bobby had seen a black van being loaded with boxes, and for a few days a black van had tailed him. The church, the center, and the Father's home were torched the same night. The chance that Bobby had surprised the arsonists was very high. If they thought Bobby could identify them, they would likely keep tabs on him. Made sense, he concluded. Unfortunately, Bobby had gone to Cat instead of the police. It was also logical that the people tailing him would then start tailing Cat after that. That would explain the car chase the following night. But after seeing him with Cat, they must have decided to turn their attention to him. That would explain why Cat hadn't seen the van while he was gone and why it had appeared outside her gym when he returned. Taj wrote his name down. Then he drew another arrow from the black van to his name.

If he could find proof that the Russians were after him because of what Bobby had seen, this case would be broken, and he could ask Cat to marry him. Until then....

He wrote down the word "accident" and then he circled it with a red pen. Why would anyone want him dead? Who had known he was going to see Cat that morning? He'd spoken to Ray that morning, but he couldn't imagine his buddy colluding with the Russians to harm him.

Who had tampered with his brakes? When? The car had responded well until after the monastery. He remembered the monk they'd brushed against when they were leaving the gift shop. Could they find out his identity and ask him what he'd seen that day? Then there were the two boys playing with BB guns outside the gym that day.

Last but not least, there was Father Forster. Where was he now? Questions without answers, Taj thought with a frown. He wrote beside the priest's name, "Talk with Cardinal Mallory."

That was it. If none of these leads panned out, he'd be in deep trouble. He had to solve this case soon, Taj vowed, or go ape. As he paused to rub his temple, his eyes fell on the computer printouts Ray had given him last Sunday. With the trip to his house and his family's impromptu visit, he'd completely forgotten about them.

He sat behind his desk, put his feet up and scanned the first article.

The first article was on St. Vibiana Center for Spirituality, its goals, and the man who had founded it, Father Robert Forster. Accompanying the article was a picture of Forster. He was a tall, skinny man with a receding hairline who wore horn-rimmed glasses. Without the priest's collar he could have passed for a college science professor, not a sixty-eight-year-old clergyman.

The next articles listed his accomplishments: "Rev. Forster Takes on Gangs in Encino"; "Rev. Forster's Community Outreach Program Benefits Immigrants"; "Rev. Forster's Neighborhood Crime-Prevention Program a Roaring Success"; "Rev. Forster Invites Businesses to Help At-risk Youth"; "Rev. Forster Encourages St. Vibiana Youth Groups to Visit Hospitals and the Elderly"; "St. Vibiana Hosts a Social Event for Immigrants"; "Learn How to Dress and Present Yourself to a Prospective Employer, Rev. Forster's Latest Initiative."

Taj smiled as he moved from one article to another. He didn't know how a man Forster's age could be so active and successful where so many had failed. Everything the man touched was successful. He encouraged parents, the police, the young, and the elderly to work together, and they did. Corporations threw money at him. Local small businesses worked with him. Everyone seemed to love him. But then again, Taj mused, why shouldn't they when he turned gang members into productive members of society? The articles also mentioned that some of the former gang members had joined monasteries, that others had gone back to school or had sought gainful employment. Why, then, had someone torched his center?

The next paper was blank, except for a brief note from Cipher, the computer whiz kid in Ray's department:

The next articles relate to cases Father Forster was involved in that earned him enemies. Thought Agent Taylor might find them useful.

Taj turned to the next page which had a list of names, and a name jumped at him. *Kovalenko,* the same name he'd heard on the transmitter when he was eavesdropping on Mother Superior at the convent in Menlo Park. It was the name of Father Forster's mysterious guest in the secret room at the center. His feet landed on the floor with a thud.

He flipped through the papers looking for the story, but the page was missing. Damn. He looked around and under his desk in case it had fallen down, but it wasn't there.

This could be the clue to break this case, he thought as he dialed Ray's number. Ray's cell phone went unanswered. After he left a message, he dialed Ray's home number. That one went unanswered too. Where the hell was he?

Ray had told him that he was on a case and couldn't be reached through his office, Taj recollected. If he couldn't reach Ray, Cipher should be able to get him a copy of the article on Kovalenko. Taj dialed the local offices of the Bureau.

"Cipher, Taj Taylor here," he said as soon as the younger man came on the line. "I hope I'm not disturbing you."

"No, sir, you're not."

"Cipher, there's no need for such formalities. Call me Taylor."

"Oh, okay. What can I do for you, Taylor?"

Taj briefly explained about the missing document.

"Just a second while I pull up the file." There was a brief pause. "Got it. Do you want me to fax it to your office or e-mail it to you?"

"Fax it." He gave him his fax number. "Oh, Cipher, have you seen Agent Delaney recently?"

There was silence from Cipher. Finally he said, "You don't know?"

"Know what?"

"Agent Delaney was released from active duty a week ago. The boys from the Justice Department are trying to pin something on him."

Shock rendered Taj speechless. When he recovered, he asked, "Why?"

"They're accusing him of manipulating witnesses. In the last two months, four witnesses in high-profile cases have refused to be placed in the Witness Protection Program. The Justice Department claims that these witnesses were handled by Agent Delaney. With twenty or more people joining the WPP per month, four witnesses changing their minds shouldn't be considered unusual. It's all bullshit."

Taj understood Cipher's indignation. The *esprit-de-corps* within the Bureau meant that the agents trusted each other so implicitly that an accusation leveled against one of them was considered an insult to the entire corps.

Cipher interrupted his thoughts. "I'm faxing the missing page now, Taylor."

Taj got up and walked to the fax machine, but his mind was still on what Cipher had just revealed to him. Why hadn't Ray mentioned the investigation when they'd met last Sunday? Why lie that he would be unavailable at the office because of a case?

"Thanks, Cipher," Taj said when the fax came through.

"Anytime, Taylor." They hung up.

Taj walked back to his chair and sat down. For a few seconds, he did nothing but stare into space. It was absurd to imagine Ray being corrupt. He knew Ray, had been by his side during the gruesome training in Quantico and when he'd mourned his fiancée five years ago. There was no way he could be dirty. Besides, the Bureau did background checks on all its agents every three years, so any red flags that might have indicated Ray had a problem would have turned up. There had to be another explanation, Taj concluded. He looked at the paper in his hand and started to read.

KOVALENKO'S DAUGHTER STILL MISSING:

TWO INDICTED FOR THE MURDER OF ANDREI, JELENA, AND PETRO KOVALENKO

TIMELESS DEVOTION

FEDERAL AUTHORITIES THURSDAY UNSEALED INDICTMENTS AGAINST THREE MEN CHARGED WITH KIDNAPPING THREE RUSSIAN IMMIGRANTS WHOSE BODIES WERE RECOVERED FROM A NORTHERN CALIFORNIA RESERVOIR. THE BODIES OF TWO MEN AND A WOMAN, ALL OF EASTERN EUROPEAN DESCENT, WERE RECOVERED FROM THE NEW MELONES RESERVOIR NEAR STOCKTON, CALIFORNIA.

THE BODIES WERE IDENTIFIED AS ANDREI KOVALENKO, 55, HIS WIFE JELENA 50, AND THEIR SON PETRO, 25. TANYA KOVALENKO, 30, IS STILL MISSING AND IS THE TARGET OF A SEARCH. NICK ANATOL, 55, AND HIS TWIN SONS, ALEXANDER AND YURI ANATOL, 32, HAVE BEEN CHARGED WITH THE MURDERS OF ANDREI KOVALENKO, JELENA KOVALENKO, AND PETRO KOVALENKO.

UNTIL TWO MONTHS AGO ANATOL OPERATED A LIMOUSINE BUSINESS CALLED TSARINA, INC. HE WAS INDICTED FOR PIMPING, PANDERING AND MONEY LAUNDERING WHEN UNDERCOVER POLICEMEN FROM THE LOS ANGELES POLICE DEPARTMENT FOUND EVIDENCE LINKING HIS BUSINESS TO A PROSTITUTION RING. HIS COMPANY EMPLOYED RUSSIAN WOMEN THROUGHOUT LOS ANGELES, WEST HOLLYWOOD AND BEVERLY HILLS, AND ADVERTISED AS AN ESCORT SERVICE IN THE YELLOW PAGES, IN NEWSPAPERS, AND ON THE INTERNET. DURING THE INVESTIGATION INTO NICK ANATOL'S BUSINESS DEALINGS, AUTHORITIES LEARNED ABOUT THE DISAPPEARANCE OF A LOCAL BUSINESSMAN, ANDREI KOVALENKO, ALONG WITH HIS FAMILY.

NICK, YURI, AND ALEXANDER ANATOL WERE ALSO CHARGED WITH THE KIDNAPPING OF TANYA AND PETRO KOVALENKO, WHO DISAPPEARED FEBRUARY 13. ANDREI KOVALENKO, WHO OWNED SEVERAL RESTAURANTS ON THE WEST COAST, RECEIVED TWO RANSOM NOTES THAT HAD BEEN FAXED TO HIS OFFICE IN WEST HOLLYWOOD, DEMANDING $500,000 FOR THE RETURN OF HIS CHILDREN. FBI INVESTIGATORS LATER LEARNED THAT THE FAXES HAD BEEN WIRED FROM NICK ANATOL'S HOME. KOVALENKO PAID $200,000 BY WIRING MONEY TO A BANK IN NEW YORK, WHICH THEN WIRED THE MONEY TO ONE OF ITS BRANCHES IN RUSSIA. KOVALENKO WAS TRYING TO RAISE MORE MONEY BY SELLING TWO OF HIS RESTAURANTS WHEN HE AND HIS WIFE DISAP-

PEARED. THE WIRE TRANSFER RECORDS ALSO LED THE INVESTIGATORS TO THE ANATOL FAMILY.

The rest of the article outlined how the culprits had been apprehended and how witnesses had come forward claiming that Tanya Kovalenko was alive. Cipher had underlined another interesting fact in the article. The Kovalenkos had attended St. Vibiana church, and Jelena Kovalenko had worked at the center as a translator.

Taj dialed Cipher's number again. "Cipher, I need to know something. Has Tanya Kovalenko been found yet?"

"Since the kidnapping? Yes. She even agreed to testify against the Anatol family and to join the WPP. Then suddenly she disappeared."

Or somebody made sure she disappeared, Taj thought. "Are the marshals trying to find her?"

"Oh, yes. They even spoke with Father Forster about her. No one knows her whereabouts."

"Thanks, Cipher."

It all made sense, Taj concluded: the woman hiding in the secret room, the burning of the center, Father Forster's disappearance. They were dealing with Russian Mafia. Were these the people who were after him now? Damn.

Taj called Mrs. D. to his office. "Bring in everyone. We need to talk."

"Even the men working on the Dorgan case?"

"Yes. I need to discuss something with everybody."

While Mrs. D. called the others, Taj paced his office. On top of worrying about Bobby's case, he was concerned about his friend Ray. He placed another call to Ray's home and left a message. By the time everyone was assembled in his office, he had reached a decision. He was pulling everyone off the case.

Mrs. D. had picked up pastries from a bakery around the corner and made coffee for everyone. As soon as they each had coffee and something to eat, Taj said, "We have a very big problem on our hands. Somehow, I got us mixed up in a Russian Mafia vendetta."

No one spoke. Taj didn't need to see the shocked expressions on everyone's face to know that he had their attention. He quickly explained what he knew about the Kovalenko case, and how Forster was involved in it. "The Kovalenko family attended Forster's church; the mother was a translator at the center. From what Godfrey and I have discovered, it appears that Forster has been hiding the Kovalenko girl. Someone working on behalf of Anatol and his sons wants to make sure she doesn't testify in their trial. They know that Father Forster has her. Unfortunately, because we're also looking for the Father, they think we're their enemy too." He studied all the faces staring at him. It was time to tell them the decision he'd made. "I want everyone off this case immediately. It's too dangerous. I can find the priest on my own."

"Are you sure, Taj?" Frank asked. "Russians are ruthless, and you may need us to cover your back."

"That may be so, Frank, but it's reached a point where people could get hurt. I can't ask you guys to do it. All I need to do is check a few things, then talk with Cardinal Mallory. If anyone knows where Father Forster is, it's his boss." A wry smile crossed his lips. "Mrs. D.? I believe you have some new cases that should keep everyone busy." He stood up, signaling that the meeting was over.

"Taj?" Frank called when everyone had left the room.

"Not now, Frank," he answered, pretending to be busy with the papers on his desk.

"I know you don't want to hear it, but I'm going to say it anyway. I think you're taking chances with this case, okay? Is she worth losing your life?"

Only the slight tightening of his jaws indicated that Frank's barb had hit home. He didn't try to defend his actions or chide Frank for the personal remark. Frank was old enough to be his father, and experienced enough for him to take notice when he spoke. But when it came to Cat, there was nothing anyone could say to him that would make him change his actions.

Taj heard the door close behind Frank. Only then did he sit back and try to relax. He rubbed his eyes. Was he getting obsessed with this case? Was he taking unnecessary chances? Sure, he wanted to help

Bobby Simmons, but there was much more at stake, the first being the identity of the person who'd nearly killed them last weekend. He had to make the person pay.

Then there was Cat and their future together. There was no doubt in his mind that he loved Cat. The two of them were meant to be together. He wanted her absolute devotion to him, her undying love. He wanted her to see him as someone she could depend on. Cat had been let down by people she trusted. Her parents had never given her the love she deserved; instead, they'd destroyed her faith in people and love. They had made her believe that loving someone was something to be shunned. Hell, she hadn't wanted a relationship or even believed in them until he convinced her otherwise. Now they were lovers, but he wanted much more from Cat. If that meant solving this case and proving to her that he was dependable, then he wasn't going to rest until it was done.

He was reaching for his keys when the door opened. He looked up to see Frank walk in, followed by Godfrey and Mrs. D. Carlton, Solomon, and Mike weren't far behind.

They all stood before his desk. "What?" Taj asked.

"We started this case together. We'll see it through together," Frank said.

Taj studied everyone's face. "Are you sure you know what you're committing yourselves to here?"

Frank, who appeared to be their spokesperson, spoke up again, "Yes. We conferred, and we all agreed that we're in with you."

Taj studied their faces for a long time before he nodded. "Okay. This is what we need to do. Frank and Godfrey, I want you to visit the Camaldoli Monastery. Find out the identity of the monk Cat and I passed on our way out of the gift shop. I want to know if he saw anyone mess with our brakes. The two monks, Brother Cornelius Land and Patrick O'Hara, should be able to help you."

He turned to the youngest member of the team. "Solomon, I want you to go back to St. Patrick's Cathedral. See if you can pick up anything new."

He glanced at Mike and Carlton. "The two of you are staying on the Dorgan case for now."

Finally, he smiled at Mrs. Dunlop. "Mrs. D., work your magic and get me an appointment with His Eminence, please. As for me, I'm going to pay my friend Ray a visit."

When everyone filed out, Taj smiled. It was good to know that he could count on his people's loyalty. Could he one day count on Cat's devotion and love or was he fighting a losing battle?

CHAPTER 18

Cat checked the clock on her dashboard as she pulled up outside Taj's office building. It was almost five o'clock. She sighed with relief when she saw his car. Thank goodness he was in. She didn't know what had possessed her to drive to his place of work, but now that she was here, doubts were creeping in. What if he was busy? What if he was at a meeting? What if he'd made other plans for dinner?

You're a piece of work, Catherine, she mused as a grimace crossed her lips. She knew what had caused her to make this impromptu visit. Just a couple of hours apart and she missed him. Actually "miss" didn't begin to cover her feelings. She was crazy about the man, so totally and irrevocably in love it scared the hell out of her.

Getting out of the car, Cat smoothed a hand over her gold sundress. Before her courage could fail her, she grabbed the paper bags containing their dinner and walked toward the entrance of the five-story building.

She looked around the lobby with interest. She'd driven past the building before, but it was her first time entering it. In the middle of the ground floor was a mounted statue of a hawk standing on top of a globe. Like the outside, the inside wall had the name "Hawkeye Plaza" written in bold letters beside a flying hawk.

Taj's middle name was Hawkeye so was his grandfather's. Could the building be his? she wondered as she took in the marble floor, the teal textured walls, and the security booth. She approached the security guard, noticed that the security system had been installed by A.P.P. Alarm and Video Security Company, the same company installing one in her house.

"Excuse me?"

The security man looked up and smiled. "Yes, ma'am?"

"What floor is Hawk Detective Agency?"

"The top floor, ma'am. The elevators are around the corner."

Cat followed his directions to the secluded elevator doors. On the wall beside the elevator were the names of the companies occupying each floor. She pressed the "up" button and waited.

She was nervous. Wasn't that something? The man was crazy about her, had said so on numerous occasions. Why, then, was she nervous?

The elevator pinged before it opened. She walked in and pressed the button for the fifth floor. She knew why she was nervous. What if he hated to be interrupted at work? What if he didn't appreciate her surprise?

When it opened on the fifth floor, she walked to the glass door through which she could see Mrs. D. at her desk. She pushed open the doors and walked in.

She had no time to appreciate the elegance of the front office before Mrs. D. looked up and said, "Catherine, my dear. How happy I am to see you looking hale and hearty."

Cat smiled. "Thanks to your brew, Mrs. D. How are you doing?"

"Could be better." She got up and picked up her bag. "You want to see *him*?"

Cat smiled. "Yes. I thought I'd surprise him with dinner." She held up the bags she was carrying.

Mrs. D. pointed at a door. "Go on ahead, my dear. He's in there working late."

"Thank you," Cat whispered. She walked to the door leading to Taj's office and pushed it open. She gave his office a quick perusal. It was elegantly done in green and tan colors. There were two plush, hunter green sofas at the corner of his office and an oak coffee table. The carpet was also hunter green, and tan wallpaper with leafy borders complemented it. His desk was pure mahogany. Certificates and original artworks adorned the walls. When her eyes landed on Taj, her wariness disappeared.

"What is it, Mrs. D.?" Taj asked without looking up.

Cat smiled. He sounded so serious, so preoccupied. "I was told you're the man to see if I have a problem, Detective Taylor."

Taj looked up. A flash of joy went through him before his eyes narrowed. He noted the gold dress accentuating Cat's curves, the spiked-heeled sandals, and the impish grin on her face. He didn't get up or smile. "What are you doing here?"

"You didn't call." She placed the two bags on his desk, walked around it to stand before him. "I thought you might want to share dinner."

Taj ignored the uncertainty in her eyes. "Why didn't you call?"

The smile on her lips wavered slightly. "I wanted to surprise you."

After he'd specifically told her not to leave the house? "Do you think the people in the black van are toying with us, Cat? What if they were laying in wait for you, huh? How would I have known? We have to work together. If I say you need to stay put, please stay put."

She shrugged. "Nothing happened. Here I am." Then, as if realizing he was royally pissed, she took a step back. "Anyway, I thought you might want to eat. But I see it wasn't such a good idea."

As she walked backwards, Taj's gaze stayed fixed on her. With the light shining behind her, he could see the outline of her body. His body stirred despite his ire. Why was he angry with her anyway? As she'd said, she was here, safe and sound. Nothing had happened to her along the way. Why, then, was he being such a jerk?

He knew the answer to that question too. He was frustrated by the fact that he couldn't solve the puzzle of the black van or find Bobby's missing priest, frustrated that he hadn't been able to contact Ray, that Cat couldn't love him or refused to love him, and that her behavior was affecting him to this extent. The list was long.

He eyed the way her dress molded her body. Was she wearing a bra?

The thought sneaked in on him. Did she have on pantyhose? His body responded to his amorous thoughts. "Why is it a bad idea?"

She looked at him with blazing eyes. "Because you're being a total jerk!" she snapped. Then the fight went out of her. "Maybe you have a right to be. I know there are people who hate to be interrupted while they work, and you must be one of them. I was going crazy at home, thought to stop by. I should have called first." She cleared her throat. "I brought Thai food, your favorite. Enjoy."

"Stay and join me," he called out.

"No, thanks, I've just lost my appetite. I'll see you at home." She turned and started for the door.

"Cat," he called in a husky voice. "Don't go, please."

Her body reacted naturally to the cadence of his voice. She stopped. She didn't turn around, though.

Taj watched the way she stood, body tense and ready to bolt if he said a wrong thing. He pressed a button and his Serenette window shades closed. He walked to the door connecting his office to his investigators' offices and locked it. He sensed when she turned around and could feel her eyes follow his every move. But she didn't say a word. Then he locked the door leading to the front office and turned to face her.

Slowly, he walked toward her, his heart filled with dread. What if his idea backfired? What if she walked out of his life forever? How do you go about forcing someone to admit that she loves you?

His body reacted to her nearness, the soft perfume she wore. He walked forward and stood in front of her. Then he waited. When she looked up, he saw the tears shining in her eyes, the vulnerability in their depths, the trembling lower lip. He wanted to gather her in his arms and apologize for being such a jerk, but he had to do this. He wanted to hear her admit that she loved him, with no fear or shame. He walked to stand behind her.

"What's the real reason you came here, Cat?" She started to turn around and face him. "No, please don't. Tell me why you had to see me."

"Taj, this is ridiculous. I had a surprise…."

"Why, Cat?" He interrupted, breathing the question in her ear.

She lifted her chin and said, "I wanted to see you."

"Why?"

She closed her eyes and whispered, "I missed you." Then she jumped when his loose hair caressed her shoulder. When his lips touched her nape, her body trembled.

Taj tasted her neck, moved slowly to her shoulder, then her exposed upper back. He felt the tremor that shook her. He breathed out in spasms. This was going to be a lot harder that he'd anticipated, he concluded. But he wasn't ready to give in, not yet. "Why did you miss me, Cat?"

Cat's body shook like a leaf. "I just did."

Wrong answer, he thought. He moved in front of her, trailed a line along her collar bone with his lips. His hands covered her breasts. She gasped. She didn't have a bra and the cotton material was no barrier to his fingers. Her nipples puckered. He smiled. *You can deny me with your mouth, but your body recognizes me, love.* But he wanted more, much more than mere physical gratification. "Why, Cat? The truth, please," he added softly.

"I spoke with the Lamberts and wanted to share the information I got from them." The words rushed from her lips, her voice shaky.

"You could have called." Everything she did indicated that she loved him. Why couldn't she speak those simple words? Didn't she trust him? Didn't she know that there was nothing on earth he wouldn't do for her? "The truth this time, Cat."

"Stop tormenting me, Taj," she whispered.

Who was tormenting who was debatable. "Tell me the truth, and I'll stop," he promised, but somehow he doubted that he could.

Cat took a deep breath. "I wanted to be with you."

"Doing what?"

"I don't know," she cried out.

Taj moved behind her again. His hands trembled as he pulled down her zipper. His fingers grazed her skin. Warm silk, he mused.

Another tremor shook her. His eyes crossed as the zipper went lower and he saw the black garter belt. She hadn't worn anything under her dress other the garter belt and stockings. Blood roared in his ears.

He stopped and took an agonized breath. His eyes closed, and he leaned forward until his lips touched her back. He bent lower and traced a line with his lips until he reached the gentle swelling of her buttocks. Why had she come to his office dressed like this? "You wanted to be with me this way?" he asked huskily.

Cat didn't speak. She stood very still, her breath struggling in her chest. With a flicker of his finger, Taj nudged the dress off her shoulder. It dropped to her hips where her arms were pressed against her body. His lips came back up to her upper back and then he moved in front of her.

She saw the look in his eyes and blinked.

He caressed her hips, her belly. "Is this what you wanted," he whispered.

"No…yes."

"My lips on you?" he asked and bit her shoulder.

"Yes," she cried out.

"My hands on you?" he asked hoarsely, his hands everywhere.

"Yes," she whimpered.

Then he stopped touching her. His breathing was labored. Finally, he looked into her eyes. "Do you want me inside you, Cat?"

Taj knew that the question was crude, but he hoped that the love in his voice and the fire in his eyes would make her see his words as what they were, the cry of a man who needed to be claimed. His fingers traced the lace of her garter belt, the curve of her buttocks, and the small of her back. "Do you?"

"Yes, Taj."

"Say it," he commanded in a husky voice. *Say that you love me damn it!* he wanted to shout.

Her lips trembled. "Please," she murmured.

"Please what? Please love me? Please kiss me? Please make me yours?"

He looked into her eyes. For a moment, time stood still. The air between them sizzled with energy, but she didn't speak. Taj waited. She still didn't say anything. Finally, Taj sighed in defeat. He took a step back, then another. What was the point? She had won. He would find Bobby's priest and leave her alone.

He turned and walked to his chair. He sat down and swiveled the chair so that he faced the windows. Defeat was a bitter pill. "Go home, Cat. There's nothing for you here."

"Yes, there is," she said in a firm voice.

Taj's head shot up, but he still didn't turn around. "Don't worry, I'll find Bobby's priest for you."

"That's not I want."

Something in her voice caused him to turn around and face her. Cat stepped forward. She gave her hips a tiny shake and the dress slid down to pool around her feet. Her chin went up a notch as her gaze challenged him. When his eyes ran over her, she said, "I want you. Please, love me, Taj. Please, make me yours. I need you."

Taj could only stare at her as she stood in his office with nothing on except a garter belt, stockings, and high-heeled sandals. Gloriously sexy and wicked, he thought. Need. Not exactly what he wanted to hear, but it would suffice for now, he decided.

Cat took tiny steps until she reached him. She pulled his shirt out of his pants. He didn't stop her. She started to undo his buttons. He just stared at her. When the buttons didn't obey her trembling fingers, she grabbed the lapels and yanked. Buttons flew across the room. He grinned at her. Then she put her hand on his chest, looked him straight in the eye, and said, "I want you inside me, Taj Taylor, now." Then she sank her hands into his hair and initiated a kiss.

For the next hour, he worshipped her in ways and places that defied description. One thing was for sure; he would never ever look at his desk, or chair, or anything in his office without remembering this day, the day Cat had called his bluff and showed him that he couldn't play games with her emotions.

They ended up in the bed in the spare room. After they were spent, he felt like a real heel, a first-class jerk for what he'd put her through. He watched her as she pulled her dress back on. She grinned at him when she caught his blatant stare. She had come to his office with seduction in mind. How often do you meet a woman that was this beautiful, and this smart, and this daring? Maybe he ought to accept his blessings and be happy.

"We need to talk," Taj said as he pulled on his pants and shirt.

"Oh?"

He sat on the edge of the bed and took her hand in his. "I behaved like a jerk earlier, Cat. I want to apologize for that. Will you forgive me?"

Cat cupped his cheek with her free hand. "Baby, there's nothing to forgive. I wish you could talk to me, though, tell me why you did it." She saw doubt cross his face. "Talk to me, please."

"No, love, my reasoning was warped. Forget it."

"Tell me anyway."

He lifted her chin and looked into her eyes. "I love you, Cat, and I want you to love me. Call me greedy or selfish, but I want the satisfaction of knowing that I have the love of the woman I adore." Wry amusement flickered in his eyes. "It was my intention to force you to admit that you loved me. A foolish notion. I apologize."

Dismayed, Cat realized that she and her insecurity had reduced this proud man to being manipulative. How could she have been so stupid? She loved this man with all of her heart. She ought to have admitted it earlier. It was too late to do it now. He wouldn't believe her. Heck, she wouldn't believe it herself if their situations were reversed.

She looked into his eyes and wanted to cry at her stupidity and insecurities. Because of those feelings, she had hurt the man she loved, the one man she would walk to the end of the world for. He wasn't foolish to want her love or to want to hear her say that she loved him. She was the one who was foolish for denying him something that had become as easy as breathing. She was the one who should be ashamed of what she had put him through.

"Don't apologize, baby, please," Cat said. "I'm the one who's been a fool. A proud, ignorant fool. And I hope with time you'll come to forgive me."

The frown on his face clearly stated that he was puzzled by her response. "I don't understand."

She was going to show him that she loved him with every breath she took. When the time was right for a confession, there would be no doubt in his mind that her declaration was genuine. She slipped her hand through his. "In due time, sweetheart. Now, where do you want to have our dinner? Here or at home?"

He smiled. "I know the perfect place." He picked up the bags of food she'd brought, grabbed her hand, and led her out of the room.

"Where are we going?" Cat asked as they left the office. She noticed that the floor was very quiet. Mrs. D. and the others were already gone for the day.

"The roof. You'll love the view."

"Do you do this often?" Cat asked as they started up the stairs.

"Eat up here? Hmm-mm. It's my good thinking spot." He released her hand to pull a bunch of keys from his pocket. He unlocked the door leading to the roof just as a security guard appeared below them. "Evening, Marcus. Is everything okay?"

"Fine, sir. Just starting my first rounds," the guard replied.

"We'll be up here for a little while."

"Okay, sir," the guard replied before walking away.

"So, how long have you owned this building, Taj?" Cat asked as he led her to the roof.

"Um, a little over three years." He explained about investing in the dotcom businesses and cashing in before the crash.

Cat looked around and laughed. "You definitely have quite a view."

"Yeah, office buildings and rooftops. You can't escape glass and concrete around here. Come on."

He led her to a wrought iron table and chairs that someone had cemented to the roof. It was the least romantic place she'd ever been and yet she was happy.

He pulled a handkerchief from his pocket and cleaned a chair. He gave a sweeping bow. "My lady."

Cat sat and smothered a giggle. "Did you put this up here?"

"It came with the building." He sat back and took a deep breath. "Fresh air, can you smell it?"

She removed the Styrofoam cups and boxes. "Are you kidding? I think pollution is at an all-time high this week. I saw it on the Weather Channel or somewhere."

He grinned. "Where's your sense of adventure, Ms. Simmons? We're in the penthouse."

"On the rooftop," she corrected.

"Sky for a ceiling."

"Smog."

"Enough room to stretch your legs."

"One misstep and you're five stories below."

He leaned forward and cupped her chin. "Has anyone ever told you that you're too literal-minded?"

Her grin widened. "Here." She passed him a plate filled with food and a fork. She'd brought Thai boneless chicken wings stuffed with glass noodles and vegetables, spicy and sour Po-Tak soup, squid salad tossed in spicy lime sauce, a Pad-Thai shrimp dish, and ginger chicken.

For a few minutes they concentrated on their meal. Despite her words, Cat loved being up on his roof. Maybe it was as close to a mountain as he could get here in Los Angeles.

"What are you doing next Saturday?" he asked, breaking into her reverie.

"Nothing that I know of." Her father's retirement party was that Friday, and that was about it.

"Want to come home with me?"

She scowled. "Simi Valley?"

"No, Montana. Grandpa Hawk is celebrating his eightieth birthday. I promise it will be fun. You've met some of the troops. They'll all be there. Mel and Blake included."

She nodded. "Sounds like it could be fun. Sure. I also need a date for my father's retirement party next Friday. Do you think you'll be available?"

Amused, he wriggled his brows while a smile played on his lips. "For you, love, I'm always available."

She smiled. "What about this Sunday?"

"Available."

"You don't know what I want to ask of you."

"Whatever it is, I'll do it."

She chuckled. "I'd like to invite you to my father's house for dinner. We should get there around four, and plan on staying until eight. Will that be okay with you?"

He took her hand in his and brought it to his lips. "Yes. Did I ever tell you that our paths—your father's and mine, that is—crossed when I was with the Bureau?"

"No."

"I didn't remember until the day I met your brother." He shrugged. "It was years ago. He might not remember me."

"I highly doubt it. Kenny remembered you."

"We'll see." He opened a bottle of iced tea Cat had brought with the food. "I learned something very interesting today."

"What?"

"The identity of the Russian woman Forster is protecting. Tanya Kovalenko."

Cat frowned. "Why does that name sound familiar?"

"Probably the news. I heard that the indictment was in the news." Taj explained what he'd learned about the kidnapping and murder of the Kovalenkos. "Not even the FBI knows where Tanya is hiding. She was supposed to be the star witness for the prosecution, but she changed her mind." Or somebody got to her, he added silently. "They were planning on getting her in the Witness Protection Program." Taj couldn't bring himself to tell Cat about Ray and the investigation, or his growing suspicions about Ray.

"And it's her prerogative to say no. I mean, she'd be living in fear for the rest of her life. The Mafia has a long memory. So the claim that she could be dead is just a smoke screen?"

"Yes. They didn't want Anatol's people getting ideas."

A shudder shook Cat's frame. "I don't blame her for refusing to testify. I wonder who Forster and Sergey grabbed from the *Santa Maria?*"

"My sources said they had two young girls with them when they crossed the border. A ten and a twelve-year-old," Taj added.

It was another hour before they left the roof. When they got downstairs, the security guard practically ran to them, yelling, "I tried to get the plate number but I couldn't, Mr. Taylor."

"The number of what plate?"

"The stupid driver that threw a rock at your car. By the time I opened the door and made it outside, the van had disappeared at the corner."

The van? Cat and Taj looked at each other, reaching the same conclusion.

Taj was the first one through the door. Cat was at his heels. The rear window of his Jaguar had a huge crack. While Taj cursed the air blue, Cat turned to the security guard. "You said "he." Did you see his face?"

The security smiled uncertainly, then he shook his head. "No, ma'am, I just used the term because...well, I assumed it was a man."

"Was it a black van?"

"Yes. How did you know?" the security guard asked.

She touched the agitated man's arm. "Lucky guess." Then she turned to Taj.

CHAPTER 19

"Baby, are you okay?" Cat asked.

"These people are getting too damn cocky," snarled Taj, a fierce look in his eyes.

Cat could see his anger escalate each time he looked at his car. "Let's go home, sit down, and analyze the situation," she begged.

"Do you want me to call the cops, Mr. Taylor?" the security guard asked.

"No thanks, Marcus, I'll take care of this. When did this occur?"

"A few minutes before you came downstairs, sir."

Taj looked up and down the deserted street. He took a step back, looked around. Then he stooped low to pick up something from underneath the car. It was the rock they'd used to smash his window. It had rolled under the car. A piece of paper was wrapped around it. "Look at this, Cat."

"What is it?"

"Looks like they've decided to leave us a note." He pulled the paper loose from the stone. It had been held with a rubber band.

Stop meddling in things that don't concern you, Taylor, or your girl-friend gets it!

They stared at the dirty piece of paper, which was slightly torn from the impact with the window and the ground, and then looked at each other.

"Let's go."

His words galvanized them both. Cat dashed to the passenger side of the car. Taj spoke briefly with the guard, then joined her. He took off with squealing wheels.

Fear clenched Cat's gut and refused to let go, but she didn't say anything to Taj. She wanted him to concentrate on his driving. Her eyes stayed glued to the words on the filthy piece of paper.

As soon they got home, she put the note on the counter. Taj joined her. The message in big letters was as definite as death. Someone was afraid of exposure. Who?

Cat looked at Taj's pensive expression. She could hear the wheels turning in his head as he contemplated the note and its implication. "Well?"

"What do you think?"

Cat looked at him, pursed her lips, then sighed. "Every time we've seen the black van, it's always been from afar. Whoever drives it has never tried to contact us or hurt us. Why tonight? Is there something or someone you are investigating now that you didn't include before? The anger is obvious. But it also smells of fear."

Taj scowled. "Ray Delaney."

"What? Your friend at the Bureau?"

"Ray is under investigation by the Justice Department. I didn't want to mention it earlier because they don't have proof yet, but they claim he's been influencing witnesses. I've tried to get in touch with him, even went to his house, but it's as though he's vanished. And the last time we met, he acted as though he found all the crap we're going through amusing. It didn't make sense."

Cat studied Taj's bleak expression. She could see that it bothered him that his friend could be dirty. She touched his hand, then took it in hers and started to rub it. "Do you think he's the one who got to Tanya?"

"I hate to admit it, but it's a possibility. When I went through the documents he gave me on Forster, the Kovalenko's story was missing. Was it a deliberate oversight? Why would he not want me to see it? I called the Bureau, and Cipher, who'd printed the original copies for Ray, got me another copy. I was shocked to learn that Ray had been suspended. When we spoke on Sunday, he didn't mention it, just told me to not to call him at the office because he was on a case." He rubbed his temple. "That was another lie. Why?"

"Maybe he didn't want you know that he'd been suspended."

"Or why, which doesn't make sense since we've been friends for years." He told her how they'd met in Quantico, how they'd been there for each other when Ray's fiancée, Diana, committed suicide and when Taj got shot.

Cat thought briefly, then shook her head. She could see that this new development was getting to him. "Baby, there could be an explanation for all this. Maybe Ray was just embarrassed to tell you that he was a suspect in an investigation."

Taj shook his head. "I don't believe in coincidences, Cat. Ray is the only person who knew that I was coming to see you that morning at the gym. When I spoke with him after the incident outside the gym, he stated that I used to be a profiler and should be able to figure out who was stalking me. I couldn't put a finger on what bothered me about our conversation at the time until now. Then there was his odd behavior when we met and discussed the black van. He was enjoying our predicament. In both cases, I ignored what I heard because he agreed to help me." Taj frowned. "Or maybe I just didn't want to question his odd behavior. Now I can't help but wonder what his motives are."

"You think he doesn't want you to find Forster and Tanya Kovalenko?"

Taj nodded briefly. "That might explain the missing paper, the accident, and tonight's warning note, but not the black van that followed Bobby."

"You're right. Lucille told me that ever since you started coming to my place, she's seen a black van parked at the end of the street. In fact, when she mentioned that, it got me to thinking about the night you helped me with my nephew. I could've sworn I saw a black van drive past my gate."

"One did. Ray doesn't own a black van, though."

This entire investigation was quickly eating away at her. She hoped they found whoever was behind the stalking soon. Shaking her head, she whispered, "Baby, let's go to bed. I'm too tired to think."

"My thoughts exactly."

Taj lifted her up from her stool and wrapped his arms around her. Cat slipped her hands under his shirt. His heart beat hard and true underneath her palm. She was beginning to see that he was her shelter. When chaos reigned, he was her haven, the one person she could always count on.

Taj had promised Cat to close the case by the end of the week, and he was determined to do it or die trying. Cat's new security system was set to go, at last. At least now he didn't have to worry about someone breaking into her home when he wasn't there. Bobby was staying with Kenny. They didn't need to worry about him, either.

On Thursday, he had another office meeting. The last two days had been hard on everyone, and the weary faces in the room were proof enough, Taj thought as he studied everyone.

He pinched the bridge of his nose and took a deep breath. "I know things have been crazy the last couple of days, and I appreciate your hard work." He made eye contact with every one. "Let's hear it. Mrs. D., anything new with His Eminence?"

Mrs. Dunlop smiled and leaned forward. "His office called. He's expecting you at eleven."

"Good. I don't know how you pulled that off, but thanks. Frank? What did you find at the monastery?"

"First, Sergey is officially in seclusion. But according to Brother Cornelius, he's helping Father Forster with a little problem. I think he's probably helping Forster keep an eye on Tanya and the two young charges. Brother Cornelius also said to apologize for the way they tried to make you two spend the night. Apparently, Forster had called and asked them to detain the two of you at the monastery."

"He must have wanted to make contact." If they'd spent the night, they wouldn't be dealing with all the mess they were now facing, Taj reflected with a frown. "What else?"

"The monk you wanted me to talk to, the one who brushed against you...." Frank looked grim. "He's nowhere to be found, but a monk's robe is missing."

"Damn!" The conclusion was obvious. "I guess we're thinking the same thing—someone pretending to be a monk messed with my brakes," Taj said.

Frank nodded. "Looks like it."

Taj grinned mirthlessly. "It's the most logical explanation." Now all he had to do was to find Ray and confront him. He had little doubt that his old buddy was working with the Russians. It was also time to tell his people everything. "I have something to tell all of you that may come as shock." He explained about Ray, the missing Kovalenko document, and the warning note. "I didn't ask Cipher if Ray was assigned to the Kovalenko case because the tension at Ray's office is running high. They don't believe he's done anything wrong." Taj stopped to study everyone's face. The room was very quiet. "I believe he did and is trying to take care of the loose ends. Ray has helped us over the years, and I still consider him a friend, but we must treat him with caution from now on. If anyone sees him, call me. Also, I don't want the fact that Ray's being investigated or that we suspect him of colluding with the Russians and masterminding this whole stalking business to leave this room. Everyone stay around the office. We'll have another meeting after I speak with the cardinal."

As they filed out of his office, he reached for his cell phone and dialed Cat's number.

—m—

Taj walked into the offices of the Archdiocese of Los Angeles. He was quickly ushered in to see Cardinal Joseph Mallory. The cardinal was in deep conversation with two men whom he quickly dismissed.

"Mr. Taylor," Cardinal Mallory said as he extended his hand toward Taj. He shook Taj's hand, then indicated a sofa.

"Your Eminence, I appreciate the time you've taken to see me," Taj stated politely.

The cardinal smiled gently. "Let's not be modest now, Mr. Taylor. I've been told a day doesn't pass that you don't either come to my office or call it. You've hounded my bishops, harassed my priests, and eavesdropped on my altar boys." He leaned back and said, "Why don't we start with your business before I explain why I summoned you here? What can I do for you?"

Summoned? Mrs. D. hadn't said anything about being summoned. "I need to know Father Forster's whereabouts, Your Eminence."

"Why?"

"I have a client who needs information from him."

"I see. Who's this client? And what's the nature of his association with Robert?"

"Robert John Simmons."

"Ah, Loretta Simmons' boy." When Taj couldn't mask his surprise, the cardinal smiled. "Loretta and Julia were wonderful servants of God, Mr. Taylor. Father Forster was their spiritual guide in New York, I believe, and here in Los Angeles. He administered *viaticum,* eh, last rites for both of them when their time arrived." He paused as he contemplated Taj. "Is that what this has been about? The calls from your office?"

"Yes, Your Eminence."

The cardinal leaned forward and shook his head. "I'm terribly sorry, Mr. Taylor. Until this morning, I'd naturally assumed you were a parishioner who was concerned about St. Vibiana. We've received numerous letters and calls about the center, some encouraging and others very unpleasant. Several people have also claimed to know the perpetrator and were willing to tell us if we would pay for the information. Private investigators have offered us their services. As you can imagine, we've been very busy."

"I have absolutely no interest in the events at St. Vibiana, sir."

"Unfortunately, Mr. Taylor, your attempts to reach Forster are why we're now here." He pushed a piece of paper across the table to Taj.

"We received this this morning."

Taj gave the note a brief glance; it was written in Russian. "Your Eminence, will you tell me the whereabouts of Father Forster?"

"Before speaking with Father Forster, we must first deal with this." He nodded at the paper in front of Taj. "It's a ransom note."

Taj started shaking his head. There was no way he was getting involved in a kidnapping situation, not when it involved Russian Mafia.

"Mr. Taylor, I wouldn't have summoned you here if we didn't need your help."

"Oh, no, sir, I can't. I'm through dealing with those crazy Russians. I'm planning on getting married and taking a very, very long vacation." Taj got up. "Contact the police or the FBI; I can't get involved in this."

The cardinal didn't stand up, but neither did he raise his voice. "Son, sit down." Taj fought with his conscience. Finally, his conscience won, and he sat. "They're threatening to kill Father Forster if we don't do as they say."

"You can afford whatever amount they're asking, Your Eminence. Believe me, you don't need me."

"But we do, son. They've insisted that we use you as an intermediary. And it's not money they are after." The cardinal waved at someone behind Taj. Taj turned to see who it was.

The man being wheeled toward them had an arm in a sling. One side of his face was swollen from a beating, and the other side had a huge bandage covering his eye. On his leg was a cast.

Taj didn't need an introduction. The ash-blonde hair and the tattoo of the Siberian tiger visible on his arm were dead giveaways. "Sergey," Taj whispered.

"Yes, they sent him with the note early this morning," Cardinal Mallory answered. "They want Tanya Kovalenko in exchange for Father Forster."

For a moment Taj just stared at Sergey. Then he asked the cardinal, "Can he talk?"

"Haltingly," the cardinal answered. "What do you want to know?"

"Everything," Taj said.

The cardinal nodded. "I'll translate."

Heavily padded again, Cat settled on the car seat, and adjusted her helmet. She was about to roll over a car. The car seat harness was tight-fitting. She wiggled her hips, but couldn't get comfortable. Then the SFX team adjusted the harness and made sure every pointed object in the car was perfectly covered with padding. When everything was to their satisfaction, they stepped back from the car.

Cat looked around the car. All the safety precautions had been taken. Nothing, she hoped, would go wrong. They'd fitted the car with a miniature gas tank, so there was minimal danger of explosion during the rollover. A roll cage had also been added inside the car to reinforce it against collapsing during the stunt.

Loren tapped her window from outside and asked, "How's the fit?"

"What?"

"Helmet and the harness…are they comfortable now?" he asked again.

"Just right," Cat answered him, giving him a thumbs-up sign.

"Pay close attention to the speed, Cat," Jed, the stunt coordinator, reminded her before stepping away from the car.

She looked through the sugar-glass windscreen at the mock street lined with cars. The pyrotechnic team had explosives taped under each car's chassis, ready to detonate them as Cat's car passed by. The last car was parked behind a pipe ramp. The ramp was set at an angle so that when the right side of Cat's car ran over it, that side would be lifted up. And at just the right speed, the car would roll over and land on its roof.

Cat understood why Jed had reminded her to check the speed. The rollover was tricky, depending very much on the ramp angle and the speed of the car. If the angle of the ramp was too steep or the car speed too high, the car would do a complete flip and land right side up again.

That wasn't what they wanted for this scene.

After a last minute pep talk, all the personnel moved back, gave the signal, and Cat started the car. As they'd done in the rehearsals, she accelerated until she reached the desired speed.

Sweat broke out on her brow and though her heart beat faster than normal, her eyes stayed focused on the other cars. Gripping the steering wheel a little tighter, she approached the first car. The pyrotechnician in charge punched the detonating button at just the right moment and the car was flung away from Cat's bigger car. The rest of the sequence went just as smoothly.

—w—

Taj arrived when Cat's stunt car was close to the last car. He watched as the explosives went off, saw her car flip in the air, roll over once and land on its roof. It skidded for a while before coming to a stop. He held his breath until he saw the safety team remove her from the upside-down car. She gave a few people hugs and shook a few hands before heading to the trailer to change. He knew that this was her last stunt for the movie, and he couldn't be happier. If only Bobby's case were concluded too. Just thinking about it was depressing.

When Cat stepped down from the trailer, Taj wrapped her in his arms, a slight grin on his face. "That's the last one, right?"

"Yes." She leaned back and studied his face. He gave her a brief kiss. She still frowned. "What's wrong?"

He took her hand and started for her car. "What makes you think something is wrong?"

"You're tense."

A wry amusement flickered in his eyes. "I saw the cardinal today."

"Ah. He wasn't helpful."

"Yes and no."

"I hate it when you say that."

A slight smile settled on his lips. "Why?"

"Because I never like what follows."

They stopped beside her car. He'd driven her to the studio that morning, then borrowed her car because both of his were in the shop. He opened the door for her. "You're not going to like this."

She rolled her eyes. "Thanks for the extra warning. What's the good news?"

"I know where Forster is."

"Really? Oh, baby, that's just wonderful. We can talk to him and forget we ever had any dealings with the Russians."

"I'm afraid it won't be that easy. The bad news is that the Russians have kidnapped Forster. They want to trade Tanya Kovalenko for him."

Cat's eyes narrowed. "The cardinal told you this?"

Taj nodded.

"Why?"

"Because he wants me to do the trading."

Cat's jaw dropped. "What? After refusing to see you for weeks, now he wants your help? The nerve. You're through dealing with these guys, baby." She gripped his hand. "Don't do it, Taj. Let the police deal with it."

"That's what I told the cardinal." Actually he'd told the cardinal that he would think about it. By the end of this evening, he'd decide whether to help them or not. Only then would he discuss the details with Cat. "I still have a few things I need to figure out."

Cat cut him a suspicious look, but she didn't pursue the subject. He knew she was thinking through everything he'd told her. The drive to her house was accomplished in silence. As soon as they got there, she busied herself with starting coffee. Then she removed defrosted pieces of chicken breast from the fridge and marinated them. She pulled out pasta and put a pot of water on the stove top.

Taj didn't say anything as he watched her. He knew she was organizing her thoughts. Every time she was worked up about something, she kept herself busy until she was ready to talk. So he waited. But after about ten minutes, he couldn't take it anymore.

"Talk to me, baby."

"I'm almost done," she answered quietly. She poured each of them a cup of coffee, added cream to hers, and then carried the cups to the counter. She sat beside him, and for a moment didn't say anything. Biting her lower lip, she studied him. "I know there's something you're not telling me. If I didn't love you so much or know you so well, I'd feel that you didn't trust me."

Taj perked up. "Say that again."

"I'd feel that you didn't…"

"The other part," he interrupted.

She reached up and touched his cheek. "I love you, Taj Taylor. I love you so very much that if anything were to happen to you, I don't know what I'd do. This thing with Cardinal Mallory…." She paused when emotions blocked her throat. "Promise me you'll be careful, okay?" she finished in a whisper.

Words seemed to fail Taj for a moment. Cat loved him. Finally! Finally she was admitting it. He lifted her chin and stared into the depth of her eyes. "I have so much to live for that I couldn't afford to be careless, love." He leaned forward and claimed her lips in a brief kiss. When he lifted his head, he murmured, "I love you."

Cat gave him a radiant smile. "I know. Thank you for being patient with me."

He caressed her cheek. "I knew you wouldn't resist me for long."

"Yeah, the Taylor charm," she murmured with a giggle and stood up. "So, what would you like to eat tonight?"

He grabbed her arm and stopped her from moving. "There's more, Cat."

She sank back on her stool with a frown. "What is it?"

"I know who was shadowing Bobby."

Her eyes rounded. "They weren't the same ones after us?"

"No. Bobby said he saw two men and a priest, right? They were actually two men and a woman dressed as a priest. The woman was Tanya Kovalenko. Father Forster waited until he felt it was safe to remove her from the center. He sent two men from Sergey's former gang to get her. When they saw Bobby, they assumed he was a member of a local gang Anatol was using to watch the center. After following Bobby for a couple of days, they realized he was a harmless student and backed off."

Cat frowned. "Who told you this?"

"Sergey, Father Forster's friend from the hermitage."

"You talked to Sergey?" When Taj nodded, Cat added, "Baby, you'd better start from the beginning. I want to know when and where you saw him and what he said."

"He was at Cardinal Mallory's office this afternoon when I stopped there. The people holding Father Forster beat him up pretty bad, but he still managed to fill in the blanks in the Kovalenko story. Tanya Kovalenko recently migrated from Russia and was waiting for her husband and their two children to join her when she and her brother were kidnapped. After she escaped the kidnappers and they were apprehended, she agreed to become a state witness and to join the Witness Protection Program. But while under FBI protection, one of the agents slipped her a note that said her family would be executed if she testified against the Anatols."

"Did she identify the agent?" she asked cautiously.

A frown crossed Taj's eyes. "You're wondering if it was Ray, aren't you? I did too, but Sergey said they never asked her. The day she left the Bureau, Tanya went straight to Father Forster for help. Forster used his connections to get her children and her husband on a ship bound for America."

"The *Santa Maria*," Cat murmured, then stood up to refill their cups. "Go on."

"While Tanya was hiding in that tiny secret room at St. Vibiana, Father Forster was receiving threats from Anatol's men that they would torch the center if he didn't produce her. Father Forster kept saying that he didn't have her. Thank you." He accepted the cup and turned around to face the counter when she sat down. "Forster evacuated the center, placed the women under the protection of the nuns at Corpus Christi in Menlo Park. Tanya was the last to be evacuated. Then he laid low until it was time to pick up her children and her husband from the

Santa Maria. They intercepted the ship before Anatol's men could get to them and brought them back to the States. By the time Anatol's men caught up with Forster and Sergey, Tanya and her family were gone. Sergey didn't tell me where they were or whether she was still going to testify. Now Anatol wants Tanya in exchange for Forster."

"Then how are you going to do an exchange when you don't have her?"

"That's where your brother comes in. The exchange is to be done tomorrow, which gives us time to coordinate things with local law enforcement. We'll use an undercover cop to replace Tanya Kovalenko. I'm to meet Kenny and Frank," he checked his watch, "in less than thirty minutes to discuss the details. I promise to be back in time for dinner." And to tell her about Ray, he added silently.

"I'll keep it warm." She caressed his cheek. "Hurry back." She saw him to the door, then went back to the kitchen and her cooking. She started on the salad.

Not twenty minutes had passed when her phone rang. She transferred the salad spoons to one hand and reached for it. "Yes?"

"Catherine?"

Cat frowned. Who was it? "Uh, yes?"

"Catherine, dear? This is Lucille Lambert."

Ah, her neighbor. Her frown deepened. "Lucille, is everything okay?"

"You tell me, my dear. Your relative is here."

Relative? What relative? "I'm sorry, Lucille, I don't understand."

"Don't you remember you told me that I should let you know if your relative with the black Honda Odyssey arrived? You said that you don't want him to go to the wrong house? Well, I was watching a movie when a black van pulled up in front of your gate. I wouldn't have called, but he's been there for at least five minutes. I wanted to make sure you were home. If you weren't, I was going to invite him to wait at my house."

The wooden salad spoons dropped from her hand as heart dropped to the bottom of her stomach. The black van was at her gate? Now?

"Thanks, Lucille. I'm home, definitely home." She put the phone down as her eyes darted around her kitchen. She was home, all right—home alone.

CHAPTER 20

Who was out there? What did they want? Her hands felt cold and clammy. Realizing that she couldn't just sit there and wait for whoever it was to break into her house, Cat got busy. She switched off the stove but left the pasta in the pot, unplugged her George Foreman grill but left the chicken in it.

Now what? She knew she ought to do something, but for the life of her she didn't know what. She took several deep breaths to clear her head. Think, Catherine, think.

The security system! Yes, she would check the monitor.

Her heart beating hard, fear clenching her gut, Cat scurried from the kitchen. The thought that they'd probably seen her silhouette against the window, knew she was home, almost overwhelmed her. She paused near the living room and chewed on her lower lip.

Get a grip, Catherine, she admonished herself. This was no time to panic. Swallowing hard, she took several deep breaths to calm herself. She was turning to go to her sewing room when her eyes fell on her cell phone lying beside Taj's jacket.

She grabbed it and bolted from the room.

As she speed-dialed Taj's number, she stopped before the security monitor and directed the camera at the front door. Then she directed the camera to the gate. There it was, the van. Though it looked menacing, seeing it somehow calmed her down. Just as she sat back on her haunches to wait, Taj picked up his phone.

"Taj…Taj, the black van is at my gate." To her dismay, her voice ended in a sob.

"What?" Taj shouted in disbelief.

"I don't know what to do or what they want. Lucille said they've been there for a while." She heard muffled sounds, as though Taj were yelling at someone.

Then his voice came back stronger again. "I'm here, baby. I'm on my way. Are you okay?"

"Yes." But she wasn't, she added silently. She was close to losing it.

"Where are you?"

"In the sewing room. In front of the security monitor. I can see the van."

"Don't communicate with them under any circumstances, Cat, okay? Don't talk…"

"Oh, no!" Cat gasped at what she suddenly saw on the screen. Bobby? She dropped to her knees and gripped the monitor. It was Bobby. How did they get to him? He looked disheveled and disoriented. Behind him stood a huge man who looked mean and dangerous.

Cat pressed the communication button with a shaking finger. She yelled, "Bobby! Bobby, what did they do to you?"

"Ms. Simmons, listen very carefully," the man with Bobby said in a heavy Russian accent. "If you want your brother to live, you'll come out now."

"What do you want?"

"Ms. Simmons, move now or he'll get it!" He pointed a gun against Bobby's head.

Where were her neighbors? Why weren't they coming out to help her brother? Tears filled her eyes.

All at once, she saw Bobby elbow the man, lunge forward, and press the intercom. "Don't do it, sis!" he yelled.

The man whirled around and slammed his gun into the back of Bobby's head. Cat's mouth opened in a silent scream as he crumpled to the ground.

"I'm coming out, you bastards. Leave him alone," she yelled.

As she turned to run outside, she realized she still had the phone in her hand. She slapped it to her ear. "Taj, are you there?"

"Yes, I heard everything. I'm coming, baby, stall them. Don't go out there."

"I have to, Taj. I have to. Bobby…oh, God."

"Take my jacket, Cat."

"What?"

"Take my jacket. I left it in the living room. Remember Menlo Park…the transmitter…I have one on the jacket. I'll hear everything you say…everything they say…just take it. I'll find you, baby. Wherever they take you, I'll find out. I promise."

Cat dropped the phone and grabbed Taj's jacket. She shoved her arms through the sleeves as she ran from the house.

Cat's call had found Taj, Kenny, Carl, and Frank formulating the best plan for rescuing Father Forster. That immediately became secondary as soon as Taj heard Cat's frightened voice. He jumped up and yelled to Kenny and Frank that the men in the black van were at Cat's.

Now they were all in Kenny's car, the siren blaring as they passed the other cars, jumped lights, and raced toward Cat's house. Seated beside Kenny, Taj had the headphones on his ears, trying to pick up any transmission from the transmitter on the jacket Cat was wearing. In the middle of electronics-ridden West Hollywood, it was a near-impossible feat, but it was better than letting fear and anger eat at him.

Tension froze his insides. All the years of training came to nothing. He didn't know how to deal with the kind of panic that was gripping him from the torturous images flashing through his head. That Cat could get hurt was something he didn't need to imagine. He couldn't afford to, not now. But his gut instinct told him that if they didn't intercept the van before it reached its destination, things could get worse, a lot worse.

"Can't find anything," he muttered in frustration. "Have you located the van yet?" he asked Frank, who was seated in the back with Carl. Frank was busy typing on a host PC laptop, trying to access the GPS tracking device that was imbedded in the lining of the jacket Cat was wearing.

"Give me a minute, boss," Frank murmured. "The mapping program is already running."

"We don't have a minute, Frank. Get us their position ASAP."

Kenny, who'd been quiet since they left Taj's office, finally said, "I still think we need to call for backup, Taylor."

Taj shook his head. "And give them an excuse to hurt her? No way. We're using the siren until we spot the van, then it goes off. I'm not about to give those bastards any excuse to act stupid."

"Okay, Taylor, I'm letting you make the call, but if I realize emotions are clouding your judgment, I'm taking over."

In a different situation, Taj would have laughed at Kenny's statement. He never let emotions cloud his judgment. No, that was a lie, he thought with a frown. He had almost driven Cat away with his self pity, doubts, and impatience. He couldn't afford another mistake like that. "You do that, Simmons."

"What are a transmitter and a GPS receiver doing on your jacket anyway?"

"I make it a rule to always wear a transmitter and a GPS receiver in dangerous situations. The same goes for anyone who works with me. Frank here is the electronics man on my team. He modifies the pieces to accommodate our needs."

Frank interrupted them with, "They just left Hammond Street and are now on West Sunset heading east."

At Frank's words, Kenny turned left on Fairfax and headed north. Then he said to Taj, "If Ray's behind this, I've got to give it to him, he's being too darn methodical. Using Bobby as a decoy to lure Cat out, making sure you were out of the house before they made their move. He must have had someone watching Cat's house."

"Lucille said there've been strange cars parked on their street since this mess started." Taj turned to look at Frank. "We'll be entering Sunset Boulevard in a few seconds. Where are they now?"

"Still on Sunset Boulevard," Frank answered.

Taj sat back. It was after seven o'clock, and darkness was quickly shrouding the city. What did the kidnappers want with Cat? Could Ray be behind this kidnapping?

Frank interrupted his musings. "They've turned left on North Fuller Avenue."

"Turn off the siren, Kenny," Taj instructed. "We don't want them to get spooked."

They followed Frank's directions—kept going for half a mile on Fuller Avenue, turned right on another avenue, went on for a quarter of a mile before parking on the side of the road.

"They've stopped somewhere up that road," Franks said, pointing to his left.

Taj read the sign. "Outpost Drive." Suddenly, Taj's body jerked when he heard Cat's voice on the receiver. "I'm getting a signal," he said. "I hear Cat's voice. See if you can find a place to park, Kenny." If anyone saw the truck, the siren on the dashboard would buy them time, but not much. In this neighborhood, they probably called the mayor or chief of police if they saw a police car was parked outside their home.

As Kenny drove and looked for a place to park, Taj removed the headphones and turned up the volume on the receiver so they could all hear what was transpiring.

—⁓⁓⁓—

When they pulled her from the van, Cat saw trees, shrubs, and more trees. Hoping for a miracle, she glanced behind them as her abductors pulled her toward a house which seemed to be part of a compound. Where was Taj? Would he find her? A shiver raked her body. Who had kidnapped her? Why? Was Bobby okay?

Two men silently appeared from one end of the compound, each carrying a rifle. Her skin chilled, and she felt the blood drain from her face. "Why are those two men carrying rifles?" she asked.

"Shut up and move!" one of her abductors snarled. "I've had enough of your nonstop chattering."

Truth was, she'd had enough of it too. It took too much energy to prattle nonstop like a giggly teenager. She'd wanted to keep Taj informed of their whereabouts, but in the process she'd kept pissing off her abductors. Wherever Taj was, she sure hoped he'd been listening. "Other than the priest, what else are you guys guarding? Surely not the mastermind of this abduction? Never knew kingpins lived in such affluent neighborhoods. But then again, what do I know of the Russian Mafia?"

"I don't care what *he* said about not touching her. If she doesn't shut up, I'll do it for her," the same abductor said, but the other one just yanked her forward.

Who had ordered them not to hurt her? She quieted when they led her through the door and into a large room with open-beamed ceiling and stone floor warmed by touches of dark woodwork and cabinetry. Wall-to-wall glass was everywhere. It was a beautiful room, one that she would've appreciated had she not be brought there under duress, Cat mused.

One of her abductors said something in Russian, and the other one laughed. The one who laughed grabbed her arm. She tried to wrench it away, but he dug his fingers into her skin. When Cat turned to glare at him, she saw in his eyes that he wanted her to give him an excuse to really hurt her; the fight drained out of her.

With the other man behind them, the man led her through a door to their left, up the stairs, and down the hall to a room that was clearly a man's private sitting area. Done in earthy colors and hunter green, the room had gas logs burning in the fireplace. Gilded lamps with golden shades glowed at the corners of the room, and paintings of wild mustangs hung on the walls. A table for two was set at a corner.

"Why am I here?" she asked, but the two men smirked at her.

Cat looked around for an escape route. The door to the hall was her abductors were in the way. Another door, partially open, clearly led to a bedroom. A king-size bed was visible.

Cat was surprised when the bedroom door opened wider and a bronze-complexioned man, early-to-mid thirties, stepped into the room. He smiled.

Could this man with immaculately groomed hair and a charming smile be the one behind the kidnapping? What about the mayhem they'd gone through these past weeks? Unless they raised them darker in Moscow, this man was no Russian.

He was dressed casually, in loose white pants and shirt, perfect attire for an evening at home, and was holding a glass of wine

"Ah, Cat Simmons. How wonderful to see you again," he said.

Cat's eyes connected with his, and her insides turned to ice. His voice might have been warm, but his eyes were the coldest she'd ever seen. Panic crept up her chest, making her fight for breath. Still, she managed to sound calm when she said, "Again? Do I know you?"

"We have a mutual acquaintance," the man answered easily. He put his drink down.

Could this man be Ray Delaney? She managed to inject amusement into her voice when she said, "I find that very unlikely. I don't make friends with people who'd know anyone who kidnapped people for a living."

The man studied her, his eyes narrowing. Then he turned to the abductors and jerked his thumb toward the door. The men grinned at Cat, then started for the door.

This wasn't good, Cat told herself as she watched the men leave. The security she'd enjoyed from wearing Taj's jacket was fast disappearing. Fear wrapped around her throat. When she turned to face her host, she found his calculating, cold eyes on her, monitoring her reaction. A slight smile played on his lips.

"I was just about to have dinner. Would you like to join me in a pre-dinner drink?"

The thought of sitting across the table from this man was enough to make her retch.

Her chin lifted. "I'm sorry, but I don't dine or drink with men who get cheap thrills stalking and harassing innocent people and then kidnapping them. I'd rather call and seek help for my brother, whom your men left unconscious at my gate or join Father Forster. I assume you have him."

"Oh, yes, I do," the man bragged. He moved closer. "I'm trying to understand what *he* sees in you. You have too much sass for my taste." He took a sip of his drink, and paused to study her face before moving to the rest of her body. "But maybe you're a tigress in bed."

A chill rushed across Cat's skin and her heart squeezed in her chest. Was he talking about Taj? "I'm sorry, I don't understand."

He moved closer. "Remove the jacket."

"I beg your pardon?"

"I want you to be comfortable, Cat. You and I are going to keep each other company for awhile, so the least you can do is let me see the merchandise. Taj won't mind. He'll probably understand the irony of it all."

Keep each other company? Merchandise? Fear twisted her gut, fast and swift. "What do you want from me? Who are you?"

"What the hell was that man talking about?" Kenny asked Taj. They were creeping behind the wall surrounding the house. They'd left their car a few houses down the road. "Who's he?"

For a beat Taj didn't speak. He hadn't uttered a word since they switched off the transmitter, but his clenched jaw and the muscle twitching in the corner of his eyes indicated his rage. He said through gritted teeth, "Ray Delaney. I thought the bastard was my friend. When I remember all the crap he's put us through, I want to…." His fist clenched. He wanted to punch Ray's face in. He wanted to rip him apart piece by piece. He wanted…. He wanted to know what he had done to make Ray want to hurt him or someone he loved.

Kenny interrupted his thoughts. "What is his beef with you, Taylor? Why has he kidnapped Cat?"

Taj didn't want to explain Ray's motives. He wanted to stay focused on what was important, which was getting into that house, getting Cat, and getting out. Even the rage he felt toward Ray was counterproductive. He said impatiently, "Ray and I were in Quantico together, then went our separate ways. We met again in L.A. The day I took a bullet, we had traded duties because he was planning on proposing to the woman of his dreams. Later, he sat by my side until my family arrived. Over the years, he's supplied me with information, and I him. I've no idea where this hatred came from."

For a few seconds, no one said anything. Then Frank broke the silence with, "I wonder how tight his security is."

"Cat saw two men with rifles," Taj said. "I'm assuming those are the ones patrolling the ground. Then there're the two abductors. Assuming Forster is here, there might be one or two guards with him. I'd say about seven and counting." Taj glanced at Carl, then Kenny, and finally Frank. "The four of us can take them."

"We've the element of surprise on our side," Kenny added.

"I hope so," was Taj's answer.

"And let's hope they don't have dogs," Frank added. "I hate dogs."

"If they have security cameras, we'll need your assistance, Frank, dogs or no dogs," Taj added as they prepared to scale the wall. "I don't know if you noticed that they use Dorgan Security systems, the very system you were toying with before this case got crazy."

"Then I have your back, boss," Frank replied. "Just get me over the damned wall."

One by one, they went over the wall and landed on the soft grass on the other side. The lower part of the compound was terraced with trees and shrubs everywhere. Like shadows, the four men moved swiftly through the compound, using the trees and shrubs as cover.

Taj still couldn't believe that he'd gotten played by his old buddy Ray. He'd thought he could convince Ray to turn himself in and take his chances with the legal system, but abducting Cat went beyond covering his tracks. The way he'd spoken to her and his words made it obvious that this was personal.

Taj pushed the thoughts aside when he saw two guards come around the corner of the house and pause to share a light. Then one started toward them while the other one headed to the back of the house. Taj pointed at the guard, then tapped his chest. "He's mine," he whispered to the others.

The man came closer until he reached the wooden steps close to Taj. Taj waited until he was at the bottom step, then leaped on him and knocked him to the ground. Before the man could recover, he rammed his head against the step. The man went limp. Taj dragged his body under a tree, took his rifle and passed it to Frank.

Then Taj signed Frank and Carl to head to their right, and Kenny to head left. "Let's get her out."

"Ray Delaney, at your service," the man told Cat with a charming smile.

Cat somehow managed to keep a blank expression on her face. "I don't think I've heard of you."

The smile disappeared from his face. "Taj never mentioned me?"

She shrugged. "We rarely discuss old acquaintances."

His eyes narrowed, then a sardonic smile crossed his lips. "You almost had me there. Of course he's mentioned me. His agency couldn't survive without me. I'm the one who supplies him with information whenever he needs it. I'm the one who bails him out whenever he gets in trouble. Everything *he's* accomplished as a private detective is because of me. *I* gave it to him. I've waited for a very long time for this moment, to have him exactly where I want him."

Cat noticed that his eyes looked glazed. He was probably remembering the past, when Taj supposedly caused him pain. She had to make him focus on the present, on her. He had to see her as a potential ally. "What did he do to you, Mr. Delaney? I know that Taj can at times be very insensitive." What a total lie, Cat thought. "And self-absorbed," another lie. "And when on a case, he becomes totally engrossed in it, to the exclusion of everything else." She would tell whatever lies she needed to find out what was going on here.

Ray studied her for a beat before saying, "It started in Quantico. Women always preferred him. I didn't mind, not in the least, until Diana came along. She was different. Special. Sensitive." His eyes narrowed. "He treated her callously—toyed with her emotions, broke her heart, then left her without a backward glance."

That didn't sound like the Taj she knew, Cat mused. "Who's Diana?"

"The woman I loved, the woman who should have been my wife. After we finished training, Diana and I stayed in touch. When I moved to Los Angeles, she moved here to be with me, I thought. But it was because of Taj. She never got over him. It was his fault she committed suicide."

Sounded as though the woman was mentally ill, Cat concluded, and had gotten fixated on Taj, but when her affections weren't returned, went crazy. Unfortunately, Ray didn't seem to see it that way, and now he wanted Taj to pay for it with his life. But not if she could help it, Cat vowed.

None of her thoughts showed on Cat's face, though, and she injected sympathy into her voice. "I'm so sorry for your loss, Ray."

His face was distorted with rage and his eyes locked on her with a burning intensity. "Taj Taylor is a terrible man without a conscience. He uses people. He would've used you too." He drained his drink. "I'm not a bad man, Cat, but it's my right to even the score. If not for me, then for Diana."

Cat's eyes widened when she saw him pull a gun out of his pocket. From the look of things, he intended to shoot her, not Taj. He meant for Taj to lose her just as he had lost Diana.

With her heart in her throat, Cat tried to think what to do, what to say. Could she count on Taj arriving in time to save her? She'd try to keep him talking, keep him drinking. "May I have that drink now, Ray?"

With a calmness that belied her terror, she removed Taj's jacket and dropped it on a chair. Ray's eyes followed her movements. Then she lifted her chin and pushed her breasts forward. Ray swallowed as his eyes touched her chest, the skin visible between her tank top and pants. "I'm parched, Ray. Do you mind?" Her hand went to her throat, caressing it. His eyes followed her hands.

"Sit." He indicated a chair with his gun. "Any preference?"

"Chardonnay is fine." Her heart racing, she looked around for a weapon. The gilded picture frame on the side table could be a weapon, but it wasn't close enough. "You have a beautiful home, Ray."

He poured her drink, carried it to her, then sat down opposite her, his eyes never leaving her face. The hand with the gun went to rest on his armchair. "Not mine. It's Anatol's secret hideout."

The man who was after Tanya Kovalenko? Ray must be Anatol's inside man at the Bureau.

As if to answer her question, Ray said, "These men are Anatol's, but presently mine to command and use until I bring in Tanya. Yes, I can see from your expression that you know who Tanya Kovalenko is. I was the inside man who made sure she didn't join the Witness Protection Program." He studied Cat, gauging her reaction. "An eye for an eye is one of the most profound sayings in the bible. Had Taylor not called me with the news that he too was looking for Father Forster, we could have had this over and done with a week or so ago, Cat. But I decided to let him do my work for me. I knew Taj would call me all along for information, and I could follow his investigation. If he found Forster, I knew we could make him tell us where Tanya is." He smiled. "I wish I'd seen his face after his brakes failed. Oh, yes," he said at her expression. "I was the monk you brushed against." He laughed maniacally.

The sound reverberated in the room, fraying Cat's already fragile nerves. The man had lost it. His hatred for Taj had eaten at him until there was nothing left but a rotten core.

He'd lost her. That was all Taj could think about as he burst through the door. There was fire in his eyes, chaos in his mind, and cold hard ice glazing his heart. He didn't give Ray a chance to react. He jumped on him and the two of them rolled onto the floor.

He heard someone scream, a woman. Cat? Pure adrenaline shot through him.

The struggle for the gun was brief. Ray wasn't a weakling, but Taj had more than brute strength urging him on. As he twisted Ray's hand, the gun went off and the sound of the shot echoed in the room. Voices and running feet came toward the room.

Taj sprang to his feet, picked the gun from Ray's hand and threw it out of reach. He turned toward Cat, expecting to see her still body lying on the floor. What he saw froze him momentarily. She was seated on the floor, tears in her eyes, but very much alive.

"Baby? Somebody call for an ambulance," he yelled. He dropped to his knees and reached for her. She looked as though she would shatter if he touched her.

"You came," she gulped. "I waited and waited."

At the sound of her voice, he grabbed her close. She felt so fragile in his arms, still, he held on tight. "I'm sorry I was late. Tell me he didn't hurt you. Tell me that you're okay."

She shuddered. "I'm fine." Her eyes went to Ray. "Is he…?"

He pressed her face into his chest. Frank was checking Ray's pulse. Frank nodded, answering Cat's half-spoken question. "He'll live," Taj said out loud.

"He was going to kill me," she whispered. "He blamed you for Diana's suicide. He wanted you to suffer, the way he'd suffered…he's suffering."

Diana? Why should Ray blame him for Diana's death? All he'd ever done was tolerate the woman for Ray's sake. "We'll talk later, baby." At that moment, Kenny and Father Forster walked into the room. Despite everything, the priest hadn't been harmed. Cat moved from the safety of Taj's arms and went to hug her brother.

Then they heard running footsteps, the door swung open, and

TIMELESS DEVOTION

Cat's father stormed into the room. For seconds, though it seemed like forever to Taj who was watching them, everyone froze. Then, as though drawn by a magnet, father, son, and daughter converged in the center of the room.

EPILOGUE

Cat sipped her drink and studied the faces at her father's retirement party. The room was filled with L.A.P.D.'s finest. Drinks were flowing, and the music was loud. The hard-working, demanding, but respected man the men had portrayed in their speeches was one that Cat and Bobby knew too well. But they were beginning to see a different side of their father now.

As long as she lived, Cat mused, she would never forget the fire in their father's eyes when he'd walked into that room, or his shaking body as he'd embraced them. The thought of almost losing one of his children had awakened something in her father that was slowly changing him. She'd seen it in his eyes on Saturday at his house. For once, he'd held his grandchild in his arms and played with him. Then there was the laughter in his eyes when they'd all paired up to play games, and the genuine interest he'd taken in Taj when Cat had officially introduced him.

"What's going on in my beautiful fiancée's head?" Taj whispered in her ear.

Cat turned and smiled. He gave her a passionate kiss, ignored the jab she gave him, and deepened it. When he lifted his head, she murmured, "Half the room's watching us. Will you behave?"

He picked up her hand and kissed her palm. The platinum and diamond ring he'd placed there yesterday winked at him. "That kiss should show them that you belong...we belong together. That ring hasn't stopped them from ogling you, the damned lechers."

"They just want to know about Ray, and how you saved me from his crazy plans."

"Could have fooled me, the way they keep looking down there." He glanced at her cleavage. Cat smothered a giggle. "Besides, you were doing just fine before I arrived. Scared me half to death, to be honest. Speaking of Ray, I hope he gets help while in jail."

The bullets had punctured Ray's lungs and passed right through. He was recovering nicely, though under constant guard. He was on suicide watch. "I almost felt sorry for him when he told me about Diana."

"Yeah, the poor, bipolar woman. Someone has to make him understand that the woman was seriously ill."

"And that the love she had for you became hatred when she couldn't have you," Cat finished.

"Did you read Ray's confession?" Kenny said from behind her. Cat turned to look at her brother, who had his arm around his wife's waist.

"Yeah, we both did," Taj said. "It's amazing what a little investigation can unearth."

"Which I started by my foolishness," Bobby said, coming from behind them.

Cat hugged her younger brother. "When did you get here?"

"Awhile ago. I was with Dad over there," he lifted his glass and indicated behind him. Their eyes turned toward the direction he'd pointed. Their father was seated with his old cronies, but his eyes were on his children. He saluted them with his drink. They saluted him back. Kenny and Brianna excused themselves soon after.

Cat could have sworn that her father's eyes were bright with tears. Yes, the old man was changing. She turned to Bobby. "Don't ever say that you were foolish to want to know the truth, little brother. If it weren't for your so-called foolishness, Father Forster wouldn't have been rescued. And if he hadn't been rescued, he wouldn't be able to carry on with his work. I hope what he told you helped with your questions. But if not, there's always DNA testing."

Bobby shook his head. "I don't need any DNA testing. I've got all of that out of my system, I'm glad to say." He turned to Taj. "I haven't yet thanked you, Taj, for everything," he said. "If it weren't for you…." A young, female officer walked by and smiled at Bobby. "I'll finish expressing my gratitude later, future brother-in-law," Bobby murmured, his eyes on the woman. "I need to discuss handcuff mechanics with that beautiful officer." He hurried after her.

"Ah, the thrill of new love," Cat mused aloud.

Taj's brows shot up. "New love?" He tucked a stray hair behind her ear. "Sweetheart, love, new or old, is synonymous with thrill, excitement, pleasure. I'd like to think that when we're old and wrinkled, you'll still bring me lots and lots of pleasure."

Cat hugged his arm. "And you me, my love. Do you want to say our good-byes, so we can start working on it?"

"Thought you'd never ask," he answered naughtily. They both laughed.

ABOUT THE AUTHOR

Born in Kenya and raised in Nairobi, **Bella McFarland** graduated with a B.S. Chemistry from the University of Nairobi. She came to the U.S. in 1991 to pursue a doctorate degree in Organic Chemistry at Utah State University. Bella is a stay-at-home mom raising her four daughters and one son.

Bella resides in River Heights, a picturesque little town in northern Utah. Although Bella likes chemistry, her real passion is reading, writing and painting.

She's already published two books, *One Day at a Time* and *Vows of Passion*. Currently, she's busy working on her next novel. She is a member of Romance Writers of America (RWA) and URWA, Utah Chapter of RWA. You can e-mail her at **bellamcfarland@netscape.net** or visit her at www.bellamcfarland.com.

BEYOND RAPTURE

BY

BEVERLY CLARK

Release Date: September 2005

CHAPTER ONE
New Orleans

"That's right, Lily pad. Turn, show us that magnificent profile. Yes, baby. Smile. Give me a pretty pout. That's it."

Lily Jordan was bone tired and could barely keep her eyes open. When this photo shoot was over she was going back to her hotel apartment and crash.

"Come back, Lily. Now, tilt your head back, love. That's it. You've got it going on, girl. Move to the left. Swing your hair over your right shoulder. Like that. Just like that. Fantastic. Now put your foot on the second rung of the ladder, then slowly climb. Take your time."

"Carey, I–"

"Just one more shot, baby."

Lily felt dizzy and shook her head to clear it. God, she was tired. Her eyes started to droop. Misjudging the next rung, she almost fell. She quickly grabbed for the sides. She closed her eyes for a moment before descending to the ground. When she started to walk away, a swirling dizziness assailed her and suddenly the ground was coming up to meet her.

Phillip pushed up the sleeve of his white hospital coat and glanced at his watch. In just fifteen minutes he would be going home for some much needed sleep. God, he was tired. He'd worked a double shift for a friend/colleague who had to leave town on a family emergency.

Just as he was taking off his coat the phone rang. He groaned. Then, letting out a tired sigh, picked up the receiver.

"Dr. Cardoneaux."

"It's Tom, Phil. We're really backed up. Can you come down and help us out."

"Look, Tom, I was just getting ready to go home."

"Man, I know how tired you must be, but the paramedics just brought in an unconscious woman. According to them, she's a model and collapsed during a photo shoot. We're really shorthanded. I wouldn't ask if I could get anyone else."

"I know you wouldn't. All right. I'll be right down."

"Thanks, Phil."

"You owe me." Phillip cradled the receiver and hurried out of his office and headed for the elevators. The hospital was always shorthanded on weekends, especially in Emergency. And even though the administrator was working on getting more doctors, the process took time and careful consideration.

Upon entering the examining room, Phillip stepped over to the sink and washed his hands. As he was drying them he started to ask the nurse about the woman's vital signs when he caught a quick glimpse of the rich honey-golden brown-skinned woman lying on the Gurney bed. It was like gazing into the face of an angel. He was almost afraid to touch her for fear she would disappear. As though hypnotized, he walked over to her and started to lift a lock of her long wavy, blonde-streaked brown hair and rub it between his fingers, but caught himself. To zap him further, the scent of wild gardenias and woman floated up his nostrils.

Phillip shook himself free of his momentary reverie.

He came down here to examine her and find out what was wrong with her, not to—he couldn't understand what had come over him. This had never happened to him before. He pulled on his professional demeanor and lifted the patient's wrist and took her pulse. It was slow, but steady. Taking out his optical light, he checked her eyes. They were a dark exotic brown. The pupils were dilated and the whites of her eyes were partially bloodshot. He'd say complete exhaustion was largely what was wrong with her. He wondered when was the last time she'd had some quality sleep.

Phillip did a quick examination of her arms, body and legs, checking for broken bones or abnormal swelling. While he was doing this, it didn't escape his notice that she had a very sexy, shapely body with long, gorgeous legs that seemed to go on forever.

Tom Crosby stuck his head around the curtain and asked in an urgent voice. "Nancy, can you help me?"

"Go ahead," Phillip told her. "I don't think our patient is going to wake up for a while yet."

You mean you hope she doesn't, Cardoneaux, he thought to himself, but knew he was lying. Actually he was more than anxious to see her fully awake.

He stepped over to the desk in the corner and picked up the woman's chart. Her name was Lily Jordan. He thought the name fit. She was definitely as beautiful and strong as that lovely flower, and although she appeared delicate, he would venture to guess that she was a lot tougher than she looked. He was sure that with some much need-ed rest, in no time at all she would get back to normal. Whatever that was, considering her line of work.

When a moan escaped her lips, alerting Phillip that she was coming around, he walked over to her.

Lily opened her eyes. It took a few moments for them to focus. When they did, she was startled by the handsome man bending over her. His eyes were a deep cobalt blue and so intense they took her breath away. And he had a tan that a tanning lotion company wished their product could reproduce. A crop of thick black curls covered his head. She could only imagine, judging from the bulge of his biceps beneath his doctor coat, what the rest of his body would look like.

She'd obviously been taken to a hospital. The last thing she remembered was the floor rushing up to meet her.

"How are you feeling, Ms. Jordan? I'm Dr. Phillip Cardoneaux."

"What am I doing here?" she demanded

"You fainted. When was the last time you had any quality sleep or rest?"

"Does it matter? She eased her body to a sitting position on the bed. "I feel fine now. Where are my shoes so I can get out of here?"

"You won't be needing them."

"What do you mean? I will since I'm leaving."

"I wouldn't advise that."

"You can't keep me here. If you won't tell me where they are, I'll find them myself."

"Look, Ms. Jordan—"

Lily saw her shoes in a plastic container on a stool across the room and, ignoring Phillip, swung her legs over the side of the bed, walked over and lifted the shoes from the container and slipped her feet into them. As she reached to pull the curtain aside to leave the enclosure, an attack of dizziness assailed her and the room spun around, then the sensation of falling into black nothingness.

Phillip had been watching her closely, and was ready to catch her when she fell. He quickly lifted her in his arms and was about to carry her back to the bed, but stopped and gazed into her lovely face. It appeared that Ms. Supermodel would have to learn things the hard way.

Phillip groaned inwardly. The feel of her soft, sexy body in his arms did things to him that it shouldn't. He was in a hospital, for God's sake, not some singles bar. He couldn't for the life of him understand why he was reacting to her this way.

Nancy returned. "What happened?"

"Our patient tried to leave and got as far as the curtain," he said, placing her on the examining table.

Nancy shook her head. "Will they ever learn that we know what's best when they're injured or ill?"

Some people maybe, but Phillip doubted that this particular patient would ever be one of them. He had a feeling that his acquaintence with the prickly Ms. Lily Jordan was going to prove an interesting and unique experience.

Lily awoke to find herself in a darkened hospital room. As she pushed the light button on the call unit attached to the side of her bed, the door opened.

"I warned you that you'd end up in the hospital if you didn't slow down."

"Carey. I don't want to hear this right now. All right? You're my photographer and my friend–not my father."

"I'm definitely not your father." He grinned. "But if you'd let me I could be much more than just your photographer or your friend."

"Let's not go there again. Okay?"

"Mimi is going to go ballistic. The delay in the shooting schedule is costing the agency big bucks. So when are they going to spring you out of this place?"

"If the doctor who examined me has his way, probably never."

Carey's brow crinkled with concern. "What did he say was wrong with you?"

"He didn't get a chance to tell me because when I tried to leave, I--ah--fainted before he could."

"You must be worse off than I thought. You drive yourself way too hard, Lily pad."

"I've told you not to call me that. Modeling is my life."

"More like your obsession. You're at the top of your game. There's no need for you to work yourself into the ground."

"Look, Carey, if you're going to lecture me, you can leave right now."

"Don't start tripping, Lily pad. Believe it or not, I'm on your side. I want what's best for you and—"

"I hear you." Lily raised herself to a sitting position on the bed and swept back the covers.

"And just where do you think you're going, Ms. Jordan?"

Phillip inquired from the doorway.

"I'm leaving this hospital."

"So you're back to singing that same song." He set the juice he'd brought with him on her tray table. "Drink this."

Clearing his throat, Carey extended his hand. "I'm Carey Graham, a close personal friend of Lily's."

"Dr. Phillip Cardoneaux."

"What's wrong with her, Doc?"

"I'd say she's suffering from an acute case of exhaustion."

"Would you two stop discussing me as if I weren't here?" Lily groused, picking up the glass of juice and draining it.

"How long are you talking about keeping her here?" Carey asked, ignoring Lily's outburst.

"As long as it takes to get her back on her feet."

"I'll inform Mimi, she's the head of the modeling agency Lily works for."

"Don't you dare!" Lily exclaimed.

"You do that, Mr. Graham," Phillip overruled her protest.

"Take care, Lily pad, I'll come see you in the morning."

"Carey Graham, don't you dare leave me here!"

"Sorry. The doc says you need rest. I'm not going to be the one to keep you from getting it. Later."

"Carey!"

"Calm down, Ms. Jordan. Don't worry, we'll take good care of you."

"I don't need a keeper, thank you very much. When can I leave?"

"In about a week."

"A week! You can't be serious. I have to get back to work. I can't stay in here that long."

"Then after you leave you'll need another three weeks or so to recover before I'd begin to consider you well enough to go back to work. If you're worried about your job, I'll call the agency and explain. What's the number?"

"Never mind. I demand to be seen by another doctor."

"That might be a little difficult. You see, we're short-handed, Ms. Jordan, so you're going to have to settle for me."

"I can call the agency myself. If you'll just get me a phone."

"What you need is rest. If I bring a phone in here you wouldn't stop at just talking to the head of your agency, so..."

"Therefore you're not going to get me a phone. Right? You're as arrogant as hell. Of all the—I demand to see the hospital administrator."

"Sorry, he's unavailable at the moment."

Her eyes narrowed. "I'll just bet he is."

"Are you calling me a liar, Ms. Jordan?"

"If the shoe fits," she volleyed back.

Phillip grinned. "You're really something."

"What do you mean by that?"

"Oh, nothing." He walked over to the door.

"Where are you going? I just told you that I want to leave now. Surely the administrator must have an assistant. I demand to speak to him or her."

"Look, Ms. Jordan. What you need is rest and I intend to see that you get it."

"And just how do you plan to do that if I'm not here for you to order around?"

"Oh, you'll be here for at least the next eight hours. You see that glass of juice you drank contained a quick-acting sedative."

"Why you sneaky son--"

"Watch your language," he chided, waving his finger. Lily threw the glass at Phillip, but it hit the door just as it was closing behind him. *The nerve of the man*, she fumed. As she started to get out of bed, a floating lethergy assailed her.

Damn you, Phillip Cardoneaux. Before she could finish the thought, her eyes closed in sleep.

TIMELESS DEVOTION

2005 Publication Schedule

January

A Heart's Awakening
Veronica Parker
$9.95
1-58571-143-8

Falling
Natalie Dunbar
$9.95
1-58571-121-7

February

Echoes of Yesterday
Beverly Clark
$9.95
1-58571-131-4

A Love of Her Own
Cheris F. Hodges
$9.95
1-58571-136-5

Higher Ground
Leah Latimer
$19.95
1-58571-157-8

March

Misconceptions
Pamela Leigh Starr
$9.95
1-58571-117-9

I'll Paint a Sun
A.J. Garrotto
$9.95
1-58571-165-9

Peace Be Still
Colette Haywood
$12.95
1-58571-129-2

April

Intentional Mistakes
Michele Sudler
$9.95
1-58571-152-7

Conquering Dr. Wexler's Heart
Kimberley White
$9.95
1-58571-126-8

Song in the Park
Martin Brant
$15.95
1-58571-125-X

May

The Color Line
Lizzette Grayson Carter
$9.95
1-58571-163-2

Unconditional
A.C. Arthur
$9.95
1-58571-142-X

Last Train to Memphis
Elsa Cook
$12.95
1-58571-146-2

June

Angel's Paradise
Janice Angelique
$9.95
1-58571-107-1

Suddenly You
Crystal Hubbard
$9.95
1-58571-158-6

Matters of Life and
Death
Lesego Malepe, Ph.D.
$15.95
1-58571-124-1

2005 Publication Schedule (continued)

July

Class Reunion
Irma Jenkins/John
  Brown
$12.95
1-58571-123-3

Wild Ravens
Altonya Washington
$9.95
1-58571-164-0

August

Path of Thorns
Annetta P. Lee
$9.95
1-58571-145-4

Timeless Devotion
Bella McFarland
$9.95
1-58571-148-9

Life Is Never As It Seems
J.J. Michael
$12.95
1-58571-153-5

September

Beyond the Rapture
Beverly Clark
$9.95
1-58571-131-4

Blood Lust
J. M. Jeffries
$9.95
1-58571-138-1

Rough on Rats and
  Tough on Cats
Chris Parker
$12.95
1-58571-154-3

October

A Will to Love
Angie Daniels
$9.95
1-58571-141-1

Taken by You
Dorothy Elizabeth Love
$9.95
1-58571-162-4

Soul Eyes
Wayne L. Wilson
$12.95
1-58571-147-0

November

A Drummer's Beat to
  Mend
Kay Swanson
$9.95

Sweet Reprecussions
Kimberley White
$9.95
1-58571-159-4

Red Polka Dot in a
  Worldof Plaid
Varian Johnson
$12.95
1-58571-140-3

December

Hand in Glove
Andrea Jackson
$9.95
1-58571-166-7

Blaze
Barbara Keaton
$9.95

Across
Carol Payne
$12.95
1-58571-149-7

Other Genesis Press, Inc. Titles

Erotic Anthology	Assorted	$8.95
Eve's Prescription	Edwina Martin Arnold	$8.95
Everlastin' Love	Gay G. Gunn	$8.95
Fate	Pamela Leigh Starr	$8.95
Forbidden Quest	Dar Tomlinson	$10.95
Fragment in the Sand	Annetta P. Lee	$8.95
From the Ashes	Kathleen Suzanne	$8.95
	Jeanne Sumerix	
Gentle Yearning	Rochelle Alers	$10.95
Glory of Love	Sinclair LeBeau	$10.95
Hart & Soul	Angie Daniels	$8.95
Heartbeat	Stephanie Bedwell-Grime	$8.95
I'll Be Your Shelter	Giselle Carmichael	$8.95
Illusions	Pamela Leigh Starr	$8.95
Indiscretions	Donna Hill	$8.95
Interlude	Donna Hill	$8.95
Intimate Intentions	Angie Daniels	$8.95
Just an Affair	Eugenia O'Neal	$8.95
Kiss or Keep	Debra Phillips	$8.95
Love Always	Mildred E. Riley	$10.95
Love Unveiled	Gloria Greene	$10.95
Love's Deception	Charlene Berry	$10.95
Mae's Promise	Melody Walcott	$8.95
Meant to Be	Jeanne Sumerix	$8.95
Midnight Clear	Leslie Esdaile	$10.95
(Anthology)	Gwynne Forster	
	Carmen Green	
	Monica Jackson	
Midnight Magic	Gwynne Forster	$8.95
Midnight Peril	Vicki Andrews	$10.95
My Buffalo Soldier	Barbara B. K. Reeves	$8.95
Naked Soul	Gwynne Forster	$8.95
No Regrets	Mildred E. Riley	$8.95
Nowhere to Run	Gay G. Gunn	$10.95

Whispers in the Night	Dorothy Elizabeth Love	$8.95
Whispers in the Sand	LaFlorya Gauthier	$10.95
Yesterday is Gone	Beverly Clark	$8.95
Yesterday's Dreams, Tomorrow's Promises	Reon Laudat	$8.95
Your Precious Love	Sinclair LeBeau	$8.95

Order Form

Mail to: Genesis Press, Inc.
P.O. Box 101
Columbus, MS 39703

Name _____
Address _____
City/State _____ Zip _____
Telephone _____

Ship to (if different from above)
Name _____
Address _____
City/State _____ Zip _____
Telephone _____

Credit Card Information
Credit Card # _____ ☐ Visa ☐ Mastercard
Expiration Date (mm/yy) _____ ☐ AmEx ☐ Discover

Qty.	Author	Title	Price	Total

Use this order form, or call 1-888-INDIGO-1	
Total for books	_____
Shipping and handling: $5 first two books, $1 each additional book	_____
Total S & H	_____
Total amount enclosed	_____
Mississippi residents add 7% sales tax	

Order Form

Mail to: Genesis Press, Inc.
P.O. Box 101
Columbus, MS 39703

Name _____
Address _____
City/State _____ Zip _____
Telephone _____

Ship to (if different from above)
Name _____
Address _____
City/State _____ Zip _____
Telephone _____

Credit Card Information
Credit Card # _____ ☐ Visa   ☐ Mastercard
Expiration Date (mm/yy) _____ ☐ AmEx   ☐ Discover

Qty.	Author	Title	Price	Total

Use this order form, or call 1-888-INDIGO-1	**Total for books** _____ **Shipping and handling:** **$5 first two books,** **$1 each additional book** _____ **Total S & H** _____ **Total amount enclosed** _____

Mississippi residents add 7% sales tax